MW00769103

ARNESTO MODESTO

THE WORLD'S MOST INEFFECTUAL TIME TRAVELER

by Darren Johnson

Contents

Contents ii

Prologue: The Original Future 1

Familiarities 7

Outed 11

Spoiler Alert 22

Intervention 29

Connections 35

Appeal to Pity 44

Words Hurt 52

Foul Play 56

Learning Shortcuts 60

Freedom of Assembly 67

Served 76

Cutting Ties 85

A City Erupts 94

Compounding the Problem 101

Piling It On 108

The Chase 111

Road Rage 115

Shady Neighbors 124

Unexpected Company 133

Too Much Power 140

Safety in Numbers 147

Barge Right In 155

Tragedy Hits Home 162

Collections 169

The Power of Persuasion 174

Ill-Conceived 179

Shaking Masses 189

First Impressions 193

Renter's Market 198

Shocking 204

Operation Panic 209

By Design 212

Making Waves 225

Bad Parking 227

Storming In 230

Traumatizing 235

Roach Trap 242

Double Down 251

Picture It 259

Chilling 267

The Keys to Success 278

Fire It Up 284

Pattern of Abuse 291

The Wrong Date 304

Breathless 310

On the Run 315

Building Violation 322

Mementos 327

Alliances 336

A Relaxing Conversation 341

Schooled 350

Sinus Trouble 354

Concessions 358

Epilogue 361

Acknowledgements 364

About the Author 365

Other Works by the Author 366

The Part Where the Author Begs You for a Review 367

Contact 368

In memory of those who will be lost.

Again.

Prologue:

The Original Future

"WHY MUST TIME TRAVEL kill you, Grandpa?"

Arnesto Modesto looked at little Jessenia and smiled. She wasn't his granddaughter but his great-great-great-great-granddaughter. Over the last century, medicine had seen countless improvements in staving off death so people were living longer than ever before. As the number of surviving generations increased, many families adopted the tradition of calling all their elders "Grandma" and "Grandpa."

"Because the nanobots have to destroy my memory cells to best extract the information before they create the impulses to send back along the curve of space-time via quantum embroilment," he said. She looked confused so he reiterated, "It's to give my brain in the past the best chance of accepting memories from my brain in the present." He tapped his frail finger against the side of his liver-spotted head for emphasis.

He overheard one of the young mothers in the room whispering to her little boy, "He's preparing to go to heaven."

"No, I'm not!" he snapped.

A few of the bystanders gasped at his sudden outburst before the room fell silent.

"There's no such thing as heaven or hell. Can't a man choose to die in peace without any religious dogma ruining the moment?"

The boy looked like he was about to cry. So did the boy's mother. Arnesto felt bad. *Must remember to be less condescending in my next life*, he thought.

He looked over at the 2130 calendar hanging on the wall. He had it special made as nobody used print calendars anymore.

The top pages of the calendar featured classic cars from the 2060s: self-driving, self-recharging, eco-friendly, and impossibly safe. They were a far cry from the cars Arnesto drove in his day. He realized he was probably the only one alive in his family who had ever driven a car. Heck, the Department of Motor Vehicles closed down decades ago.

The bottom page showed April with that day's date circled. He loved that circle. His day had come at last. Less exciting were the marks filling every day before. The nurse put another mark inside that day's circle then looked at Arnesto with a mild sneer. It was part of their arrangement that she would mark the calendar every time he was snarky to someone.

From his deathbed, he looked around the room. Besides the nurse and Arnesto's assistant, Marcus, everyone was somehow related to him. Descendants, descendants-in-law, cousins a number of times removed, cousins he wouldn't mind seeing removed. They were all awkwardly looking at him. Even though it was his big day, he never got used to being the center of attention. He made an attempt at some damage control.

"I mean, we all have our own ways of coping with death. Besides,

2

I'm not going anywhere except to the past, where I will get to live my life all over again. Does anyone have any questions?" he asked.

"If the impulses go back in time, couldn't they recreate your memories in a dinosaur?" Jessenia asked. Several people chuckled, easing the tension in the room.

"A great question! Who read and understood my research and wants to answer that?" The adults looked around the room at one another, but nobody volunteered. *Idiots.*

Arnesto had no choice but to answer for them. "I'm kind of oversimplifying things, but the impulses are grounded in my brain. That means I'm the only one who can receive them. But if one of them escapes and lands in a dinosaur's puny brain, the impulse would be incompatible. The energy would simply float away. Anyone else?"

A middle-aged man spoke up. "Would you like us to pray for you?"

Arnesto glared at the man. "You listen—"

"Arnesto, your blood pressure," Nurse Pearl said, placing her hand on his frail arm and nodding to the marked-up calendar.

"Who cares, I'm about to frigging die anyway!"

"It might affect the experiment." She was good. She knew how to handle him. He looked over at his assistant, Marcus, who shrugged. The experiment was unique, built upon layer after layer of wild conjecture. Both memory extraction and quantum teleportation had their geneses early in the twenty-first century, but no one had ever attempted to marry the technologies like *this.*

Arnesto centered himself, again looking around at his guests. "I think it's time," he said. He looked again at Marcus, who gave him a quick nod. He then turned back to the crowd.

"I'd like to thank you all for coming. Despite my brilliance, I've made some mistakes, but seeing all of you here, I know I've done something right." There were a great number of smiles, but Arnesto focused on the gaps between those present, picturing in his mind the many who weren't. "I've had a great life, but now my time has come. It is my dying wish to make a final contribution to the world of science, and my experiment should do just that. At the same time, it will allow me to execute my Twenty-Ninth Amendment right to humanely terminate my life with dignity — as if I had any left." A few chuckles. "A tiny percentage of the nanobots are there purely to observe. Marcus will be displaying the feed on one of the monitors on the wall there. I encourage you to watch and ask questions. However, those of you who are embarrassed, squeamish, or easily offended may wish to look away or even leave the room. I guess that's it. I wish you all the best. Goodbye."

Marcus handed him the specially marked vial, then Nurse Pearl assisted his shaky hand as he inserted it into the injector port leading directly to his bloodstream. It didn't take long for the first nanobots to reach the blood-brain barrier and cut their way inside. In no time, they were tracing their way along the synapses to the memory center of the brain.

Marcus selected the most interesting-looking view on the multi-cam display and made that the primary display on the viewing monitor. It was mostly the children who watched as a nanobot found an isolated memory cell and attached itself. There was a pause, then a bright flash filled the monitor. The camera nanobot had to reorient itself, but once it did, it panned over the area where the flash happened. A few people gasped. The memory cell was all but gone and in its place were a bunch

4

of damaged nanobot parts.

Jessenia looked at Marcus, who explained in a respectful, hushed tone, "It's a violent reaction on a very tiny scale."

She then looked at Arnesto. "Does it hurt?"

"Not at all," Nurse Pearl reassured her. "We gave him some medicine to make him feel completely relaxed and pain-free."

Marcus considered mentioning the stimulation nanobots that had nothing to do with the experiment but were there solely to interact with the brain's pleasure center, but thought better of it. He found a camera near a large cluster of cells and put that up on the viewing monitor. It took several seconds as many more reactor nanobots appeared and secured their positions. Another big flash. This time the camera nanobot remained far enough away to hold stable. There were more oohs and aahs as the aftermath of the orchestrated reaction revealed itself.

The microexplosions were coming faster now. Marcus shifted his entire display to the viewing monitor. Like the end of a fireworks show, flashes appeared in many of the individual windows on the screen.

The children delighted in the carnage of nanobot parts floating in the newly empty spaces. Arnesto had opted out of the decomposing variety. What was the point? He was going to die anyway. Might as well go for broke and use a sturdier compound. At least that way, he had reasoned, he didn't have to worry about some nanobots crapping out before they could finish their job. Marcus wondered if Arnesto's additional aim was to enhance the viewing pleasure of his audience.

With Arnesto's increasingly compromised blood-brain barrier, the hemorrhaging began to overwhelm him. Nurse Pearl watched as her patient's brainwaves turned to flatlines on the small monitor by his bed. Through watery eyes, she noticed one of the men looking at her.

"He's gone," she said to him in a whisper, though the room was so quiet, nearly everyone heard.

There were hugs and tears and final goodbyes as people slowly filtered out of the room. Marcus clicked off the viewing monitor. The nanobots were all but gone, too, having completed their mission.

"Did it work? Is he in the past?" Jessenia asked, lingering at the foot of her grandfather's bed.

Marcus crouched down to meet her at eye level. "Arnesto told me the experiment was so tricky, that even if it worked, there would be no way for us to know." He glanced at Nurse Pearl who looked up as she pulled the sheet over Arnesto's head. Marcus then looked back at Jessenia. "Your grandpa tried something that's never been done before. If anybody could make it work, it was him." Jessenia seemed to accept this answer and met her mom who was waiting for her in the doorway.

"Do you think he did it? Is it possible?" Nurse Pearl asked when the girl left.

Marcus looked at his monitor and saw a piece of destroyed nanobot float by in one of the windows. He shrugged, "If he did, the past had better watch out."

On the outskirts of Arnesto's memory center, one last reactor bot found and attached to a memory. It extracted the information and unleashed an enormous localized burst of energy, and then the memory was gone.

Familiarities

Modesto Residence
Massachusetts
Late Twentieth Century

THE ENERGY BURST ARRIVED as an impulse, which Arnesto's brain interpreted and saved as a memory. The memory was of Arnesto at the DMV when he was twenty-eight. Not the most exciting memory, to be sure. However, it was a moot point. Arnesto would never have cause to recall this particular memory. Even if he could, even if he knew it existed, his young brain was too immature to handle it.

Arnesto giggled as the toy racecar left the track and landed on the shag carpeting. It didn't take much to entertain him. He was, after all, only four years old. His mother kept an eye on him as she prepared his snack of apple slices.

"Are you excited to see the boats?" she asked. They were about to drive into Boston to see the tall ships arrive in celebration of the nation's bicentennial.

He nodded, unaware of both the significance of the event and the fact that he had just made history of his own. One couldn't blame him; there was no trail of flames, no ball of lightning, no fanfare of any kind.

Still, it was there — a remnant from the future, harmlessly locked away inside the mind of a preschooler. Young Arnesto was now leading the world in time travel by exactly one memory's worth of brain cells. As if in celebration of the event over which he had no control or even knowledge, he ate his apple slices.

At age five, Arnesto was relieved to hear his town included in the long list of school closings broadcast over the radio during the Blizzard of '78. He headed outside with his parents, where he climbed the enormous snowbank left behind by the snowplows working nonstop. He knew just where to jump to break through the thick layer on top of the three feet of powder covering the lawn. He knew because he remembered seeing his dad do exactly that on the 16mm projector they got out when family came to visit. Alas, he didn't weigh enough and landed disappointed on top of the icy crust. His father had better luck, breaking through and now caught in snow up to his waist while his mother recorded it on camera. Just like he remembered.

When he was seven, and it was down to him and his neighbor, Cathy Gross, in the first-grade spelling bee, he somehow knew she was going to misspell "brown" as "braun" right before she did. He didn't give it another thought. He was too excited about winning to reflect on what happened. Excitement that faded when his prize, disguised as a sugar cookie, revealed itself to be a damn oatmeal cookie.

He was ten when the family took a trip to Niagara Falls. Standing by the rail atop the American side, a bee appeared out of nowhere and stung Arnesto on his wrist, causing him to yelp in pain.

"Ow! Again?!" he said. Nobody was sure why he said, "again." Had he been stung recently? No one could recall. Later, they were in the car when Arnesto's mother, Nancy, turned around from the front

8

passenger seat to ask how he and his little brother Gerald were enjoying the trip, aside from the insect attack.

"I saw the twins from soccer," Arnesto said.

"You did? Where?" Nancy asked.

"Outside the Ripley's Museum." Confused, Nancy looked at her husband, Karl, then back at Arnesto.

"We haven't been there yet. We're going there now," she said.

"Oh, right." She was right, they hadn't been there yet. He kept his eyes open as they arrived, parked, and headed into *Ripley's Believe It or Not!* Museum. Arnesto was excited. After all, it had been his idea to go there. Though reluctant to go at first, his parents caved in and wound up also enjoying the oddities and exhibits.

When they finished their tour and were pulling away in the car, Arnesto took one last look at the museum, where he saw the twins Karen and Katherine Mitchell and their parents walking up the sidewalk to the entrance.

This was no big deal to Arnesto, who figured his earlier memory must have come from seeing them somewhere else in the area the day before and confused that with the museum somehow.

Two years later the family was watching the opening ceremonies of the 1984 Summer Olympics in Los Angeles. "Oh, look, Karl, that man is flying in on a jetpack! Do you think we'll all have jetpacks soon?" Nancy asked.

"I don't know," Karl shrugged.

"No, they're too expensive, impractical, and especially dangerous for everyday use," Arnesto said.

"Gee, way to kill my dreams," Nancy laughed. "How do you know that?"

"I must have learned it… sometime," Arnesto said. Try as he might, he couldn't recall when he had acquired this information. On the other hand, he felt confident his future would be disappointingly devoid of jetpacks.

And so Arnesto would continue to have these rare, sporadic moments of foresight that he couldn't explain. They were harmless, inconsequential, and quickly forgotten. They never appeared to affect anyone, least of all him.

Until one did.

Outed

Sophomore Gym Class
Monday, October 12, 1987
B Period

IT WAS COLD OUTSIDE, especially for one standing around in a field waiting for someone else to hit a ball at them. For some reason, the coach decided they were going to play softball for gym class that day. He chose the field closest to the school where there weren't any benches. This meant one team stood in the field waiting for anything to happen while the other team stood around home plate waiting for their chance at bat. It was a large class. When his team took the field, Arnesto saw that they already had six or seven outfielders, so he chose a spot partway between shortstop and the left fielders.

As had been happening all period, there wasn't a lot of action. There were many fine athletes at the school, however, few of them made it into the early morning sophomore gym class. Todd Shea happened to be one of the few present with any skill.

After a wise choice not to swing at his first pitch which landed on the ground five feet in front of the plate, he was given a perfect second pitch. The crack of the bat turned a few heads as he connected with a long fly ball to left field where Jon Kelley snagged it on a bounce. Arnesto saw Jon start to pull his arm back and quickly turned to first base where Todd had no intention of stopping. Arnesto wasn't particularly concerned with the play, as he knew Jon could easily throw the ball to second. He became concerned, though, when he heard Jon shout his name from behind him. In that split second, Arnesto started to turn his head to the right, but then flinched and moved it the other way as he brought his glove up to where his face had nearly been, blindly catching Jon's throw.

He stared in disbelief at the ball in his glove for a moment, but then became aware of the multiple people yelling at him. Snapping back to reality, he started to throw the ball to the second baseman — who wasn't there. Becoming only the third player to recognize his team didn't have anyone covering second — after Todd and Jon — he had no choice but to run for second himself. Todd realized he wasn't going to make it and tried to turn around to return to first, but couldn't reverse in time and Arnesto tagged him out.

"Good out," the coach yelled. He enjoyed throwing praise to students he felt seldom deserved any. "Alright, let's bring it in. Somebody grab those bats."

"Who won?" a kid named Josh asked.

"You did," the coach said. "Only you though, nobody else."

"Sweet," Josh said.

Arnesto sauntered inside the school to his locker, still mulling over what had just happened.

"Golden Glove Boy!" Josh yelled at Arnesto while strutting by. Arnesto's best friend Pete Morgan was at his own locker a few feet away. Pete looked at Josh then at Arnesto.

"What was that about?" Pete asked.

"I made a good play in softball," Arnesto said.

"Wow, what's that like?"

"Kinda weird actually. I'll tell you about it after school," Arnesto said, shutting his locker.

"Wait," Pete called after him. "We're playing softball today? It's freezing out there!"

* * *

"You've got five red lines in a row coming up," Pete said.

"Good," Arnesto replied. Having enjoyed a nice dinner at Pete's house, the boys had retired to the basement, where they waxed philosophical while playing split screen Tetris. It was always a friendly competition to see who could survive the longest. Pete, being better at the game, got ahead of Arnesto, meaning he could warn his less skilled friend about upcoming tetrominoes. In this case, the news was quite welcome, as the series of straight, red line pieces would help Arnesto clear out some of his uncomfortably high tower.

"So you made a good play in gym?" Pete asked.

"Dude, it was weird. I was playing short, and Jon Kelley used me as a cutoff from left."

"What happened?"

"I tagged out Shea."

"Ooh," Pete winced. "I wouldn't piss off Shea."

"The weird part is I never saw Jon throw the ball. I saw him start to, but I looked away, he hummed the ball right at my head, and I caught it," Arnesto said.

13

"That's cool. All this video game playing must have given you good reflexes."

"No, Pete," Arnesto said, pausing the game. "I never saw the ball. The crazy thing is I don't think I was supposed to catch Jon's throw. I think — I think I was supposed to get hit."

"What do you mean? Is that why you've been rubbing your nose all night?"

"Yeah. I think it hit me right here," Arnesto said, rubbing his index finger down the bridge of his nose.

"But it didn't. You caught it. Can we unpause the game now? I was in the zone."

"Yeah, sorry," Arnesto said and unpaused. "Don't think I'm crazy, but it's like I saw it happen. Well, I never saw the ball hit me, but I saw the aftermath. Being on the ground, blood on my shirt, my nose hurting like hell, somebody helping me to the nurse's office... Also, the ridge of my nose gets permanently flattened. Not a lot, but if you saw it in before and after pictures, you could tell the difference."

"So, you had a vision? Damn it. Seven squares in a row. Seven fucking squares," Pete moaned.

"I don't think so. It's more like... like I *remembered* it."

"How is that different from a vision?" Pete asked.

"Because I *still* remember it." Arnesto looked over at Pete, who quickly glanced over and then back at the television with a concerned face.

"You're looking at me like I'm crazy," Arnesto said.

"I'm not looking at you. I'm looking at all the squares building up on your side."

"Shit." Arnesto was already in trouble, and the square pieces put

14

the final nail in the coffin. He finished with 392 lines, while Pete was still going strong at 405. Knowing there wouldn't be time for him to start a new game, Arnesto put down the controller and leaned back against the couch. They both watched Pete's side of the screen for a while until Pete finally broke the silence.

"Do you remember the lottery numbers?" he asked, joking.

"It hurt like hell!" Arnesto said. "You know what, forget I said anything. I must be losing it."

"Okay," Pete said, still focused on the game.

* * *

The next day, Arnesto was still troubled by his good softball play that he felt shouldn't have happened. He stopped by the nurse's station after his last class and peered in from the doorway. His eyes scoured the room, looking for something, anything that would help him remember. This would have been the first place he would have gone with a smooshed nose, and he felt like he *had* come there. So why couldn't he remember anything new? Was it possible he had an overactive imagination?

"Can I help you?" the nurse asked.

"Just browsing," Arnesto said as he turned around and headed for his locker. He was starting to realize how absurd it all sounded and regretted mentioning it to Pete. When he reached his locker, he saw Pete was already there. They had gone the whole day without broaching the topic and Arnesto hoped it would stay that way.

"Hey," Arnesto said.

"Hey," Pete said. "I almost forgot, how was gym class today?"

"Fine," Arnesto said dryly. "How was *your* gym class?"

"You know why I'm asking."

"Look, about what I said last night, I was messing with you," lied Arnesto. "Can we pretend we never had that conversation?"

"I don't think you were lying," Pete said.

"So, you believe me?"

"Do I believe you had a... precognition? Hell no. But I believe something happened. Nothing supernatural — probably a crossed wire in your brain — but you sure sounded sincere when you were telling me." Arnesto looked mildly uncomfortable but didn't say anything, so Pete continued. "You said you still remembered being hit by that softball. Wouldn't that mean you have two memories? To make it easier, let's say we're making up a story for writing class."

"So, hypothetically?" Arnesto asked. Pete nodded. "Well, in this hypothetical world, my amazing friend... Blarnesto had this odd experience — this *one* time." He held up his index finger for emphasis. "And yes, he has both memories."

Pete chuckled. "Then *my* amazing friend, Blete, asks him what else is different about the memories besides the obvious hit/no-hit action."

"Well," Arnesto said, "Blarnesto clearly remembers making the catch. But while he also remembers getting hit and the ensuing aftermath, it's not as clear."

"Is it more fuzzy, like a dream?" Pete asked.

"More like... faded. Like the memory is old."

"Very interesting. Oh, look, it's Blosh," Pete said, motioning toward an oblivious Josh walking by. By now the increased jocularity had dissolved any tension Arnesto felt. "Blete requests Blarnesto inform him should any further incidents occur."

16

"Blarnesto agrees as long as Blete promises to *never* mention this to anyone. Ever."

"Fine, Blete promises," Pete said.

"Okay. Wait, I think I'm having another one now." Arnesto put his hand to his temple. "Yes. See Stephanie Summers over there?" He motioned toward their attractive classmate gathering her things from her locker across the hall. "I'm going to go ask her out and she's going to say — hold on, I'm remembering it now — yes, she's going to say, 'Piss off, loser.'" Arnesto looked her up and down but otherwise remained motionless. A few moments later, she shut her locker and walked away.

"Well, why didn't you talk to her?" Pete asked.

"I obviously knew what she was going to say. I'm not going to let her reject me *twice*."

"Ha ha, well damn, I'm convinced!" Pete said.

Arnesto spent the next few days trying to see if he could have any more flashes of memory, but none came. He would look at someone and think, *She's going to say this!* or *He's going to do that!* But he was always wrong. One time he thought he predicted the exchange student arguing with the teacher, but as he couldn't recall any details, he quickly dismissed the idea. Besides, she was generally argumentative.

No recalled conversations, no more surprise athletic plays in gym, nothing. Arnesto gave up. High school reverted to its usual boring state, though perhaps not for Clarence Hudson, who was holding his girlfriend Jamie Mann at her locker and moving in for the kiss.

He's a lucky guy, thought Arnesto, *though not that lucky. She's going to turn her head away each time he tries to kiss her then laugh uncomfortably before saying, 'Get out of here!' Ugh, why am I still trying to remember future events* — Before he could finish his thought, it happened.

First dodging right then left, Jamie denied Clarence a kiss, then laughed and said, "Not here!" Arnesto froze, his mouth fell open. Jamie noticed Arnesto watching them and led her boyfriend away. Arnesto felt embarrassed that they had caught him watching and gave them a head start before following them to Trigonometry.

Arnesto sat in the middle of the back row where he could observe everyone, thinking about what he had just witnessed. Fate seemed to be teasing him. The scene had almost played out the way he imagined, but the wording was off. He felt sure she had said, "Get out of here!" He wished *he* could get close enough to a girl to be told, "Get out of here!"

He tried paying attention to the lecture. Mr. Massey was a great teacher and friendly with the students, but that day, Arnesto couldn't focus. He was lucky that math came easy enough to him that he could get away with not paying attention, but he would gladly trade in some of that skill for better luck with the ladies. He looked at Jamie seated at the right side of the class then at Clarence in the front row talking to his friend next to him. Hold on, the guy has a girlfriend and doesn't even sit with her? *Get out of here, Clarence!*

"Get out of here!" Mr. Massey yelled at Clarence, in a voice loud enough that most of the class jumped. Nobody moved, not even Clarence, who was as dumbfounded as everyone else. Mr. Massey pointed a finger at him, flicked it toward the door, and said, "Go."

The teacher everybody liked had yelled at — and kicked out — a student in Honors Trig. People started looking around to verify that everyone was witnessing the same thing. But that wasn't Arnesto's focus. All he could think about was how Mr. Massey had used the exact words from his memory. Somehow the two memories had mixed.

Mr. Massey reverted to his usual self like nothing happened. "Can anyone tell me what this is?" Nobody volunteered, either because they were still in shock or they didn't know the answer, or a combination of the two. Arnesto felt a sense of foreboding. Sure enough, Mr. Massey called on the one student he could usually count on to answer questions that eluded the rest of the class. "Arnesto?"

Arnesto panicked. He didn't want to disappoint his teacher by being another student not paying attention. He hastily scanned the blackboard but found no clues. What had Mr. Massey been talking about? He couldn't remember, and he didn't even know what "this" meant. He was taking too long. *Quick! Say, "I don't know."*

Arnesto opened his mouth, but he did not say, "I don't know." Instead, he asked in a strained voice, "The Fibonacci sequence?"

Mr. Massey laughed, "Very good" and resumed his lecture as every other student in class turned their head at Arnesto in unison.

Arnesto was even more incapable of focusing now; his mind was all aflutter. *Did all that really happen?! Jamie's head-turning, "Get out of here!", Fibonacci. Sure, I got some of the details wrong, but I couldn't have guessed the rest. But did I remember them before they happened, or am I only remembering them after the fact? The former isn't possible, though I still remember my nose getting flattened.* He decided he wouldn't tell Pete about this. He wouldn't mention anything to anyone until he had hard evidence of what was happening to him, which he had no idea how to collect.

Arnesto resumed trying to remember things, but his efforts were again in vain. Still, Arnesto remained ever vigilant. The problem was high school was *boring*. Sure, there were a few moments here and there that seemed familiar. But there was nothing as strong as Clarence's rejection/ejection combo and even *that* feeling was flimsier every time

19

he thought about it.

A few weeks passed without any results, and Arnesto had again all but given up. That was until the powderpuff game between the junior and senior girls.

It was a cold November night, and Arnesto and Pete were shivering in the stands. Pete suggested they walk around to warm up a little. As they walked amongst the crowd watching from the track surrounding the football field, they steered clear of a group of senior boys carrying an inflated crocodile balloon for some reason.

Arnesto looked back at the crocodile and stared. Then his mouth fell open.

"Pete! Do you have a piece of paper and a pen?"

"Why would I bring those to a football game?"

"I'll be right back. I need to get something from my locker. Don't move!" Arnesto shouted as he ran down the hill to the school. Five minutes later, Arnesto returned out of breath.

"Did you get what you needed?" Pete asked.

"Oh yeah. Keep your eye on that balloon crocodile."

"Why?"

"You'll see soon enough."

"Whatever."

Halftime ended. The third quarter came and went. Arnesto grew restless. Finally, a few minutes into the fourth quarter, he saw it.

"Watch!" Arnesto yelled at Pete, pointing at one of the junior boys who had stolen the crocodile and was now sprinting across the field in their direction with an angry senior close behind and gaining. A few feet in front of Pete, there was a mom with her son, who looked to be around eleven.

"Kid, watch out!" Arnesto said as he nudged the young boy out of the way, making sure to also keep clear himself. A split second later, the senior caught up to the junior and tackled him. On the way down, the junior's free hand went whizzing by where the young boy's face had been a moment before.

"Thank you, that was kind of you," the boy's mom said to Arnesto before walking her son away.

"You're welcome," Arnesto called after them. He reached into his back pocket, pulled out a folded sheet of paper, and handed it to Pete.

"Don't freak out and remember you promised not to tell anyone," Arnesto said as Pete unfolded the paper.

Some of the color left Pete's face as he read the note to himself:

After a junior steals the crocodile, a senior tackles him right in front of us. During the tackle, the junior's hand breaks the boy's nose. The seniors then proudly carry their deflated crocodile back to their side of the field.

"That's freaky. But you only got one out of three. The boy's nose is fine," Pete said.

"Yeah, at the last second, I decided I couldn't let them smash the kid's face. Partly for him, but partly because I didn't want to watch it happen again. It was gross."

"That's quasi-noble of you, though it doesn't help your credibility." He read the note again. "What about the last item? I don't see the seniors carrying—"

"Look," Arnesto interrupted. Pete looked up and saw the seniors carrying away the damaged crocodile, their fists triumphantly punching the air.

"Well... shit."

Spoiler Alert

Morgan Residence
Sunday, February 7, 1988
Early Afternoon

PETE STILL WASN'T CONVINCED of Arnesto's power. Arnesto must have set the whole thing up. Somehow. Yes, he must have convinced the junior to steal the crocodile, knowing this would anger the seniors, aim for the boy, then allow himself to be tackled. On the track. Which probably hurt like hell. Maybe Arnesto paid the junior a good sum of money. There had to be a logical explanation.

They wouldn't get much opportunity to argue about it as Pete became bedridden with mono. While he was laid up, he received a letter from Arnesto, which Pete's mom left in his room for him. He didn't open it; he didn't have the energy. All he could do day after day was lie on the couch and play Contra. In fact, it wasn't until two weeks later when his energy finally started coming back that he even thought of the letter again.

He opened the envelope and saw another sealed envelope inside. The inner envelope had written on it in big letters, "DO NOT OPEN until you're feeling better!" Pete sighed and opened it. Inside was a note:

Hey, slacker, glad you're feeling better. I can't believe you beat Contra in one life, very impressive! Now quit faking and get back to class!

P.S. ¡Bienvenido, Pedro!

Great, now Arnesto was spying on him. How else could he know that he beat Contra in one life? Pete shivered. How *did* he know? Pete hadn't told anyone about it. The only one who would care was Arnesto.

He walked downstairs and sat on the couch where he had spent almost every waking hour of the last two weeks. There was no window through which one could see the television screen. He looked around but didn't see a hidden camera anywhere. Arnesto wouldn't cross the line like that anyway. He walked into the kitchen where his mom was drinking coffee.

"Mom, did you talk to Arnesto?"

"No, why?"

"Never mind." She was the only one who stayed home with him, but she had never played Nintendo. It seemed very unlikely that she would have been aware of how many lives he had left at any given time, much less called up Arnesto to inform him of his achievement. Oh well, he was still recovering. He would figure it out when his strength returned.

When he walked into homeroom, Arnesto was sitting at his desk looking smug. Pete walked one column of desks past, then sat in his own desk next to Arnesto's.

"Seriously, though, good job," Arnesto said.

"Okay, tell me. How did you—"

23

"Hold on, here it comes," Arnesto interrupted, watching the door. In walked Mrs. Gonzalez, who was both their homeroom and Spanish teacher as well as one of their favorites. Arnesto waited until she closed the door and put down her bag before looking at her students. Arnesto then turned to Pete and with a flair, raised his right hand to his right ear while making an expression indicating he was listening for something.

"¡Bienvenido, Pedro!" Mrs. Gonzalez exclaimed. Arnesto couldn't help but laugh at his own brilliance.

"Gracias," Pete said.

"Do you believe me now?" Arnesto whispered.

"No," Pete said, hoping Arnesto wouldn't hear the lack of conviction in his voice. He still didn't accept that Arnesto could predict the future, but the wall of disbelief was beginning to crack. It wasn't how Mrs. Gonzalez said what Arnesto had written that bothered him; it was the way he seemed to know exactly *when*. But it still wasn't sufficient evidence to convince Pete. That would come soon enough.

After surviving his first day back at school, Pete returned home. He did some homework, had dinner with his family, then turned on the television. He was watching *Night Court* when he saw an ad for *Saturday Night Live* featuring Tom Hanks. A minute later, the phone rang. His dad said it was for Pete.

"'Oh, a stumble!'" came Arnesto's voice.

"What now?"

"Tom Hanks on SNL. He does this Olympic skating bit, it's hilarious!" Arnesto must have seen the same commercial.

"Are you inviting yourself over Saturday night?" Pete asked, getting the hint.

"Do you want irrefutable proof that I'm a god?" Arnesto asked.

24

"Fine, you can come over."

* * *

Saturday night arrived and the boys prepared to watch the show. Arnesto couldn't wait to show off, even revealing in striking detail information about the skit that was about to begin. Pete, on the other hand, wanted it to be over.

During the sketch, Arnesto frequently quoted the lines right before they happened. "'Oh! A tempo change! Very dramatic.'"

"Please stop," Pete said, struggling to contain his frustration.

"One more. '0.0 — that's the Russian judge.'"

"...the East German judge," Phil Hartman's character said.

"Oh, 'East German,' huh, I remembered that wrong. I'm not a very good god," Arnesto said.

"You're not a god at all! You must have hacked their system or they sent you a script or you saw a rehearsal or something." Pete was rattled.

"Well, let's keep watching. Maybe someone will make a mistake I can point out before it happens," Arnesto said.

"No! Fuck." Pete shook his head. "If I say I believe you, will you stop spoiling shows for me?" he asked. Arnesto had to think about it. Besides keeping his and the spectator boy's faces intact, he had made little use of his skill other than showing off and getting on Pete's nerves.

"Fine," Arnesto said as if the compromise was in any way unfair to him.

"Why is it so important that I believe you anyway?"

"I don't know," Arnesto shrugged. "You're the only one who knows. There's nobody else I can talk to about it."

25

Pete looked at Arnesto and saw something he had never seen in his friend before: fear. Arnesto was afraid. He was also alone. In that instant, he knew things would be different. His friend had, for lack of a much better term, some kind of superpower. And who could Arnesto possibly go to for help? Arnesto came to him. Pete's sense of pity for his friend turned into a swelling of pride.

"No there isn't anyone else you can talk to," Pete said at last. "And there can't be."

Arnesto turned to face him. "What?"

"You can't tell anyone. Can you imagine what would happen if word got out about this? People would never leave you alone. *Ever.* My god, the masses would stop at nothing to question you — or kill you. What about the government? If they found out, they would lock you in a cell for the rest of your life. Or perform experiments on you."

"Shit!"

Pete stood and began pacing. "Arnesto, we will have to be extremely careful. No more talking about this stuff in homeroom unless we are sure nobody can hear us. And no talking about stuff from the future, including movies and television shows."

"I already said I wouldn't!" Arnesto protested, though with a smile because he was no longer alone. It was clear now that Pete believed him.

"Wait a minute, why didn't you warn me about getting mono?" Pete sounded miffed.

"I didn't know."

"So you can remember an SNL sketch almost verbatim but couldn't remember me lying on my deathbed for two weeks?"

"You weren't on your deathbed," Arnesto said. "I don't know how it works. It seems random."

"But this all started with your great play in gym class way back when?"

Arnesto sat bolt upright. "No, it didn't! This has been happening for... years. They were little things, though. I always sort of shrugged them off."

"Is there any sort of pattern you can detect?"

"It seems like they're increasing in frequency."

"That's good... I think," Pete said, scratching his head. "Is there anything you can remember about the future right now?"

Arnesto looked straight ahead and unfocused his eyes. After a few seconds, he turned to Pete. "No, nothing."

"Hmm. Maybe you need to think about something specific. Like high school. Concentrate hard and see what you can remember."

This time, Arnesto closed his eyes. He took a deep breath and let it out. At long last, he opened his eyes, looking disappointed.

"Nothing?" Pete asked.

"Dude, nothing *ever* happens at school." Pete nodded in agreement.

"It's late," Arnesto said. "I should get going."

"Alright, we're not making much progress tonight anyway. I'll see which of my parents will drive you home. I'll check in with you on Monday."

Come Monday morning, Pete checked in with Arnesto. No new memories. Tuesday, Wednesday, nothing. Soon Pete stopped checking in and soon after that, they stopped talking about it altogether.

Finally, three weeks later, Arnesto grabbed Pete and pulled him aside after Trigonometry. "I had one — a future memory. We have to go to the mall!" he said.

"What? Why?"

27

Arnesto looked around to make sure the coast was clear. "There's a chick with enormous knockers!"

"What... the *hell* is wrong with you! For fuck's sake, I thought somebody was going to die or something. Well, what mall? When?"

"I don't know," Arnesto said.

Pete's shoulders slumped. "Do you remember anything else?"

"No. I was checking out Stephanie Summers in class — as always — and she stretched, arching her back, sticking out her chest like this—" Arnesto mimicked the motion.

"Arnesto, stop! People can see."

"And I remembered the girl at the mall. Dude, you have to *see* this chick!"

"How will we find her if you don't know where or when she'll be?"

"Hmm," Arnesto said. "I guess we'll do what we did last time and we'll run into her sooner or later."

"But now we can't. The first time, it happened naturally. Now, I'm always going to be thinking, 'Is this the day? Should we go to the mall today?' Our thought process has been altered because you had to go and alter the timeline."

"You're right... damn it."

"No offense, but so far your skill only seems good for depriving me of pleasure."

Intervention

School Entrance
Monday, March 28, 1988
Morning

PETE WAS WAITING for Arnesto at the school entrance when he arrived Monday morning. Arnesto knew it was important if Pete couldn't even wait for him at their lockers.

"Do you remember anything about Chris Wood?" Pete asked as they walked down the hallway. Arnesto shook his head. "Anything about a tree?" More head shaking. "What about a car?"

"No. What's going on?" Arnesto asked.

"They're saying Chris Wood borrowed his parent's car Saturday night without permission, lost control, and hit a tree. He's alive, but he hit his head pretty hard. They're saying he may not be the same after this, even if hc makes it."

"Wow, that sucks." Arnesto knew who Chris Wood was, but they didn't have any classes together and never crossed paths.

"How about now? Remember anything now?" Pete asked.

Arnesto shook his head. "No, nothing. Why?"

"If you had remembered before it happened, could you have

29

prevented it?"

"Interesting. How would that work? Walk up to him and tell him he's going to get into an accident? If his joyride was a spur-of-the-moment decision, he would have thought I was crazy. Or if he planned it, he would have wondered how the hell I knew."

"Right. Either way, he doesn't believe you and drives anyway. Maybe he avoids the accident but thinks you're a freak and tells everyone. Or worse, he still gets hurt and thinks you tampered with the car somehow." They sidestepped a couple football players walking the opposite direction. Pete continued, "The trick is to help without getting caught."

"We could have anonymously called Chris's parents suggesting they hide the keys. Or blocked their driveway that night. Or—"

"Or chopped down the tree, if we knew which tree. Wait, the accident would have still happened, never mind," Pete said.

"Actually, that's not bad, depending on what was behind the tree. If it was a field, then losing control of the vehicle while not having a serious injury might have scared some sense into Chris. My solutions would have worked that night, but maybe he would have tried again later and hit a different tree on a different night."

"Phew!" Pete said. "It's enough to make your head spin. Let's say you were able to save him and get away with it. Here's a bigger question: should you? I keep thinking about that kid whose nose you saved at the powderpuff game. What if getting hit would've started him on the path to becoming a world-class plastic surgeon?"

Arnesto laughed. "Or maybe the trauma of the event would've turned him into a supervillain. I can tell you this: life is not a zero-sum game. If I do something good, the universe isn't going to compensate by making something bad happen. It could even lead to more good, like the woman who saves a drowning baby that grows up and becomes a doctor and saves the woman's life many years later."

Pete smiled; he liked what he was hearing.

"It's kind of a moot point. There's no way I could exactly reproduce my former life even if I wanted to. Everything I do and say, for example, this very conversation, may bring about changes that I couldn't do anything about even if I knew about them. So yeah, may as well try to help people. Wait a minute. Did you just talk me into becoming a do-gooder?"

Now it was Pete's turn to be amused. "I guess it's true, 'With great power, comes great responsibility.'" Pete noticed Arnesto's confused look and said, "Voltaire."

"I know," Arnesto said, lying. "You just reminded me that they're making a Spider-Man movie… someday."

"Spider-Man, huh? Is it any good?"

"Yeah, it's great. They had this cool trailer of a helicopter caught in a giant web between the towers of the World Trade Center. No, wait, they pulled the trailer... I can't remember why. But anyway, they keep making more and more Spider-Man movies and they only get worse."

"So I'll only see the first one." Pete smiled. "See? You *can* use your power for good!"

"Let's see about that," Arnesto said, noticing the situation escalating outside their homeroom door.

"You don't hit a girl!" Todd Shea yelled. He was arguing with Nicholas Montgomery about some incident that occurred the previous summer. Apparently, Todd had just found out about it and decided to voice his concerns. Todd also had backup: three of his intimidatingly large jock friends whose names Arnesto didn't know.

"She gave me a bloody nose!" Nicholas said, standing alone.

"I don't care. You don't hit a girl!"

Despite Todd's well-crafted rebuttal, Arnesto knew — from experience — that the conversation was about to turn physical. He maneuvered around the jocks and positioned himself alongside Todd and Nicholas, who were only inches apart.

"Guys, teacher's coming," Arnesto said. They looked around but didn't disperse as Arnesto hoped they would.

"*What* teacher?" one of the jocks asked.

"Come on, guys, you don't want to get suspended over something that happened last year, do you?" Arnesto asked.

"He hit a girl!"

"Well, you make a good point. But still, this is not the place. You'll get suspended," Arnesto said, hoping to reinforce his point through repetition.

"Teacher," one of the jocks said as Mrs. Gonzalez approached.

"Fag," another jock whispered as he bumped into Arnesto's shoulder.

"Fagesto," the first jock said.

"Heh, Fagesto," the second jock repeated. They chortled back and forth at their hilarious new insult.

They did it. They actually found a way to make my name worse.

"Thanks, Arnesto," Nicholas said with a smile as they watched the jocks leave for their respective homerooms.

"Guess they're not fans of gender equality," Arnesto said, rubbing his shoulder where the jock had bumped him. Nicholas left for his homeroom as Arnesto and Pete walked into theirs.

"That was brave," Pete said after he and Arnesto took their seats. "What would have happened if you hadn't stepped in?"

"Nothing." Arnesto put his A-period books on his desk then resumed rubbing his shoulder. "Seriously, there would have been a minor scuffle, then they both would have gotten suspended for a week. That's it."

"Oh." Pete sounded disappointed. "Then why did you intervene?"

"Nicholas is a friend of mine. I always regretted not backing him up."

"Well, you made up for it. How do you feel?"

"Kind of good. I hope I didn't make it worse somehow."

* * *

As their sophomore year dragged toward its final days, Pete started to enjoy coming to school in the morning. Arnesto's memories were coming in faster than ever before, and Pete never knew which of Arnesto's faces would greet him. Usually there was neutral-face, which meant no new memories. Sometimes there was giddy-face, which meant Arnesto remembered something interesting, though usually not useful. Finally, there was concerned-face, which meant Arnesto remembered something negative.

But this time, Arnesto was wearing a new expression which made concerned-face look paltry by comparison. Arnesto stood motionless, staring blankly with his head leaning into his closed locker. He had bags under his eyes. Pete looked around the area to verify the coast was clear.

"Rough night?" he asked. Arnesto replied with a weak nod. "I can tell. You look like shit. You remember something?" Another nod.

"What? What did you remember?" Arnesto stood up, turned, and lifted his heavy eyes toward his friend. He muttered a single word.

"Everything."

Connections

Morgan Residence
Saturday, June 25, 1988
Late Evening

THE BULLFROG LEFT the pool skimmer and went flying over the chain link fence into the woods behind Pete's house. Arnesto was impressed. "Good distance."

Pete wore a satisfied grin. "That might be the winner. Here, you get the last one while I get the snacks." He handed the long pole to Arnesto who walked toward the deep end of the pool as Pete disappeared into the kitchen. Pete reemerged as Arnesto raised the final trespasser out of the water. The deal was they could only use the hot tub if they cleared out all the bullfrogs first.

Arnesto took slow strides around the pool toward the fence as he balanced the amphibian at the other end of the skimmer. "For the championship," he proclaimed as he brought the skimmer end back before swinging it forward. However, the bullfrog slipped off the end too soon and only landed about ten feet behind the fence. "Damn it, I still don't have the touch." He put the skimmer down by the pool and stepped into the hot tub where Pete was already waiting. Pete handed him a root beer popsicle. "Thanks, I needed this," Arnesto said, taking a bite.

"So let me get this straight," Pete said. "You have the memories of an old man — excuse me, an older version of *you* — thanks to a brain procedure involving some *Star Trek* shit that *you* came up with that also kills you."

"That's correct," Arnesto said, taking another bite of his popsicle. "Well, I'm like ninety-nine percent sure it killed me. My final moments wouldn't have made it out of my hypothalamus into long-term memory. Believe me, at that age, I was ready to die."

"I have so many questions."

"I grant thee three."

"Hell no! You come into my hot tub eating my popsicles and lay this shit on me. I'm asking you *everything*," Pete barked. Arnesto laughed so hard he almost choked on his popsicle.

"Okay! Ask away," Arnesto said, once he regained his composure.

Pete sighed. "At least you're getting your sense of humor back." He thought for a few moments then smiled. "O wise oracle, when do we get laid?"

Arnesto quickly turned to Pete. "What, together?! *Never*, you sick fuck!" he said, feigning disgust.

"You know what I mean!"

"Let me think. Senior year. Well, yours is toward the end of senior year. Mine is soon after."

"Damn, that's two years away. Is it... with Sylvia?" Pete asked anxiously. Unlike Arnesto, who crushed on a great many girls, Pete spent most of high school fixated on one unknowing Sylvia Bowers.

"No, you haven't met your first yet. You meet her at work. That reminds me, have you applied for that hospital kitchen job yet?"

"I... was working on it," Pete said. "I guess I shouldn't be surprised that you knew I was applying. This is going to take some getting used to. So nothing ever happens between me and Sylvia?"

Arnesto sensed Pete's pain. "No, sorry. Well, you didn't make anything happen before, but that doesn't mean you can't this time."

"Nah, I can't talk to her. She makes me too nervous. Let's change the subject. Ooh, what's the greatest invention of the next century or so? After your time-traveling memory thing, of course."

"Good question." Arnesto had to think about this one for a bit, then he smiled. "Yoga pants. They're like tights, except women wear them *everywhere*, even to work."

"The future sounds awesome! Who wins the election?"

"Bush."

"Who wins the *next* election? Bush again?"

"No, he loses to Bill Clinton, from Arkansas. I should probably warn him against sleeping with his interns."

"I won't ask. Are there aliens?"

"From space? No." They both looked disappointed. "But there are planets. Like metric shit-tons of planets. They find so many that most scientists believe it's highly likely that there's life out there. Space travel's still a bitch, though. Hey, do you want to know how you die?"

"*Hell* no! Please, I don't ever want—"

"Autoerotic asphyxiation. Pretty impressive for a man of your years. Don't worry, I'll erase your browser history."

"I don't know what a browser is, and I don't care. Please stop being a dick, and promise me you won't tell me anything about my future. If you do, I'm going to fret about it until it happens."

"Okay, I promise," Arnesto said.

"Thank you. So... why now? Why did your memories all come back at once?"

"My best guess is that it was some sort of feedback loop. The more electrical impulses phased in, the more my brain became a grounding station — a focal point — until it reached a critical mass. Then it was done. I was complete."

"A complete *tool*," Pete corrected. "Well, at least now we know why it all happened. But dang, I'm still sad about Sylvia."

"Well, if it's any consolation, I'm 99% sure the Celtics never invite me to a tryout."

"Their loss." They sat melancholy for a bit. Pete suddenly chimed in. "How do they do without you warming the bench?"

Arnesto realized what Pete was insinuating. "Let's see. Next year will be the '89 playoffs. I'm not positive, but I think they lose. I'm pretty sure they get run over by the Pistons in the first round." They were now both sitting up perfectly straight, smiling from ear to ear.

"Would you be willing to bet on that?"

Arnesto stretched his arms along the back of the hot tub. "How could I *not*?"

"Another popsicle, good sir?" Pete asked as he got out and headed inside the house.

"Indubitably, good sir!"

Pete returned not thirty seconds later with fresh popsicles. "So... how do we do it? Do we find a bookie?"

"No, they're always bad news in the movies. What about Atlantic City?" Arnesto asked.

"There's a casino in Connecticut that's much closer."

"We have no way in."

"We have no way in in Atlantic City."

"Don't you have family in Jersey? What about your cousin... Barry?" Arnesto asked.

"Larry."

"Didn't he turn twenty-one a while back?"

"Yeah, he did. I don't know if he'll want to place a bet for us, though."

Arnesto took another bite of his popsicle. "I've got it," he said. "Well cut him in for a share of our profits. It's hard to argue with free money. We'll have to convince him *why* we think the Pistons will go all the way this year. Then we'll keep betting on them every game, and we're guaranteed to win more than we lose. We'll have to lose some, though, to avoid arousing suspicions."

"It's not just about winning or losing; you need to factor in the vigorish."

"Oh, I intend to bet *vigorishly*."

Pete groaned. "Get serious. Why do we have to go to Atlantic City? Can't we call him?"

"How would we get him the money to bet and how would he get us our winnings? Besides, my memory — it could be wrong. If I suddenly remember a different outcome, or a different game to bet on, whatever, we might need to contact him to cancel or increase a bet. Look — if those kids in *Stand by Me* can hike twenty hours to see a dead body, we can drive four hours to make a fortune. C'mon, it'll be *fun!*"

"Alright, fine," Pete said. "But I know you really want to see the attractions."

"Don't you?"

"Yeah, kinda."

* * *

Junior year began and Arnesto, being a few months older than Pete, was the first to get his driver's license. This worked out well, as Arnesto could drive them both to their new hospital kitchen job. With evening and weekend differentials, not to mention the extra shifts they picked up in preparation for their future sports betting, they would have rather decent bankrolls with which to later build their fortunes.

"I hope we don't get Eugene today," Pete said, referring to his least favorite boss. "Have you worked with him yet?"

"No, not yet," Arnesto said, merging onto the highway. "You know, he starts off gruff with new people, but once you get to know him, he's alright."

"So you *have* worked with him, just not in *this* lifetime." Pete looked at Arnesto, who shrugged. "I don't know if I'll ever get used to this superpower of yours." He turned toward the passenger side mirror then turned and looked out the back window. "Hey, this guy is right on your ass."

"Jesus, where did *he* come from," Arnesto said, looking in the rearview mirror. They were in the left lane going fifty-five in a forty-five-mile-per-hour zone with a pickup truck tailgating a few feet behind them.

Pete pointed to a vehicle several car-lengths ahead of them in the other lane. "Catch up to that car, don't let him pass."

"Ha ha, yeah," Arnesto agreed, pushing down the accelerator.

However, a few seconds later, Arnesto instead pulled into the right lane behind the car and slowed down almost to the speed limit. The pickup sped past, flipping them off.

"What'd you do that for? Why'd you let him pass?" Pete asked.

"Because," Arnesto said, "he was going to try to kill us."

Pete knew Arnesto wasn't kidding. "Shit, what happened?"

"Nothing, thankfully. First he cut us off and slammed on the brakes trying to get us to hit him. Then he tried to engage us in a game of chicken, but we were able to avoid it by hanging too far behind him. We got lucky."

"Huh. Well, if you know nothing happens, why not do it again? I mean, it could have been interesting."

"Pete," Arnesto said, turning to Pete and sounding more like a disappointed father than a cocky teenager, "I told you, that's not how it works. There's no way I could exactly reproduce what happened the last time. My timing would be at least a tiny bit off, perhaps causing us to ram him... or worse."

"Alright, forgive me for being an actual teenager and not Nostradamus, like you."

"Tell you what," Arnesto said, getting back into the left lane and hitting the gas, "we'll follow him from a safe distance and make sure he doesn't kill somebody else in our absence. Maybe he'll put on a show for you."

The "show" wasn't much, only some weaving in and out of traffic and more vulgarities.

They made it to work and had a wholly uninteresting shift. Pete was on soups and salads followed by washing dishes while Arnesto was stuck on "floors," widely known as the least desirable of the kitchen

41

jobs. The other ten or so jobs, while in no way glamorous, all required some element of teamwork and thus, social interaction. But not "floors," where you not only spent the bulk of the shift mopping, you did so alone with almost no interaction other than Eugene pointing out spots you missed. Arnesto didn't even realize Jacqueline was working in the cafeteria that night until he saw her sign out her timecard at the end of the shift.

Jacqueline was two years older, a college freshman, and a babe, the kind who has an instant chemistry with everyone she talks to. She was the kind that engages you in conversation so casually and naturally that men find themselves thinking about her and wondering why they can never meet someone like her.

"Hey, we're having burgers tonight, let's go," Pete said with great insistence.

"Hold on, I'll meet you at the car," Arnesto said, running after Jacqueline.

"Where are you going?"

"I'm going to have sex with her real quick. Be right there!"

Pete lingered behind as he watched Arnesto catch up with her.

"Um, Jacqueline?" Arnesto asked.

"Hi!" she said with her smile which lit up the room.

"Uh, yeah, I saw you driving the other day—"

"I didn't hit you, did I?" she joked.

"This is going to sound weird, but it looked like you weren't wearing your seatbelt."

"Aw, you're worried about me. Sometimes I forget."

"Jacqueline, you have to remember to wear it." Her smile left. The conversation had turned awkward. "A cousin of mine was just killed in

a car accident. He would've lived if he had been wearing his seatbelt."
She didn't say anything, so he continued. "I'm sorry, this is weird. I just
wouldn't want anything to happen to that pretty face of yours."

"I'll try to remember. Goodnight, boys," she said to both of them,
somewhat patronizingly before turning to leave.

"And if a rodent jumps in front of your car, it's better to hit it and
maintain control than to swerve into oncoming traffic!"

"Okay!" she yelled back.

"That was quite specific," Pete said. "Come on, my family's
waiting."

"I hope she listens," sighed Arnesto. "We'll find out soon enough."

"You did the right thing."

"God, I can't wait until we have self-driving cars! But that's like
decades away still. Even if I saved Jacqueline, so many more are going
to die in auto accidents before then."

"Seriously? Self-driving cars?"

"Yeah, they virtually eliminate drinking and driving, texting and
driving, road rage, you name it."

"How do they work?" Pete asked.

"Lots of lasers and path-finding and... stuff, I'm not sure."

"That's cool. What's texting?"

"It's how people communicate in the near future without having to
actually talk to one another. It's awesome. I'll explain in the car."

Appeal to Pity

Atlantic City, New Jersey
Sunday, November 6, 1988
Afternoon

NOVEMBER ARRIVED, and that meant it was time to start gambling their earnings. They would make the drive to Atlantic City on a weekend day, meet Pete's cousin Larry, and give him the money. He would disappear into the casino, then return ten minutes later with their betting slips. The next week they would return with the winning slips and leave with new slips and some money. And then they would leave with *more* money. And then they… stopped.

The long drive got old in a hurry, but that wasn't the problem. The problem was they were sixteen and still bound financially to their parents. They couldn't even open up new bank accounts without their mom or dad's signature. They also didn't have much to spend the money on — what big purchases could they make that they wouldn't have to hide them from their families? Once they turned eighteen, they reasoned, they would be free to do as they pleased.

For the most part, high school plodded along. With the extra money, they were able to cut back on their shifts at the hospital, which gave them more time to goof off and talk about girls. One difference was that Arnesto's grades were climbing. Naturally, this concerned Pete.

"Is everything alright with you?" Pete asked, after scoring a layup on Arnesto.

"Yeah, why do you ask? Check." They were playing losers-outs, so Arnesto was now on offense. He tossed the ball to Pete to check it. Pete tossed it right back.

"In homeroom, you didn't ask me what book we were reading for our book report due *today*." Pete guarded Arnesto who drove to the left. "And I didn't see you frantically reading the Cliff's Notes either," referring to the popular study guides of which Arnesto had built an impressive collection.

Arnesto smiled. He drove quickly to the right before yelling, "Kareem Abdul-Jabbar skyhook!" The ball clanged off the rim to the left, giving Pete the rebound. "God-*damnit* I used to make those."

"In which lifetime?" Pete taunted as he dribbled to the top of the key.

"This one, ass. Anyway, I finally realized — or I guess remembered — that it can actually be fun to put a little effort in. I was thirty when I finally learned this."

Pete's three-point attempt hit the back of the rim and went flying back out to him. "Good for you," Pete encouraged. "Is that why you're acing Advanced Chem?"

"Well, partly, but in that class I'm mostly doing better from experience. Chemistry becomes a big part of my later research. Hey, do you want to know which elements the periodic table is missing?"

"Not particularly. But I can see how high school being little more than a beginner's review would make things easier for you. So are you a super genius now?"

"No, of course not. I don't cure cancer until at least my fifties," Arnesto joked. "Nine-ten, check."

Pete rolled his eyes. Arnesto had gone on a five-point tear after being down four-ten. This made Pete particularly adverse to his jokes. However, Pete's well-timed block and Arnesto's subsequent swearing returned a smile to Pete's face. It was short-lived.

They heard the hallway door open and watched as Stephanie Summers walked across the gym floor toward the side entrance. "See you tomorrow, Stephanie," Arnesto said.

"Bye!" Stephanie said, exiting the gym to the east parking lot.

Pete's lower jaw dropped as he turned to Arnesto. "You're talking to Stephanie Summers now?" Neither Pete nor Arnesto had any trouble talking to the girls they worked with at the hospital, but the girls there were mostly from other schools. But this was *their* high school, where one didn't start conversing with those who spent more than a decade forming cliques and ignoring guys like Pete and Arnesto.

"Yeah, we both got to Social Studies early, so I braced myself and said hi to her. We only talked a little, but she seems pretty nice. Truth is, most everybody feels at least a little awkward at our age."

Pete reflected on this before replying. "Well, shit, dude, ask her out."

"I — I don't know," Arnesto said.

"What? What is it?"

"She seems kind of... young. She's still in high school," Arnesto said in earnest.

"*So are you!*" Pete screamed before powering his way to the hoop to win the game 11-9. "Come on, let's go get some grub." They grabbed

46

their bags and headed back into the hallway then out the northern exit to the teacher's lot where Arnesto had parked his car ("because I can").

"'She's still in high school.' For fuck's sake!" Pete repeated, shaking his head as they strode into the lot.

"Hey, can we catch a ride?" asked a couple girls, standing on the sidewalk. The boys didn't recognize them. They might have been sophomores. It was a big school.

"Sorry, I have a two-seater," Arnesto lied.

"We'll sit on your laps," the same girl offered.

"Sorry, I can't."

The boys walked in silence. Pete waited until they were both inside Arnesto's car before asking, "Why didn't you want to?"

Arnesto put the key in the ignition but didn't turn it. He thought about it. He had no reason to turn them down aside from a weak gut feeling about what, picking up hitchhikers? From his own school? He realized that, for once, he had made the exact same decision the last time, in his previous life. This meant he had no other experience on which to inform him in *this* life, other than knowing that if he did nothing, nothing would happen.

"Ah, what the hell. We'll try it your way this time around," he finally said, starting the car. They drove around and pulled up to the sidewalk next to the girls. After a brief conversation, they picked up Amy and Sheryl, who were so grateful for the lift, they didn't mention the fact that Arnesto's car had magically grown a backseat. Aside from Amy's directions, the short ride to her house was mostly filled with awkward silence.

"Thank you so much," Amy said before she and Sheryl disappeared into Amy's house.

"See? You did a good deed and nothing bad happened," assured Pete. "Let's go eat!"

They ordered their burgers and fries. Pete got a Coke while Arnesto got a water, to Pete's surprise, as Arnesto loved soda as much as anyone he knew. Arnesto explained how horribly unhealthy soda was and how it gave him kidney stones in his thirties. "I will *die* before I go through that again," he said as they grabbed a table and sat down.

"Speaking of death, our debate is tomorrow," Pete said. They both enjoyed their Speech, Discussion, and Debate class, as the homework was unusually light, a small price to pay for the occasional embarrassment of having to speak in front of the class. They had been given the task of arguing against gun control versus Michelle Parker and Nicole Clark, two of the better students in class, who were arguing in favor of gun control.

"Oh my god, no. We need to prepare." Arnesto said, looking distraught.

"Don't worry," Pete said. "I'll pretend I'm sick and then we can work on it over the weekend."

"Pete, no. We tried that. It didn't work. We got shellacked."

"What happened?"

"You fought bravely, my friend," Arnesto sighed. "Really, I remember this all too well. You try to convince Mrs. Spencer that you aren't up for it, but she doesn't back down. She's not mean or anything about it. You give it a shot, and it seems we're in the clear, but then she comes back at you, repeat. Your debate with her about whether you're fit to debate lasts twice as long as the actual debate! And then we wind up having to have the stupid debate anyway!"

"Jesus," was all Pete could say. After a couple bites of his burger, he continued, "I guess we'd better prepare then."

"Good. It's not like we have to bust our asses. We only need to spend a little time—"

"Unless," Pete interrupted, "I can talk our way out of it this time. No, hear me out. Now that I know I will lose the battle, can't we prevent it? What do you remember us saying exactly?"

"Nothing! I don't remember what either of you said because it was so painful to watch that I blocked it from my memory as soon as I could. All I remember is a lot of back and forth." They were now debating the debate of whether they would debate.

"Come on, let me try. I know I can get us out of it this time. *Please*," Pete said.

Arnesto thought about it. What did it matter anyway? It was one graded assignment for one class. Did it ever affect their lives after that? Not really. But it did give them something to laugh about down the road.

"Fine," Arnesto said at last.

* * *

Less than twenty-four hours later, it was time for battle.

"Next up: gun control. Who's debating?" Mrs. Spencer asked.

"Uh, Mrs. Spencer? I'm not feeling well," Pete said.

Here we go, thought Arnesto, while remaining steadfastly silent like the rest of the class.

"I'm sorry, Pete, but it won't take long," Mrs. Spencer said in her usual encouraging tone.

"I can't — I'm really not feeling well today."

49

Go, Pete, go, Arnesto thought. *No, what am I saying, don't get your hopes up.*

"You don't look that sick, are you sure you can't give your debate?" Mrs. Spencer asked.

"I'm sure. I can't do it, I'm sorry."

"It will only take ten minutes. Could you please try?"

While history was awkwardly repeating itself, Arnesto tried to think. He could rattle off the names of dozens of subatomic particles, many of which had yet to be discovered, but he couldn't remember any decent arguments against gun control, other than gross misinterpretations of the Second Amendment. All he could come up with were slogans from bumper stickers, like, "If guns are outlawed, only outlaws will have guns" and "Gun control means using both hands." Well, if history was going to repeat itself, and it sure seemed like it was, it couldn't hurt to join in. Maybe *he* could save them.

"Mrs. Spencer? Pete's really sick, I would like to motion for a continuance." Pete turned and glared at Arnesto while Mrs. Spencer and half the class turned their heads toward him in bewilderment.

"I'm sorry, boys, I must ask you to try. And this is a school debate, not a courthouse hearing." Several students snickered.

"Alright," Arnesto said, getting up and walking to the front. Pete had no choice but to follow.

Michelle and Nicole went first and gave several well-thought-out and articulate arguments. Though unprepared, Pete did a surprisingly good job arguing. Arnesto's rebuttal, on the other hand...

"Statistics, statistics, statistics. Sure, we can cite statistics all day, but then we'd be ignoring the *human* element." It only got worse from there.

50

When it was all over, the remaining students voted on whether they were in favor of gun control. Like Arnesto remembered, they lost twenty to one.

"I *had* it. Now we're screwed," Pete hissed at Arnesto.

"It's over now," Arnesto whispered back. "Besides, you get a B+."

"Oh," Pete said, feeling satisfied. The following Monday, they would, in fact, receive the same grades Arnesto remembered, a B+ for Pete and a C- for Arnesto.

Words Hurt

Homeroom
Thursday, March 2, 1989

EAGER TO PUT the debate debacle behind them, the boys chose to focus on other subjects. Pete was already seated in homeroom and engrossed in a textbook when Arnesto walked in and sat down.

"Hey," Arnesto said.

Pete abruptly turned. "Oh, I didn't hear you swish into class. You're wearing jeans?! What happened to your corduroys?"

"I wanted to be prepared for when cords go out of fashion," Arnesto whispered.

"Yes, it's good to be prepared for *five years ago*. Hold on, something else is different about you. Your eyebrows..."

Arnesto smiled and rubbed the freshly shaved spot between his eyebrows. "I have two of them now."

"Look at you making yourself over. I'm impressed. Any other surprises?"

"No other shurprishes." Arnesto quickly covered his mouth with his hand but then slowly lowered it when he realized Pete wasn't about to stop staring him down. Arnesto gave a fake smile, revealing the metal underneath.

"You're wearing your retainer again? Why?"

"I didn't wear it enough," Arnesto said, "and I have the feeling my teeth might get a little crooked later in life." He removed the retainer from his mouth. "It's still annoying, though. Excuse me while I go rinse this off in the drinking fountain." Arnesto left and returned a minute later.

"What's that?" he asked, nodding toward Pete's book.

Pete flashed him the cover of the SAT prep guide he was reading.

"Ah, the SATs," Arnesto said. "An excellent measure of one's ability to... take the SATs."

"Here," Pete said, "let me ask you one. Yogh is to Futhorc as Kalian is to...? Is the answer, A) Witenagemot, B) Cacomistle, C) Simoom, or D) Chaulmoogra?" He saw Arnesto's deer-in-the-headlights look and laughed. He held the book so Arnesto could read it for himself.

"Are you serious?" Arnesto asked. "What did they do, read Shakespeare and say, 'Oh, hey, guys, here's another word that's never been used anywhere else in history, let's hit them with it!'? It's bullshit."

"I concur, it's retarded."

"I haven't heard of any of these, and I mean, *ever*. Alright, I'll pick 'A', wine-age-moth or whatever."

"Witenagemot? I'm thinking it's 'B', Cacomistle, but who knows. Let me see," Pete said, flipping to the answer guide in the back. "Aha, it's 'C', Simoom. 'Just as a yogh is a single letter as opposed to a futhorc which represents an alphabet, along the same scale, a kalian, which is a pipe, draws in a small amount of smoke, as compared to a simoom, which is an entire wind.'"

Arnesto simulated flipping his desk in rage. "Is there an answer guide for the answer guide? I guess they expect us to read the dictionary?"

"If they do, that's pretty retarded." Pete resumed reading.

Arnesto looked around, then leaned over and tapped Pete on the shoulder. "Why do you keep saying the r-word?"

"What? What r-word?" Pete thought for a moment. "'Retarded?'"

"Yeah, it's offensive. It's like the n-word," Arnesto said.

"Just because you got that question wrong doesn't mean you're retarded."

"No, not me, people who are… specially abled."

"You're saying," Pete said, "the *r-word* is offensive. Wait a minute." His eyes narrowed into slits. "Since *when*?"

Arnesto thought for a little while. "I'm not sure. One of these days. Or years. Wouldn't you like to get a headstart on it though?"

Pete rolled his eyes. "Okay, any other terms that suddenly become offensive?"

"Just you wait. After 2010, people get offended by *everything*."

* * *

Two Saturdays later, they took the SATs, and three weeks after that, they received their results in homeroom. Arnesto opened his envelope and after a quick peek, put his results down.

"1250. I cannot believe I got the same exact score." Though it was a good score, he was still disappointed.

Pete finished looking at his own score and grabbed Arnesto's. His eyes widened as he slumped back in his seat. "You're an idiot," he said. Still slumped and looking downward, he grudgingly held out Arnesto's results. Taking a closer look, Arnesto's own eyes widened when he saw his score: 1520. He couldn't believe it. He was only eighty points from what in 1989 was a perfect score of 1600, placing him in the top one percent nationwide.

Unable to show his ebullience (one dare not boast about academic achievements in school), he decided to focus on Pete.

"How did you do?" he asked. Pete meekly raised his open palm toward his own results. Arnesto accepted the invitation and grabbed them off Pete's desk. "1340. That's great." It was. "You improved 10 points, I think," he whispered. Pete finally turned his head and looked at Arnesto.

"Fuck you."

Foul Play

Arnesto's Bank
Tuesday, May 2, 1989
Lunchtime

ARNESTO LIKED to run errands during lunch. This gave him the chance to get off school grounds for a bit, even though it was against the rules to leave campus during school hours. You could get suspended for sitting in your own car with the engine off. Even so, he never got caught. On days when he planned on making his "prison breaks," as he called them, he parked in the wide-open east parking lot. Faculty must have thought no one would be foolish enough to try to leave from that lot, so it was the least patrolled.

On this particular day, Arnesto escaped to the bank to deposit his work check and some cash. He and Pete had just started betting again and with each paycheck, he snuck a little more of his gambling winnings into his account. It was safer in the bank than one of his hiding spots in the woods behind his house.

With all other variables equal, Arnesto had managed to walk into the bank at roughly the same exact time as he had in his previous life. However, the extra cash increased the duration of his transaction by a few seconds. It was that small but important extra time that allowed Norma, the teller in the next window over, to finish up with her customer before Arnesto's business concluded.

"I can help the next person," Norma said as Arnesto was being handed his receipt. Eula Romero was that next person. "Well, hi, Eula, how are you?" Eula and Norma knew each other from way back and had a nice chat. This put Eula in a better mood, making her less of a bitch, according to Ashley.

Ashley Morris was a sensitive, teenage nurse's aide working her first part-time job at the retirement home. She was not happy to be working that night with Eula, who was the charge nurse. Ashley felt Eula was particularly hard on her, while Eula felt Ashley needed more discipline. However, that night, Eula's mood seemed slightly better than usual.

Normally when her shift was over, Ashley left in a hurry before Eula could nag her any further. Instead, Eula let Ashley go early, so there was no need to rush. Perhaps that's why Ashley caught something moving out of the corner of her eye as she passed Doris Cook's room.

Doris Cook was suffering from dementia and wasn't long for this world. She was also a fall risk and trying to get out of bed to fetch her glasses, unaware they were already within reach on the tray table right next to her bed. One can hardly blame a senile, old woman with poor vision for such a mistake.

"Mrs. Cook!" Ashley exclaimed, reaching Doris just in time to catch her before she fell. Ashley helped Doris get back under the covers then handed the old woman her glasses before returning to the nurse's station to inform Eula, who was grateful, though she didn't show it.

Eula wanted to transfer Doris to a bed with sidebars, for Doris's protection, though she was still trying to wrangle permission from Janet Howard, Doris's daughter. It was a fine line between protecting the patient and patient rights. Since Ashley caught her in time, Eula wouldn't have to fill out an incident report, nor would she have to call Janet, who would undoubtedly have been upset and rushed right over.

Having not received any unexpected phone calls from her mother's nursing home, Janet Howard was now free to drive her son David to the game. David Howard would have made it in any case, as his father would have driven him. But Janet, being more uptight than her husband, helped David get there sooner.

David was thirteen years old, and found it hard to contain himself, especially as he and his mother were allowed into one of the employees-only entrances at Boston Garden. It was the third game of the first round of the playoffs, and the Celtics were already down two games to the Pistons.

As David's dad told him, "You're going to get more time on the floor than Larry Bird!" This was true, as Bird had quit the season early due to medical issues. David was ready. Once he arrived on the floor and the game began, he was so focused on his job as towel boy, he didn't even know who fouled whom. All he knew was that it was only the first quarter and this was his chance to shine. After the whistle, he ran out with his towel and wiped up the players' sweat off the parquet floor. He did a fine job, then ran off the court even faster than he had run onto it. And that was all it took.

If David had instead arrived at the arena a little later, due to his father's driving, then Philip would have been the one mopping up the sweat that time. And Philip, being less conscientious, would have missed one little spot which one of the Pistons would have pointed out to him. The Pistons player would have subconsciously altered his position as a result, and in doing so, would have been in a slightly better position to catch the rebound of the missed free throw. But that didn't happen. Instead, the Celtics got the rebound.

That one little extra rebound changed the entire flow of the game from that point on. The Celtics scored more than they should have, and the Pistons scored fewer. In the end, some chaos theory-induced series of events caused the Celtics to barely claim victory in a game they were not supposed to win.

This was upsetting to Pete, who had bet a couple thousand dollars on the game. "What the hell?!" he yelled at Arnesto the next day after school.

The results were even more upsetting to Arnesto, who had bet the same amount. "I don't know!" Arnesto yelled back.

"You told me," Pete said, gritting his teeth, "that the Pistons sweep the series."

"They — they did!"

"Obviously, they didn't!"

"I don't understand. I clearly remember them winning all three games. As a Celtics fan, I would remember something like that."

"Arnesto, are you sure it was this particular series? This season?"

"Well — yeah. Something's wrong. One of us must have... changed history. Did you drive over Isiah Thomas on the way home from school today?"

"I don't think so. Fuck. How can we ever bet on anything ever again?"

"Pete, I'm sure this was an isolated incident. I hope. The Pistons are still favored to win. I'm still going to bet on them."

"Not me. I'm out."

Learning Shortcuts

Shopping Mall
Thursday, June 29, 1989
Afternoon

AT LAST, they were in the home stretch. It was the summer after junior year and senior year was coming. Pete was excited, not to be going back to class but to be that much closer to the freedom of college.

"Are you looking forward to Mr. Hinkley's physics class?" he asked Arnesto as they browsed the video game selection at Babbage's. "I get the feeling it's going to be hands down our most interesting class this year."

"I'm… not taking it."

"What? You told me you were, C period, like me."

"Pete, I have to tell you something. I got accepted to State Commonwealth University of Massachusetts. Early entrance."

"What?! I mean, congratulations. When are you going?"

"September," Arnesto said.

"*This* September?! I guess it would have to be. What about high school? Are you not going to finish?" Arnesto shook his head. "Jesus H. Christ. So you're done? You're not going back *ever*?!" Pete asked. Again,

Arnesto shook his head. "Well, I knew high school wasn't your favorite thing, but I didn't know you hated it *that* much."

Arnesto gave Pete a quick head jerk to indicate they should walk out into the mall where they could expect a little more privacy. "It's not that exactly," Arnesto explained. "Pete, you have to understand. You've had three years of high school. I've had *seven*. Seven years at that place. I'm ready to get my life rolling. I'm also eager to meet my wife."

"Your *wife*?!"

"Technically, my first wife. We had many great years together, and I can't wait to see her again."

"I guess I can understand that. Why didn't you tell me sooner?"

"I didn't want to tell you until it happened. I just got in finally."

"And your parents are alright with this?" Pete asked. Arnesto winced. "You *didn't*. They don't know? Are you kidding me! Wait, they must have had to sign something."

"The process does require a parent's signature, yes," Arnesto confirmed. Pete stared at him in disbelief.

"You *forged* their signature?! Oh ho ho, you are in deep shit, buddy boy. There's no way you can pull this off. What's going to happen when, oh I don't know, you don't come home from school?" Pete was incredulous.

They paused by the top of the escalator outside Waldenbooks at the far end of the mall and looked around.

Arnesto shook his head. "She's not here." They went down a level then started walking back toward the main entrance. Arnesto resumed their conversation. "I have a plan," he said, smiling.

"Here we go," Pete said, not hiding his sarcasm.

"My parents are splitting up. I mean, not yet, but right before the start of senior year, assuming I haven't mucked up the timeline. But judging by their increasing animosity toward each other, I feel pretty confident it will still happen. My dad's going to move out. I figure after they announce it to me and my brother, that's when I can swoop in and be like, 'Hey, I have some good news. I'm also moving out because I got accepted to college early. Yay!'"

"Your parents are getting divorced? Wow, I'm sorry to hear that."

"No biggie," Arnesto said. Pete gave him a look, the kind of look a person gives their friend who's revealed his parents are getting divorced and then says, "No biggie." Seeing Pete's face, Arnesto felt compelled to explain, "They weren't meant to stay together. They each marry someone better for them and even make amends down the road. It all works out in the end. Now, what do you think of my *plan*?"

"It's atrocious. You're kind of hitting them while they're down," Pete said, feeling a couple of loops behind on this emotional roller coaster Arnesto was making him ride.

"Hitting them with *good* news," Arnesto corrected.

"Won't they *miss* you?"

"No. They might think they will. Or maybe not. We aren't getting along well at this point, and we definitely won't next year."

"Well," Pete said, "this sounds like the dumbest plan ever made, but knowing you, you might actually make it work. It's not like they can kick you out of the house, that's what you *want* for crying out loud. You know, I kind of want to see if you can pull it off."

"Thanks," Arnesto said, beaming.

"And I am sorry about your folks."

"No biggie."

* * *

Sunday, September 3, 1989
Late Evening

Arnesto grew restless as he listened to the heated argument coming from upstairs. *Come on, let's get this over with,* he thought. He was dying to know if his plan was going to work. What would he do if it didn't, go back to his high school and say, "Hey, my stupid parents wouldn't let me go to college early, can you give me some classes?" He shuddered at the thought.

Could he pretend to still go to high school while secretly attending college? He'd have to make that long commute back and forth almost every day. As he contemplated the logistics, he heard his parents' bedroom door open.

"Kids, come upstairs!" Arnesto's mom shouted.

Oh boy, here we go. Arnesto exhaled and headed toward the stairs. At the top, he met his bratty little brother Gerald, who had just come from his bedroom down the hall, and followed him into their parents' bedroom. His mom, Nancy, was sitting on the bed with a tissue in her face, distraught and crying, while Arnesto's father, Karl, packed a suitcase. The tension was palpable.

"Well? Tell them!" Nancy shook her tissue at Karl.

"I'm moving out."

"Tell them *why!*"

"Your mother and I have been fighting for a while and finally realized we're not compatible anymore." Gerald started crying and ran to his mother who held him. This left Arnesto as the only one without anything to do except stand there looking and feeling awkward.

"It's okay, Gerald," his mom said through tears of her own.

"I'll still be around," Karl said, "I've rented an apartment a few miles down the road. Look, nobody's hurt. It's not like anybody has cancer."

After an insufferably long silence, Nancy asked her sons, "Do you have any questions or anything?"

Arnesto shuffled his feet. This was the moment he had been waiting for. *Okay, here goes.* "Actually, I have some good news. I got accepted early admission." The other Modestos turned to look at him.

"What do you mean? When do you start?" Nancy asked.

"Next week." *Crap! Why did I say next week? I leave in two days. I'm choking, hold it together!*

"What?! What do you mean, you're leaving next week? What about your last year of high school? What about your diploma? Your friends? Karl, what do you have to say about this?!" Arnesto had difficulty keeping track of his mother's rapid-fire questioning, but wanted to have the answers ready, should he once again be allowed to speak.

"How are you going to pay for this?" Karl asked pragmatically. "We have a little bit of money saved up, but with our situation—"

"That's the best part. I got a full ride! Full scholarship, stipend, the works. It's all paid for!" There was no scholarship, but Arnesto had already taken care of the first semester with his gambling winnings. He had enough to cover at least three semesters after that, with plenty more opportunities to win more money during that time.

"Do you still plan on studying computers? Programmers only make about eighteen thousand a year."

Arnesto fought the urge to laugh. "I believe I'll find a way to make it work."

"What about your brother?" Nancy asked.

"Are you going to miss me, Ger? Do you want me to stick around another year so you and I can hang out all the time?" Arnesto's sarcasm was peeking through. He couldn't help it; anyone else's parents would have been proud. But not his. No, they had to put up a stink about *everything*, even something as impressive as this.

"No!" Gerald said. At least his brother was — in his own way — on his side.

"You know I was going to go away to college next year, right? What's the big deal?" Arnesto asked.

"Why didn't you tell us? Karl, what do you have to say about this?" Nancy asked. Arnesto was grateful he wasn't given the chance to answer, as he still hadn't come up with a good response. The answer he had given Pete, "I just got in," was no longer true; he had known for months.

"I'll still be around, too," Arnesto said before Karl could speak. It's only an hour away." *More like an hour and a half and still not nearly fucking far enough.* "I can come back and hang out with you every weekend, Mom." It was a threat.

"That's not the point," she said.

"Or if you really don't want me to go, I won't go. Maybe you're right. Maybe I should spend another year here at home. Of course, the school said they can't guarantee I'll get the scholarship again next year. So, I'll have to pick up extra shifts at the hospital. It won't be easy, but it shouldn't affect my grades too much if I'm careful. I was excited about going, but if it means that much to you, I can stick around here another year." *You mess with my life, I mess with YOU.*

"Now hold on," Karl said at last. "Your mother and I need to discuss this privately."

"Not tonight. I can't deal with anymore tonight," she said.

"Don't do anything until we discuss it. Now goodnight, both of you," Karl said.

Arnesto turned and walked out the door. As he walked toward his room, he smiled to himself. He knew his parents. There would be no discussion.

He had won.

Freedom of Assembly

Arnesto's Dorm Room
Tuesday, September 5, 1989
Afternoon

FREEDOM. THOUGH HE WAS still a minor at seventeen and therefore not truly independent, it was close enough. He was at long last out of the house and it was *sweeeeeet*.

No more getting up at 6:30 every damn morning (which is ridiculous for teenagers) to get to homeroom by 7:30. Now he had one class at 9:00 a.m. twice a week in his own dorm building and everything else was at least two hours after that. No more lectures from his parents, at least until he visited them again. No more getting grounded every time Gerald decided to start a fight with him.

Just like high school, college was easier the second time around, though the disparity was less. Having been a professional programmer for countless years in his previous life helped with his programming classes, however, he was having to relearn languages he had only ever used in college. He was used to C++, Python, and Java, but was now being forced to relearn LISP, ADA, and Fortran 77. He also had to take Assembly language programming, which, if it was any easier this time around, didn't reflect in his grades.

Then there was the matter of his wife. He didn't know what to do about her. First of all, he couldn't even *find* her. He was a year ahead of schedule and wasn't destined to meet her for another thirteen to fourteen months. He was pretty sure she was taking classes at the time, but if she was, he never saw her around campus. He periodically stopped by Mona's, the restaurant where she worked, or at least would a year from then, but still didn't see her. And he had another problem — he still had some growing up to do. Literally.

Arnesto was a late developer. Though he was her type — there was no question about that — would she, a nineteen-year-old hottie, still find seventeen-year-old, five-feet-seven Arnesto as attractive as she would a year from now when he was five inches taller? Hadn't she once confided in him that she preferred tall guys? And even if they did start dating, they were at different points in their lives. Would they still hit it off? More importantly, would she still be willing to sleep with him? Great. One of the primary reasons for coming to college early, and he might wind up having to wait anyway. Still, it wouldn't hurt to keep an eye out for her.

Weeks passed without any luck. New England was getting colder by the day. He could have called Mona's to see if Katrina was working, but that felt too creepy. Besides, what if he then came in and somebody recognized his voice? How would he explain that? So, if he wanted to see her, he had to leave the warmth of his dorm, walk a half mile to the only campus parking lot for which he had a pass, drive downtown, find a place to park, then peer into the front window of Mona's to see if he could spot her. By the time that failed and he reversed the process, it was a good forty-five minutes wasted.

He knew where she lived, too. Or would soon. He had also lived there, only a couple months after they had started dating. Still, he couldn't risk stalking her like that. Then again, was it really stalking knowing how she would feel about him?

* * *

Soon, it was Thanksgiving, and Arnesto and his brother Gerald were invited to an awkward Thanksgiving dinner at their dad's apartment. At least he would get to spend part of the weekend with Pete.

He went over the next day. While the rest of Pete's family was at the mall enjoying Black Friday, Pete had stayed home. He invited Arnesto downstairs into his father's office.

"Check it out, my dad got it through work," Pete said.

"Wow, is that a 486?!"

"Yup! Twenty-five megahertz, four megs of RAM, forty-megabyte hard drive, both five-and-a-quarter *and* three-and-a-half inch floppy drives."

"Damn! That must have cost several grand."

"Go ahead, boot it up." Pete grabbed another chair while Arnesto sat down at the keyboard.

Arnesto turned on the machine and waited for its long load time to complete. "Windows two point one?"

Pete smiled. "Two point one *one*."

"Nice! Let's see, still no Minesweeper, but they have Reversi, cool." Arnesto eagerly began playing.

Pete's smile faded. "What do you mean, 'Still no Minesweeper?'"

"Mild spoiler, but they add Minesweeper to Windows three or three point one or something."

"Did you use computers your whole life?"

Arnesto played, capturing two blue pieces, but then the computer recaptured his red pieces, plus three more. "I'm good at math. How am I losing on the lowest difficulty? Yes, I used computers extensively for all my decades."

"Does processing power continue to double every couple years?"

"Moore's Law? Yes, for many years to come."

"So, you must have had computers, what, *thousands* of times more advanced? Or more? This computer must seem so quaint to you."

"Fuck! I lost because I was rushing. Doesn't count." He started a new game but then noticed Pete waiting for a response. "Not at all. I mean, sure, if I think about it, I can recall using one of my many computers from the future, but they're a distant memory at this point. This" — he pointed toward the computer — "is about the best personal computer in the world right now. I am honestly as excited about this machine as you are. Except for the fact that I'm losing *again!*"

Some of Pete's smile returned. "You can't keep giving up the corners. Let me see that!" He reached for the mouse, but Arnesto waved him off.

"Wait, let me finish!" he snapped. He inevitably lost again, then switched seats with Pete, who started a new game.

"How's senior year going?" Arnesto asked.

"It's not the same without you. Well, physics is fun, even better than we thought it would be. Mr. Hinkley has this large magnet, but Josh took it and—"

"Stuck it to the ceiling vent! Mr. Hinkley couldn't get it down. I remember; that was hilarious!" They enjoyed a good chuckle together. "Did anyone notice I was gone?"

"Actually, yeah. Every now and then somebody asks where you are or what happened to you. And no, I don't tell them you're touring with Aerosmith. Did you find your wife yet?" Pete asked.

"No," Arnesto sighed. "I wish I had. I could have been boning her by now. I keep looking, though. How are things with Min-seo?"

Pete groaned. "She ended it last weekend. There!" Pete said, clicking with extra gusto on the last square to give him the game.

Arnesto stood up. "My turn."

"No way. You played twice, I get to play twice." Pete changed the skill from "Beginner" to "Novice."

Arnesto sat back down. "Sorry to hear about your breakup. But like they say, 'Better to have loved and lost than to have missed out on some poontang.'"

"Ugh, we never made it that far. We came close a couple times. I thought for sure she was going to be my first. You know what frustrates me the most, though?" Pete asked.

"People who say, "It happened *on* accident,' rather than '*by* accident.'?"

Pete furrowed his brow, Arnesto having interrupted his train of thought. "I have never heard anyone in my life say, 'on accident.'"

"I guess it hasn't started yet. Maybe it's a generational thing."

"Why in holy hell would people suddenly start saying, 'on accident?' That doesn't make any sense whatsoever. Things happen *by* accident. How can something possibly happen *on* accident?" Arnesto shrugged. "Jesus, how else do future generations defile the language?"

Arnesto thought for a second. "They add 'at' to everything. It's not,

'Where are you?' anymore, it's, 'Where are you *at*? Where is this at? Where is that at?' I know, it's awful. I never got used to it," Arnesto said, noticing Pete's disgust. "'Said' gets replaced by 'was like.' I was like, 'Pete let me tell you about the future,' and you were all, 'Hells to the no.'"

"People don't talk like that, do they?"

"Don't throw shade just 'cause bae caught me slippin'. Ship it crucial, he lit af, fam!"

"If they want to sound like idiots, good for them."

"Good *on* them."

"This is literally the most depressing conversation I've had this week, and that includes the one where Min-seo dumped me."

Arnesto didn't have the heart to tell him that "literally" would also come to mean "figuratively" around 2013. He also felt guilty about commandeering the conversation. "Anyway, what were you about to tell me? Something that frustrates you?"

Pete shook his head back to reality. "It was the way she ended it. She came up to me at work and said, 'Peters, we done now, bye.' I spent the whole shift trying to talk to her, to ask her why, but she wouldn't talk to me. Just like that."

"Jeez, that's rough. Which... which, um... What number..."

"My god, spit it out, man!"

Arnesto wanted to get the phrasing right. "Is this your first breakup?"

"Yeah..." Pete said with a hint of suspicion. "You know what, I'm already at peak frustration level, go ahead and spill it, spoil my whole life if you need to."

"Min-seo *is* your first. Or will be, if you want. I'm positive about that."

72

"But she dumped me."

"Yeah, she tends to do that."

"Jesus, how many times?!"

"I don't remember. At least a few. But hey, this is good news!"

"How the hell is this good news?!" Pete asked.

"You get back together with her *and* you get laid!"

Pete digested this for a moment. "Huh. I guess it *is* good news. I'm going to get me some!" He perked right up. It wouldn't last long.

"How's the rest of the hospital gang doing?"

"Fine," Pete said, suddenly looking uncomfortable.

"What is it, what happened?"

Pete sighed. "Jacqueline — she died exactly like you said. Someone at work saw her obituary in the newspaper. I'm sorry."

"Goddammit. It's my fault. I could have saved her," Arnesto said, throwing his hands in the air and feeling like someone had punched him in the gut.

"It's not your fault. You're in no way responsible. You warned her, remember?"

"It was too soon," Arnesto said.

"Yeah, she was only a little older than us."

"No, *I* was too soon. I warned her months in advance. Maybe if I had warned her that day…"

"Did you remember the date?" Pete asked.

"No, but I knew I was way early. If I had been closer…"

"Forgive me, but without even knowing the date, I don't see what you could have done. Look, how's college going?" Pete asked, eager to change the topic.

"It's good. My programming classes are harder than I remember,"

73

Arnesto said. Pete couldn't resist smiling at this. "My favorite class is Poly-Sci, believe it or not. We have the class in this auditorium that used to be a movie theater. The seats are *so* comfortable. I go to class, fall asleep, and wake up when it's over."

"Aren't you missing vital info from the lecture?" Pete asked.

"No, he pretty much reads from the textbook. When the Berlin Wall fell a couple weeks ago, I thought for sure we would at least discuss *that*, but no. The textbook is hilariously out of date, by the way."

"Is it, or are you biased because it's all ancient history to you?" Pete asked. Arnesto took a moment to consider this until Pete interrupted his train of thought. "I just heard the garage. My family must be back. I'm sorry to have to kick you out, but I have a history paper due. I'll walk you out."

As they headed toward the garage through the dining room, they saw Pete's mom reading by herself in the corner.

"Arnesto, how's college going?" she asked.

"Fine, thank you, Mrs. Morgan."

"Pete misses you at school," she said.

"Mom, please, I'm walking Arnesto out to his car."

Arnesto noticed the cigarette in her hand. She wasn't overt about her smoking — she only smoked three cigarettes per day, and only at night, away from the rest of Pete's family.

Arnesto and Mrs. Morgan said goodbye, then the boys walked out through the garage. Arnesto opened his car door and leaned on it. "Hey, Pete. If I did remember something else about you or a family member—"

"No! I was kidding earlier. You've already told me too much, thanks. Please never tell me any more about my future, including my family. I want to be ignorant like everybody else."

"But what if it's... important?"

"Then I *especially* don't want to know. I don't want to spend my life fretting about things I probably shouldn't know in the first place. Besides, with you mucking up the timeline, who knows what will actually happen?"

Arnesto saw the seriousness in Pete's face and felt he had to respect his friend's wishes. "Okay," Arnesto nodded, then got into his car and drove off.

Served

Downtown, Near University
Sunday, November 26, 1989
Early Afternoon

THANKSGIVING OVER, Arnesto returned to school early. He spent his first day back in his dorm alternating between cursing the gobbledygook that is Assembly programming and cursing the airship levels in Super Mario Bros. 3, which was most likely programmed in Assembly. *How did I ever beat this game?* he wondered.

Needing a break and confident he still had some time before thousands of his fellow students returned and ruined the parking situation, he decided to venture downtown. Parking was better there, too. For once, it was a sunny day and the sun felt nice and warm on his face. It also made it harder to see into the front window of Mona's. There was nobody seated at the two window tables closest to the door, so instead of walking by like usual, he stopped there and pressed his face to the window.

"The food looks even better from the inside," a familiar voice said, startling him.

It was her. Katrina, the first true love of his lives.

76

"Oh yeah?" he said, returning her smile. He got these words out despite not being able to think.

"If you're hungry, you should come in. It's delicious food."

"Will you be my waitress?" he asked. She smiled, then looked inside briefly, surveying the situation.

"If you wait a minute, I can clock in, get my apron, and seat you in my section." Instant chemistry.

"Okay." He watched her disappear inside, which gave him his first chance to really look at her, at least her backside. She had long, silky smooth black hair which she had pinned up for work. She was also wearing stylish clothes as part of her work uniform, which fit her athletic nineteen-year-old body very nicely.

He waited, then walked in. Right on cue, she met him at the hostess station and led him to his table. The dinner rush wouldn't start for a while, so throughout the meal, they had ample opportunity to flirt with each other until, finally, she brought him the bill.

"Oh," he said, looking over the bill with a confused expression. "I don't see your phone number on here."

She laughed. "Aw, you're totally my type, but I'm kind of seeing someone right now."

WHAT! Oh, right, she did have boyfriends before me. She's probably still seeing that one she told me about. What was his name, Sean? What do I do now?! he thought.

"You deserve better," he said.

"Why? Do you... know him?" she asked.

"I know... *better*," he smiled. She laughed but didn't seem to know what to say, so he continued. "Tell you what. Here's *my* number," he said, writing down his number and handing it to her. "No pressure, but if things don't happen to work out with Billy Bob or whatever—"

"Sean," she said after a chuckle.

"Right, if things don't work out with Billy Sean, you can call me. Bye for now." He left feeling taller than he ever had in his life — partially assisted by his final growth spurt, which had come at last.

One week later, a newly single Katrina called to invite him over to watch a rented copy of *Rain Man* on VHS.

* * *

After dating her a couple weeks and feeling secure their relationship really was happening all over again, Arnesto decided to call Pete to let him know the good news.

"I found my wife!"

"Congratulations! Dude, I'm so happy for you. Did you bone her yet?" Pete liked to get straight to the point.

"I did! You know, I always remembered enjoying sex, but my memories did not do it justice. It's amazing. I mean... goddamn."

"Stop rubbing it in," Pete said. "Min-seo is still holding out on me. Wait a second. Tell me the truth. Did you invent time travel so you could go back in time and lose your virginity before me?"

"What?! No!"

"You did, didn't you. Oh my god, I knew you were hyper-competitive, Arnesto, but I didn't think you were this petty."

"Dude, I'm not—"

"Admit it. This is exactly the kind of thing you would do."

"Okay, I'm immature now, but—"

"Aha!"

"Pete, let me finish, goddammit. It was a much older version of me that invented time travel, one who couldn't care less about something like that."

"It doesn't matter anyway."

Arnesto liked the sound of that. Maybe their bickering would end. "Right, it doesn't matter."

"Because I was first."

Arnesto didn't know what to say. It might be best to drop it. But how could he? "I have lost my virginity, and you haven't. So I am first."

"You're first *now*, in this universe. But this is your second go-around. Which obviously happened after your first go-around, in which I lost mine first. I was the *first* first, the absolute first."

Pete was either envious or in desperate need of having his pipes cleaned. Arnesto remembered being both when the situation was reversed. Still, Pete had a point. "Okay, Pete. You were first."

"Thank you."

"But I didn't invent time travel just to get laid before you, I mean, this go-around."

"Okay," Pete said.

"It's astounding to me that we remain friends," Arnesto said. "Then again, that was the *other* us, and they never had *this* conversation. I have to go. I'm seeing her again tonight."

Arnesto and Katrina were inseparable after that. He spent almost every night at her place. They didn't even have their first argument until his birthday the following spring.

* * *

79

"I'm glad you're only a year younger than me again," she said, grabbing another one of the cupcakes she had baked for his birthday. She had turned twenty in February. "That month I was two years older made me feel like I was robbing the cradle," she laughed.

Arnesto had decided he would tell her the truth that day — how mad could she get on his birthday? "Yeah, you know what, though, Snuggleblossoms?" he asked. They hadn't had nicknames in their former life, but Arnesto thought it would be fun this time around. Still, he hadn't yet found a nickname for her they could agree upon.

"No," she said, taking a bite out of her cupcake. The quest for the nickname would not end this day. "What?"

"I'm actually eighteen, well, now."

"What," she said, the joy of the occasion having left her face. "Today is your nineteenth birthday," she said.

"Eighteenth," he winced.

She slumped into the couch, staring straight ahead. "I can't believe this," she said.

"The good news is that if we ever have sex again, it will finally be legal."

"Oh my god, you are not helping!" She stood up and crossed her arms. "Why did you lie to me? You've been lying to me this whole time!"

"Would you have gone out with me if you knew I was seventeen?" he asked.

She looked at him, still pacing. "Yeah... maybe... I don't know."

He got up and put his hands on her shoulders. "No, you wouldn't."

"Don't tell me what I would or wouldn't have done," she said, pushing him away.

"Does it matter anymore? Look, we're here now, the same exact people we were yesterday. We're two people lucky to have met and formed this wonderful relationship," he said, taking her in his arms. She started to push him away, but then gave up and put her arms around him.

"You're lucky you're tall," she said. He had grown another two inches since Thanksgiving. "And yes, we will have sex again... maybe even tonight if you can refrain from pissing me off any further." He snorted at her remark. "It's not funny! You'd better promise not to lie to me ever again!"

"I only lied for the sake of our relationship," he said. She looked up at him expectantly. Realizing just in time that the period for logical discussion had passed, he continued, "But I promise, I will not lie to you ever again." This was perhaps the biggest lie he would ever tell her, and he knew it. He had no choice. He wanted to tell her everything and impress her with his ability, but he couldn't risk her safety by bringing her into his insanity. How would she react to him being a time traveler... if she even believed him? He also didn't want to lose her if she *didn't* believe him. It was hard enough convincing Pete, and *he* was logical.

"Let's go to bed," she said at last, leading him into the bedroom. "You're sure you're legal *now*, right?"

"Yes, you can no longer statutorily rape me."

"Oh my god," she said, tossing his hand away before disappearing into the bathroom and shutting the door behind her.

"I was only a *child!*" he yelled, falling into bed.

* * *

The end of spring brought the end of Arnesto's freshman year of college. He was a sophomore now — and then some. Between advanced placement exams, earning foreign language credits in high school, and taking an extra class each semester, Arnesto now had fifty-four college credits — only six credits shy of becoming a junior — and there was no slowing him down. He was able to squeeze in another overloaded semester during the summer break. By the end of fall semester, he was a senior. The next spring consisted of the end of his computer science program. All he had remaining by that summer was some general education classes which he completed easily. And then he was done.

"What do you mean, you're done? You're *graduating*?!" his mom asked. She had called from southern California, where she had moved with Gerald after the divorce.

"Yes, Mom."

"Arnesto, I can't believe this. I am so proud of you. You're only nineteen!"

"Thanks, but it wasn't a big deal. I just took an extra class here and there."

"A college graduate at nineteen, wow. When is the graduation?"

"It's in a couple weeks. But Mom, I know it's short notice, and it's a long trip—"

"I'm coming to your graduation. You denied your father and me your high school graduation; there is no way we're missing this."

"But Dad is going to be there. Will you two be alright?"

"Don't be silly, we're civil now," she said. This was news to him. He had mostly avoided family interactions since he first attained his independence two years earlier. One of the benefits of obsessing over school was that it always gave him an excuse to avoid family drama. He always had to "head back to school and work on that project."

"Great," he said, unable to fake any enthusiasm. Just because his parents were civil with each other didn't change the fact that he was still nineteen and didn't want them fretting over him.

"I'm going to go see about plane tickets," she said. "This is so exciting! I'll call you back once I know my itinerary. Bye, honey."

"Bye, mom," he said, hanging up the phone.

"It will be fine," Katrina said.

"I didn't say anything," Arnesto said.

"I could tell by the look on your face."

"What was the point of them getting divorced if they're still going to get together and harass me every time I do something amazing?"

"Well, I don't think you're going to have to worry about *that* too often," she kidded him. "Besides, I *like* your parents. They're nice."

"They're the ones that named me Arnesto," he grumbled.

Katrina disappeared into the bedroom and came out a few seconds later carrying a present.

"Maybe this will help," she said, handing him the package. "I thought you could use this now that you'll have some free time on your hands while you're looking for a job."

Arnesto tore off the wrapping.

"A Super Nintendo?! No way! I *loved* the SNES!" He cringed internally the moment he said it.

"You... what?"

"I said, 'I love the SNES!' Someone brought one into the computer lab the other day. I got to play it briefly and meant to ask you if we could get one." It was an outright lie. "I can't believe you already got it! Thank you so much! C'mon, I'll hook it up and we can play." He was already tearing into the package.

"I was going to start making dinner—"

"Pleeeeeease!"

"Okay, fine," she said, unable to resist his enthusiasm. She sat on the couch and waited for him to connect everything.

To her surprise, it took him no time at all to set everything up, as if he had done it many times before. He was both excited to play and relieved she believed his falsehood. He would sooner lie and tell her he had already played two-player with Saddam Hussein than tell her truthfully how he had already spent hundreds upon hundreds of hours playing the SNES in a previous life.

"Here, you have to be Luigi," Arnesto said, handing her the second controller.

Cutting Ties

Outside Katrina's Apartment
Wednesday, September 18, 1991
3:30 p.m.

"IT'S GOOD NOT OWNING a lot of stuff, isn't it?" Arnesto asked, looking into the fifteen-foot U-Haul barely a third full despite containing all their belongings. "What time is it?"

"About 3:30," Katrina said. Arnesto shut and locked the cargo door. "Perfect. Time for one last lap around the college before heading to the highway. You can drive, I have one loose end to take care of," he said, tossing her the keys. After a quick stop at the manager's office to turn in their apartment keys, they left the complex, drove downtown past Mona's, and arrived on campus.

They drove past the dorm where Arnesto had paid $440 each month for one of the creaky twin beds in a shared bedroom he had hardly seen since moving in with Katrina more than a year and a half earlier. Despite having moved out, the university still forced him to pay because he was younger than twenty-three. *Somebody* had to pay for the new sports arena. "College: America's greatest racketeers," he said. Katrina ignored him. She was busy getting used to driving the truck, which was much bigger than anything she had driven before.

They drove past the administration building, where employees were trained in the fine art of extortion. Next came the student union. Things were quiet at this particular time; there were only *two* visible student protest groups marching outside. Arnesto watched them for a moment, then lost interest and resumed his search.

The quad came after that, followed by the library. Arnesto had gone in once for a few minutes his freshman year. As a computer science major, he had little use of the place and never returned. On one side of the library was the buyback area, where if one had managed to keep his eighty-five-dollar textbook in pristine condition the entire semester, the university would happily buy it back for a buck and a half.

On the western edge of campus, and a full mile from his dorm — a long walk during the lengthy Massachusetts winter — sat the computer science building. Inside was the computer lab, where Arnesto spent many evening hours hunting for errant semicolons. Across the hall was the printer area, where after emailing their completed projects, students could wait in line for other students paid two dollars per hour to retrieve their printouts from the row of dot matrix printers behind them.

At last, driving past the soccer fields on the final leg of their loop, Arnesto saw what he was looking for. He eyed the skinny young men jogging alongside the road in their matching uniforms, including shorts revealing far too much of their long, twiggy legs. Arnesto felt a little embarrassed for them, even though it was the current fashion. They passed the bulk of the team before Arnesto saw a familiar mullet on the head of one of the frontrunners.

"Slow down a little," he said to Katrina as he rolled down his window.

86

"What are you doing?" she asked.

"Hey, Terrance!" he yelled out the passenger window as the truck began overtaking the mulleted runner. "Stop shoplifting! You're going to get kicked out of school, idiot!"

Katrina was almost as surprised as Terrance, who didn't recognize the person who had just yelled at him. "Friend of yours?" she asked.

"He was once," he said, rolling up the window. "It's complicated. We can go now. On to California!"

* * *

The cross-country road trip to the Bay Area took about a week. A week after that, he was scheduled for an interview at Smiling Axolotl Games, his old job. He arrived ten minutes early, parked, and walked in.

"Hi, I'm here for my interview. I'm Arnesto Modesto." The receptionist invited him to take a seat. He was a little concerned that he didn't recognize her. After all, he had worked for the company for many years. *Must've been before my time,* he thought. In his previous life, he had applied there in 1994 after he graduated college. Now it was almost three years earlier. Of course he wouldn't recognize everybody.

He looked around the hallway. The walls featured large cardboard cutouts of some of the company's more popular game characters. There was Doodler Dude from *Doodler Dude & the Noodling Noodlers,* a puzzle game; Sproinger from the *Sproinger* series of platform games; and Rock Stone, the no-nonsense, one-liner-spouting badass, whose motto was, "Unused ammo is wasted ammo." However, there still weren't any cutouts of Chimp & Zeke, from their ever-popular adventure game series — the first game was still in pre-production.

Though he wasn't quite as excited as he was the first time around, he was still thrilled to be there, about to get his start in the games industry. He hadn't even considered doing anything else. Why not come back to his first post-college job where he had several great years and made many lifelong friends?

The interviewers were not his friends. They weren't enemies or anything, in fact, they were great people in their own right. It's just that they were people who had moved on from Quality Assurance into other parts of the company, as so many people did back then, before Arnesto had arrived in 1994. There was Maggie (who was a *hottie* back in '91), Don, and Isaac. Both Maggie and Don would one day move into the sound department, while Isaac would move into production.

The interview went smoothly enough. There weren't many nineteen-year-old computer science graduates applying to be testers, which gave Arnesto an immediate edge. He knew all about editing autoexec.bat and config.sys on boot disks, often a requirement to run certain PC games. He knew and loved video games more than Maggie and *way* more than Don, though possibly less than Isaac. And of course, he was affable, using some of the techniques he had picked up from his many interviews over the decades of his former life.

"I'm sure you already know this," Isaac said in a tone more serious than he had shown thus far, "but testing does not mean, 'getting paid to play games all day,' as many people outside the industry seem to think." Maggie and Don both nodded in agreement. "It's like they think we're in here doing nothing but playing Civilization — if only! The truth is, most of the time you'll be testing an unfinished, unpolished, buggy-as-hell game—"

"With placeholder art," Maggie said.

"And no sound," Don said.

"—that crashes all the time and that you may not even like in the first place," Isaac added. "And you'll be testing it all day, every day, for months until it ships."

"Are we scaring you off yet?" Maggie asked.

"Not at all," Arnesto said. "I knew some testers from… *before* who warned me what's it's like. I'm ready to do this."

"Good! By the way, I like your tie," Maggie said, as the interview seemed to be coming to a close. Arnesto looked down at his tie. He hated it; it was ugly.

"I'm sorry, am I dressed too formally? I promised my dad I would wear a tie, even though I told him the games industry is too informal for that."

"No, it's fine. Better to overdress for an interview than underdress," Maggie answered.

"Do you want to cut it?" Arnesto asked.

"I'm sorry?" Isaac asked.

Goddammit. Too soon. There was a tradition at Smiling Axolotl that when someone wore a tie to an interview, they cut it. The company was about freedom of creativity. Ties were seen as stifling and best left for bankers, lawyers, and the like. The problem was, they hadn't yet started that tradition. He had to think fast.

"I want to show you guys that I'm Axolotl material. I want to be a game developer, not a member of Congress," Arnesto said, flicking his tie in disgust. "Game devs don't wear ties. Axolotls don't wear ties. Do you have a pair of scissors?"

"I'll go get one!" Maggie was enjoying the gesture, at least. Don and

Isaac merely smiled, perhaps unsure how to react.

"Maggie, would you please do the honors?" Arnesto asked when she returned. She laughed as she cut his tie a couple inches below the knot. Arnesto dropped the bottom parts on the table. "When do I start?" he asked with a great, big smile. They all laughed and told him he would hear within a couple of weeks and if he didn't, to call human resources and ask.

Four days later, he received an offer letter in the mail. He had been accepted to start as a Quality Assurance Tester, Level One, for eight dollars an hour. He signed and mailed the acceptance letter and started the following week.

When he arrived for his first day of work, he walked into the tester area and inhaled deeply. The Test Pit smelled better than he remembered, perhaps because there were fewer testers. More likely, it was because it was Monday morning, and some of the smell had dissipated over the weekend.

The Test Pit sat in the center of the building with no windows and only the one door in the corner for ventilation. Along every wall was a series of shallow desks with barely enough room for the 13-inch CRT monitors on which they tested the PC games in development. The chairs were a random selection of rejects from other departments. QA would grow along with the rest of the company, but still wouldn't come into its own until 1995 or so. That was the year IT finally set up email servers for the PC, which meant the testers could stop fighting over the one Mac to check their email. Not that testers got many emails in those days, but occasionally someone from another department announced that they were giving away free gear or something. Heaven help you if you were in the hallway between the kitchen and the Test Pit when someone

90

emailed the company about free donuts.

Arnesto was eager to meet (or re-meet) his coworkers and also eager to find out what his first project would be. That latter eagerness would fade in a heartbeat.

"I'm sorry to do this to you, but we need people testing SASS," Isaac said. SASS stood for Smiling Axolotl Screen Saver. It had been before Arnesto's time, but he had often heard the complaints from senior testers, years after it had shipped. At least he would be able to add his own grumblings to the mix.

SASS was a collection of a half-dozen screen saver modules based on games the company had produced. There was the Noodler module, consisting of Noodling Noodlers gradually slithering onto and filling up the screen. There was a module of Sproinger bouncing around the screen on his own. Then there was a module of Rock Stone's face. Every so often, he would shout one of his one-liners, but that was it. There was no animation or anything else, just his face. Having a static image would do absolutely nothing to save the screen. Thankfully for the user, the default setting was to randomly alternate between modules every few minutes. Thankfully for the tester, there were settings at all, though they didn't help much.

That's what made SASS so awful. Unlike an adventure game where you already know the solution to every puzzle and have to invent new ways of breaking the game, there were no puzzles in SASS. There wasn't anything, only some lame screen savers. The only interaction was in the settings. Did you want the modules to switch every 30 seconds (crazy!) or every minute or two? Did you want Sproinger to bounce around slowly, quickly, or somewhere in between? It didn't take long to test every possible combination, and that meant you were left to watch. Just watch, hoping to replicate that one crash bug Don found that one time that nobody could reproduce. It was mind-numbing.

And so Arnesto's career in games began again.

He spent the next couple of months testing the screen saver until it went out the door to the great relief of everyone involved. They spent the month after that testing the international versions, to the great *pain* of everyone involved. When the final foreign version shipped, the testers were elated. They could finally get back to testing actual games!

They started with one game, then a second and a third. They gradually hired additional testers as well. The company was ramping up, and they soon invited Arnesto to be a part of the interview process.

There were a couple of applicants who concerned Arnesto but only in hindsight. Unfortunately, they still interviewed well. What could he do? Try to warn his coworkers? "Hey, this guy is going to break the expensive new art scanner scanning naughty pictures of Counselor Troi, but not for another two to three years?!" No matter. They would figure it out eventually.

Besides, he had greater concerns.

One day after work, he went to his car, drove around to the back of the lot where he could have some privacy, and called the one person who could help.

"Pete! Suit up, we got one."

"On my way."

"Really?"

"No, I have no idea what you're talking about. How's the games biz?"

"Good. I'm actually part of the hiring process now. It's weird interviewing someone who originally interviewed me. But that's not why I called. You know those four white cops who beat Rodney King?"

"Of course, their trial is about to end. It's all over the news every day. Why?"

"They're about to be acquitted," Arnesto said.

"Are you freakin' kidding me?!"

"That's not the bad part. After that, the shit hits the fan. There's going to be rioting and looting, fires and killing. It's going to be awful. You told me way back when that I should use my power for good. I was thinking maybe I could help in this case, but I don't know how."

"My god," Pete said. "I appreciate you wanting to get involved, but this is a trial by fire if there ever was one, so to speak."

"So you think I should stay out of it? Let history take its course?"

"Hell no. If you can do something, anything, then you probably should, albeit from a safe distance. Hmm. I don't see how you can prevent them from being acquitted. Can you warn them somehow? Anonymously, of course," Pete added.

"Who, the jurors? The police?"

"I don't know. Somebody. There's got to be some way to warn the people."

"Warn the people..." Arnesto said.

A City Erupts

Arnesto's Hotel Room
Los Angeles, California
Wednesday, April 29, 1992
1:03 a.m.

ARNESTO TURNED OFF THE TV. He had finished watching a rerun of *Cheers*, and now it was time to move. He grabbed his knapsack and left his hotel room. He was only a block or so from Koreatown in Los Angeles. It was just after one o'clock in the morning, and only an occasional vehicle drove past.

He had told Katrina he was driving down to LA, but under the pretense that he was helping his grandmother move into a retirement home. In reality, she had already been living there a month.

Upon arriving at his target area, he walked a few more blocks, feeling an outward spiral pattern would work best. To him, it seemed less likely he would be caught walking in a spiral than if he simply went back and forth. He could also keep turning left while avoiding crossing his own path. And should he need to bail, due to a mugger, an irate store owner, or a suspicious police officer, he could do so easily, knowing more people would have seen his flyers at the center of

94

Koreatown than the fringes. Who was he kidding, a spiral pattern was more *fun*.

At last, he arrived at the epicenter. Ground zero. *Time to strike*. He made sure the area was clear, then pulled a staple gun and a flyer out of his bag and stapled the flyer to a telephone pole.

BEWARE RIOTERS
TODAY, 4/29/92
If the officers who beat Rodney King
are acquitted, the people may riot.
Protect yourself and your family.
Good luck.

He tagged another telephone pole, then taped a flyer to a store window, keeping watch all the while. It took a few attempts, but soon he could rip off a piece of tape in his pocket, stick it to a flyer still in his bag, then remove the flyer from his bag and stick it to a store window in one smooth motion. Usually he could do this without stopping (except for high-value targets like bus stop billboards on which he posted more than one flyer), and eventually he could do it without even looking.

He thought about the anonymous letter he had written to the defense team imploring them to plead guilty. This had understandably been ignored. He thought about the other letter, sent from a fictional local business owner and addressed to the court. This one implored the judge to read the verdict "at a time inopportune for public outcries," but this letter, too, appeared to be ignored. And so Arnesto had found himself at a Kinko's on Wilshire Boulevard during their slow hours discretely making a couple hundred copies of his prescient flyers.

He tagged doors, too, hanging flyers over the locks. While a rushed business owner might not see a flyer on their window, there was no way they could miss a flyer blocking their lock. They might rip it off and toss it aside without a glance, but at least they wouldn't miss it entirely. He imagined a business owner looking at the flyer, taking it in his hand and reading it, then going home. Arnesto was jolted back to reality. The door he had just tagged moved. Not much, less than an inch, but it was open. It wasn't a business.

It was an apartment building. He peered inside and saw rows and rows of those thin little mailboxes that can only hold mail inserted vertically. Feeling bold and not seeing anyone around, he opened the door and stepped in. It was the perfect spot for him to deliver his message. While his other flyers might be read by no one, here he was virtually guaranteed a much larger audience. He put up several flyers, more than a dozen in total. He felt satisfied as he reached the back door of the long hallway. Just in time, too. He heard footsteps coming down a stairway from above, two, maybe three floors up. The bottom of the stairs was right behind him on his side of the building.

He pulled on the back door, but it didn't budge. He pulled harder with the same result. The footsteps were getting louder and coming fast. He paused in disbelief. *What the hell?! What am I doing wrong?* He tried twisting and turning the handle, which didn't move, before attempting one final yank with no better luck. He peered out one of the small windows on the side and saw a garden area. *It's a private area. That's why it's locked.*

He turned to see feet appear at the top of the stairs. He sure as hell didn't want to go up the stairs and pass someone who wouldn't recognize him on the way up. His only option was to retrace his steps and go out the way he had come in. He ran as quietly as he could toward the front door but knew he wouldn't make it. He heard a loud *thud* as whoever was running behind him must have jumped down the last couple of steps and landed on the ground floor. Slowing to a casual but hustled walk, the footsteps behind him closed in on him, then slowed. It allowed Arnesto just enough time to reach the front door first. He lunged at the door handle, then stepped back, holding the door wide open.

"Gomawo," the man said, thanking Arnesto in Korean before running out the door and pedaling away on his bike. Arnesto noted the uniform. The man was simply making a late-night food delivery. He wasn't pursuing him. In fact, being in a rush, the man was probably oblivious. He would never be able to identify Arnesto as having been there on the morning of the first day of the riots. *As if with all the rioting, looting, and killing that's about to happen, anyone would care about one late-night trespasser. What is wrong with me?!*

The stress compounding his exhaustion, Arnesto finished up his route and headed back to his hotel. Along the way, he found a newspaper dispenser where he dumped his remaining stack of flyers; there were quite a few left. Half a block away, he realized whoever filled the dispensers would probably toss the flyers. *Oh well, there's no turning back now. I don't have a better option anyway.* He made it back to his hotel room and crashed.

The acquittals came at 3:15 that afternoon. Arnesto hung out downtown and waited. An hour passed, then another. Maybe he had done it. Maybe he had actually prevented one of the largest riots in

American history. He headed back down the busy street toward his car. He didn't notice the fast-moving van pass him in the opposite direction, but he did hear its tires make a faint screech as it took the corner. Arnesto spun around and saw a logo on the side of the van as it disappeared behind a building. He ran back to the intersection and watched the news van roar down the street for a few blocks until it got lost in the traffic. *Damn, it's happening.*

His eyes shifted upward to the helicopter crossing overhead, several intersections down. *Damn.* Against his better judgment, his better judgment being to get the hell out of there, he ran after it. After running only three blocks, he saw the smoke. One more block and he saw the fire. "Damn it!" he yelled.

He made his way to the pay phone he had carefully selected days earlier. Just as he had hoped, there wasn't anyone in range to overhear the call. He took out his tape recorder and adjusted the volume to the highest setting. With his left hand, he picked up the receiver and dialed 911. Arnesto hit "Play" on the tape recorder and held it up to the mouthpiece, holding both at arm's length in front of him. After a few seconds of blasting the sounds of a riot mixed with gunfire into some poor emergency responder's ear, he hung up and stopped the tape. He rewound and recorded over the tape and then without touching the tape itself, he ejected it into a nearby trashcan and headed back to his car. He made it north of the Grapevine on Interstate 5 before stopping for gas.

"You're not driving into the city, are you?" the female cashier asked.

"No, I'm heading north."

"Well, you picked a good time to get out of town. Sounds like there's trouble down there. Some nasty fires, too."

"Is that right?" *It's going to get a whole lot worse, lady. Businesses are going to burn to the ground, people are going to die, and I couldn't save them. I could have prevented this, all of it.*

Arnesto Modesto, the world's most ineffectual time traveler.

He had no way of knowing many of the flyers had gone unnoticed. Many had gone straight into the garbage, both read and unread. Of those that were read, many were immediately forgotten. But there were some, not many, but some that weren't ignored. Some businesses closed early, losing less merchandise to looters. Fire extinguisher sales in the area were about the same, except that the sales came a little earlier in the day and were used to slightly greater effect. He had saved no lives, but in the end, he had saved a few businesses. Not that he would ever know.

It was getting late by the time he returned home, but not too late for a debrief.

"Why focus solely on Koreatown?" Pete asked from the other end of the phone line. "It seems like a huge chunk of LA is burning to the ground. Do you... hate blacks?"

"No! I couldn't remember where all the incidents happened. I only remembered finding it odd that four white cops beat a black man and a bunch of Koreans lost their businesses."

"That *is* odd. So what was on the tape?"

"Part of the riot scene from *Police Academy*."

"You can't be serious," Pete said. "What was your plan there?"

"I thought if they heard riot sounds and machine gun fire, the police would react a little quicker."

"I... don't even know how to respond to that. Anyway, don't beat yourself up over this. You had no time to prepare. We'll catch the next one."

Compounding the Problem

Arnesto's Home
Silicon Valley, California
Saturday, April 3, 1993
Evening

"THIS WACO STANDOFF seems like it's going to last forever," Pete said over the phone.

"No, only another couple weeks," Arnesto said.

"It's not going to end well, is it?"

"No, I'm afraid not."

"Is there something you can do?" Pete asked.

"Like what? Call up Janet Reno and tell her that a siege is going to leave scores dead, including the children, as they burn the place down from the inside?"

"Jesus. It's been almost a year since the LA riots. You must have picked up some tricks since then. What if you tip off the FBI or a news station or something? At least *try* to warn them."

Arnesto closed his eyes and pinched the bridge of his nose. "I suppose I should."

"Why are you not gung-ho on this?"

"Waco's not the end of it." Arnesto chose his words carefully so as not to prematurely announce a major event to his friend. "I know it sounds terrible, but when it ends, I will know exactly when to prevent a future act of retaliation that kills twice as many people — people that didn't willingly join a dangerous cult."

"No, it doesn't sound terrible. I'm sure you're doing the right thing. Most people in your circumstance wouldn't lift a finger to help those people — in either scenario." Pete heard Arnesto sigh. "Then again, you're not most people. Do you know who will retaliate?"

"Yeah, a psycho named… just some psycho."

"Couldn't you watch this guy? Hire a private investigator to keep an eye on him or something? That way, you could try to warn folks in Waco, but still prevent the retaliation?"

"Yeah, maybe. Let me sleep on it. One thing's for certain — I am *not* going to Texas. Too far to drive to mess with a bunch of gun-totin' cowboys," Arnesto said.

"You could fly there then rent a car."

"I just turned twenty-one. You have to be twenty-five to rent a car."

"No, there's a lot of places that will rent a car to twenty-one-year-olds. You'd just have to pay a fee," Pete said.

"I didn't know that."

"Look," Pete said, "I'm not telling you to go. But if you do and get into trouble, act like you love gun racks or hate abortions or something. Good luck, pardner."

A few days later, Arnesto drove a rented sedan that smelled like cigarettes from Austin to the compound in Waco. Knowing he wouldn't be able (and had no desire) to get past the ATF checkpoint, he instead chose a spot behind a bunch of other cars on the side of the road with a view of the area.

He surveyed the scene. There were cars, pickup trucks, press vans, and military vehicles. Locals and looky-loos, members of the press, and more agents than one could count. Then there was the compound itself which, from three miles away, appeared quiet.

Arnesto spent his time ambling about aimlessly, avoiding conversations while eavesdropping on others, and watching the press for any signs of action. Once the sun started to set, he noticed people leaving and decided to follow suit. As he was walking back to his rental, one pickup slowed down as it passed him.

"Best get the lead out, boy! The feds'll start their concert any minute!" the driver said, then rolled up his window as he drove off. Arnesto sped up his walk, not sure what the man was talking about. He wouldn't have to wait long to find out.

As Arnesto came within thirty feet of the car, the FBI started blaring music at the compound. Though Arnesto could barely make it out from that distance, he could tell the FBI had chosen the most annoying music possible: Christmas carols. Arnesto got in his car and cranked up the radio. Even country music was preferable to Christmas carols.

The next day was like the first: not much in the way of progress.

It wasn't until the third day that Arnesto finally caught something of a break. He was walking up the dusty hill by the compound again when he spied a man in his mid-twenties with a short, military haircut sitting on the hood of his car. The young man looked familiar.

"Want to buy a bumper sticker?" he asked.

Arnesto looked at the stickers, which all had pro-gun and/or anti-government sayings like, "Ban Guns, Make the Streets Safe for a

Government Takeover."

"The government sure messed up this situation, didn't they?" Arnesto asked. *Why does he look so familiar?*

"ATF had no business being here in the first place, and they have made nothing but mistakes since they arrived. The government wants to control everything. They want to take away all our guns and turn us all into socialists. I'm sorry some of them got killed, but they should have had the sheriff go in with a warrant."

"I hear that. I'll take these two," Arnesto said, picking up two bumper stickers off the hood. He held out his hand. "Name's Bob."

"Nice to meet you, Bob. I'm Tim," said the man, shaking Arnesto's hand. Until that moment, Arnesto wasn't one hundred percent sure who he was talking to. Now he was. It was Timothy McVeigh, the future bomber of the Alfred P. Murrah Federal Building in Oklahoma City which left 168 people dead, including nineteen children.

Arnesto paid and then they chatted a bit more, with McVeigh doing most of the talking. Finally, Arnesto's nerves got the better of him and he excused himself. Once a respectable distance away, he looked back and with McVeigh looking the other way, jotted down his license plate number.

Back at the hotel, Arnesto quickly called Katrina to let her know how the "game conference" was going. They had a nice chat, then they hung up and he dialed Pete.

"I met him!" Arnesto said.

"Who, David Koresh? How the hell did you do that? And why?"

"No, the other guy, the one who retaliates if Mount Carmel burns down."

"What... he was there?!" Pete asked.

"Yeah, selling bumper stickers that say things like, 'A Man With a Gun is a Citizen, A Man Without a Gun is a Subject.' I bought a couple. Didn't want to do anything to anger the man. He *really* hates the government," Arnesto said.

"Wow, could've used him in our gun control debate. For fuck's sake! You were supposed to gather intel, not start hanging out with these guys. Next thing you know you'll be playing poker over steaks and whiskey with him, Koresh, and the Unabomber. Did you make any progress with Koresh?"

"Not really, but — holy shit, I know who the Unabomber is — anyway, check this out. Koresh not only convinced the other men he should sleep with their wives; he convinced them they couldn't."

"You wish you had that power, don't you?" Pete said.

"No," Arnesto said. "I don't want to go around stealing other dudes' wives, but if I'm ever single again, it would be nice to have a fraction of that guy's charisma."

"David Koresh is a megalomaniac. He loves the sound of his own voice. They keep playing some of his recordings on one of the stations here. I'm watching one now."

"What channel?" Arnesto picked up the remote and went through every channel on the bolted-down television. "They don't seem to have it here. Listen, can you record it for me? I have an idea, finally. Record as much as you can, then send me the tapes by the fastest delivery possible."

"You got it," Pete said.

Over the next week, Arnesto remained in his hotel room glued to the TV. After many painstaking hours of listening, transcribing, recording, and editing, he felt like he had what he needed. He rewound and played the cassette tape for what seemed like the thousandth time. It was David Koresh saying a bunch of words that Arnesto had spliced together. It didn't exactly flow, but the multiple layers of recording obscured the choppiness.

"If they come in here," the tape said, "we will burn this place. Everyone will burn. The children must die before God." The recording gave him chills. He made a few copies to mail to the local news stations but wasn't sure if he should give one to the FBI. It wasn't out of disrespect. He simply feared the FBI would recognize a fake and stomp it out before it could do any good.

He mailed two of the tapes then drove a short ways north toward Dallas to discard the now-broken VCR and a few other items before heading back to Austin. But once on the highway, he had this nagging suspicion that kept growing larger. What if the news stations didn't do anything with the tape? He simply couldn't depend on them like that. It would be a huge risk, but he had to call the FBI.

First, Arnesto drove back into Waco where he made a brief stop. Then, he continued to Austin and found a payphone near the airport. He called the diner in Waco where in the past week he had witnessed no small number of agents. He didn't want to call 911 or the FBI's hotline which may have been recording their calls. The confused server who answered brought one of the agents to the phone.

"Agent Whiteside," a voice said. Arnesto had second thoughts. Talking to the feds suddenly seemed like a decision that could haunt him the rest of his life. And what was with that name - *Whiteside*? It sounded evil. "Is there someone there?" Whiteside asked.

Then again, who was Arnesto to judge someone else's name? He had to warn him. It was the right thing to do. "They'll burn it down,"

Arnesto finally said.

"Excuse me?"

"If you try to enter the compound, they will set the place on fire. They're not planning to surrender. Ever."

Whiteside glanced over at his fellow agents. "Who is this?"

"I'm sorry, I mailed the other tapes to the media. I left yours at the Dr Pepper Museum, first floor, hidden behind the soda fountain on the right side. He's going to kill them all. Listen. To. The tape."

"Look, why don't you come in and we'll... hello?"

It was actually the FBI who decided to play the tape — doctored to a more professional level — on their loudspeakers. They targeted the women in the compound, incorrectly believing their motherly instincts would kick in at the last moment, sparing the children.

Instead, according to the FBI's final report, it was Steve Schneider, Koresh's right-hand man, whose growing suspicions about his leader were confirmed by the tape. He shot Koresh dead before turning the gun on himself. As the FBI's final assault had not yet begun, nobody inside the compound had any reason to start the fire. With their fearless leader gone, a few of the confused followers decided it was time to leave. This gave the other followers someone else to follow, and most of them left en masse. Even the most stalwart of the men, initially prepare to fight until the bitter end, realized the awkwardness of being the only ones left and they, too, surrendered.

The Waco Siege was over. The day was April 16, 1993, three days earlier than the last time and far fewer dead.

Piling It On

FBI Field Office
San Antonio, Texas
Friday, April 23, 1993 (One Week Later)
11:20 a.m.

AGENT WHITESIDE WAS GLAD to be out of Waco, but not thrilled to be back at the office. He still had a mountain of paperwork to complete. And now the phone was ringing again. He picked it up. "Agent Whiteside."

"You used the tape," said a synthetic computer voice from the other end of the line.

"Excuse me?"

"In Waco, the tape I left you at—"

"I'm sorry, is there something wrong with your voice?" Whiteside asked. He could make out the sounds of a keyboard clicking and clacking away.

"Acute pharyngitis. Am I in trouble?" the computer voice asked.

"I could charge you with obstructing a federal investigation." Whiteside held his hand high and snapped his fingers urgently to get the attention of another agent to run a trace. "Two people may have died because of you."

"More than seventy people are *alive* because of me," came the computer voice after more clicking and clacking. "Leave me alone and I can save more. Many more."

"Sir, you pull a stunt like that again and I can guarantee you prison time. You have information, you call the hotline, you do not—"

-click-clack-click-click-clack- "I promise no more interference, just hot tips." Even the pleasant computer voice no longer sounded sincere. "Do we have a deal?"

"I can't—"-clack-click- There were only a couple keys pressed this time. Whiteside could tell the caller's next words had already been recorded or copied and pasted into some text-to-speech program.

"There was a man selling anti-government bumper stickers at Waco named Timothy McVeigh. He is extremely dangerous and openly vowed revenge for what happened at the compound. You need to watch him."

"Alright, thank you for that. We will look into it. Anything else?"

-clack- "The Unabomber is Dr. Ted Kaczynski. He lives off the grid in a cabin in Montana." Before waiting for a reply, Arnesto hung up the pay phone, shut his laptop, and nonchalantly hustled away.

Whiteside hung up the receiver and wrote down the names the mysterious caller had given him. Computer voice or not, there was something haunting about the finality of the informant's words. He debated adding the caller to the notes but decided against it. It wasn't the tips that dissuaded him. For all he knew, they were bogus. It was the fact that they had found stockpiles of lighter fluid and other fire accelerants at three different locations within the compound. It appeared that while the tape was phony, its message had been genuine. A rumor had formed within the Bureau that the tape had prevented a far worse outcome. Perhaps fueled by the Christmas music they had blasted, a few agents had even called it, "a gift from Santa."

A fellow agent walked up to Whiteside's desk. "Payphone in San Francisco. Want me to look into it?"

Whiteside looked up at the agent. "No, but I have something else for you to look into."

The Chase

Smiling Axolotl Games
Silicon Valley, California
Friday, June 17, 1994
5:57 p.m.

ARNESTO SMILED as he logged out of his work computer. It was the end of the workweek, and the project he was working on was between crunches. He was going to leave at a decent hour for once. But first, it was time to check in with QA. He was approaching his original hire date, so it was time to get reacquainted with his old friends.

That included Hiromi, who Arnesto nearly bumped into as he was leaving his office. "Pardon me, sir. Thank you very much," Hiromi said in a deep southern drawl as he sauntered by in a jumpsuit and pompadour. Hiromi did a couple hip gyrations, then danced down the hall, stopping in each doorway to do a quick impression.

Arnesto was thrilled. In his past life, this moment had occurred before Arnesto had been hired, but Hiromi's impersonation was almost as famous as the company screen saver was infamous. He watched until Hiromi disappeared around a corner, then made his way into the test pit.

"Guys, you're not going to believe this. Elvis is alive *and* he works here." There was a muffled reaction from the five testers remaining.

Kabir spoke first. "Hiromi did that to lighten the mood. Today was Brenton's last day."

A tester named Chad said, "He was fired for breaking the new art scanner with pictures of a certain Star Trek counselor that were 'inappropriate for a professional work environment.'"

Kabir shook his head. "Thanks for the discretion, Chad."

"They weren't even real," Chad chimed in, looking up from his workstation. Kabir shot him a look, causing Chad to put his arms up to indicate he was done talking, while adding, "I'm just saying, the pictures were clearly fake. Give me Photoshop, I could do better in five minutes. *Five* minutes."

"Can we help you with something?" Kabir asked Arnesto.

Arnesto pointed at himself with his thumbs and said, "I came here to see if any of you whiny, little amateurs want to take on the greatest Squid Wars player who ever lived."

"Ooooooohhh!" the testers shouted.

"Let's do it," Kabir said. They both sat down in front of the television and grabbed a controller as the other testers gathered round.

Arnesto felt confident. It was the second game he had tested in his past life, and he was one of only a few people who could beat the punishing single-player mode. However, not having played it in over a century, he was feeling a little rusty.

Arnesto controlled Icer, a glacier squid, against Kabir's Whiplash, a whiplash squid. Whiplash was on the ropes so Kabir bailed and was now a tiny human diver, swimming defenseless. Arnesto chased him around the level, but Kabir found an undamaged bush-club squid named Clubber and jumped on. Arnesto groaned.

Now Kabir was on the offensive as Arnesto looked for a replacement squid of his own. They traded blows for a while, then both Arnesto and Kabir gasped when they saw an unused fire squid named Pyrotooth. With a quick freeze blast from Icer, Clubber was rendered immobile for a second. Arnesto's diver bailed from Icer and swam his little heart out toward Pyrotooth, but Clubber defrosted and fired an ink shot killing Arnesto's diver and giving Kabir the round.

"Drink the ink," Kabir said, taunting Arnesto.

"Oooooooohhh!"

"This game is awesome, I hope it does well," Kabir said. Arnesto knew it wouldn't. For some reason, it never caught on, despite good reviews. It didn't help that the company gave it almost no advertising. At least its memory would live on as Arnesto and Kabir would break it out from time to time, years down the line.

After several more rounds, the score was tied three apiece, and Arnesto had the clear advantage in the seventh round. His squid was about to deliver the fatal blow when the game crashed. Arnesto remembered there having been a recurring split-screen crash bug that persisted right up until the game shipped a few months from then, but he couldn't recall any details that might help them fix it.

This was annoying, but for Arnesto, it was offset by the fact that he was getting to know these guys again. Better, they were getting to know him. It had been one thing to be in the trenches, finding bugs alongside them; it was another to be a programmer and one of those who *caused* the bugs. Bonding over Squid Wars helped quite a bit. He only needed more time, but it wasn't going to happen this evening.

As Kabir reached for the reset button, Hiromi burst into the room and announced, "There's a huge car chase happening in LA right now. They say O.J.'s making a run for it." The other testers ran after Hiromi to watch the television in the kitchen.

Arnesto puffed his cheeks and exhaled in disapproval. The "trial of the century" had failed to hold his interest in his previous life. It would be even worse this time around. How long had the chase lasted? If it ended soon, they might be able to go back to playing. He put his controller down and sauntered into the kitchen. Everyone watched as the white Ford Bronco ambled down the highway with around a dozen police cars in pursuit. From what he remembered, Arnesto could tell it wasn't going to end for a while and decided to head home. His bonding with the testers would have to wait.

"You're leaving?" asked a surprised Hiromi as he caught Arnesto heading out the door.

Arnesto smiled, happy that someone cared about his departure. "I'll catch the miniseries," he said. He would have several to choose from.

Road Rage

Silicon Valley, California
Thursday, April 13, 1995
Morning

THE UNABOMBER HAD BEEN CAUGHT soon after Arnesto's tip. However, Arnesto felt uneasy. Unless he had missed it, there had been no mention of the capture of McVeigh, the would-be Oklahoma City bomber. Of course, McVeigh wasn't yet big news; if he had been captured, it's possible he had been brought in quietly. Maybe the FBI confiscated his truck bomb and wanted to keep a lid on it to prevent copycats. Still, the two-year anniversary of the end of the Waco Siege was quickly approaching. It probably wouldn't hurt to check.

Arnesto called the FBI from a public place on a burner, the new, disposable cell phone of choice for drug dealers and time travelers.

"Agent Whiteside, please," he said to the woman who answered.

"I'm sorry, Agent Whiteside is out on assignment. Would you like to leave a message? I'll make sure he gets it."

"Is there any way you can transfer me? He'd really want to talk to me personally." *Especially under the circumstances.*

"I'm afraid I can't do that."

115

"Alright, I'd like to speak to whomever is in charge of the McVeigh case," he said.

"I'm sorry?"

"Timothy McVeigh." He spelled out the last name.

After a long pause, the woman on the other end of the line said, "I'm sorry, I can't find a reference to a McVeigh. Would you like to talk to someone in investigations?"

Why were these things always so difficult? "Actually, could you transfer me to someone at the Oklahoma City office? Thanks."

Once transferred, he spoke briefly with the male agent who answered the phone. From the conversation, Arnesto felt that either the FBI never looked into McVeigh, or looked into him, found nothing, and terminated any inquiries. It was also possible they were watching him and staying tight-lipped about it, but that seemed unlikely.

But if they had no interest in McVeigh before Arnesto's call, they certainly did by the time he told them about the yellow Ryder truck filled with explosives coming from Kansas to their very doorstep in a few days' time.

Unfortunately, that was all he could remember. When they started asking Arnesto questions about himself, he hung up, then destroyed the burner and threw it away.

He felt relieved. Surely, they wouldn't need his help anymore. But as he looked at the people around him, his relief evaporated. What if they didn't believe him? There had never been an attack like Oklahoma City before. It would remain the deadliest act of domestic terrorism for decades to come. Even if they didn't believe him, they had to check it out. But what if they came up empty? What if there was some breakdown in communication somewhere? *Argh.* Still, what could he

116

do at this point? There wasn't any sane reason to travel to Oklahoma himself.

Right.

He grumbled, drove home, and started packing.

Katrina insisted on driving him to the airport.

"I'm sorry about the timing of this," he said.

"Not at all! These people need your help," she smiled. "Go. Help them integrate your network code or whatever." He had told her that he was flying out to one of their partner companies to help with a last-minute crunch. She believed him.

"I was supposed to help you with our wedding plans this weekend."

"I know, and you've been a big help so far. Huge, in fact. But I can handle the rest myself," she said. "This is a free out. You should take it."

The first time they got married, she chided him for not helping enough. This time, he exhausted himself trying to help and she didn't even want it. It was a hit to his pride, but he had far graver concerns.

During the flight to Oklahoma City, he reminisced about Waco. There weren't nearly as many deaths this time around; maybe McVeigh wouldn't seek retribution? But then he remembered their conversation. McVeigh had seemed so bitter even before Waco had turned tragic. No matter. If there was even the slightest chance of history repeating itself, Arnesto had to try to stop him. He was sorry he had bought those bumper stickers and had shredded them at the first opportunity.

He tossed and turned in his hotel bed all that night. When the alarm went off at five o'clock, he awoke with a fright and jumped out of bed. He ate his bag of airline peanuts and some other junk food he had purchased from the snack machine the night before, then got himself

117

together and checked out of the hotel.

He drove past the Alfred P. Murrah Federal Building and was delighted to see it was still there, though he was concerned with how easily he drove by it. After his warning, shouldn't they have set up roadblocks or brought in tanks or something?

Before long, he was on I-35 North. He traveled about an hour north without seeing any yellow Ryder trucks coming the other way. This made sense as most do-it-yourselfers probably wouldn't have been up at that hour.

He found a good stakeout point at a gas station alongside I-35 South. From there, he could see a little ways north without McVeigh noticing him in return. Around the corner from the gas station entrance, away from foot traffic he kept at least one eye on the road, trying to look busy for appearances. He looked over his road map, flipped through the car manual, and even had a few pretend conversations on his phone. More than once he was tempted to get back on the road and move to the next gas station to the north, but decided to wait until someone at his location got suspicious of his presence.

Before anyone noticed him, he noticed someone else.

Something yellow was headed his direction on I-35 South. As he put his phone down, he watched as a single-occupancy, yellow Ryder truck grew in size then disappeared under the overpass. Arnesto only caught a glimpse of the driver, but he looked clean-cut and possibly young. It wasn't definite, but it was likely his man.

Arnesto started up the car and pursued. It didn't take long to catch up; the Ryder was going two miles under the speed limit. Arnesto looked to see if the truck was sagging under the weight of all the explosives that might be inside, but he couldn't tell. His heart racing, he steeled himself as he began to overtake the truck. As he approached the front, he let up on the accelerator to bleed off a tiny bit of speed.

Closer, closer, any second now… It felt like slow motion as he passed the cabin of the truck, peering inside as he did.

He hated being right all the time.

There was no doubt in his mind. It was McVeigh. He restored his previous pressure to the gas pedal, reclaiming the tiny amount of speed he had given up and increasing the distance between them until finally pulling into the right lane about one hundred yards in front of the Ryder. *So far, so good.* McVeigh had neither tried to run him off the road nor started firing at him. Given McVeigh's outstanding skill as a sharpshooter, this was not out of the question. However, in all likelihood, McVeigh probably hadn't given Arnesto any thought at all. If nothing else, he would have been distracted by the black-and-white coming up behind him.

Arnesto, feeling he was a safe enough distance in front of McVeigh, pulled out his phone to call 911. Instead, seeing the police lights were meant for *him*, he put it down.

You've got to be kidding me… Wait, maybe this is a good thing. He pulled over and got his license and registration ready. Though he had never been pulled over in *this* lifetime, his former self had received a few tickets, so he knew the routine. He made every attempt to ignore the Ryder as it passed, heading toward its obliteration; one suspicious glance from him could alert McVeigh. *What is taking this cop so long? Come on, come on!*

Arnesto rolled down his window. He knew better than to get out of the car, but it was tempting. Instead, he held his arms out the window with papers in hand and tried motioning the officer to approach.

119

At last, the officer got out of his car and sauntered over. "Are you in some kind of a hurry?"

"Listen, there's a yellow Ryder truck up ahead that's filled with explosives." Arnesto half expected to be interrupted at this point, but since he wasn't, he continued, "Here's my cell phone, I was about to call 911. You need to stop that truck before it reaches the city."

"Hold on. How do you know it's filled with explosives?" the officer asked.

"I... saw it," Arnesto said. It was mostly a lie, though it's possible his former self saw a recreation on some crime show at some point. "We left the same hotel in Kansas early this morning. I was returning my key to the front office when I caught a glimpse of him putting something in the back. He turned and saw me and quickly shut the back door like he was hiding something. I didn't think much of it, but something about the way he acted seemed odd, so I chased him down and was about to call the police when you pulled me over." These were all lies.

"And what did you see exactly?"

"It looked like some big containers full of liquid toward the front. He and another guy were moving some large bags of something from a pickup into the Ryder, too. I think it was fertilizer."

"What makes you think it was a bomb?"

Arnesto wasn't sure how to answer this. "Who rents a Ryder to transport stuff like that? I can tell you, there was no furniture in that truck. If nothing else, you've got him on illegally transporting dangerous goods, right?" The officer seemed to be debating whether to believe this preposterous story. "Look, give me a ticket, that's fine. I will happily take a ticket and slow down. I'm not in a rush anymore, but you are. Please, call this in. Ask someone to check with the FBI."

That seemed to strike a nerve. "Wait right here, don't move," the officer said. He hustled back to his squad car and got in.

Arnesto sat back in his seat, still holding his license and registration. He looked in the rear-view mirror and could tell the officer was talking over the radio, though he couldn't hear what he was saying. Thirty seconds passed. *Come on, hurry up!* Arnesto looked down the interstate, but the Ryder was long gone.

Finally, the flashing lights disappeared from the rear-view mirror as the police car took off, accelerating with considerable speed. Arnesto smiled wide as he watched the black-and-white roar down the highway.

"Yes! Go get him, copper!" Arnesto yelled. He rubbed both his hands through his hair as he exhaled. He shoved the registration back into the glove box and put his license back in his money clip, which he then put back in his pocket. He breathed one more heavy sigh of relief, then started the car.

He stuck to the speed limit at first, but then went a little faster. He was hungry. After about fifteen minutes, he noticed there were a couple vehicles pulled over to the side of the road. As he approached, he saw the flashing lights from a police car pulled way over to the side. There was no Ryder truck present. With a sinking feeling in his gut, he slowed down and pulled off the road ahead of the civilian vehicles.

Only then did he see somebody attempting CPR on the lifeless, bloodied police officer thirty feet past the squad car.

"Motherfucker!" he yelled. With a death grip on the steering wheel and gritted teeth, he pushed down hard on the accelerator. This was it. This would be the day he would wind up on the news.

He was going to ram the truck off the goddamned road.

Sure, he would have a lot of explaining to do. Maybe they would go easy on him, seeing as how it was a truck bomb. Or maybe the truck would explode and he would be vaporized. That would suck, especially with so much more to do, so many more lives to save. What would his family think? Was he having second thoughts? *No! Catch up to the truck, do the PIT maneuver you see the cops doing on television, then drive the hell out of there as the truck fishtails, flips over a few times, and explodes. Oh, God.*

His rental car screamed down the interstate. It was the fastest he had ever driven, at least in this lifetime. Or maybe both, he wasn't sure. *Take that, former me.* The miles were flying by, but the road signs reminded him that the distance to the city was shrinking in a hurry. Ten minutes passed. Twenty. *Where is the truck?!*

Suddenly, brake lights. Everybody was slowing down. *An accident?* It must have been big; there were several police cars, but where were the vehicles involved? There weren't any; it was a roadblock.

At the speed he was travelling, Arnesto had to hit the brakes hard to come to a safe stop. People were merging into the right lane, but he had learned to drive in Massachusetts, where etiquette is frowned upon, so he took the opportunity to get farther ahead in the left lane. In so doing, he caught sight of a yellow truck peeking out in front of a semi way up ahead.

Now what? If they somehow let McVeigh through, Arnesto would be unable to catch up to him in time. But clearly, they were here for McVeigh. Should he get out and run ahead to the police to warn them, hoping they wouldn't shoot him as he did so?

He never had time to decide.

The police ahead all ran off to the right side of the road. Arnesto could just make them out as they chased McVeigh, who had taken off running himself. Police officers and federal agents alike were waiting

122

for him, however. McVeigh, desperate to escape, chose to ignore the orders to halt. Still running, he drew his gun at an officer in the way. Arnesto heard the hail of gunfire that came next.

As a result of his twenty-nine gunshot wounds, McVeigh was dead.

Agents handcuffed McVeigh's lifeless wrists, holstered their weapons, and walked back to their vehicles. Two people were dead, but at least it was over.

Still, something didn't feel right. Arnesto had a sobering thought: hadn't McVeigh been caught without resistance right after the bombing? Why did he run this time when he knew his chances were slim at best? Just as an agent climbed into the driver's seat of the Ryder, Arnesto knew the answer.

Oh no.

In that moment, the two-minute fuse McVeigh had lit before fleeing ran out.

The explosion sent officers and truck parts hurtling through the air while the shock wave blasted through vehicle windows, sending broken glass everywhere. In an instant, everything seemed to be on fire.

Arnesto, dazed with loud ringing in his ears, tried to assess the situation. The cars around him, protected from the blast due to distance, were now crossing the center divide to leave the scene on I-35 North. Arnesto followed their example, checking the map for an alternative route back into the city.

One carwash and a flight later, Arnesto was back home watching the news. Although he had saved more than one hundred and fifty lives, all he could think about were the seventeen who had perished.

Shady Neighbors

Arnesto's Home
Silicon Valley, California
Thursday, July 17, 1997
3:12 a.m.

"YOUR TURN," KATRINA MUMBLED, nudging Arnesto awake. He could hear baby Melissa crying in the other room. He looked at his alarm clock. 3:12 a.m. He continued to lay there for a moment, unable to move. How many other twenty-five-year-old men were dumb enough to willingly become a father so young?

Actually, it was the *first* Arnesto who was willing; *this* Arnesto felt obligated to keep his family history intact. And so he recreated Melissa and was grateful for his success. Just a little less so at 3:12 in the morning. And she was the easy one. She wasn't even colicky like Carlos would be after his birth in a couple years, assuming Arnesto would also be successful in recreating *him*.

Arnesto forced himself out of bed and into Melissa's room. He braced himself for the worst, but her diaper didn't smell. *Yes!* That was the win he needed right now. All she wanted was to be held.

He gently bounced her in his arms as he walked back into the

124

master bedroom to report the good news to Katrina, but his wife was already sound asleep.

Taking the opportunity to compare the two most important women in his life, he could tell even in the darkness that Melissa's hair, though rather a dark shade itself, was still lighter than her mother's. Katrina's hair was also straight, while Melissa had some curls coming in.

Curls? Melissa's hair is curly? Since when?! The first Melissa didn't have curly hair. Who the hell was he carrying right now?! Had they brought home the wrong baby from the hospital?

Please tell me we didn't abduct somebody else's child! he thought. He carried her back into her room, turned on the light, and examined the rest of her. It still seemed like Melissa... *Curses, why must all babies look so alike?!* Maybe he should wake Katrina and ask her? No, of course not! What would he say, "Hey, hon, do you know why this baby has curly hair when our first Melissa from the other universe had straight hair?" It was probably some change in history: different experiences, different physiology. He and Katrina had minute differences between them and their former selves at this point; why shouldn't their child? He put Melissa back in her crib and decided he would keep a close eye on her. As always, time would tell.

He turned around and heard a loud meow coming from right in front of him which startled him. "Froggy! Hey, buddy!" Arnesto said as he knelt down to pet the most talkative cat of all time. "And where's your brother? There he is. Hey, Schmedley!" Schmedley was larger than his brother (as well as their two littermates) and lighter colored as well. He was also more reserved, only deigning to meow when he not only wanted attention but deemed it an urgent matter.

Getting these cats had been one of the most critical moments for

Arnesto to recreate. He had looked forward to it for years. He smiled as he remembered how easy it had been. All he had needed to do was wait for his coworker to send the email that she was looking for homes for her new kittens, walk into the conference room, and take them home. Katrina, who had wanted cats for a long time, had been overjoyed and had named the little one Froggy for no reason at all. Arnesto had named the bigger one Schmedley to "take him down a notch." Now they were back in his life and he knew they would give the whole family years and years of joy.

Yes siree, Bob, if there were guidelines to reliving one's life in an alternate universe, one of them had to be: "Make sure to reacquire any beloved pets!"

Arnesto returned to bed and when he reawoke, Katrina had already left for work, dropping Melissa off at daycare along the way. Arnesto still felt tired, though, and this was unfortunate as he was about to have a very long day.

There was no telling what might trigger Arnesto's memory, allowing him to recall some future event. It could be something small, like a word or an image, or something big, like a disaster. Today, it was breakfast.

While Arnesto poured milk into his cereal, he noticed the picture of the lost child on the back, a little boy named Cyrus Mosher. Try as he might, Arnesto couldn't remember any details about Cyrus. This was the first he had heard of him. Still, while he ate, he focused on Cyrus's picture and tried to remember if he had any information about other missing children he could leak to the police.

He went through his mental catalog of newsworthy kidnappings. Angie Daniels had already been found. Lino Banes was another high-profile victim, but try as he might, Arnesto couldn't recall any information about him.

Then there was Violet Gordon.

Arnesto froze mid-chew. Violet was currently missing and he knew where she was. Sort of.

In his past life, he and Katrina had taken numerous day trips to Napa Valley to tour the vineyards. On one of those trips, one that wasn't scheduled to happen for a few more years, Arnesto was going to take a wrong turn and get them temporarily lost.

When Violet was found, many years after that, the news would show the house where she had been held and abused for the majority of her life. All Arnesto could remember was watching the news report and realizing they had driven by a house that looked suspiciously similar during their unexpected detour.

In other words, he remembered remembering seeing a house that they *may* have seen... while lost.

He finished eating and getting ready, left a voicemail for his boss that he was calling in sick, and hit the highway.

Less than two hours later, he was in wine country. He wanted to retrace his steps but wasn't sure which steps to retrace. He ruled out wineries he had seen recently, but that still left several potential starting points. He marked them on a map and began the arduous task of driving to each one, then heading back out of town, looking for places where he might make a wrong turn. As navigationally challenged as Arnesto was, the routes out of these wineries were too simple — they only had a few, well-marked turns onto major roads to get visitors back onto the main highway.

He tried some other wineries in the area to no avail. He also tried expanding his search, but still no luck. It was time to call in the big guns.

"Hey, Katrina."

"Hey, Babe."

"I might have to stay late again tonight. Also, I was talking to one of the guys at work about wineries. I can't remember — which ones did you like best?" She mentioned a few of the ones he had already covered. "Okay, are there any he should avoid?"

"No, not really. I guess it depends on his taste more than anything."

Thanks, honey, you're a big help. "Are there any still on your wish list?" She mentioned a few, including one he hadn't been to yet that day. *Aha, a lead.* "Alright, thanks, Sugarmuffin!"

"You're welcome! Hey, maybe he and his wife would like to join us next time. Is he married?" she asked.

Is my fictitious wine buddy married? "Nah, I don't like him that much."

"He can't be that bad if you're getting all this information for him."

"Ngh... I... you know..." Arnesto stammered.

"Well, if you respect him at all, don't tell him about Arnucci's."

"What?! Just because your spaghetti was soggy one time—"

"Sorry, babe, I have to go. Love you!" she said, hanging up without waiting for him to reply.

There was *nothing* wrong with Arnucci's. It was a small, old-fashioned Italian restaurant that served delicious food, especially after a long, hard day of tasting wine. And the bread, sweet jumping Jesus, the bread, so soft and warm... The hell with it. He was in the area. Might as well eat there without her.

The sun was starting to set when he pulled into the strip mall parking lot. He smiled as he parked right in front of the entrance, then got out of his car and went up to the door, which to his surprise, was locked. He tugged again, but it didn't move. He looked around and saw the business hours in the window.

Closed Tuesdays?! Who does that? Who closes Tuesdays?! "This is bullshit!" he said to no one. Hungry and dejected, he got back in his car and looked at the map to reassess. He didn't know what else there was to eat around there. He could take a guess on the next winery having some sort of deli, or since he was close, get back on the main highway.

Only he wasn't close. As the crow flies, the highway was ten minutes away. In a vehicle taking the optimal route, closer to twenty. For a navigationally challenged driver deciding to take a "shortcut" that looked like it lead to the highway but instead got the driver lost, at least fifty.

It wasn't a wrong turn from the winery. It was a wrong turn from Arnucci's!

He quickly started the car and headed for the "shortcut." It wasn't hard to retrace his steps; there wasn't much choice but to stay on the main road with only the occasional side street that looked like it led nowhere. Eventually, the road he was on ended at a crossroad. Heading west didn't feel right and also went the wrong direction, so he turned east. There were only a couple more houses before the barren land ended at the trees behind the dead end. He turned around and started heading back, scrutinizing every homestead along the way.

None of them looked right. They were the right type, and Arnesto felt like he was literally in the neighborhood, but none of them were quite the one. That's when he realized he wasn't tracing his path exactly. He turned around again and headed back toward the dead end. Only this time, instead of driving all the way, he pretended he was actually trying to find the freeway and turned around at the point one could see that this particular road led nowhere.

As he made the first point of a three-point turn, he saw it. From his current spot, parked perpendicular to the road, he was able to look past the side of the house on his left, and, through a small clearing in the trees, see the house he'd been looking for. It was off one of the side streets.

He completed the turn, headed back the way he originally came, and drove down the first side street he found. He got a chill when he saw the house up close. Though still not positive, it looked awfully like the house he remembered from the news. It was not a good neighborhood. There was nowhere he felt comfortable parking and though the plots of land were large, the houses looked run-down and unfriendly. He imagined people with raised eyebrows peeking out from behind curtains watching him creep through their neighborhood. Someone was likely to respond to a strange car parked on the street.

He went back to the main road and turned down the next side street. Besides looking for a spot to park, he wanted to check out the house's backyard where Violet was likely being kept. No luck: still no place to park, and no access to the yard.

He wanted to go home. He was tired and still hadn't eaten, though his hunger was offset by his anxiety. He had the address now. He just had to find a pay phone and make an anonymous call. The only problem was he still wasn't sure it was the right house. If it wasn't, at worst, the police would show up and scare the crap out of some innocent elderly couple. Even so, Arnesto's anal-retentiveness wouldn't let him leave. As he debated this in his mind, he once again returned to the dead end and parked, killing the engine and turning off his lights.

After waiting a few minutes, he stepped outside into the warm, dusty air. Though it was dark out and only a partial moon, there was hardly any light pollution and no cloud cover. He could see well enough, but it also meant he could be seen. Fortunately, there was nobody around. The people in the nearest house probably wouldn't notice him from this distance, especially if he stuck to the woods on the edge of their property.

He slunk through the woods quickly, making sure not to stray too far from the edge lest he get bitten by something large and venomous. Once he made it to the side street, he was able to stay hidden as he passed the house in question in order to survey their back yard. It looked more like a junkyard. There was an ancient rusted Chevy truck on cinder blocks, stacks of worn out tires, a swing set that looked like a strong gust would knock it down, some faded lawn ornaments, and lots of tarps covering firewood and who knows what else.

And a shed. That's where she would be. Maybe.

His heart racing, he took a few deep breaths in a misguided attempt to calm himself. The fence enclosing the backyard wasn't too high, so he was able to jump over using a post as support without making much noise. He then scuttled behind the shed where he couldn't be seen. He waited a bit, but the house remained dark, so he peeked around the edge of the shed, then crept around the side of the shed to the front.

There was a latch on the door, but no lock, only a wire hanger bent into a U-shape inserted upside-down through the latch. If Violet was indeed inside, would the kidnappers be this careless? Maybe they were just lazy. It was certainly easier than fumbling with a lock if you were drunk or hooked on meth and in the mood to do unspeakable acts to an innocent little girl. *Assholes.*

Okay, open the door, take a quick peek, then run back to the car. One, two, THREE. He removed the hanger and pushed open the door enough to squeeze inside. *Please don't let there be a silent alarm.* Even in the darkness, he could tell there was very little in there. Broken old lawn mowers and other junk, nothing of value.

Using his flip phone as a light source, he kept it low and out of line of sight to the house. He did a quick but thorough scan and didn't see anything. He took another couple steps inside to make sure he covered every corner. There was nothing behind the door or elsewhere save a small tarp in the back right corner. He snapped his phone shut and turned back toward the door. Then he froze.

Had he seen a foot under the tarp? He stepped back and looked toward the tarp, but had to reopen his phone for light. It was still hard to see. He peered closely at the edge of the tarp where he thought he had seen the foot, but if he had, it wasn't there now. The rest of the tarp was obscured by one of the dead lawn mowers, so he leaned in and slowly scanned upward from the bottom of the tarp to the top.

When at last his eyes met hers, he nearly screamed.

Unexpected Company

Napa Valley, California
Thursday, July 17, 1997
9:30 p.m.

"WHO ARE YOU?" came a hushed, young voice.

He stared at her in silence for a few seconds, though it felt like much longer.

"Violet Gordon? I'm going to call the police and get you out of here. They'll be here soon, okay?"

"No, you have to get me out of here."

"I will, I'm calling the police."

"No! They won't help," she said.

"What do you mean? They'll save you." Arnesto was confused and not thrilled to be having this conversation.

"They came before. I've seen them come to the house at least twice. They never come out to the back yard," she said.

That's right. The police had mishandled the case. The kidnappers, Len and Ceola Cornett, were already on police files for other crimes related to children in their past. The police came by to check up on them from time to time but weren't thorough enough. However, they were only doing routine checks at the time. Surely if they got an emergency call about a child locked in a shed...

"Please, get me out of here," Violet said again. "Please. Please." It was her eyes. They reminded him so much of his daughter's. How could he turn her down?

"Okay, let's go," he said.

"I can't... look." She uncovered her legs from the tarp and showed him the steel cable connecting a metal shackle securing her left ankle to a spike embedded in the floor.

"Fuck," he said, wincing at the realization he had just sworn in front of a child. Then again, after all she'd been through, one little f-bomb probably wasn't going to hurt. He examined and pulled on the cable, but it didn't budge. He looked around for something he could use, but for fairly obvious reasons, there wasn't a hacksaw lying around. "Where's the key?"

"Inside the house, probably. They might catch you, though."

"I need a tool and I don't have one. Violet, I don't see another option. I have to go call the police."

"No, I want to go with you." Again with the eyes. "There's a hardware store in town. Mr. Cornett goes there sometimes."

"You want me to leave you, go buy a tool, and then come back and hope we don't get caught?"

"If the police come, there could be a shootout and they might lose. Then Mr. Cornett will either kill me or take me some place else. Please, Mister." She had thought this through. Still, it didn't mean her plan was good. Under normal circumstances, he would have already been calling in the cavalry from a safe distance. However, her plan had another benefit: he could maintain his anonymity.

134

"Okay. Wow. If I'm not back in... thirty minutes, call 911 and tell them everything. Do you know the address here?" he asked, pulling a burner out of his pocket. He opened it and handed it to her.

"Yes," she said, before reciting it. Then she shut the burner and shoved it back into his hand. "But if it gets to the point I need to call 911, it's too late. If they catch me with that, I'll be in even worse trouble. Please hurry," came her hushed voice from the dark. Arnesto heard the rustling of the tarp, presuming she had already covered herself back up.

"I'll be back as quick as I can, I promise," he said as he stepped outside and replaced the hanger.

He really hoped the hardware store stayed open until ten o'clock. He was already cutting it close. If he was late, or they closed any earlier, so help him, he was going to break in and run like a madman down every single aisle until he found something he could use. He could not let that little girl spend one more minute in that shed than was absolutely necessary. He already felt like shit for leaving her.

Traffic was pretty light in town. Judging by the neighborhood, it seemed unlikely the residents had bustling social lives. He arrived at the hardware store at 9:55. As he got out of the car and rushed toward the entrance, he made it to the sidewalk and froze.

There was a payphone on the corner.

One little phone call. All he had to do was pick up the receiver, dial 911, disguise his voice, and tell them Violet Gordon was chained up in a shed behind the Cornett residence, and give them the address. It was the smarter play.

But no, he had made a promise. *Damn that kid.*

He ran inside the store where a few employees were preparing to close up for the night.

"Are you looking for anything in particular?" asked an associate, hoping to expedite Arnesto's last-minute shopping experience.

"Bolt cutters? My, uh, friend got drunk... long story," Arnesto said.

"Aisle fifteen."

He ran down the aisle, grabbed the bolt cutters, and headed toward the register, keeping an eye out for anything else that might help. He stopped briefly in front of some boxes of blue shoe covers, like the ones they wear in an operating room, but decided they were all too big for Violet's tiny feet. Besides, the purchase might make him look even more suspicious.

As he pulled out his wallet, he realized he had made a mistake he swore he'd never make: he was short on cash. Actually, he had enough for one of the smaller bolt cutters, like the 12-inch or 14-inch, but he had grabbed the 24-inch model. As the cashier watched him consider grabbing a smaller model, Arnesto spied the ATM by the wall near the counter. If the police ever investigated bolt cutter purchases occurring right before Violet Gordon was freed, they would find Arnesto in an instant if he used his debit card. However, they probably wouldn't go so far as to check ATM logs that occurred right before a cash-based bolt cutters purchase.

Arnesto held up his index finger, giving the cashier the "be right back" symbol and withdrew a bunch of cash from the ATM. Then after paying, he left and made the return drive back to the dead end.

He felt even more conspicuous skulking around with the large bolt cutters, but the neighborhood was as quiet as it had been before, and he returned to the shed without incident.

"Violet, it's me. I'm back," he said as he slipped inside. Her tarp came off. "Can you walk?"

"Yeah."

Opening his phone and laying it on its side gave him enough light to examine the cable holding her prisoner. It was no match for the bolt cutters. With just a little effort, Arnesto managed to cut through the cable outside the shackle.

She was free.

He grabbed and shut his phone in one smooth movement then joined her just inside the door. As they peered out of the shed, he whispered instructions. "I'll help you over the fence, then we'll sneak down to my car in that direction," he said, pointing. "Are you ready?" He was not prepared for her response.

"What about the others?"

Arnesto felt like he was going to pass out. Before he could even ask her what she was talking about, she had scampered off to one of the tarps by the tire pile. Before he could reach her, she was already walking back to him with a two-year-old fast asleep in her arms.

"Take Brenda," she commanded, handing the baby to Arnesto. "She won't wake up; they drug her every night. Tonya might put up a fight, though."

He followed her behind the rusted Chevy. She checked a couple tarps before finding Tonya.

"Tonya, wake up, we have to go," Violet said as she gently shook Tonya awake.

The six-year-old stirred and rubbed her eyes. "Violet? How'd you get out? Where are we going?"

"Come on, we're going to the hospital, let's go."

"I don't wanna. Len will be mad," Tonya said.

"We have to leave. *Now*," Violet said.

"You're trying to get rid of me because I'm his favorite wife."

Arnesto felt nauseous. He realized all three of the girls were wearing little white dresses. Len Cornett "married" each new girl he kidnapped. Only his favorite "wife" could call him Len, as Tonya just had. Arnesto looked at the back door. For a moment, he wanted somebody to come out. For the first time in his life, he wanted a confrontation. He was prepared to take the bolt cutters and swing them as hard as he could into the Cornetts' skulls. Instead, he shook off the impulse and returned to reality.

"Tonya, get up," Violet said.

"Leave me alone or I'll scream."

"Go ahead. Nobody will hear you. Len and Ceola are at the hospital. That's why we're going. But I guess if you want to stay, that's okay. Len will probably be angry that you were the *only one* who didn't come. But at least you won't get any lashes until he gets back."

"Okay, I'm coming," Tonya said, getting to her feet. She must have earned the right to not be bound.

"Anybody else?" Arnesto asked, suddenly realizing why he didn't remember there being more than Violet. Violet had been rescued alone. Something must have happened to the other two girls. The media frenzy had decided to focus solely on the good news of Violet's rescue, ignoring the fate of the others.

"No, just us three," Violet said, shaking her head. She took Brenda from Arnesto so he could carry Tonya.

When they reached the fence, they put down the two youngest girls. Arnesto helped Violet over the fence, then handed her Brenda, then gently lowered Tonya over the side. Arnesto hopped over after them, then he and Violet once again picked up the others. They hugged the tree line as they crept back through the neighbor's yard to Arnesto's car. There was no way they could carry the girls through the trees, especially with Violet being barefoot. Soon, all three girls were huddled together in the back seat as Arnesto drove off.

"If it's alright with you, I'll drop you off at the emergency room, but then I have to leave," Arnesto said looking in the rear-view mirror. Violet looked at him in the mirror and nodded. Other than her first words to him, she never questioned him or his motives. Maybe she didn't want to know. Maybe she had long ago been beaten into submission. Or maybe she was simply exhausted. They all were.

"Thank you," she said a few moments later.

When they got to the ER, Arnesto parked right out front, hoping there weren't any security cameras recording. With the two littlest being carried, Violet followed Arnesto into the waiting room. He gently set down Tonya in an empty chair then turned to Violet.

"You did amazing tonight," he said, looking into her eyes one last time. He thought her eyes looked a little watery, but couldn't be sure. "You're going to be okay." Then he yelled over his shoulder toward the desk. "Nurse!" When he saw a nurse get up and begin to hustle over, he yelled, "Be right back, there's two more!" then ran out the exit to his car.

He drove around the loop in front of the emergency room and looked in through the glass to see the first nurse crouched down examining Violet's ankle while two more nurses ran over to assist. Then he drove off.

Too Much Power

Massachusetts
Friday, July 16, 1999
8:08 p.m.

"YOU'RE TALKING ABOUT CHANGING the presidency of the United States." Pete was incredulous.

Arnesto drew back and swung. He hit his blue ball with the right amount of power, but his aim was a tiny bit off and it hit the edge of a rectangular block in the middle of the path. "Damn it! Don't talk during my backswing. And I'm talking about doing what's right. Are you going to hit, or what?"

Pete put his red ball in the right dimple of the thrice-dimpled rubber mat at the start of the hole. His form wasn't quite as clean, but he easily bypassed the block, leaving his ball inches from the hole. "Who's to say what's right?" he asked. "Wait, is any of this going to matter? You didn't come back east just to hang out one last time before Y2K wipes out all of civilization, did you?"

"Y2K is fine, people fix most of the problems in time. Nah, I came back to slash JFK Jr.'s plane tires."

"Did you not like his so-called cameo on Seinfeld, or…?"

Arnesto snickered. "Trying to save lives."

"I see. Speaking of, I didn't hear anything about Columbine. I assume congratulations are in order?"

"All I had was a yearbook photo," Arnesto beamed. "All I remembered, besides the date, was the would-be murderers making finger guns in their class picture. Thankfully, it was enough to intervene."

"Excellent! How's Carlos?"

Arnesto sighed. "Another reason I was eager to get away. Baby Carlos is colicky... *again*. He has a birthmark behind his right shoulder that he didn't have before. I was so hoping he wouldn't have colic this time around, but no, he keeps that and gets a birthmark. I swear I can hear him screaming from here. Oh, well, he's Katrina's problem right now."

Pete shook his head. "I'm a little surprised you became a family man, I mean, at such a young age," Pete said.

"Katrina is a couple years older, she wanted kids, I couldn't say no."

"Sounds like you didn't have much choice. But that was in your previous life, right? I mean, this time around, you didn't *have* to have children again so young."

"Yeah, I did. They're my kids. I had to recreate them as exactly as possible. I can't imagine not having Melissa and Carlos," Arnesto said, smiling. "Oh, and Preston, but he comes later."

"I never thought about it that way, but right, that makes sense. Still, what about all the diapers and crying and lack of sleep and stuff?"

Arnesto's smile faded. "Yeah, it sucks. Again. I won't lie, children are not much fun at first. But they get better after the first, oh, twenty years or so."

141

A break in the dialog gave Pete a chance to absorb everything Arnesto had told him. Arnesto finally broke the silence.

"The essence of the game is to hit the ball closer and closer to the hole. But if you mess up your first shot on a volcano hole, that's it. You're fucked. Game over." They took turns moving around the base of the volcano, each hitting the ball ever so slightly too soft or too hard or too much to one side.

While in agreement, Pete couldn't resist the urge to passive aggressively taunt his friend. "It's part of the game."

"It's bullshit! Give me a six!"

The next hole was the loop-de-loop, where one has to cream the ball to get it through the waist-high, red, metal loop. Pete hit the ball a little too softly, causing it to bounce against the hard metal surface creating a wonderful cacophony of loud clanks before rolling back to the start. His next shot made it through but then rolled into a corner. Pete used his putter to move the ball out, but it rolled right back. "So, the election?"

"Sorry for the spoiler," Arnesto said, looking around for potential eavesdroppers, "but while Gore wins the popular vote, he loses the electoral vote. Bush becomes president."

"Well, that's too bad, but that's the process." Pete's ball was in Arnesto's way, so he tapped it in for par.

"There's more. Do you know what a hanging chad is?" Pete shook his head, so Arnesto explained all about how Florida's votes were tabulated by archaic, punch-card-based machines prone to counting errors. He had a nice second rebound off the wall, but his third shot rimmed out of the hole. "Argh! Give me four," he said, finishing the hole.

"So Gore should have won?" Pete's ball hit the trap door at the top

142

of the ramp inside the castle as it closed, sending his ball all the way back out. "Oops."

"I'm not sure. Some sources say Bush still would have won, but it's impossible to be certain. It's close, *very* close. There are other shenanigans as well. Factor those in, maybe Gore was supposed to win." After Pete's second shot made it into the castle, Arnesto hit a perfectly timed shot, but it was a little too hard and bounced back out of the pit, causing it to also roll all the way back. "Jesus!"

"Okay, so you warn people in time, maybe they actually listen to you and fix the system. You save Florida some embarrassment, but Bush wins anyway. Are you happy?" Pete asked as he wrote down a couple threes on the scorecard after they finished the hole.

"Here's the thing."

"Oh boy."

"When it's all said and done, George W. is not regarded as one of our finest presidents. The economy tanks, yes, partly due to the dot-com bubble bursting, but he certainly doesn't help. He creates a *huge* deficit, unemployment shoots up, and he invades Iraq."

"We go back to Iraq? The Bush family must really hate those guys," Pete said.

"There's more. There's going to be a terrorist attack on American soil. It's rumored that Bush ignores certain warnings and—"

"Wait, can't *you* do something about the attack?" He was frozen in place after moving his ball away from the wall, awaiting Arnesto's response. He looked as scared as someone might when they've received such grave news.

"Yes, in fact, I already have a plan," Arnesto said, assuring Pete who resumed his shot. "Should be an easy one, too."

"What's easy about it?"

"Well, for one thing, I know exactly when it is. It was nice of them to name the event after the date. For another, the bad guys aren't exactly hidden..."

"Okay, but if Gore gets elected, the attack might happen on a different day."

"True, but Gore might not ignore the warnings," Arnesto said, picking up both balls out of the hole and handing the red one to Pete. Their scores remained close with some back and forth over the last few holes. "I could still try to warn them besides."

"Unless the terrorists decide to go with a different attack than the one you're expecting. That sounds like quite a gamble," Pete said.

"Many more U.S. soldiers are going to die if Bush gets elected. And even if I prevent the attack, they may try again later," Arnesto sighed.

"You know, Arnesto, there was a time when I envied your ability. That time has long since passed. No offense."

"None taken. It *can* be kind of fun. Sometimes."

"So what happens after Bush?"

"Bush gets reelected in another close election."

"That tends to happen with wartime presidents. Okay, so the people *do* like the guy."

"He helps plunge us into another recession," Arnesto said.

"Jeez. So we're screwed."

"Well, the *next* guy helps us recover quite a bit." Arnesto refrained from spoiling any more than was necessary. "Though his weak stance on curtailing surveillance isn't going to help *me* any." *Thanks, Obama.*

"So you could help Gore get elected, but maybe he messes up, then Bush runs and wins after that, and makes things even worse, and... you

144

could keep going forever."

"Exactly. Where do you draw the line? Oh, man, we're at the stupid hanging log thing." Arnesto pushed the log hanging vertically over the hole. He hated the log since it caused many otherwise decent shots to get knocked away, another violation of the essence of mini golf.

"Okay, how about — and this is just my opinion, mind you — unless a Bush or a Kennedy or someone comes along and literally starts World War III, you let the people vote and deal with the consequences? Gore still has to lose many states on his own. That doesn't mean you still can't try to save the soldiers who'll die under Bush's leadership. Plus, on a personal level, you maintain a higher level of future predictability."

"Okay," Arnesto said.

"'Okay'?! That's it? That was easy." Pete prepared to putt, but then stopped. "Wait a minute. You already decided this, didn't you."

"Sorry, old friend. I pretty much came to the same conclusion a few minutes ago, but I still wanted to hear what you had to say. I appreciate your input. With regards to the election, I am going to... do nothing. Too many unknowns, too many variables, too much playing God."

* * *

A year later, the election unfolded close to how Arnesto remembered it: Florida still managed to make a complete mockery of the voting process, and there was still recount after recount. However, this time, they were in Gore's favor. First, Gore won by 382 votes, then he led by 1,204 votes, then 1,966 votes. Arnesto had no idea what he had done to cause this change, but he didn't completely mind it either.

However, just when it looked like Vice President Gore was going to be President-elect Gore, a shipment of more than eighteen thousand absentee ballots that heavily favored Bush was discovered, leading to still more motions and lawsuits. Despite the ballots having arrived after the deadline, Florida Governor (and Bush's brother) Jeb Bush signed an executive order stating the votes would count. Though the order was immediately challenged, Florida chose to add these ballots to the tally, giving Bush a final lead of more than three thousand votes and the presidency.

Safety in Numbers

San Francisco, California
Sunday, September 9, 2001
2:30 a.m.

ARNESTO PARKED his car and opened his laptop. He looked for unsecured wireless connections and found the same three networks he had found there a week earlier. Once his computer connected to the first network on the list, he created a new Hotmail account. He then opened up the text file he had been working on for years and copied the contents into the email. First came the list of recipients which he had acquired over the past many months. The list began with high-ranking members of the security team at Logan and Newark International Airports and included a smorgasbord of names from the FBI, CIA, the White House, the World Trade Center, the Pentagon, and others, twenty-nine names in all. Arnesto, initially concerned with having "too many cooks in the kitchen," thought the call to action would be more likely heeded with a larger number of readers.

Next came the subject and body of the email. The email detailed, as best as he could remember, events set to unfold just two days later. The information was incomplete, to be sure, but what could he do?

He read the email over a few more times, but the words were so familiar to him now that it was difficult to be objective. It was the wee hours of the morning, and he was in a poorly lit neighborhood more than fifty miles from home. However, with the light from his laptop screen illuminating his face, he didn't want to linger.

Arnesto looked around but didn't see anyone spying on him. Even if he did get caught, how much trouble could he possibly be in for tipping off a major attack? *Too much.* Even the slightest notice could hinder him going forward, and he had some big events coming up.

He took a few deep breaths as he read the email one last time. Why was he hesitating? Did he subconsciously remember one more detail he could add? He closed his eyes and tried to relax, but nothing new came to mind. In fact, he hadn't remembered anything new about this particular incident in eight years. It was for the best. At this point, he was risking planting some fake memory in his head. Memories are fickle that way.

He opened his eyes, took one more deep breath, and clicked, "Send."

* * *

Security Officer Ray Carroll was already getting ready for work when the call came.

"Are you coming into work now?" It was the chief.

"Yeah, I was just getting ready," Ray said.

"I figured. Do what you gotta do, but get here as soon as you're able. See you soon."

"Roger that." Ray hung up the phone then saw his wife Erin

looking at him with a concerned expression on her face.

"Trouble at work?" she asked.

"Sounds like it."

"Are *you* in trouble?"

"No. Well... I don't think so. Why would you jump to that conclusion?"

"I'm sorry!" she chuckled. "But be safe today, okay?" He smiled as he walked over to her, placing her arms around his waist then laying his hands on her shoulders.

"Only today?" he asked with a wry grin.

"Go," she said as she gently pushed him away and walked back into the kitchen.

After a long commute through the insufferable Boston morning traffic — *Will they ever finish the Big Dig?* — Ray arrived at his workplace in the security offices of Logan International. The chief spotted him right away.

"Ray! Here, I need you to read this." The chief shoved a chair at Ray while handing him a printout. The chief's tone made Ray uncomfortable, but his discomfort was about to get much worse. He looked down at the printout and read:

Subject: IMMINENT THREAT - 9/11/01 ~0800 AM - MULT. HIJACKINGS

Body:
Two days from now, on September 11, 2001, no fewer than 19 terrorists will attempt to hijack four passenger aircraft from Logan International and other airports in the northeast shortly after takeoff. Their aim is to fly these aircraft into major targets along the east coast.

The terrorists are members of al-Qaida working under Osama bin Laden. They are all Middle Eastern men in their twenties and thirties. They are well-trained and well-armed, and intend to carry knives, box cutters, and mace past security. Shortly after takeoff, a signal will be given. The terrorists will get up from their seats in first-class and rush the cockpit, gaining entrance by any means necessary. Once inside the cockpit, their intent is to kill the pilot and copilot and then blockade themselves inside. They will then alter course toward their target, using the aircraft as a weapon of mass destruction. They will not hesitate to kill anyone who gets in their way.

Partial Intel:
- Tuesday, 9/11/01 between 0800 and 0900, Eastern Daylight Time
- American Airlines flight 11 out of Logan International Airport
- United Airlines flight 93 out of Newark International Airport
- 19 hijackers divided among four aircraft
- Islamic extremists, members of al-Qaeda led by Osama bin Laden
- Seated in first-class
- May be wearing explosive devices (may be decoys)
- Armed with box cutters, mace, knives
- May don red headbands at start of attack
- Target #1: World Trade Center, North Tower
- Target #2: World Trade Center, South Tower
- Target #3: Pentagon
- Target #4: Washington, D.C., possibly the White House

Sincerely,
Anonymous

"You shittin' me, Chief? This a prank?" Ray asked as he reread the bullet points, though he felt pretty sure he already knew the answer. He felt even more sure when he looked up at the chief.

"Not a prank. FBI and NTSB are already here. Word is they've got the names of seventeen of them and should have the rest confirmed by early afternoon. A couple of them were already on the FBI's terrorist-alert list," the chief said.

An FBI agent walked into the room. "Gentlemen, briefing in the situation room in five minutes," he said, displaying the number five with his hand.

"Be right there," the chief said. "Ray, this is all need-to-know, top personnel only. Baggage handlers, screeners, even the pilots are being kept in the dark. The plan is to let these assholes board, then surprise them from behind. We'll talk about the specifics in the meeting. Ray, two of the flights are out of Logan. I'm going to recommend you take point on one of the task forces. C'mon, they're waiting for us."

* * *

"All first-class passengers may now board at this time," said the cheery woman at the check-in counter. She had no idea what was about to happen. All she knew was that she had been told to delay boarding the rest of the passengers until she was given the all-clear.

Terrorists, undercover agents, and unsuspecting passengers alike took their seats and settled in. Then, as had happened innumerable times in practice over the past thirty-six hours, the task force took action and the yelling began.

"FBI!"

"HANDS IN THE AIR!"

"DON'T MOVE!"

"GET DOWN!"

Agents and security officers poured in from behind the coach section while more ran in from the boarding area. Some threw themselves on top of passengers to try to protect them from any would-be blast. A couple of agents directed the flight attendants, shoving them into the kitchen area. One agent ordered the pilots to lock themselves in the cockpit before taking position outside.

The would-be hijackers were yanked from their seats and tackled to the ground. One managed to yell, "Allahu akbar!" just before a taser was shoved into his neck.

Ray maintained control of the left arm of one of the terrorists as he, the terrorist, two agents, and another security officer went down in a heap on the cabin floor. The terrorist's right arm, however, was still not restrained and as Ray landed on top of the hijacker, there was nothing he could do to keep the hijacker's box cutter from piercing his carotid artery.

The agent on top of Ray had no way of knowing that Ray's life was slipping away. Precious seconds were lost as the task force focused on pulling the terrorist out from under Ray and subduing him.

The situation contained at last, the terrorists were taken off the plane and down the stairs to the apron where they were placed in custody away from the main airport. Agents tried to control Ray's bleeding, assisted quickly by paramedics who had been waiting below. Ray was rushed to a medevac helicopter, where he was airlifted to Massachusetts General Hospital, but it was all for naught. He had already lost too much blood.

* * *

Arnesto stared at the television through eyes red and puffy with large bags underneath. He kept switching channels between the main news networks, waiting for the horrific news that would never come. Every now and then, one of the programs showed the New York City skyline, causing Arnesto's heart to skip a beat, but there was never any news behind it. It was shown purely as a backdrop.

One of the channels mentioned flight attendants, which caught Arnesto's attention. However, instead of talking about how they were murdered in a hijacking, the piece was about whether stewards working for Delta were going to unionize.

Nothing else came close. Mariah Carey released her soundtrack to the movie *Glitter*. Michael Jordan was possibly (definitely) coming out of retirement again. Outfielder Paul O'Neill was placed on the Yankees' disabled list.

Arnesto's apartment grew brighter. *Sunrise*. He smiled. He probably would have heard something by now, but it was still too early to be sure. A couple more commercial breaks and it was the top of the hour. Seven o'clock in the morning for him, ten o'clock for Manhattan.

And still no mention of any terrorist attack.

Had he actually been successful in warning them or was the news just slow? He knew what he needed. He went to the window and looked up at the sky, but that didn't work. So he went outside and made the short walk up the hill a couple streets behind his house until he had a nice view of downtown. As he looked out over the city, way off in the distance, he spied what he was looking for.

Contrails.

He followed them to the source, and while he couldn't see the airplane, he knew it was there. Such a beautiful sight on such a perfect morning. He remembered all the people who had been stranded after all air traffic in the United States had been grounded for the first time in history. But that was 9/11. Today wasn't 9/11; today was plain ol' boring September 11, 2001, and aircraft were still flying overhead. Thanks to him.

Arnesto looked around to see if anyone was watching, then did a little victory dance.

Soon he made it into work, where everything seemed brighter. His coworkers smiled and walked about the place with a sense of purpose. Arnesto walked by the main conference room, but instead of it being full of people glued to the television, it was empty and the television was off. And as the day progressed, there never came an email from management offering to match employee donations in honor of the victims.

That Tuesday, Arnesto had a regular, boring, wonderful day at work.

Barge Right In

"DO THESE THINGS ALWAYS happen so early in the morning? Over." Pete sounded tense over the walkie-talkie.

"A lot of them do. I'm not a big fan of it either, but it does provide more daylight for subsequent rescue operations. Over." Arnesto realized he wasn't helping to ease the tension and added, "Not that they'll need one today."

Pete's shaky voice came back on. "Roger. What was that rattling noise I heard? Over."

Arnesto looked at the cup in his hand. "That's my McSalad Shaker. Too bad these things get discontinued. I guess if it doesn't cause heart disease, Americans won't eat it. Over."

So far, it was a cool morning in Oklahoma, though Arnesto felt the humidity was hurting the taste of his salad. He turned his eyes to the maritime scanner.

"Love is coming," Pete said, watching his own scanner. They both

155

saw the towboat Robert Y. Love approaching from the south.

"Too soon. Stand by." Arnesto understood Pete's eagerness. He felt the same way. But like he explained the night before, being too early wouldn't help. It would only arouse suspicion and raise unanswerable questions. Too many of those and it could be all over. For everyone.

"Still sounds like a question to me," Pete said. "Robert Y. Love. Like, 'Robert, why love?'"

"That's exactly how I remembered it. Alright, cut the chatter, Blocker Two. I am rolling. Stand by, over." Arnesto started up the RV he had rented.

"Roger." Pete started his rented moving truck but sat tight. He wanted to puke.

Arnesto drove up the onramp to I-40 East. Traffic was increasing, but it wasn't an issue, and he merged onto the highway without difficulty.

Pete looked at his walkie-talkie. Shouldn't he have heard something by now? He looked at the scanner but wished he hadn't. The Love was closing in a hurry.

As Arnesto drove under the small overpass by mile marker number 289, he gave the command. "Blocker Two, you are go, over."

Pete dropped the walkie-talkie and scrambled to pick it up. "I don't — I don't know if I can do this." He was practically hyperventilating.

"Pete, all you have to do is park the truck. If you don't, people are going to die. Go. *Now!*"

Pete switched the vehicle into drive and inched forward. "Roger, on the move." He pressed the accelerator and found himself getting up to highway speed as he merged onto I-40 West.

"I'm about there," Arnesto said. "You must be, too. Remember, just

156

like we practiced. Get to your spot, put on your hazards and block 'em."
He made it sound easy. The physical part *was* easy. It was the mental
part that was difficult. In reality, Arnesto was only slightly less nervous
than Pete, despite being far more experienced. But he had to sound calm
for Pete's sake. *Heh, "for Pete's sake." I'll have to tell him that afterward.
Surely, he's heard it before though? What am I doing, focus!*

Hazards flashing, Arnesto weaved back and forth a little for effect
before coming to a stop at an angle before the median. He got out and
looked east as he ran to the right side of the road. After a quick check to
make sure nobody could pass the RV on the right and run him over, he
looked out at the water and saw the Robert Y. Love and the two barges
it was pushing upstream.

Pete likewise parked his moving truck at an angle. He looked out
the driver's side window and saw traffic approaching from the rear,
which didn't help his nerves any. At least they appeared to be slowing
down. He waited for the angry honking to start, but it never happened.
Arnesto was right; people show odd restraint in unusual situations like
this. He was grateful Arnesto had given him the "easy" side. He had a
closer on-ramp as well as a smaller shoulder, making it easier to block
traffic. "I'm in position," he said.

"Excellent. Thirty seconds to impact. Stand by."

Pete was impressed. The last car heading eastbound over the
bridge had just passed. "Which side's getting the collision, can you
tell?"

"Actually, when a ship collides with a stationary object, it's called
an allision."

"Really?! You're doing this now?!" Pete thought his head was
thumping, but then he realized it was the bass coming from a car stereo

blasting music at full volume. He looked out and saw a dark Camaro stopped behind him.

"It's my side, he's hitting the west side," Arnesto said. Among the few details he remembered, the exact location of the accident was not one of them. They were both relieved to learn the allision was going to happen closer to Arnesto. "Oh shit, here we go, stand by!"

CRUNCH!

The barges slammed into one of the piers supporting the bridge. The impact was enough to cause a 503-foot section of the bridge to fall partly onto the barges and partly into the Arkansas River below.

"Holy shit, dude! That was awesome." Arnesto surveyed the scene for a few seconds. "It's over. Now we go dark, turn off and hide the walkie-talkies, and do not move until the authorities tell us it's okay. Over," Arnesto said.

Pete let out a sigh of relief. He held up the walkie-talkie to his mouth, but then the Camaro's bass sounded different like it was lowering in pitch. He looked out the window and saw the car accelerating toward the bridge.

"Arnesto, one got by! There's a car heading your way on the bridge, over!"

Arnesto jumped out of the RV and ran in the direction of the approaching vehicle. He didn't have far to run as all four lanes of the bridge disappeared at a sharp angle into the river. He got to the edge and waved his arm at the approaching car. "Get out and wave your hands," he said to Pete over the walkie-talkie. "Maybe he'll see you in the rearview mirror!"

Pete did just that, but it had no effect.

Arnesto waved frantically at the car from his side, but the driver

158

couldn't see the gap until it was too late. He hit the brakes hard, but the car went flying off the bridge head-first into the water. A couple fishing boats involved in a nearby fishing tournament sped toward the car but were unable to rescue the driver in time.

"I don't know how he got by!" Pete said.

"Return to the truck and back it up. Make sure nobody else can squeeze through."

"I can't see. What happened, did he stop?"

"Yeah. He stopped," Arnesto said. It was technically true. "Close that gap and go dark."

Pete looked at the gap in disbelief as he got back in the truck. He still didn't know how the Camaro squeezed through. He backed up until not even a motorcycle could fit. This left more room on the left side, but he would block that with his body if he had to. He turned off and hid the walkie-talkie, then got out and waited.

* * *

Hours later, they were eating take-out pizza in a couple lawn chairs outside the RV Arnesto had rented.

"He died?! You told me he stopped!" Pete said in shock at the news.

"I'm sorry I deceived you, but it was for the good of the mission. I needed you to focus. You kind of scared me when you hesitated at the beginning."

"Oh my god, if I hadn't hesitated, he might still be alive."

"No. That's not true. You only hesitated a few seconds. He would have wound up behind you anyway," Arnesto said.

"I still fucking killed him. 'All you have to do is park the truck.'

159

That's what you said. 'All you have to do is park.' And I couldn't even do that right."

"Pete, listen to me. This is not your fault. You didn't build that bridge or choose not to put pier protection cells in front of all the piers. You didn't cause the accident. You sure as hell didn't tell the driver of that car to squeeze past you. What you *did* was save around a dozen lives, maybe more. You're a hero."

"So why do I feel like absolute shit?"

"Because someone still died. That's one thing I've finally learned. You can't save everyone. Trust me, I know."

Pete thought for a moment. "Jacqueline. That girl from the hospital."

"And others."

"That was more than ten years ago. And you couldn't have done anything else. She wasn't a great driver and she didn't wear her seatbelt. Jesus, you still think about her? It's a completely different situation."

"Is it?" Arnesto asked.

"Yes, what could you have done, follow her around everywhere? Wait, that wouldn't have worked. You would have had to drive ahead of her — no, that wouldn't work either. There was nothing you could have done. But today, we could have — I don't know — put up roadblocks or signs saying, 'Bridge Out Ahead!' or something."

"You have some lying around?"

"We could have made some or bought some," Pete said.

"Then what? What happens when they start investigating and ask where the signs came from? And people in other cars tell them it was us? And then they ask how we knew to put up 'Bridge Out' signs before the bridge was out?"

"We could have rented a motorboat, then pulled up alongside the Robert Y. Love and blasted an air horn into the cabin until somebody noticed, or even climbed aboard ourselves. We could have prevented the accident altogether," Pete said.

"But then someday, someone else would have hit the bridge and killed *fifty* people," Arnesto said. Before Pete could argue, Arnesto continued, "Okay, *maybe* nothing would have happened or maybe someone decides to upgrade the bridge before something does. It's like you told me at the very beginning, 'Don't get caught.' Even a tiny little thing that gets one or both of our names in the paper is leaving a trail. And I really don't want to get caught. Especially with some — I'm sorry to say — nasty events coming up."

"Well, hell, I'd listen to me. I'm a smart man," Pete said, mumbling in the most depressed tone Arnesto had ever heard from another human being.

Arnesto laughed. "I *do* listen and yes, it's true. I feel terrible about the Camaro driver. But we exposed a critical flaw in the system through an event that was going to happen anyway, didn't raise any eyebrows that we know of, and saved a bunch of people."

Pete nodded but Arnesto could tell he was unconvinced.

"Tell you what," Arnesto said, "I won't call on you for any more missions for a while."

"Good. Now if you're finally done eating, can you give me a ride back to the airport?"

"One more slice."

Tragedy Hits Home

Arnesto's Home
Silicon Valley, California
Friday, January 17, 2003
Late Morning

"IS SHE GOING TO LIVE?" It was Pete calling. He sounded upset.

"Who? Is who going to live?" Arnesto asked.

"My mom. She's been diagnosed with lung cancer. Is she going to live?"

Arnesto cursed himself. One need not be a time traveler to have seen this coming. Pete's reaction was new to the timeline, though, so he couldn't have remembered it, but still, he should have expected it. He thought for a bit before answering.

"Are you sure you want—"

"Just fucking tell me! Is she. Going to. Live!"

Arnesto struggled to speak. After a long silence that only prolonged the agony, he finally said, "No."

"Goddammit. God fucking damn it. How long?"

"About three months. But that's what happened last time — maybe if she tries more aggressive therapies right from the start..." Arnesto said.

"They already said they're doing everything they can. You're an asshole, you know that? You knew this was going to happen, and you did nothing to stop it."

"I'm sorry, I really am, but you told me you didn't want me to—"

"You're a fucking asshole." —click—

Arnesto heard the dial tone and hung up the receiver. Was there anything he could do for her now? He had never studied oncology, much less effective turn-of-the-millennium cancer-fighting techniques. For once, he felt certain about the best course of action, which was, sadly, to do nothing.

Even worse, he had lost the one person he could go to for advice. This was particularly bad timing, as he needed some now. The Space Shuttle Columbia was currently in orbit for its final, doomed mission. He had wanted to ask Pete if he should warn NASA, and if so, how.

NASA had already ignored Arnesto's first warning, emailed months in advance of the launch, about the dangers of foam insulation breaking off and damaging the spacecraft. Who could blame them for not responding? Why would they, a bunch of rocket scientists for crying out loud, listen to an anonymous source from the internet offering a vague warning without any evidence to back it up? After all, they had contradictory evidence — other incidents of foam shedding which had only caused minor damage.

And these warnings were a big risk. Every time, every single time Arnesto tried to warn someone, he left one more clue out there which could lead to him being caught and possibly unable to help anyone else. And this was a special case. These were seven astronauts — seven specialists who knew the risks of space travel better than anyone. Was it worth attempting to save seven — who in all likelihood could not be saved — at the risk of losing tens of thousands? Every one of the seven was no doubt smarter than he was. What would they do in his position?

Whatever they would have done would have been more intelligent than *this*. He crafted another email:

> I regret to inform you that Columbia will be lost upon re-entry. Upon close examination coupled with rigorous simulations, the foam which dislodged during takeoff caused catastrophic damage to the left wing. With a compromised wing structure, the spacecraft will become unstable and ultimately disintegrate.
>
> Please initiate whatever preparations you deem necessary. Hopefully, your operation will be one of rescue and not salvage. We have all failed this mission.
>
> Regretfully,
> Anonymous

Though he had a dozen email addresses of various NASA officials, he only emailed three of them. He wanted to get someone's attention without creating too big of a ruckus. They would have their hands full soon enough. He waited until it got dark, then made the short drive to a residential area close to the NASA Ames facility in Mountain View. It was from there he sent the email on someone's unsecured network.

Arnesto never found out if they had acted on the information. It likely wouldn't have mattered in the end anyway. Without another shuttle ready to launch, and without equipment with which to dock at the International Space Station, rescue was never a viable option.

On February 1, 2003, Arnesto and the rest of the nation mourned the loss of the Columbia crew.

* * *

In mid-April, Mrs. Morgan's funeral concluded, and people were doing that awkward thing of lining up to pay their respects. Arnesto felt even weirder because he hadn't spoken to Pete since their hostile phone call.

"Arnesto, thanks for coming," Pete said.

"I'm really sorry for your loss."

Pete nodded then said, "Hey, come over to my dad's house afterward."

They caught up in Mr. Morgan's living room. Pete talked about his mom, how she had withered away due to the cancer. He talked about how he wished the priest had spent more time talking about her and less time preaching about God.

"I agree," Arnesto said. "And why was he the only one to get a snack?"

"The communion wafer? Who knows."

"So... are we cool?"

Pete took a long time to answer. "I guess. I think I'm in too much shock to be mad at you anymore." He looked around to make sure they were alone and added, "So, what's happening in the future?"

"Are you sure you want to talk about this, I mean, today?"

"Please, I could use the distraction."

"Pete," Arnesto said, pausing, "there's going to be an earthquake. Actually, a series of earthquakes around the world. I need your help."

"What can I do?"

"I don't know what to do, how to warn people. Maybe it's time I came forward, revealed who I am. I always used my foreknowledge of these quakes as an excuse to stay anonymous. Maybe that's over now."

"Well, if that's what you feel is best," Pete said.

"So you agree?" Arnesto asked.

"No, you idiot, I was being sarcastic. Jeez, you go a few months without me and you turn into *this*," Pete sneered. "First of all, what do you know about these quakes?"

"Dates, places, magnitudes, *casualties*." Arnesto noticed Pete's confused expression and explained, "Years from now I was a programmer on an earthquake game. Actually, the project was scrapped early on when the team realized all we had was a weak setting for yet another post-apocalyptic first-person shooter, but not before I had done a lot of research on the subject. I still thought it would be cool to do an earthquake game, so I reviewed my notes from time to time—"

"Reinforcing those memories, making them stronger."

"Right."

"And you can't email those governments because they won't believe you until after the fact, at which point, you may have done little more than cause an international incident." Pete understood.

"If I go public, then at least there's a face..."

"Why not go to the president, anonymously? Give him the list, then after the first one or two, he or his people will probably believe you."

"But will anyone believe *him*?" Arnesto asked. "What happens if they find out he ignored the first couple of entries? Or if he decides to let certain countries suffer or tries to sell them the information?

Involving the government might mean a death sentence for countless civilians."

"What about paying somebody off the street?"

"A patsy? Still unrespected and probably too unreliable."

"Scientists then. Give them the list. Maybe they —"

"They won't accept something without evidence. Even when the list starts coming true, they still might be hesitant to report it without proof," Arnesto said.

"Damn. Sounds like you need some sort of… faith healer," Pete said, snorting at his own suggestion. He waited for Arnesto's rebuke. When it didn't happen, he said, "Oh, come on! Faith healers are only great at deceiving the masses for their own personal gain. They can't be trusted to actually help people. In fact, as con artists, they're probably the last people on earth who would believe you anyway, no matter how accurate you were or how much money you promised them."

"What about an actual priest?" Arnesto asked. "Some salt of the earth guy who actually believes what he's preaching. Somebody pure of heart and well-spoken. Somebody truly willing to sacrifice in order to save thousands of lives."

"He *would* already be starting with a flock of sheep willing to believe his every word."

"Exactly," Arnesto said. "If we can get him to believe me, maybe we can warn people from the get-go."

"Hmm, relying on people's gullibility to tell them the truth. But you can't talk to this person. *Ever.* He can't be able to identify you even by your voice."

"I need to find another do-gooder to act as an intermediary," Arnesto said.

"Exactly. Are you sure about this, though, letting religion take all the credit?"

Arnesto had to bite his tongue to keep from revealing how religion would turn the United States into the laughing stock of the civilized world in the decades to come. "Believe me, I'm not happy about it, but for now, I don't see a better way. Now I have to find these people."

"Remember the LA riots?" Arnesto's scowl answered Pete's question. "Duh, of course, you were there. Wasn't there some guy in the midst of it all who was trying to calm people down? He got people to stop and listen and was hailed as a hero."

"Sounds like the anti-Arnesto," Arnesto said. "I missed it. I was too busy running for my life, followed by avoiding all news for the next few weeks. Besides, that was eleven years ago, I probably couldn't find the guy now even if he *was* a religious leader."

"Right, maybe you can find somebody from an event that was more recent."

Or one that hasn't happened yet.

Arnesto felt some relief as a plan began to form. He even had somebody in mind. When it came time to say goodbye, he gave Pete his sincere condolences and returned to his own dad's house where he was staying. However, instead of waiting a few days for his flight home to California, he went to the airport early the next morning and got on the first flight to Louisiana.

Collections

New Orleans, Louisiana
Sunday, April 20, 2003
11:30 a.m.

AFTER A BRIEF SEARCH and several phone calls, Arnesto believed he had a hit on a location: the Lower Ninth Baptist Church in the Lower Ninth Ward of New Orleans, only a couple miles away from the French Quarter. That neighborhood would also become one of the worst-affected areas hit by Hurricane Katrina, with standing floodwater depths of over ten feet in some places.

It was during the aftermath, when he and his wife, Katrina, were watching the horror on television, when they aired a piece on "The Heroes of the Hurricane." This included one person in particular, a preacher, who pulled several people out of the rising water to safety. Then he saved an old woman trapped in the wreckage of her home. Finally, he interrupted and ended a conflict between two rival gangs at the Superdome — while he was reclined on a gurney donating blood. While Arnesto had been impressed as hell, all Katrina had said was, "Why is he called, 'Father' if he's a Southern Baptist?"

Arnesto stopped for some delicious gumbo followed by an even more delicious beignet as he waited for church to let out. He didn't dare attend himself, but was able to hang out on the corner and eavesdrop as the man he was looking for, Father Martin, said goodbye to members of his congregation. Person after person gave the father a hearty handshake, high-five, or fist bump.

A frail, elderly woman said, "I'm sorry, Father, I didn't have anything to put in the coffers today. With my prescriptions—"

"Miss Louise, what did I tell you about that? You need to take care of *you* first. I even see you looking at the collection plate, I'll kick you out of my church." She and a few of her friends who were standing behind her all started laughing. "I mean it, I will kick you out. I will kick you *all* out." The group howled with laughter.

"Thank you, Father," Louise said. "You know, you remind me of my late husband. Except you're tall, strong, and good looking."

"Oh, Louise. If you were eighty years younger." She pinched his cheek, but he gently swatted her hand away. "Get out of here." Every word was pure amusement to everyone within earshot.

Arnesto himself laughed at the banter as he slunk away. He couldn't help it. The group's laughter was contagious. The rapport Father Martin had with his congregation was clear. Arnesto knew he had his man.

He now had the first half of his team, but he still needed to find the second half. He had it in his head that a social worker might be what he needed, so he started calling homeless shelters in the area. The man he talked to at the first place he called was polite but too busy to stay on the phone answering Arnesto's odd questions. At the second place he called, a woman answered.

"Hello, Lower Ninth Mission," she said.

"Hi, I was hoping to talk to a social worker."

"Of course, who is your case manager?"

"Oh, I don't have one. I just wanted to ask—"

"Are you in any immediate danger?"

Arnesto was taken aback by the question. He looked out the windows of his rental car, then said, "I don't think so."

"What I mean is, are you safe with yourself? I hope that doesn't offend you, but sometimes people call us as a last-ditch effort before hurting themselves."

"Oh, I understand. No, I'm fine, thanks. I wanted to talk to someone about the mission and the work they do there."

"We work one-on-one with people suffering from drug and alcohol abuse, or victims of domestic violence, people with illnesses, and of course, people who are homeless. I don't mean to be presumptuous, but do any of these apply to you?"

Arnesto considered each one briefly. "No, I'm doing fine, I promise. I just wanted to— wait, why do you ask?"

"I sensed a pause both times I asked about you. That usually tells me something is going on. Don't get me wrong, you sound fine, but I detect a lack of certainty in your voice."

"Yeah, that's true. You must be a good judge of character. Are you ever wrong?"

"Yes, I am, and yes, I'm wrong a lot. Listen, why don't you come in here so we can talk face-to-face? Are you nearby?"

Arnesto looked down the block. He could probably walk there in thirty seconds, and he was curious to hear what she had to say. But no, as tempting as it was to get some counseling from this woman, that would defeat the whole purpose of trying to find someone — someone like her. She had taken control of their conversation from the beginning, but now he needed to take charge. "Yes, I'm nearby, but I can't come in. And before you use your Jedi mind powers on me again, tell me the truth. Do you like helping people, are you good at your job, and is your shelter accepting donations?"

His sudden change in demeanor caused her to reflect a moment, but then she answered, "Yes to all three."

"Excellent. I promise, I will be in touch. Oh, I almost forgot, what's your name?"

"Isabel."

"Isabel, thanks for taking the time to speak with me today and I'll talk to you again soon." He hung up before she could reply. *As soon as I figure out what the hell the plan is.*

He spent the flight home brainstorming and came up with a simple plan. The hard part would be convincing Isabel, so he spent much of the next work day figuring out what to say to her. The next day, he overnighted her a package consisting of several packs of brand-new socks, one of which contained an envelope with cash inside, and a burner.

Then he took a drive during his lunch break to call her at the shelter and warn her about the package. Though she was cautious and confused by his actions, they agreed to talk the following night after the package had arrived.

The next day, when the time for their call was almost at hand, Arnesto headed for the door, but his daughter intercepted him.

"Dad, can you help me with my math homework?"

"Oh, I'd love to, sweetie, but first, I have to help work with something. Should take no more than forty-five minutes or so, tops."

He saw Katrina give him a look. "I'll be back as soon as I can."

Once a suitable distance away from home, Arnesto called Isabel's burner from his own, and they had The Conversation. It began with her thanking him for the socks and money, though he could tell she was dubious. She became even more so when he described the purpose of their interaction. It took even more cajoling than he expected, and he had expected quite a lot. He left out everything regarding his memories and time travel, but he also couldn't explain how he knew what he knew. Still, in the end, she decided to help him.

He arrived home exhausted from the conversation. The rest of the family was fast asleep, as he would be soon. He and Isabel would remain able to contact each other if they needed to, for example, if Arnesto had forgotten some detail, but he felt he had told her everything she needed to know. Still, he had this nagging suspicion that he had forgotten something.

The Power of Persuasion

Lower Ninth Baptist Church
New Orleans, Louisiana
Sunday, April 27, 2003
1:05 p.m.

"EXCUSE ME, REVEREND MARTIN?" Isabel asked after the sermon. Isabel Durand was a black woman in her early thirties who lived with her mother and fourteen-year-old son. As a pregnant teen, she had dropped out of high school, but later completed her GED and earned her bachelor's in night school. She was kind and generous but also tough as nails should the need arise. She was also an excellent judge of character and excelled at her job as a social worker.

"Please, call me, 'Father.'"

"Isn't this a Southern Baptist church?"

He smiled. Father Martin was a black man in his mid-fifties but looked ten years younger, especially since shaving his beard which was disproportionately gray. He was immensely likable, and this came out in his sermons. He loved preaching, giving back to the community, his lifelong hometown of New Orleans, and jambalaya.

"There's a special boy in our congregation who kept calling me

174

'Father' by accident," he explained. "I got tired of people correcting him, so I adopted the title. I like it, sounds less pretentious."

Now it was her turn to smile. She knew she had the right guy.

"What can I do for you?"

"My name is Isabel Durand and I need your help. May we speak privately for a few minutes?" she asked.

"Of course, let's speak in my office." He led her to his office and held out a chair for her, then closed the door and sat behind his desk. He could tell whatever she had to say was important and gave her a few moments to collect herself. He had no doubt he could help this woman, as he had seen it all in his many years at the church, at least, until now. "How can I help you, child?"

"This is going to sound strange, but I was paid a lot of money by an anonymous stranger to come here and ask for your help in saving thousands of lives around the world, including many right here in New Orleans," she blurted out.

"Whoa, slow down a little bit. How exactly do you expect me to do that? Do you mean save them with prayer?"

"No, save them from earthquakes," she said, watching his smile turn to a look of confusion. "My — employer — claims to know about some earthquakes coming up and wants you to make a video to warn people. Will you do it?"

"Hold on a second, this is quite a bit to take in all at once. You're laying a lot on an old man," he laughed. "Earthquakes: are we talking about the rapture?"

"No, it's not the rapture. Just some earthquakes. Powerful, deadly earthquakes."

"My child, there are many unsavory types who would take

advantage of you. Anyone who says they can predict earthquakes is, forgive me, full of—"

"I know. I don't exactly believe it either."

"You don't? Then why are you here?"

"Partly because I was paid a hefty sum of money. But also — there was something, I don't know, *sincere* about him, in his voice. What I can't figure out is — what's the catch? What does he have to gain from this? Moreover, what if he's... *right*?"

"The Bible says, 'Satan disguises himself as an angel of light.' Don't be tempted by false prophets," he said.

"You're probably right, Father. I'm sorry to have wasted your time," she said, standing up to shake his hand.

"Talking to one of God's children is never a waste of time."

"Oh, I almost forgot!" she said, ruffling through her purse. "He wanted me to make a donation to the church. This is for meeting with me today." She handed him an envelope. His eyes widened as he saw the stack of hundred-dollar bills inside. "And this is for thinking about it." He noticed she was holding out another envelope, which he grabbed much more slowly than the first. "Also, let me give you my card in case you change your mind or have any questions. If you call — and I hope you do as he says he's prepared to make considerably larger donations to us both — sooner would be better than later."

"Why is that?" he asked, at last finding his voice.

"The first earthquake is May 21 — just a few weeks away. Algeria, I believe he said."

"I see. Well, the church and I both thank you profusely for your generous donations here today," he said, shaking her hand again. "Is there anything else I can do for you?"

"Yes, he said to tell you — and I'm a little uncomfortable repeating this — the Algerian earthquake is going to happen no matter what we decide. It's unlikely we'll have much of an effect even if we do warn people, sadly. However, he believes that not only will it make believers out of you and me, but it will give us a chance to build up 'street cred' — his words, not mine — so we can save a lot more lives later on. Good day, Father."

* * *

A couple of days later, after much contemplation, Father Martin invited Isabel over to chat.

"I can't believe I'm doing this," he said as he watched her set up the laptop next to him.

"We're saving lives," Isabel said, picking up the digital video camera. "Okay, I'm recording, you may begin anytime." Father Martin nodded, then turned toward the camera.

"Hello, I'm Father Martin. As you can see from this live feed of CNN.com, it's a little after three o'clock on April 29, 2003. It is with great sadness that I must report that there is going to be an earthquake on the northern tip of Algeria on May 21st of this year, just over three weeks from today. The quake will have a magnitude in the high sixes, just under seven. There will no doubt be many injuries and deaths, and many more will be left homeless. That is all for now." He waited a second then asked, "How was that?"

"Let's see." Father Martin walked over and watched the display over Isabel's shoulder as she played it back. "That was great. I see why my employer picked you — you have an honest face."

"I have an *old* face. Even that little camera adds ten pounds."

Isabel laughed. "You look fine. But are you sure you want to go through with this? You will either look foolish to a handful of newsroom assistants or you'll become black Jesus."

"Blasphemy, child. I am simply the messenger's messenger. This wouldn't be the first time I looked foolish, nor will it be the last. But I will be *damned* if I waste what God gave me by failing to warn others. Send the video to whoever will listen. We should pray that I am merely a fool and not a harbinger of doom."

"Thank you, Father. If all... *heck* breaks loose, I will see you on the twenty-first."

Ill-Conceived

Arnesto's Home
Silicon Valley, California
Friday, May 2, 2003
9:47 p.m.

ARNESTO FELT SICK to his stomach. Any moment now, his lovely wife was going to finish up her nighttime routine in the bathroom and join him in bed. They were supposed to have sex. Tonight was the night they were supposed to conceive Preston. After much painful deliberation, Arnesto decided he wasn't going to let that happen.

He already had two wonderful children. It's not that there wasn't room for a third child; it's that there wasn't room for *this* child. Preston. Preston the Terrible. For some reason, Arnesto never quite bonded with the boy in his previous life. Preston was an unruly child, then a juvenile delinquent, then he was in and out of prison.

It wasn't his upbringing, Arnesto figured. Melissa and Carlos had turned out fine. Amazing, in fact. As parents, Arnesto and Katrina did everything they could to straighten out Preston. They read every parenting book and tried every strategy, but nothing seemed to work. They heard plenty of suggestions. People as a whole *love* to give

179

unsolicited parenting advice. Unlike others, including Katrina, Arnesto was never offended by this. He welcomed it, hoping that just once someone would offer a tip he hadn't tried a thousand times before. No, it wasn't anything to do with how Preston was raised. Some people were just born evil.

This was not something Arnesto could change. Even with an entire lifetime's worth of experience, Arnesto knew there were no new tricks that would help. Preston would still be trouble. In fact, this time around, things would be *worse*. The first time, there was always hope. After every incident, after every call from the school principal, there was hope it would be the last time. But this time, he knew. There was no hope. And without hope, Arnesto wouldn't be able to put all that time and energy into trying to fix an unsolvable problem. And that would mean Preston would probably be even worse. So how could Arnesto knowingly unleash his evil spawn upon the world?

And yet, this was his *son*, his own flesh and blood. He felt so *guilty*.

No, he mustn't back down now. After saving so many lives and improving so many others', the universe owed him one. Anyway, he was doing the universe a favor. The stress of raising Preston had worn him down last time. This time he didn't need the distraction while he was out saving the world. Heck, maybe without Preston, Katrina wouldn't file for divorce several years from now. It was nice to think about, but he needed to focus on the present.

Maybe she wouldn't want sex anyway. Just because the first Katrina wanted sex on this particular night in his other life didn't mean this Katrina would necessarily repeat the pattern. Hadn't he already seen countless other examples where things were different from how he remembered them? From the get-go, he had irreversibly altered the universe. It would have been impossible not to. Every time he breathed he was inhaling different air molecules, creating microscopic ripples in time. And yes, sometimes, he threw himself into the pond yelling, "Cannonball!" He was the Harbinger of Chaos. No, he *was* Chaos, and she was Katrina, Wife of Chaos. Maybe he had nothing to worry about.

"Hey, Babe." Katrina stood in the bathroom doorway in her red nightie. She looked good. She got into bed beside him where she began kissing and caressing him. For a moment, he forgot his mission. But then he remembered and started to push her away. "What's wrong? Don't you find me attractive anymore?"

"I'm sorry, my stomach hurts." He wasn't lying. "I need to go to the bathroom. Don't move, I'll be right back. Have some wine!" *Alcohol always makes her drowsy*, he reasoned as he sat down on the toilet. Not many men would try to get their wives drunk in order to *not* have sex with them, but Arnesto was willing to go that extra mile.

He waited several minutes, then flushed for effect, washed his hands, and returned to bed. Katrina was facing away from him but immediately rolled over when she felt him get under the covers. To his surprise, she was even more aggressive than before. If he had any complaints about his marriage, and he generally had few, it was that over the years she more and more relied on him to initiate sex, and more and more turned him down when he did.

"Ngh," he grunted, grabbing his stomach, then headed back toward the bathroom.

"Babe!" she whined. He mentally added her lack of sympathy to his complaint list.

"I'm sorry! Have some more wine!" he shouted as he closed the door.

This time he sat there even longer. He considered masturbating Sperm Preston out of his body, but was afraid she might barge in on him or even if she didn't barge in on him, she would still know somehow. Then there would be a fight. He couldn't risk a fight with his lovely, horny, drunken wife. That might lead to make-up sex.

"Are you coming out?!" she whined.

"Just a minute!" he yelled back, lying. Did she think he somehow had expert control over his bodily functions under the circumstances? *Hmm, a new complaint, "Expresses impatience over unknowingly fictitious bowel movements."* He imagined that being one of the options to check on a list on some official Wife Complaint List form. She was racking them up tonight. He tried focusing on her shortcomings to keep his mind straight, but this inevitably led to him picturing her lying in bed in her red nightie. He switched to analyzing how he could have handled this mission better, in case he suddenly remembered having other demon children he'd like to avoid.

Finally, legs going numb, he stood up and left the bathroom. For a split second, he panicked when he realized he forgot to flush. "Just gas," he would say if she asked. She wouldn't. She had already given up on him some minutes earlier, evident by the fact that she was now wearing pajamas and was sound asleep.

* * *

The next day, with Katrina off to work and Melissa and Carlos off to school, Arnesto tried playing around on his computer. Not feeling it, he tried reading, then playing video games for a while. Deciding a nap might be just what he needed, he shut off the console and television and headed to the bedroom.

He paused to admire the family pictures on the wall. There was one of him and Katrina taken at a friend's party before the kids were born. In it, he and Katrina both wore big, genuine smiles. Arnesto smiled back. There was one of Katrina with baby Melissa, the most beautiful baby ever born. There was one of Carlos by himself as a toddler. They had pretty much every combination, including a couple of pictures of all four of them. But no Preston.

Arnesto decided to remember what those pictures had looked like. What could it hurt? It was an innocent comparison between timelines. For one thing, a few of the current pictures had to be removed in order to squeeze in Preston's photos. The one with Carlos making a funny face got replaced by one with all three kids. There was one of Arnesto that he was only too happy to replace with one of Melissa trying to teach Preston how to play catch. And Preston's baby photo would be right about *there*, the fourth picture in succession if you were walking down the hall toward the back of the house. *Oh, that picture.* It was a fine photo of a handsome baby boy and one of the larger pictures on the wall, more of a close-up than the others. Arnesto remembered that the picture's prominence had amused him. He had always wanted to ask guests what they thought of it.

"Do you think it's a giant baby, or merely a regular-sized baby with a giant head or even a regular ol' baby caught in a tiny parallel universe?" he wanted to ask, but never did.

He chuckled which quickly gave way to a smile, which in turn gave way to a frown. He never did unleash his giant-baby-related humor on anyone, and now he would never get to. He burst into tears. Did most fathers who murdered their sons cry, he wondered? No, stop that, it wasn't murder. What was it then? What do you call it when a man, using his own unique form of prescience, chooses to not give birth to a son he's supposed to have because he's so selfish that he doesn't want to raise a child who happens to be a little *rowdy*? And how could he deny Melissa and Carlos the brother they were supposed to have? Who was the monster now?!

He stopped crying, but now his head was spinning. It was time for that nap.

* * *

He tried to seduce Katrina that night, and the next, and the next, but she wasn't feeling it. He couldn't even tempt her with wine. And then it was too late. Sperm Preston gradually absorbed back into Arnesto's body.

Though depressed, Arnesto came to terms with his loss over the next few weeks. What else could he do?

One day, feeling back to his usual self, he decided to make a pass at his wife. He walked up behind where she was sitting on the sofa and put his hands on her shoulders. She shrugged them off.

"Arnesto..." Something was wrong.

"What is it?" he asked, walking around to sit down next to her. She had a most serious look about her. Arnesto silently tried to guess what was going through her head, but none of his guesses were even close.

"I'm pregnant."

Arnesto opened his mouth but couldn't speak. Did he miscalculate? It was certainly possible, though he didn't think so. He wasn't thrilled by the news. Sure, Preston might get his chance at life, but Arnesto had accepted that it wasn't going to happen. This was going to take time to process. There was another reason he wasn't thrilled, however. Something else was wrong.

It was Katrina. The last time she told him this specific news, she had been smiling, looking for his approval. This time, she was not smiling. She looked serious and even a tiny bit disappointed. He had to know what was going on.

"When—"

"It's not yours."

All the air rushed out of the room. Arnesto was shocked. How could this be? Despite barely being able to think, he did some quick calculations. It was just too unlikely that she happened to get knocked up by someone else on the same day he was supposed to have impregnated her. Then he figured it out.

Oh my god. Preston was never mine.

Realizing the implications of this only crushed him further. Finding out your wife was pregnant with another man's child would be devastating under normal circumstances. Finding this out and realizing you spent a fraction of your previous life playing the fool, raising another man's demon child made things so much more difficult. It was one of the few times his special gift had worked to his disadvantage.

This was why she had been so aggressive that night. It wasn't because she was feeling frisky; she was attempting to cover up her mistake. She must've had unprotected sex with this other person earlier that day. *At least things can't get any worse,* he thought.

"I've fallen for someone else. I'm leaving you. I'm sorry," she said.

This was too much. He leaned forward and put his head in his hands. He didn't know what to do or say. He didn't know what to *think*. It felt like he had been run over by a herd of wild horses who were now taking turns kicking him in the gut.

"Please say something," she said at last. He ran his hands through his hair and then leaned back and sunk into the couch.

"Who is he?" he asked without looking at her. He *couldn't* look at her.

"It doesn't matter—"

"*Who?!*" His anger surprised him and startled her.

"His name is Mike. He works at the restaurant."

"The bartender?!" Why would she choose Mike over him? He wasn't particularly impressive, physically speaking. Arnesto racked his brains trying to remember what he could about Mike, whom he had only met once or twice. His job wasn't very impressive. He had a few stupid tattoos. He did mention playing the guitar or something. *Fucking musicians.* Arnesto tried to remember if there was anything about Mike's future he could use to destroy him. He couldn't recall anything; he barely knew the guy.

"He's a real nice guy—"

"How could you cheat on me?!" Arnesto asked as he turned to face the woman who was breaking his heart.

"It just sort of… happened. We close the restaurant together a few nights a week, and we hit it off. We're in love." He couldn't believe how stupid she sounded, like a fourteen-year-old girl falling for the first seventeen-year-old boy who compliments her mind while staring at her tits.

"I can't believe you fucking cheated on me."

"It's not like I was the only one," she said.

186

"What?!"

"Where do you go, Arnesto? Where do you go at night? You say you're working late, but I've driven by your work, and you weren't there. The parking lot was empty!"

He didn't say anything. He hadn't cheated on her. He had lied about his whereabouts many times, but only to go on his own secret missions to save lives and try to make the world a better place. He had always lied to her for her own protection.

And now there was no point in telling her the truth. His marriage was over. But there was still one thing he had to know.

"When did you decide to end it?" he asked.

"What?"

"I'm guessing this wasn't the easiest decision you've ever made. I'm hoping you debated it, at least. Was there a point at which you finally said, 'This is it.'?"

"Arnesto, that's a weird question—"

"Please!"

She sighed. "The other night. You were supposed to help Melissa with her homework, but you weren't there. She asked why you hadn't come home yet. I told her you were working. You made me lie to my own daughter, Arnesto. That's when I knew."

Of course. He had never thought about it before. In the other lifetime, he had helped Melissa. Katrina had appeared and leaned in the doorway, watching with a smile. Arnesto had looked at Katrina, and they had smiled at each other. Katrina had seen how good he was with their children and realized she wanted to make it work, at least, a little while longer.

But not in this lifetime. This time, he had abandoned them. That night, he had taken a drive to put distance between him and his home in order to make a secret phone call to Isabel Durand to convince her to help him save people from earthquakes. A worthy cause, sure, but it didn't help matters at home.

"I still think you're a wonderful father. I want you to continue to be a huge part of their lives. I know we can keep this amicable."

And they did. He wound up being the one to move out. He felt it would be easier for the kids to stay with their mom in the house. He felt it far better to err on the side of generosity than to risk fighting in the courts where the husbands traditionally got their asses handed to them. He also didn't want anyone looking too closely at his financial statements.

Even though the whole situation felt like a kick to the nuts, deep down, he knew it could always be worse. At least he wasn't in Algeria.

Shaking Masses

Lower Ninth Baptist Church
New Orleans, Louisiana
Wednesday, May 21, 2003
6:30 p.m.

"THEY SAY THE DEATH TOLL is over three hundred already," Isabel said. She was a little out of breath from rushing over to the church.

"They just upped it to five hundred... and climbing." Father Martin was transfixed on the television. The two of them sat in silence watching the broadcast.

"What does it mean?" Isabel asked during a commercial break.

"It means," he said, turning off the television, "that we must continue God's work. Let's make that next video before the phone starts ringing."

"I don't know if I can do this, Father. It really happened. I want to help — I do — but maybe this is too much. They are going to ask us so many questions. And you, you're going to be scrutinized by everyone. It's going to be worse for you. Should we bail?"

"My child! We can't run from this. I don't *want* to run. Can't you see all the good we're about to do?"

"But our source said that if we can't handle this, to get out. You can find someone else to record you."

"My child, breathe," he said, taking her forearms in his hands. "Do you believe in God?"

"Of course, Father."

"God gave this mystery man a gift and led him to us. We were chosen by God to do His work. If anybody comes after you, you tell them to talk to me. As He watches over us, I will watch over you. Together, we will save so many lives. Can I get an 'amen'?"

"Amen."

"Good. Do you have the script? Great. Tell me when you're ready to record." He took the script from her and read it as he walked behind the lectern. "Lord have mercy," he said to himself.

"Recording, Father," she said from the front of the aisle.

"Hello, I'm Father Martin. First of all, as predicted in my previous video, Algeria was hit by an earthquake earlier today. Please join me in sending our thoughts and prayers to our brothers and sisters in North Africa searching for their loved ones beneath the rubble.

"Now I have good news and bad news. The bad news is that the worst is far from over. There are going to be several more large earthquakes over the next few years. I will detail them in a bit. The good news is that we know about them *now*. If people start making preparations today, then we can make some attempt to evacuate the people and minimize the damage to buildings.

"Now here is the list of upcoming earthquakes, along with projected casualties. August 14 of this year, Lefkada, Greece, magnitude 6.3. This is not one of the bad ones. It's on the list mainly to warn them, but also to give credence to the rest of what I'm about to tell you.

"December 26 of this year, Bam, Iran. Magnitude: 6.6. Sadly, even though it's about the same size as the one that will happen in Greece, the devastation will be far greater. Estimated casualties — again, only if we do nothing — in the tens of thousands.

"And then there is December 26 of next year, 2004, off the northwestern tip of Sumatra, Indonesia. Magnitude: 9.3, again, that's 9.3. This earthquake will cause a massive tsunami that will hit many countries before it's done, with Indonesia and Sri Lanka being hit the hardest. Estimated casualties: in the hundreds of thousands.

"October 8, 2005, Pakistan-administered Kashmir, 7.7 magnitude, casualties in the tens of thousands.

"May 12, 2008, Wenchuan County, Sichuan, 8.0 magnitude, casualties in the tens of thousands.

"January 12, 2010, west of Port-au-Prince, Haiti, 7.0 magnitude. Another horrible one, casualties in the hundreds of thousands.

"March 11, 2011, Tohoku, Japan, 9.0 magnitude, tens of thousands of casualties.

"These are all the earthquakes for which I currently have information. Please, *please* share this information with as many people as you can. Let's get the word out to the people and governments of these cities so that their lives may be spared. Thank you and God bless."

Isabel closed the camera. "That was perfect, Father. No need to do another take."

"Thank you, child. When you're making your CDs for all the news stations, could you make me a copy?"

"Of course. I'll get started right now," Isabel said, putting away her camera and hustling toward the front door.

"Thank you. And Isabel?"

"Yes, Father?"

"We were chosen to save these people."

First Impressions

"TODAY WE HAVE a very special guest on our show. He sent our producers a video detailing the earthquake in Algeria. The catch — he sent it more than two weeks *before* it happened. What's more, he's made a second video detailing even *more* earthquakes — some years away. Please welcome the man behind these incredible videos, Father Lester Martin!" The Marlene Turner Show wasn't the most popular morning program in New Orleans, but that didn't matter: Father Martin would appear on all of them eventually. The show's host, Marlene Turner, was an up-and-comer in the business, and this particular broadcast would greatly contribute to her career as she and her producers were the first to invite Father Martin on air.

"Father Martin, thank you for joining us. You have our producers scratching their heads. The question on everyone's mind is how — *how* did you predict this earthquake would happen?"

"Marlene, thank you for having me. The truth is, I did not, in fact,

193

predict anything. An anonymous source contacted me and gave me the information I provided in the videos."

"An anonymous source? You have no idea who it is?"

"None whatsoever. And frankly, I prefer to keep it that way. Why shouldn't we respect the privacy of someone whose only intent is to save lives?"

"So this person contacts you with this seemingly impossible information — were you skeptical?"

"Yes, unfortunately, I was. You can probably tell the difference in the videos. In the first one, though I was sincere, you can tell I lacked the conviction that I had in the second video," Father Martin said. Despite this being his first television appearance, he was eloquent and perfectly comfortable as a guest on the show.

"We'll get back to the second video in a second. Why you? Why do you think your source chose you and not the government or a seismologist?"

"I don't know. All I know is that somewhere out there, my source, who may very well be an angel, has chosen me to be his or her vessel. Frankly, we are trying to do God's work and save as many people as we can." The largely religious audience responded with great applause.

"Father Martin, at latest count, over seven hundred people are reported dead from the Algerian quake, and that number may still climb even higher. Could those people have been saved, and why weren't they warned?"

"Well, first of all, we did attempt to contact their government. One of my trusted associates sent them a copy of the video and warned them via phone and email. However, there is no one to blame here. Someone you don't know from a foreign country tries to warn you about an earthquake in the future with zero evidence to back it up. Can you blame anyone for not taking it seriously? We sent the video to yours and two of the other networks and never heard back—"

"Yes, and *someone* here is getting demoted," Marlene said, angrily looking around the room to laughter.

"But that's exactly my point. All things considered, it was a preposterous claim, or so it seemed. Blame won't help anyone. All we can do with regards to the Algerian quake is to make a donation and/or send our prayers to the victims and do better next time." Applause.

"Yes, let's get back to that second video. Can we get the list up there?" The screen cut away to a list of the seven upcoming earthquakes, which showed the dates, cities, and magnitudes, but left out the potential casualties. "There it is. My goodness. Father Martin, I'm looking at these numbers, and I'm frightened. Look at that: 9.3."

"Marlene, those are indeed scary numbers. But they should be less scary when you realize time is on our side. Now people have a chance. It's up to the people and governments of those cities and countries to decide what level of preparedness they are going to have. There is no reason anyone should be hurt or killed from these earthquakes."

"Let's talk about the first one on the list. In the video, you didn't sound too concerned about the earthquake you say will occur in Greece in August, even though its numbers are comparable to the one that just happened in which hundreds have died. In fact, you even mention 'giving credence' to the rest of the earthquakes."

"That's correct. Not to belittle the event in any way, but I believe that, unlike the other earthquakes on the list, we are simply not going to see much in the way of casualties, especially if they take precautions."

"Father Martin, you are not a seismologist, is that correct?"

"That is correct."

"Well, we thought it would be prudent to bring one in for this discussion. I'm told he just arrived backstage. From the University of New Orleans, please welcome Dr. Hans Bergman!" Dr. Bergman was tall and thin and a little on the pale side, but he had a pleasant demeanor. He shook hands with the other two while an assistant quickly set up a chair for him next to Father Martin's. If Father Martin was at all startled by the surprise guest, he didn't show it.

"Hello, thank you for having me," Dr. Bergman said.

"Dr. Bergman, what do you make of all this? Can someone predict earthquakes?" Marlene asked.

"With all due respect to Father Martin and his source, no. We currently lack the technology to predict earthquakes."

"So how do you explain this?"

"Again, I mean no disrespect, but the most logical explanation is that this is some sort of elaborate prank." The crowd booed.

"Hold on, Dr. Bergman is a well-respected seismologist and we're proud to have him on the show," Marlene said, admonishing the audience. "Dr. Bergman, what do you think about the claim that an earthquake in Greece, of the same magnitude as the one that just happened, will be so much less dangerous?"

"That actually wouldn't surprise me. Greece is no stranger to earthquakes. They've had plenty of experience on which to draw and prepare. They construct their buildings with earthquakes in mind, as well as teaching earthquake preparedness in their schools."

"Even if it's a six on the Richter scale?"

"Actually," Father Martin said, "they don't use the Richter scale anymore. They say, 'moment magnitude' or just 'magnitude.'"

Marlene exaggerated a look of surprise in Father Martin's direction to everyone's amusement. She then turned back to Dr. Bergman, who smiled and nodded.

"As there's no way to predict an earthquake, there's no way to predict the fallout afterward, but if Greece were hit, I would expect the results to be far less devastating than they were in Algeria."

"So the scientific community will not be setting up their instruments and camping out in Greece, waiting for the earthquake to happen."

"I can't vouch for everyone, but I cannot see a mad rush of seismologists packing their bags, no. However, and this is one of the beauties of science, we are open to it. If an earthquake *does* happen as predicted, then you can bet the scientific community will be stampeding over itself to get to the next one."

"Well don't hurt yourselves. In case it does happen, we'll be needing you. Dr. Bergman, Father Martin, thank you both very much for coming today." The crowd applauded one last time before filing out of the studio.

Within a week, Father Martin appeared on the other stations that had received his video. His congregation increased quite a bit as well, but only through the first half of June. Once people realized Father Martin wouldn't predict the lottery numbers or make any other predictions for them, once he told them he couldn't give away his source even if he wanted to, the newcomers stopped coming. In fact, attendance dropped even *lower* than normal when some of his regular worshipers stopped attending due to their annoyance with the newcomers "taking over the place." He never was invited to any national news broadcast, and soon his phone all but stopped ringing.

Renter's Market

Nina's House
Silicon Valley, California
Monday, July 14, 2003
Night

SHE WAS GONE. Finally.

Arnesto was tired of stalking her. Her name was Nina something, one of the servers who Katrina managed at the restaurant. She was a younger woman of Indian descent and pretty, though that's not why Arnesto kept driving by her house to see if she wasn't home.

Even more frustrating was that the information he needed was sitting right there in the back office at the restaurant, but he and Katrina had just separated. He couldn't ask her when Nina was taking her vacation to Santa Monica. Still, it was important he know when she left.

Now that she had, he could stop stalking her. He also knew the date of the accident — July 16, 2003, two days from then. He remembered an old man in a maroon sedan crashing through the farmers' market, killing ten and injuring countless others. He also remembered Katrina complaining about Nina repeatedly talking about the incident; Nina had been a firsthand witness to the horror.

The next day, he made the tedious five-hour trek down the most boring part of I-5 between Merced County and Los Angeles. It was also a smelly stretch of road due to the thousands upon thousands of cows fertilizing the ranches off the east side of the interstate. Once in Santa Monica, Arnesto checked into his hotel, then took a taxi to the moving truck rental where he rented a fifteen-foot truck. He found a place to park it near his hotel then turned in for the night. He was tired. That section of I-5 takes a lot out of a man.

When he awoke the next morning, he ate the free continental breakfast at his hotel, then checked out. He left his ample belongings in the trunk of his car, then went out to the truck. It was still dark out but wouldn't be for much longer. Opening the back, he pulled out the loading ramp. He didn't have anything to put inside but he wanted some cover as he inspected the rear left tire. As he did, he stealthily leaned a nail against the back of the tire. He then replaced the ramp, closed the back door, got into the truck, backed up a foot, then rolled forward a foot. He got out and checked again. The nail had embedded itself nicely into the tire.

Satisfied, he drove down 4th Street until he reached Arizona Avenue, where the farmers' market would soon close off the street at one end. He turned his hazard lights on, then pulled the truck slightly into the entrance, still aligned with 4th Street but perpendicular to the market itself.

He got out and looked for the nail in the tire but couldn't see it or the hole, so he got back in and pulled forward several inches. This time, he found the nail easily. The tire had already lost some air but wasn't going flat quickly enough, so with a little effort, he removed the nail. He then stuck his ready-made sign in the driver's side window: "Flat tire

— Don't tow, out buying sealant."

It wasn't a lie. He had to wait until the store opened. He could have bought some beforehand, but wouldn't that have looked suspicious if someone ever looked into the matter closely enough? *Play it true, cheat as little as possible.*

When he returned from the store, he was a little disappointed to see everything was the way he had left it. That meant he still had to wait.

And wait. And wait some more. Rewriting history is seldom glamorous.

Hunger finally reared its ugly head, so he quickly grabbed some food from the farmers' market, then returned to the truck to eat. He didn't dare sit inside the truck, but rather, hung out by the flat tire, always keeping an eye on Arizona Ave., and always prepared to dash behind the rear of the truck if needed.

It wasn't until 1:43 that something finally happened. Unfortunately, it was the last thing he wanted. It was help.

"Is this your vehicle?" the police officer asked, walking over to the rental truck from his cruiser parked just behind.

"Yeah. Flat tire. Was about to try sealing it up," Arnesto said.

"The truck's been here all day. I've already driven by a couple times."

"Yeah, sorry, took me a while to find a store with sealant, then I got hungry." *When did he drive by?* Arnesto took the sealant out of the plastic bag, then looked around for a trash bin but didn't see one close enough, so he stuffed the plastic bag into his pocket.

"I need you to move this truck. The market closes in fifteen minutes. Need any help with that?"

"No, thanks, I got it." Arnesto looked down Arizona Ave., but only saw a Mercedes and another car behind it that he couldn't make out. As he turned back toward the truck and bent down, there was a loud crunch sound. He instinctively stood up and turned around as he saw the Mercedes roll to a quick stop in the intersection.

As the maroon-colored Buick pulled around the Mercedes, Arnesto felt a tug on his arm as the officer yelled, "Watch it, get back!" The Buick accelerated as it drove around the road closure sign in the middle of 4th Street, and accelerated as it continued its short journey before plowing into the side of the rental truck.

The crunching sound of the crash was awful to hear, but the eighty-six-year-old driver appeared uninjured, though quite confused. He would never drive again.

Arnesto smiled as he applied the sealant to the tire. He had achieved nearly the same outcome, namely getting a deadly driver off the road, but with far less destruction and none of the casualties.

Once the Buick had been towed and all the accident paperwork filled out and exchanged, Arnesto returned the rental, explained what happened, then was given a shuttle ride back to the hotel. Then it was a matter of getting back into his car and making the long, boring, smelly ride back up I-5.

* * *

But first, he decided to make a pit stop. Arnesto's mom had taken his separation from Katrina even harder than he had. While she meant well, her constant calling to see if he was okay had only made a difficult experience even worse.

But now she was only thirty minutes away. He could stop by, pay a quick visit, then get on his way. The timing was good, since saving those lives that day had him feeling better than he had in a long time. Yes, she would see how well he was holding up, feel better about things, and both their lives would improve.

His mom was delighted to see him. In fact, after asking him if he was *sure* he was okay for the hundredth time, she even seemed to accept his situation. She and her new husband, Roland, asked to take Arnesto out to dinner but relented when he said he didn't want to be out driving on the highway too late. They settled for eating cookies in the kitchen while they played a game of cribbage.

Toward the end of the game, when she should have been playing her turn, Arnesto's mom again brought up his impending divorce. "I'm still sorry she left you, but it's good to see you're handling it so well." She turned to Roland. "He always was a smart one. Did you know he graduated college at nineteen?"

Roland, ever the polite one, said with a laugh, "Yes, honey, I believe you've mentioned that before."

"I know, I've mentioned it many times. I'm proud of my little Arnesto."

"You know, Mom," said Arnesto, who normally avoided adding to game-delaying conversation, "I've always wanted to ask: Why the... *heck* did you name me Arnesto?"

She looked surprised by the question. "I thought it was cute."

"Okay, but what's the story behind it?"

"That's it, I thought it was cute. 'Arnesto Modesto.' It rhymes."

Arnesto stared at her in disbelief. "Yeah, I got that. Okay, follow-up question: Why in the love of all that is good and holy in this world did you spell it with an 'A'?"

She looked even more confused. "That's not how you spell it?"

He put his elbows on the table and hid his face in his hands. "It's spelled with an 'E'."

His mom looked at him and Roland and burst out laughing. It wasn't at Arnesto's expense, she thought it was hilarious. He conceded that her spelling was not unheard of, though it was by far less common.

Soon after, they finished the game. As Arnesto put on his sneakers, his mom took one last opportunity to remind him to visit more. "We're so glad you were able to visit. When do you think you'll be able to come see us again?"

"Soon, I'm sure."

"I know it's a long drive. What if you took the train?"

"The train takes twelve hours."

"Wow, never mind. I only mentioned it because this woman from my book club said her son takes the train to work every day. She said he loves it. I don't know how safe they are, though. Then again, if he's been taking it for years without any problems, it's probably fine."

"If you didn't think it was safe, why did you suggest — ah, crap!"

His outburst startled them. "What is it?"

"Nothing. Sorry. Just remembered something I need to do." He stopped himself before asking her if she knew which train her friend's son took. It wouldn't matter for a year and a half or so, but he couldn't risk her remembering him asking. He would get the info he needed another way. Ugh, he couldn't even celebrate preventing one accident before being reminded of another.

Shocking

Lower Ninth Baptist Church
New Orleans, Louisiana
Thursday, August 14, 2003
Morning

FATHER MARTIN was not forgotten, merely "put on hold," as he described it. This was no more evident than on the morning of August 14, when he awoke to what sounded like chanting outside the church and, peeking out through one of the stained-glass windows, saw a large crowd gathered outside. Some of them were chanting, "We want Father Mar-tin! We want Fa-ther Mar-tin!" Some were holding signs. There were also camera crews. "Lord have mercy!" he said to himself. *Something went wrong. I've led them astray*, he thought.

He returned to his rectory and turned on his TV. It took a few tries, but then he found what he was looking for. A reporter was talking to a man in front of a fallen building. The subtitles said his name was George Petropoulos from the Greek Committee for Earthquake Preparedness.

"...one of a number of buildings that was destroyed by the earthquake earlier today. George, how bad is it out there?" the reporter asked.

"Some roads and buildings like this one were damaged, which you never like to see. There were also some injuries," George said.

"Injuries, but no deaths."

"That's correct."

"All things considered, that doesn't sound that bad for an earthquake of this magnitude," the reporter said.

"We can always do better, but you're right, our dedication to earthquake preparedness definitely saved many lives and structures today. We were also fortunate to have received help from the United States, who warned us in advance," George said.

"The United States?"

"Yes, a Father Martin from New Orleans. Thanks to his warning, we were able to get the word out and vacate the most at-risk structures—" Father Martin turned off the television and smiled. He stood up and walked outside to address his adoring fans. That night, his predictions were mentioned on every news program in America. Father Martin became a household name overnight, except for people stuck in the Northeast blackout of 2003; they would have to wait a little longer.

* * *

Bam, Iran
Four months later

Worldwide pre-relief efforts began immediately for all the nations on the earthquake list. However, there was none more so than for the Iranian city of Bam, who was now next in line for disaster. At first, the

Iranian government reacted negatively, claiming this was merely a trick by the Americans to infiltrate their country and subvert their leadership. They quickly changed their tune once they realized how popular a destination Iran was becoming. Scholars, academics, seismologists, and other scientists from around the globe began pouring into the country. And they weren't alone.

There were film crews. From Hollywood to Bollywood, it seemed everyone wanted a piece of the action. Some were there to film the spectacle for big-budget action flicks, others saw the opportunity to make award-winning documentaries, and a few had the honorable intention of recording life in Bam simply for posterity.

They all paid handsomely for the honors.

Many celebrities arrived to assist with the effort, though some were grateful for the opportunity to help the public forget their latest DUI back home. Tourism in general exploded in Bam. Many wanted to see the city for themselves before it changed. Some stayed to help with preparations, and a few thrill-seekers merely wanted to experience the rush of an earthquake.

Temporary shelters were constructed outside the city in preparation for the aftermath. Any attempts to retrofit buildings in the city itself were abandoned; there wasn't enough time.

Evacuation efforts also hit a few snags as people didn't want to leave their homes. Father Martin himself was flown in as a special VIP specifically to assist in this matter. While he had a huge positive impact, there was only so much he could do. Why should they believe this stranger telling them in a foreign language to abandon their homes? As the earthquake drew closer, the government made evacuations mandatory. Even so, many were able to hide or sneak back into the city after they were removed.

In truth, Father Martin wasn't all that excited to be there. Though he had no question it was God's will he do all he could for these people, he had never been so far from New Orleans before — he had never even left the country — and here he was about to experience a devastating earthquake halfway around the globe.

On the bright side, people were more respectful in Iran. As homesick as he was, it was nice to not be asked for a picture or an autograph every five minutes. Back home, he didn't like the way the tabloids captured his face and felt sure they were intentionally making him look older. And then there were the invitations — *everyone* wanted him to baptize their baby, officiate at their wedding, or perform last rites for a terminally ill loved one. He wasn't even Catholic!

So Father Martin slowly acclimated to his temporary new home. He felt proud to be a part of this historic moment and was glad he could be there to help, wavering only slightly when the first foreshock hit on December 25.

The second foreshock hit that night. People weren't as scared as they might have been had the foreshocks been a surprise, but they had been predicted by the experts, so they were more appreciated than feared. They not only served as final warnings of what was to come, but also helped silence any non-believers.

The main event happened as predicted the following morning. With a magnitude around 6.6, Bam lay in ruins. News outlets around the world had their pick of the footage — the event had been recorded by too many cameras to count. There were still many injured, killed, or missing, but they numbered in the dozens rather than the tens of thousands.

As relief efforts began in Bam, the world quickly turned its eye toward Sumatra.

* * *

Arnesto couldn't wait to discuss the results with Pete and called him the following night.

"Hey, Arnesto 2.0, Happy Holidays! I'm sorry, but I can't talk right now. We're about to watch Firefly."

"Again? I thought you watched them all."

"How could I? We're only partway into the second season."

"*Second* season?!" Arnesto was skeptical. "Are you absolutely sure?"

"Positive, we've already watched several episodes. Why?"

"In my first life, it was canceled after one season. I don't know what happened, but I must have done something right!"

"Don't get too cocky — they canceled Family Guy." Pete sounded cross.

"Don't worry, it comes back in a couple years. Go enjoy your show." They hung up.

Arnesto felt good; he was on fire! It was a wonderful feeling he was not accustomed to.

It wouldn't last.

Operation Panic

"My son's in surgery," Pete said in a tense voice, though trying to sound calm. "Daniel has an inguinal hernia. They said it would be a simple operation, but my wife is freaking out. You know Christine."

"That's understandable," Arnesto said, trying to be reassuring.

"Is it? Does she have reason to be freaking out? I mean, I'm sorry to trouble you with this, but could you give me a hint how this turns out?"

"Oh, you want a spoiler! Of course, Pete, anytime. Let me think." Arnesto lowered the phone and closed his eyes, recalling what he could. After several seconds, he opened his eyes and continued the conversation. "You can tell Christine that this surgery has a ridiculously low chance of even the slightest complication." Arnesto smiled both at being able to help his friend and that it was good news besides.

"But there is a chance."

"Well, in any surgery there's a chance of something going wrong, but I'm pretty sure that won't happen here."

"You're not sure though?" Pete asked.

"Okay, I'm sure."

"Hmm. Could you tell me what you remember?"

"Yeah, I remember you telling me he had the surgery, and that everything went fine." There was silence from the other end of the line, so Arnesto continued, "Do everything you did last time. Except for the worrying part. Trust your instincts."

"Right. I'll try." Pete still didn't sound convinced.

"Pete, what's going on? Why don't you believe me?"

"I do, I trust you. It's just..."

"Yes?"

"You're not making any lame jokes!"

Arnesto looked at the phone in disgust. "What are you talking about?"

"You always joke around. Always. No matter how dire or inappropriate the situation. And now I tell you my son's in surgery and you're being serious. It's weird."

"I don't always— alright, hold on, let me think." Arnesto paused for several seconds, but he wasn't attempting to recall anything; the pause was purely for effect. "Okay, I did remember something, but I wasn't quite sure how to tell you."

"What, what was it?!"

"Daniel — he survives the surgery fine. However..."

"WHAT?!"

"I'm sorry, Pete. Daniel grows up looking like his father."

"You're a dick."

"Think about it. He'll lose any last hope that he was secretly sired

210

by another man, one who is more handsome and perhaps taller as well."

"Okay—"

"No, wait! I remembered — the first successful face transplant is only a few years away. Daniel is saved!"

"Fuck you. I'm hanging up now. Bye." Pete hung up. Arnesto put down his phone, then it beeped. He had a new text from Pete that simply read, "Thanks."

By Design

Smiling Axolotl Games
Silicon Valley, California
Friday, July 9, 2004
8:53 p.m.

"SHIT!" ARNESTO BARELY RESTRAINED himself from slamming the controller down on his desk. It was approaching nine o'clock on a Friday, and he wanted to go home. However, he still had bugs to fix, including one that occurred after defeating the game's final boss. To reproduce the bug, though, he had to actually *beat* the boss.

This was proving difficult as he had cheated to the final level, not having had time to play the game all the way through, so he lacked the powerups he would have acquired along the way.

The player's name was Sand Stone, either Rock Stone's brother or his cousin, depending on which way the wind was blowing. Even in this late stage, the game's design changed frequently.

However, what irked Arnesto most was the fact that each time he fought the boss, he had to reload to the previous save point and watch the same damn, tediously long cutscene again.

Finally, the cutscene ended, and Sand was teleported to his starting boss fight position. This would have been discombobulating enough, but thanks to another bug where all spawn points defaulted to facing north instead of the direction they were populated in the levels, Sand started off facing a wall.

Wham!

Half of Sand's life was instantly gone as the boss knocked him into the corner. Now Arnesto had to wait while the game played Sand's standing-up animation.

Come on, come on, come on, get up, Sand!

Sand Stone stood up facing left, so Arnesto prepared himself to run that direction. Unfortunately, due to another bug in the animation system, the code thought Sand was still facing right. When control returned to Arnesto, Sand's character instantly rotated the other way, causing Arnesto to run Sand into the wall for a split-second, which was just enough to—*Wham!*—allow the boss to hit Sand again, ending his virtual life.

"Argh!" Arnesto hit the button to reload. He closed his eyes and tried to calm himself, but he couldn't focus with the idiotic cutscene dialog coming from the console in front of him.

"Whoa, that feels like something big!" Sand Stone said as the screen shook. "I've got a bad feeling about this." Who the fuck was he talking to? There wasn't even another character there!

Cue the big boss smashing through the wall, a couple long, slow camera pans, and one more pearl of wisdom from Sand, "You're never too big… to be SANDED!"

Cut to Sand Stone facing the wrong way, and… nothing. The game had frozen. Arnesto swiveled around to his monitor and sighed. One of the other programmers on the team was trying to catch a bug in the graphics code. Even though the bug itself was relatively harmless, the programmer had put in an assert which forcibly stopped the game for anyone who happened to get it, even though the programmer was the only one who could fix it.

That meant Arnesto had to restart the level.

From the beginning.

It was a twenty-minute level.

Arnesto stopped to think if there was any way he could speed up the process. Sure it was late in the project and everyone was exhausted from crunch mode, but there was one simple change he had always wanted to inquire about...

He stood up and walked down the hall, turning into Randy's office. Randy was the project leader on *Sand Stone vs. the Plutonians*. He was a nice guy with a wonderfully creative mind, but he was terrible about signing off on aspects of the design then changing his mind.

Randy's eyes were glued to his television while he fumbled through the second level of the game.

"Hey, Randy," Arnesto said. "Can we let the player skip the cutscenes?"

"Hmm, I don't know. The player might be confused as to where to go next."

"The radar points them toward their next objective."

"They might miss out on the story."

"It's a shooter," Arnesto said.

"Yeah, I don't know," Randy said. "Here, have a seat. Do you think the inventory icons are clear enough?"

Arnesto sat down. "Yeah, I haven't heard anyone complain about them." *Except that they've already gone through four iterations.*

"I think they're still confusing. I need to change them again."

"What if the player doesn't want to watch the cutscenes and just wants to get in there and shoot things?" Arnesto asked.

"He can shoot things when the cutscene is over. Do you hate cutscenes or something?"

"No, actually, I love cutscenes. I will always watch them. *Once.* But I have friends who, for whatever reason, don't care about cutscenes. For them, games are about the interaction, and when you take that away from them..." He watched Randy's avatar walk back and forth down the same hallway a few times, apparently lost. To be fair, the radar only worked from a top-down perspective; it didn't indicate that the player needed to climb up. "See, your way forces the player to play the game the way you want them to. By letting those who want to skip cutscenes skip them, we'd be letting them play the game the way *they* want to." Arnesto allowed a few seconds for his words to sink in, then pointed to the television. "You need to climb up the filing cabinet there."

"Ah, right, I always forget that. See, there would be a good place for a cutscene." Randy maneuvered Sand Stone up to the next floor where he encountered more deadly Plutonians. "Wouldn't skipping the cutscenes require extra coding?"

Aha, maybe Arnesto was actually getting somewhere. He considered Randy's question. "There would be a hair of scripting in a few of them, but I could handle every case myself." What Arnesto said was true; the game wasn't that complicated.

"I'm still afraid the player would miss something."

My god, man. There is nothing to miss. Nothing!

Perhaps it was time to compromise.

"Okay, how about if we let the player skip a cutscene after the first time?" A few people felt this way, though Arnesto still felt it was bullshit. Why force it on the player at all? Why make them sit there and watch something they don't care about? To some players, cutscenes are akin to tampon commercials interrupting their favorite show.

"I don't know..." Randy said.

"Hey, guys!" Jeff said, waltzing into the room and standing inside the doorway. Jeff was the scourge of the project — the producer.

"Hey, Jeff," Randy said, "how would you feel about being able to skip cutscenes?"

"Sure, sounds okay to me."

"But the player might miss out on some information," Randy said.

"Oh. Right. Nah," Jeff said.

Arnesto didn't know what his cortisol levels were but assumed they were climbing dangerously high. "Okay, last question. Can we at least put the final checkpoint *after* the cutscene?" Nobody responded. "Have you guys played the final boss? He's hard. And then you have to watch that boss-intro cutscene over and over—"

"Are you kidding? I can't get to that level," Randy said.

Jeff shrugged. "Actually, Arnesto, I came in here to ask you something," he said, changing the topic. "Do you think you can get multiplayer up and running this weekend for the demo Monday?"

Arnesto waited for the laughter, but to his chagrin, none occurred. Jeff was serious. "You want to add multiplayer? *Now*? Also, we have a demo Monday?" Communication was not the project's strong suit.

"The Rock Stone guys gave me some code," Jeff said. "They never committed it to the project, but they said it should pop right in. I emailed it to you."

Arnesto was in shock, but what could he do, say no? His voice now meek, he said, "Okay, I'll take a look."

"Great, see you guys Monday!" Jeff said, already three steps out the door.

The next day, Saturday, Arnesto strolled into work around noon. At least the building was quiet. He almost had the whole place to himself. It would help him focus on hooking up multiplayer which had shown up out of nowhere and become his number one priority.

With any luck, the other team's code would be incomplete or wouldn't compile or something. If he couldn't get it working, then he could focus on all the other tasks he needed to get done.

No dice. Their code plugged right in, which made sense since it was their engine being used in the game. Still, with all the changes his team had made to the project, Arnesto couldn't believe the new code worked. They were much more talented than him.

However, just because the code was there didn't mean Arnesto had anything to show for it. For one thing, he needed a test level. The debug room they used for testing and the tutorial level were both much too small, and level three and beyond were all too large, but level two? If he duplicated level two, limited players to the main outpost, and blocked off exits to the Plutonian landscape, it might work.

He stripped the new multiplayer level of all its single-player content. Then he made new, regenerating versions of weapons and health kits and populated those in several places within the level.

He threw a few Plutonians in, made them also regenerate after a few seconds, and replaced their models with human ones. Now, he had Sand Stone, Sand Stone (Clothes Torn), Corporal Tide; the man in charge of the whole operation, and Dr. Rebecca Tide, Corporal Tide's xenobiologist daughter who frequently had to be rescued by Sand

Stone. He also changed their behavior so they would attack each other and not just the player.

Finally, he updated the main menu so that he had a way to actually access multiplayer and voila!

It was still very rough, but if someone who had never seen the project and who wasn't too good with video games walked by and watched the screen for only a few seconds, it would have looked like a remotely decent four-player battle.

It had taken most of the day, but it was a decent start. He left around eight o'clock that night, tired and famished but feeling a little bit better about the situation.

The next day, he returned and set to work improving it.

Since the code was already there, it wasn't too much more work to add different gameplay modes to the existing deathmatch style, such as king-of-the-hill and capture-the-flag.

He also had to expand the interface to match these expanded options. Fortunately, thanks to Randy's incessant redesigns, Arnesto had written code to streamline the process as much as possible.

He hooked up the score and player rankings.

He added the level timer and countdown.

He put in player taunts and special sound effects and voices, harvested from the game's existing assets.

After another long day, he had done it, and all without any new art or even so much as a design spec!

It was all temporary work that would have to be redone by the sound department, artists, and level designers, and there would be countless bugs, tweaks, and fine-tuning, but that was nearly all out of his hands now.

He went home happy and returned the next morning. It was Monday, so the building was bustling with activity. He overheard a couple of the level designers excitedly trying out the new multiplayer option. After a minute, one of them popped his head over his cubicle wall and flashed Arnesto a big thumbs-up. Arnesto smiled wide in return.

Their enthusiasm almost made up for the seven new bugs assigned to him in the bug database. Maybe it was Jeff who, not having anything better to do, went through and assigned this latest batch. If so, then Arnesto's bug count was probably artificially inflated since Jeff seemed clueless about who actually worked on what and was a terrible guesser.

Jeff suddenly appeared in Arnesto's doorway. "Hey, Arnesto, can you revert your changes?"

"What changes?"

"Multiplayer."

Arnesto did a double-take. "I just put multiplayer in. You mean you want me to take it out for the demo?"

"No, we're not going to ship with multiplayer. It wasn't quite what we were looking for."

"Did you see it? Did you and Randy try it at all?"

"Yeah, we played it together. We realized there was too much left to do and too little time to do it. So, can you revert your changes?"

Arnesto stared at him for a moment, dumbfounded. "Yeah, I'll take it out."

"Thanks." Jeff disappeared down the hallway.

Arnesto sat motionless, staring at the spot where Jeff had been.

This. This is how people have aneurysms.

Fearing they might change their mind again, Arnesto didn't dare revert his changes. Instead, he commented out the line of code that added multiplayer as an option to the main menu. That was all it took. One change to a single line to undo his entire weekend and remove the most enjoyable feature of the game, rough as it was.

Something flashed on his monitor. It was an email from Randy, with a whole new slew of interface art that needed to be implemented.

Arnesto examined them and then replied. "Hey, I did these last week," he replied. "They're already in the game."

A minute later, he received Randy's reply: "No, these are brand-new as of this morning. You can see they're a little shinier than the old ones. They'll make this game pop!"

Arnesto opened up one of the existing icons in a separate window and compared it to the new one from the email. Only looking at them side-by-side could he see the minute difference: a few pixels representing some sort of glare coming off the object in the upper-left corner.

He compared another and another. By Zeus, Randy was right; they were all different! He began the onerous task of renaming and replacing each one while composing a list for the artist of which icons were now the wrong size.

The seventy-hour workweeks continued in this fashion for a couple more months, at which point they finally reached Beta. In theory, this meant only bug fixes, no more feature changes, not even from Lead Design Changer Randy. But Arnesto felt the chances of Randy restraining himself were about as likely as the company sending him a fat royalty check — a practice the company had phased out years earlier.

In actuality, the changes did come to a halt, but not for the reasons most people would have guessed.

The night the first beta version was officially burned and passed by QA was followed the next morning by a special project meeting.

"As you know," Jeff said once everyone was squeezed into the conference room, "last night we officially reached Beta." There was some mild hooting and hollering and some quick applause. "However, I regret to inform you the project's been canceled."

Silence. People looked around at each other. Was this some horrible producer joke?

"Is this... real?" a level designer asked. "What happened?"

"It's real," Randy muttered from his seat in the corner. He usually had such an energetic presence; Arnesto hadn't even known he was in the room until then.

"The higher-ups played the game and felt it still needed too much work," Jeff said.

"But we just hit Beta," an artist said. "We could hit Gold Master in a month or two."

"The higher-ups felt like even if we shipped it out the door, it wouldn't be competitive in the current first-person-shooter market, especially without multiplayer."

A couple heads turned to see Arnesto's reaction, but he was too numb to have one. When he had signed on to the project, he had hardly remembered anything about it. He hadn't worked on it in his first life, nor had he ever played it, and now he knew why. The only thing he felt was a rising anger at Jeff for saying, "higher-ups" every two seconds.

"So two years' worth of work, poof!" another level designer said. Seems like everyone felt the same punch to the gut. Funny how even a mediocre project that everyone was sick of can still feel like such a loss to those involved.

"Sorry," Jeff said. "But you all get to leave early today."

Ooh, we get to leave early, thought Arnesto as he followed the depressed masses back to their desks. *We put in hundreds and hundreds of hours of overtime, for free, and now we get five of those hours back. Whoopee.*

A couple days later, Arnesto was playing Nethack at his desk when he got the call to come to the office of Harold, the Technical Director. Since Harold was in charge of all the programmers, Arnesto thought he was going to tell him what project he would be joining next. Instead, the conversation was not so upbeat.

"We're putting you on probation," Harold said.

"What?! Why?!"

"We feel your work has been slipping. You're not putting in the effort that you used to."

"Respectfully, I busted my ass on Sand Stone. Could you be more specific?"

"We know you had some trouble keeping up with the changes to the UI..."

"How could I not? Randy changed every aspect of the interface every day!" A slight exaggeration, Arnesto admitted.

"You could have streamlined the process more to make those changes easier to implement. Some more effort up front could have saved you lots of time down the road. Time that could have been spent implementing multiplayer, for example." Arnesto had about a thousand responses to this, but before he could pick one, Harold continued. "We're going to have you work with the tools group. They said you could work on an art integration tool, but you will be closely supervised. If we don't see solid improvement from you in a week or two, then we might have to let you go."

222

Holy crap, had it really come to this? Arnesto had to think. How would one of their better programmers have handled Randy's constant interface changes? Of course, if he knew that, he would have *been* one of their better programmers. Still, to be suddenly put on probation and thrown into the Tools group, away from games? Something didn't add up.

"I'm not the only one being put on probation, am I... The company's downsizing. Projects canceled close to the end, people put on probation so the company won't have to give them severance during all the layoffs... I get it now. Well, there's no point in me working on a tool for a week or two only to get fired afterward. I hereby resign." He stood up and held out his hand for a handshake.

"Now hold on, Arnesto. You've been here for years, we don't want to lose you like that. Let me ask around and see if we have another position for you. Let's talk again tomorrow."

Arnesto didn't understand Harold's sudden change-of-heart but also didn't care. He remembered that soon there would be several external emails, each containing the many names of those laid off and sent to the growing group of ex-employees. He knew no matter what that his time at Smiling Axolotl was over.

The next day, Harold said he couldn't find anything, so Arnesto made his resignation official.

He took a couple weeks off to decompress by doing nothing but sleep in and play video games, but then decided to look for work before his former coworkers got laid off and started competing with him for jobs. If he had followed in his own footsteps, right now he would be working for Cumulonimbus Electronic Entertainment where the pay was better, but the crunch modes were even worse than they were at

Smiling Axolotl. That would make it even harder to break away should history require his attention. On the other hand, if he didn't work there, he would never meet his friends from that particular company.

He opened a new tab on his desktop and started to type in, "Cumulonimbus," but then changed his mind and decided to check his financial status and entered the name of his bank instead. When he saw his balance, his jaw fell open. It seemed some of his investments had done rather well. He wasn't insider-trading-congressman rich, but he was in the ballpark. That made his next decision simple.

Arnesto leaned back, reached his arms out toward the ceiling, and yelled, "I am retired!"

For the moment, he felt as free and happy as he had since he was a child the first day of summer vacation. It would take the plight of those less fortunate than himself to ground him again.

Over the next few months, the dreaded layoff emails flowed into his inbox. They were as sad to read the second time around.

A couple more months passed and the gaming sites announced the acquisition of Smiling Axolotl by a much larger conglomerate. The company was saved!

A week later, the day before Christmas, the entire studio was shut down.

This didn't bother Arnesto as much as he expected. For one, he already knew it was coming. For another, it was hard to worry about a game studio shutting down when one of the world's worst natural disasters was less than forty-eight hours away.

Making Waves

Coastal Waters
Sumatra, Indonesia
Sunday, December 26, 2004
7:59 a.m.

AROUND EIGHT O'CLOCK in the morning on December 26, 2004, the third-largest earthquake ever recorded began off the coast of Sumatra.

It wouldn't stop for ten minutes.

The entire earth vibrated about a centimeter.

Arnesto and the rest of the world remained glued to live coverage of the event. Arnesto started with the channel featuring Father Martin as a special guest and watched with pride as the priest spoke with eloquence and diplomacy. It couldn't have been easy to answer the same questions over and over with no new answers to give. Sometimes they would ask him how humanitarian efforts were going in the countries that hadn't been hit yet, which gave him some respite. Once they turned to the subject of his source, Arnesto felt uncomfortable hearing about himself and changed the channel.

He was astounded by what he saw this time around.

He remembered from his past life the shocking amateur videos of the huge tsunami waves smashing through everything in their path, but those videos were nothing compared to the countless hours of professional, high-definition video taken this time. There were waves up to one hundred feet high! The best part, though, was how few people were seen in the videos.

Still, there were many casualties. Not all evacuations were successful, often due to miscalculations on the part of the people in charge. Some underestimated the speed and/or power of the water. Some evacuations of the more remote villages took longer than expected. A few were unwilling to leave their homes which they had known all their lives, and of course, there were those who thought God would protect them while others thought it was God's will that they perish. Some just flat out didn't believe the warnings.

All in all, hundreds were confirmed dead or went missing. Arnesto was grateful his warning via Father Martin had saved ninety-nine percent of those involved. But the event was still a tragedy, and after seeing images of the dead and the widespread damage and homelessness, it didn't feel like a win.

Bad Parking

Glendale, California
Wednesday, January 26, 2005
5:58 a.m.

ARNESTO CALLED THE POLICE and Metrolink to warn them about the SUV parked on the tracks. The only problem, if you can call it that, was that there was no SUV. He parked his own car a little ways down Chevy Chase Boulevard and walked over to the tracks to verify this. It was dark and rainy out, but he could see well enough to know the area was clear… for the moment. A Union Pacific freight train sat stationary on the third set of tracks.

Not wanting to look any more suspicious than he already did, Arnesto started back to his car. He passed by a sign that read, "DO NOT STOP ON TRACKS." *If only!* He heard a vehicle coming up the street behind him. He kept walking but listened for the sound of the vehicle either passing him or stopping. Instead, he heard gravel.

He spun around and saw a Jeep Cherokee Sport that had just turned off the road and was now driving on the gravel parallel to the tracks. About fifty yards down, the Jeep turned and put its front wheels between the rails.

"Hey, train's coming!" Arnesto yelled, waving frantically as he ran toward the vehicle. Arnesto knew the driver knew that, but the driver didn't know that Arnesto knew the driver knew. Arnesto hoped that seeing a freak running toward the Jeep screaming and shouting would confuse the driver and prompt him to drive off. Instead, the driver got out and fled on foot earlier than expected.

Arnesto ran to the Jeep. It was unlocked, but the engine was off and the keys were missing. He couldn't even put it into neutral in order to push the vehicle out of the way. Still, nothing to worry about. Arnesto's anonymous call from minutes before meant the police would arrive soon. If nothing else, somebody must have notified the trains' conductors by now.

He noticed the smell of gasoline. Was the Jeep leaking? It didn't appear so, but it was wet, and not from the rain. The vehicle had been soaked in gasoline. As concerning as this was to Arnesto, it wasn't as bad as what he heard.

It was a train horn. He couldn't see it, but he could hear it coming from the north. And it wasn't far off.

His confidence in his plan was crumbling. What if emergency services hadn't passed along the information? Or what if they thought it was a prank? Wouldn't they still investigate, though? Was he willing to risk the lives of eleven people?

As if to answer for him, the train blared its horn a second time. Arnesto couldn't be sure in his excited state of mind, but it sounded louder, closer this time. He squinted his eyes and looked down the tracks where he could just make out the approaching train's headlights.

He looked inside the Jeep for something he could use, like a spare set of keys. *Ha, wishful thinking.* There was, however, a lighter in the glove box. He grabbed it and the vehicle registration, then using the cuff on his sweatshirt, quickly wiped away all his fingerprints, just in case.

He heard another train horn, but this one sounded different. To his chagrin, this one was coming from the south.

How many freakin' trains are coming here?!

Knowing it was what the driver intended anyway, he lit the registration on fire, then holding it at arm's length, used it to catch the hood on fire before sprinting as fast as he possibly could back to his car.

They would say a few years from then that, "Cool guys don't look at explosions." This did not apply to Arnesto, who instinctively turned around, mouth wide open, upon hearing the blast behind him. After several seconds staring in shock, he resumed his hustle. As he ran from the scene, he could make out the front of one of the trains coming down the tracks before he turned down the road toward his car.

The train conductors must have seen the smoldering wreck on the tracks ahead of them. Arnesto could already hear the squealing of brakes as he sat in his car and closed the door.

The northbound train stopped in time; however, the southbound train had too much momentum. It slammed into the Jeep, pushing it southward but stopping right before the train switch which would have caused the Jeep to become lodged under the leading car. The extra bit of braking time meant there was no derailment or collision with the other trains.

More importantly, there were no deaths or injuries, though there were plenty of frayed nerves, particularly on the part of Arnesto, who was fleeing the scene as fast as he could.

Storming In

Downtown
New Orleans, Louisiana
Saturday, March 5, 2005
3:00 p.m.

"MY FELLOW NEW ORLEANIANS, I have some bad news. In late August of this year, our wonderful city is going to be struck by a hurricane named Katrina. It's going to hit, and it's going to hit hard. The levees that keep the water out of our lovely city... will fail. New Orleans will be flooded. I encourage everyone to make whatever preparations are needed to steer well clear of the storm. I will now open the floor to questions."

Every hand in the press conference went up in a flash. Father Martin had wanted to keep this a local matter but knew that was impossible. He was one of the most famous people on earth now. The mere fact that he had decided to hold a press conference made him, once again, the top story. Now that he had made his announcement, all hell, much like the levees, was about to break loose.

The questions came fast and furious.

"Did you get this information from your anonymous source?"

"Yes, I did," Father Martin answered.

"How does your source know the levees will break?"

"I don't know."

"Is your source running some sort of elaborate computer simulation?"

"I don't know."

"Will you be evacuating before the storm hits?"

"Yes, absolutely."

"How long have you known about this?"

"I just found out about it myself."

"What do you think will happen to property values as a result of your announcement?"

Father Martin sighed at this one. "I can't speculate on that. I'm not here to guess on what *may* happen; I'm only here to warn people what *will* happen," he answered.

"Is this some sort of ploy to get more people to attend your services?"

"Of course not."

"Father Martin, while your earthquake list has no doubt saved thousands of lives, how do you explain the fact that hundreds of people have since died from earthquakes that were not on the list?"

Father Martin leaned in slightly. "I want to make this clear. I know for a fact that if my source had even a *clue* about those earthquakes or any other disaster, I would have been notified, and I would have informed all of you. The fact that so many have come together to save tens — if not hundreds — of thousands of lives is nothing short of a miracle. Next question, please."

"If the levees were strengthened, could New Orleans be saved?"

Finally. This was the question he had been waiting for. After a brief pause for effect, he began, "Again, I don't want to speculate; I'm not an engineer. However..." He gave another brief pause and for the first time since the briefing began, mustered a slight smile. "It stands to reason: if you build a wall strong enough, it will be able to hold back the water.

"We know what will happen if we do nothing. I know it will take time and resources and money, and it may still not be enough, but isn't it worth taking that chance? I know as a community, we can work together to make the levees strong. I will do my part to raise funds for what I'm sure will be a huge undertaking. But isn't it better to regret having made the levees too strong than to regret having made them too weak? Thank you, there will be no further questions at this time. God bless."

The meetings between officials began immediately. If anyone but Father Martin had delivered the news, the number of denials would have been higher. It only took an external review board three weeks to determine that, "Given a hurricane of sufficient force, either a direct impact or water overflowing the tops of the levees and subsequently eroding the soil on the other side would lead to a catastrophic failure of the majority of the levees protecting New Orleans."

The Great Levee Rebuild Project was initiated at once.

On April 23, a brand-new video-sharing website called YouTube appeared. A recording of Father Martin's press conference became the second video ever posted to the site, after co-founder Jawed Karim's, "Me at the zoo." Father Martin's two video warnings about the earthquakes were posted the following day, and before long, his videos became the first on the site to go "viral."

Though the number of homes for sale in New Orleans did increase,

232

there was no mass exodus, only a temporary evacuation. In fact, property values *increased*. Savvy investors realized that either the rebuild project would be successful and home values would go up, or the levees would still fail and they would be eligible to partake in the class-action lawsuits.

On the other hand, homeowner's insurance was hard to come by. Several insurance companies began to preemptively cancel policies.

Sandbag companies sprang up overnight. *Legitimate* sandbag companies took a little longer.

And as with the other Father Martin disasters, there was the influx of tourism.

On August 23, 2005, a tropical depression formed over the Bahamas.

The next day, it intensified into Tropical Storm Katia. It was named Katia instead of Katrina at the government's insistence as if that would somehow undermine Father Martin's warning and prevent the inevitable.

Hurricane Katia hit Florida the day after, enraging Floridians that they had failed to receive the same warning as New Orleans.

Katia headed back out to sea and gained strength over the gulf for the next few days before finally turning northward and slamming into Louisiana and the Gulf Coast on August 29. That afternoon, the storm tore a hole in the Superdome, but nobody was inside. At that point, most of the city's inhabitants had already been evacuated.

There also was no mass flooding of the city as the new levees held. In fact, the only levee that failed was from the original set, which was left in place as a test as the new wall was built behind it.

Though not flooded, New Orleans was still scarred by Katia, which left behind billions of dollars in damage and dozens of deaths across multiple states.

Traumatizing

Santa Clara International Airport
Santa Clara, California
Wednesday, September 13, 2006
5:45 a.m.

OWEN PORTER PARKED his car on the top level of the airport parking garage. At that early hour, there were plenty of open parking spaces on all but the lowest level. However, the top level was uncovered and offered the best view of planes arriving and departing. He got out of his car and walked over to the ledge where he watched as a 747 crabbed slightly into the strong crosswind.

Being a pilot himself, he knew quite a bit about aviation, though he hadn't flown in years. He had served many years in the air force before flying as a civilian. His daughter loved flying almost as much as he did and was once his favorite passenger in the Cessna he rented. How long had it been? Four years? Five? Those were better times, happier times. A DC-10 rolled onto the runway, accelerated, and took off for a destination unknown.

It was time. He removed his hands from the ledge. That's when he noticed he wasn't alone. There was another man leaning on the ledge about thirty feet to his left. *Where did HE come from?* Owen thought.

The stranger smiled and waved. "Good morning!" he said. Owen said nothing but gave a subtle nod in return. "Quite a crosswind today!"

What an idiot, there's almost always a strong crosswind at this airfield. Owen rested his hands back on the ledge. *He's gotta leave soon.*

"You look like a pilot. Are you a pilot? I've been thinking about getting my license." Owen looked at the stranger in disbelief. On any other day, he'd have chatted the stranger's ears off about the wonders of flight. But today, he wanted to be alone.

It was clear that wasn't going to happen. "Excuse me, I have a plane to catch," Owen said, turning to walk back toward his car.

"I... uh... I don't think you do, Mr. Porter!" the stranger shouted, struggling to be heard over a departing 737. Owen quickened his pace. "Mr. Porter!" Owen ignored him.

Of all the days, I had to be recognized by this clown. Do I know him? Doesn't matter. I'll get in the car, drive around for a bit, and come back — is he following me?

"Owen Porter, I'm here about your daughter, Jenna!" That was enough for Owen, who stopped as he was about to reach for his car door handle. He spun around and glared at the stranger.

"What *about* Jenna?!" Owen growled, his hands balling into fists. He was ready. For what, he wasn't quite sure. The stranger didn't appear to be a threat. In fact, he seemed oddly nervous.

"Jenna is about to suffer a traumatic event, namely, the death of her father." After a brief but uncomfortable pause, the stranger continued. "Please, sir, help me spare your daughter years of grief."

Owen eyed the stranger. *How does he know this?* "She hates me," he finally said, looking down.

"No, sir. I know she yelled at you last night, but really, you're the only—"

Owen unlocked his car, sat in the driver's seat, and slammed the door shut. After a moment he rolled the window down. "Get in," he said.

The stranger hesitated, then walked over and sat in the passenger's seat. "The name's Troy. Troy Clark," Arnesto said, holding out his hand.

Owen took it. "Jenna's okay?"

"She's fine, but she won't be if... you kill yourself."

"She'd be better off without me. I'm a burden to her," Owen said, staring straight ahead.

"I know she's supporting you. That can't be easy on a man's pride. I also know you owe the government some money. A debt that would become hers in the unfortunate event—"

"It would?! That's bullshit! Are you with the government?! Is that why you're here?!"

Arnesto held up his hands. He wasn't about to piss off a suicidal veteran attempting to martyr himself. "No no, I'm not with the government! I'm an independent. I'm here to save your life. Look, I brought you these." Arnesto produced and handed Owen a book on curing one's gambling addiction and a money order for twenty thousand dollars. "I also signed you up for Gamblers Anonymous. They meet Tuesday and Thursday nights, 8:30 at the rec center. That money is a loan, by the way. I'm guessing you don't take too kindly to charity. Interest is one percent per year, to provide some motivation. Pay it back to the stem cell research company of your choice." *Might as well try to cure Alzheimer's early while we're here.*

"How do you know so much? Why are you doing this?" Owen asked.

237

"I can't tell you that. All I can tell you is that I sort of stumbled upon your situation by mistake and realized I could help. Consider it my way of making it up to you for spying on you." Arnesto was getting better at this lying thing.

He continued, "I don't think you realize how much you mean to Jenna. You are her rock. You are the only one she feels she can count on." Now he was being truthful.

"You sure seem to know a lot about me," Owen said, handing his gifts back to Arnesto, "so how is it you don't seem to know about my cancer?" Arnesto's confused look told him all he needed to know. "Yeah, you government boys suck at your jobs."

"I'm not with— how long?"

"Doctors say three to four months. But they're never right. Could be more, could be less. And what am I supposed to do, sit around in more and more pain waiting to die, using my last days on earth to make Jenna miserable? Forget it, I'm going out my way." He pulled out a gun.

"Waitwaitwait! What about hospice care, checking with the VA, Medicaid, Medicare, something like that?"

"I'm not old enough for Medicare, you dumb shit."

"Sorry, having a little trouble thinking right now. What about the rest?" Arnesto asked.

"The rest of what?"

My god, he's as difficult to argue with as... Jenna. "Have you looked into them? They have services, they can help you."

"No. What's the point," Owen said, raising the gun to his temple.

"Hold on! Where's your note?! You at least need to leave a note."

Owen lowered the gun again. "Are you serious?"

"You don't have a note, do you." It wasn't a question. "You didn't plan this. Most suicides are committed on impulse. Give it twenty-four hours. Take some time, write a note, see how you feel tomorrow."

"No. I'm done talking," Owen said, again raising his gun.

"*Wait*, motherfucker!" Arnesto brought his own empty hand up to his ear, mimicking a phone. "'Hello, Jenna? Yeah, we need you to come down to the morgue and identify your father. It might take you a while since he blew his brains out. Also, you're going to have to handle all the arrangements and the funeral and everything. Your extended family won't lift a finger to help, but they'll complain about it all. Oh, also, they'll expect you to pay for everything since they're assholes like your father. By the way, do you remember your last words to him during your fight last night? Well, enjoy blaming yourself for his death for the rest of your life.'"

Arnesto glared at Owen who stared back out of shock. One man on the edge of death, the other having never felt more alive.

Slowly, Owen lowered the gun to his side. Arnesto suddenly became aware of his heart pounding in his ears.

"'I want you out of my life,'" Owen said. "That was the last thing she said before hanging up on me last night. 'I want you out of my life.'"

Arnesto nodded. "She said it, but she didn't mean it. She was at a party with friends, she had a few, she blurted it out. You can't let it end like this. You can't let those be her final words to you."

Owen shook his head in frustration. "How do you know all this?! You're not a spy. You didn't follow me here. I was watching out. No car drove up here after I arrived. That means you were here before me. How did you know I was coming to this exact spot to kill myself? Wait a minute. Do you work for Father Martin?"

Arnesto barely managed not to gasp. "Who?"

"Don't play dumb. You young people are always online. Stories have been popping up ever since Hurricane Katia. People claiming to be helped by some mysterious stranger."

Arnesto realized this could be the answer. Owen was clearly good at keeping secrets, had some odd sense of honor, and didn't have long to live besides. "I'm not supposed to talk about it."

Owen slapped his knee. "I knew it! Can you tell me anything about Jenna? I mean, she does have a good life after I'm gone, right?"

"Have you noticed you and I are a little bit alike?"

"There's some similarities, I guess."

Arnesto shrugged. "Sometimes women marry men that remind them of their fathers." He gave Owen a moment to let that sink in. "Funny thing is, I haven't even met her yet. That won't happen for many years down the road. But then we meet, get married, and every year after that we visit your grave on the anniversary of today. At least, that's what I'm told. So, any chance we can push that date back a few months?"

Owen let out a long, slow breath. "You called me a motherfucker."

"Yes, I'm sorry, it was—"

Owen held up his hand. "No, don't ruin it by apologizing." He turned his gaze forward out the windshield. Then he gave the subtlest of nods. He put the gun away and reached over and opened Arnesto's door.

"Take all that crap with you," Owen said.

"Sure, I'll take the gun, too."

"No."

"Alright, the bullets then."

"No. Relax, I'm not going to do it. You don't work at one of them suicide hotlines, do you? You kind of suck at it."

"No," Arnesto said, getting out of the car, "I couldn't handle the stress."

Arnesto wasn't kidding, but Owen must have thought it was mildly amusing since he smiled. "I forgot your name," he said, leaning over and holding out his hand.

"That's okay, so did I," Arnesto said, as he leaned in and shook Owen's hand.

"You're alright, kid," Owen said. "Take care of Jenna." He pulled the passenger door shut and started the car.

Arnesto stepped out of the way and watched as Owen drove away. He then sauntered behind a pillar and barfed.

Roach Trap

Arnesto's Apartment
Silicon Valley, California
Friday, April 11, 2008
Evening

ARNESTO WAS ANXIOUS. He felt like a little kid waiting for Christmas. Except in this case, he didn't know when Christmas would finally show up and come into his life. The best he could do was narrow it down to within a few weeks.

Any day now, he would meet his second wife.

He logged on to his dating profile for the umpteenth time in a row. There were no new messages. Not surprising as he had stopped communicating with other women a while back in anticipation of Her.

And one day, there she was.

RoachMotel66 wasn't online, but she had completed her profile. She only had two pictures. One was a few years old when she had longer hair, ignoring the site's recommendation of only posting recent pics. The other was recent, however, it was only a profile shot of her face. Neither pic revealed anything about her body. It didn't matter. Arnesto knew she was tiny. He knew she was five-feet-three and thin

242

with a blonde pixie cut.

And frigging adorable.

He sighed with relief at finally seeing her again. He took the time to read her profile, knowing he shouldn't take too long. Soon she would be inundated with messages, like, "Hey," or "Sup" from guys who posted pics of themselves shirtless or in front of their cars. Arnesto always wondered if that ever worked.

She might even receive a dick pic or two. Arnesto hated this tactic. Sure it made his lack of vulgarity look much better in comparison, but it was a classless move that hurt everyone.

The waiting period was over. It was time to strike.

He wrote her the following message, responding directly to several points mentioned in her profile: "Hi! I didn't read your profile, but I'm opposed to the environment. Want to come over and watch me play Halo for the next 6-8 hours?" He checked it over, then giggled as he hit, "Send."

He played video games to keep himself busy while he waited. He had a feeling she would be back soon.

He refreshed the window to update his favorites list. She appeared at the top — with a little green circle in the corner. She was online.

He clicked on her picture to bring up her profile again. He only did this so the site would send her a notification that he was checking her out.

At last, she responded, "Okay, you made me laugh. Its good to see there's at least one guy on here with some intelligence." Another response came right after, "Typo, ugh! It's, not its. Not my fault, I was eating a burrito while I typed. ;-)"

That's my girl!

Arnesto wrote back, "It's okay, I made a typo once." He got the notification that she viewed *his* profile and added, "Are you checking me out? My eyes are up here!"

He eased off the jokes and let the conversation flow more naturally. They talked about her job in I.T. She was the only female in a small group of technicians that worked for a sales company. They had fun there, but sometimes things got a little *too* slow. They played online games together during their downtime, except for Barry, who wasn't into it.

She and Arnesto talked about other things, too, sticking to the usual topics. Where they were from, how many siblings they had, what colleges they went to, how glad they were college was over, and so on. When it looked like things were slowing down, Arnesto decided to kick it up a notch. "RoachMotel66. Is that Roach as in Rachel or Rochelle?"

"Wow, you are the first person to guess Rochelle! No one guesses that. They always guess Rachel," she said.

"Booya! Ten points to Gryffindor!" he said.

"Definitely! But I can only give you nine. It's actually Rochel, not Rochelle. Still, nobody else has any points, so..."

"Your parents spelled it Rochel? Are you sure? Get them on the line, I need to speak with them. Just kidding. Nice to meet you, Rochel. My name is — and this is no joke — Arnesto."

"Arnesto? With an A?! That is hilarious! Wow, we'll have to let all our folks have it. We can get back at them in front of everyone at our wedding. KIDDING!"

Not if we elope again.

"Your profile says you're divorced?" she continued. "How many times have you been married?"

Let's see. Katrina, you, Jenna, Katrina again. Four times now, damn. Wait, the first three don't count. "Just the one time. I'm not in a rush to make that mistake again."

"That's good to hear. And on that note," she wrote, "I have to get to bed. I have to get up early for my long day of doing nothing. But I enjoyed our conversation. :-)"

"Wait, what's your number? I want to ask you out to sushi."

There was a noticeable pause before she responded, "I don't know if I should give out my number to someone I just met on the internet. I hope you're not offended."

This felt new. Did he not get her number during their first conversation last time? Had they exchanged more messages through the site before he made his move?

"Not at all! I understand," he wrote. "But I would love to talk with you again. You can have my number," which he typed in, but added, "No pressure! Otherwise, maybe we can chat online again soon. Have a good night!"

"I'd really like that. Goodnight, Arnesto with an 'A'!"

A couple late night chat sessions and several text messages later, and they were ready to meet. He wanted to get to the restaurant before her this time, so he arrived ten minutes early. However, as soon as he walked in, he saw her already seated at a table. That was her way. She smiled and gave him a little wave.

She even stood as he approached, neither taking their eyes off the other. He started to go for a hug, which she was about to return, but he chickened out at the last second and offered a handshake.

"I'm sorry, didn't I warn you? I'm a little awkward on the first date," he said as they sat down.

She smiled her bright beautiful smile. "That actually makes me feel better."

"How so?"

"I kind of have a type. I'm usually attracted to thin, awkward guys."

He held out his arms and said in his best sarcastic tone, "Hello!"

"When I looked at your profile, I thought you were good-looking, but you looked a little buff. And then in chat, you seemed a little too smooth. I'm glad to see it was all a façade!"

Arnesto looked a little stunned. It wasn't an act. "Nobody's ever called me any of those things before." He held out his hand for a high five. "Five points to Slytherin!"

"Slytherin?! I'm going to pretend you said Ravenclaw."

"What about you?" he asked, feigning disgust. "Neither of your *two* pics shows your body. I came here hoping to meet somebody morbidly obese, and instead you surprise me with your perfectly fit little figure?!"

She tried hard to resist smiling but failed. "I can see we're going to have a grand time." The word "grand" came out sounding ever so slightly like "grond." Anybody but someone who already knew everything about her would have missed it.

Arnesto straightened up and stared at her. He wasn't expecting this so soon, but here it was. She noticed his reaction and looked down at her silverware and then outside, avoiding eye contact. Should he bring it up? It was a gamble, but things were going very well. As if he could possibly resist. "We're going to have a *what* time?"

"A *grand* time." Now there was no accent. Nor was there any indication she wanted him to press her on the matter.

"I don't mean to pry," he said. She rolled her eyes. He decided to

246

go soft. "I have always wanted to visit Ireland." Her softened expression told him he had made the right choice, but it wouldn't hurt to continue treading lightly. "I've heard it's beautiful and would love to hear about it from someone who may have gone and may have picked up the accent. And if they have, they shouldn't be embarrassed because it's the sexiest accent ever. Well, second to the French accent."

She stared at him a long time before speaking. "I did spend some summers there with extended family as a child. And yes, it is beautiful." She waited for a response, but Arnesto said nothing. "I *may* have picked something up and blurt it out every once in a great while." Arnesto held steadfast. "Aren't you going to say, 'Aha!' or something?"

"*That* would be immature."

She couldn't help but burst out laughing. Neither could he. When she was able, she said, "Don't worry, I'm American, born and raised. I'm not dating you for a green card."

"Prove it. How many assault rifles do you own?"

"*Three*," she said, holding up three fingers for emphasis.

He nodded. "Correct. Minor infection: take doctor-prescribed antibiotics and heal, or try to pray the problem away?"

"Make an appointment to see my doctor. Wait an hour and a half for a five-minute visit. Pay an eighty-dollar co-pay, plus another hundred and thirty for the pills that probably cost sixty cents to manufacture. Take the pills and heal, but then feel sick a week later when I receive a three-hundred-dollar bill not covered by my already huge deductible or my insurance. Consider next time asking for a million likes on Facebook."

Arnesto was shocked. "Holy shit. You're American. No more questions, Your Honor."

They talked for hours. Afterward, they went for a walk around a nearby park. He pleasantly surprised her by taking her hand. The next day, she woke up and checked her phone. There was already a text from him thanking her for a wonderful time and telling her he really wanted to see her again soon. She appreciated it but wondered if he was this way with all the girls. She went online to review his profile, but he had already disabled it. Now she was impressed.

They went on more dates, which quickly turned into getting take-out and playing video games or watching old horror flicks or documentaries. They became lovers, and he was the best she had ever been with. Somehow he seemed to know exactly what she liked.

"I love how much you love my breasts," she said as they lay in bed after one particular love-making session.

"They're perfect."

"They're only B-cups. Rounding up."

"Yeah, but look at them. So perky and… breasterific." He did have a way with words.

"Nobody's ever given them more attention than you," she said. "But, and I know you won't take this the wrong way, sometimes it feels a little more like… you're feeling for something. For a brief moment there, you reminded me of my doctor."

Arnesto got quiet.

"What?" she asked.

"I don't want to worry you," he responded, "but I thought I felt a tiny bump." This was a lie; Arnesto hadn't found anything at all. He leaned up so they could see each other. "But then I lost it. Even if I had felt something, it could have been a harmless fibroid or something. Still, it wouldn't hurt to get checked out. Is there any history of breast cancer

248

in your family?"

"Now you *sound* like my doctor. What gives?"

"Nothing. I… have some experience with this. I lost someone once."

She put her hand on his chest. "I'm sorry. There's no history of cancer in my family."

"No aunts or great-aunts or anybody had it?"

"I promise... No, wait, I think my great aunt Gladys had it. But *I* don't."

"I know. I'm sure you don't," he said. "I'm sorry, I'm paranoid about that sort of thing. Still, I would consider it a huge favor if you got checked out. Just to rule it out."

She hadn't seen him like this. He seemed… serious about something. "Fine," she said, pushing him off.

The next day, she pleasantly surprised him by telling him she had made an appointment for late the following week. It was the earliest they could get her in.

The following Thursday, when she got home from work, she had a sheepish grin. "I have something for you," she said, handing him a CD.

Arnesto looked at the disk, which had the date and Rochel's initials scribbled on it. "You didn't!"

"My X-ray. Clear, like my breasts. No cancer."

"How did you…?" He started to ask as he inserted the CD into his computer.

"Please, you're the only person I've met more anal-retentive than me. I knew you'd want to see it."

"Uh huh." He was fixated on the image as if it was artwork. He looked for tumors but gave up. Even if there had been something there, he lacked the skills to find it.

"You're not going to find anything. And you could at least turn around and face me to let me rub it in," she taunted.

He ejected the disk and turned to face her, smiling wide. Holding his arms out to his sides, he gave her a quick chin-up nod and said, "Come at me, bro!"

She ignored him. "Actually, it wasn't all good. Dr. Kim told me to tell you she appreciated you being proactive. She said more of her patients would be alive if they had reacted this way, and you did the right thing. Oh, and to keep on top of it."

"I'm so sorry you had to tell me that," he said. "I know it had to be tough. Now give me a hug."

She walked over and embraced him, resting her head against his chest. "You scared me, you big jerk."

"Good! I kind of like you and want to keep you around, and that fear might just keep you alive."

Double Down

Doctor's Office
Silicon Valley, California
Thursday, December 4, 2008
11:40 a.m.

"...ADJUVANT CHEMOTHERAPY possibly followed by radiation therapy after that," Dr. Ganesh said. She was the consummate professional, the right combination of confidence and competence. She was not afraid to speak her mind, yet had a superb bedside manner. She was definitely someone you wanted on your side in a fight against cancer. What did she say that one time? Oh, right, "I'm going to make your cancer my bitch."

Arnesto almost smiled at the thought but stopped himself. Now would not be the time to look amused. Rochel might not see it, sitting next to him clutching his hand, but Dr. Ganesh would from behind her desk. She missed nothing, and he didn't want to give her the false impression that he was aloof. That said, he was only half listening to their conversation. He had heard all this before and besides, if he got his way, it would all be moot. He had to wait until it was his turn.

At last, there was a lull in the conversation. "Arnesto, how do you feel about all this?" Dr. Ganesh asked. "Do you have any questions?"

"Bilateral mastectomy," he said with enough conviction that one might have thought he was solving the final puzzle on a game show. Rochel, at least, was taken aback. It was harder to tell with Dr. Ganesh.

"You... you want to have them chop off my breasts?! We're not nearly at that stage, are we, Doctor?"

"Like I said, we caught this very early," Dr. Ganesh said, turning toward Rochel then back toward Arnesto. "While a double mastectomy is an option, it would be overkill at this point. We should save that option until—"

"Forgive me, Doctor, I know I lack your medical expertise, and I value your opinion more than you know, but I want to... *nuke* this thing. I want to hit this cancer so hard, all memory of it is erased from existence."

"Arnesto, what's gotten into you?" Rochel asked.

He ignored her. "Survival rate's like ninety percent, she wouldn't need radiation, and it would all be over and done with, right?"

Dr. Ganesh nodded. "Sometimes radiation is still needed afterward, but probably not in this case, *if* you decide to go this route." She wasn't putting up much of an objection but wasn't in complete agreement either.

"Excuse me, patient here," Rochel said, waving her hands at Arnesto. "I'm sorry, Doctor, this is a lot to take in."

"Not at all. I would like to get moving on this sooner rather than later, but there's no need to make a decision right now. Take a couple days, discuss it amongst yourselves, and call my office anytime."

They thanked her and left. Rochel wouldn't look at Arnesto as they made the short walk back to the car in silence. They got in the car and put their seatbelts on. Rochel stared straight ahead while Arnesto looked at her for several seconds before finally starting the car and taking them home. When they arrived, she went in and sat on the couch, still in a silent daze. He didn't know what to do, so he sat down next to her. Again, he got no response when he looked at her, so he did what any man would do in that situation: he reached for the remote.

"What was that?" she asked, still not looking at him.

"What?" he asked, setting the remote down.

She looked disgusted. "What do you mean, 'What?' What was all that back there?! I've never seen you act like that before." She was *mad*.

"I don't want you to die."

That seemed to reduce her frustration a little. "I don't intend to die, but I also don't intend on chopping up my body for no reason." With that, she was finally able to look at him.

He turned to her and took her hands in his, but she violently flicked them off. "You are so strong and young and healthy, well, otherwise. But cancer doesn't care. Cancer don't give a fuck. Would you risk your life over a one-in-a-hundred chance? What about one-in-a-thousand? No, right? So let's not give cancer that chance. A bilateral mastectomy is the surest—"

"Stop calling it that!"

"Fine, 'hacking off your pleasure domes' is the surest, safest way to beat this thing."

"Ugh. So you know more than the doctor now."

"She's terrific, an excellent doctor, but... she doesn't know everything."

"And you do."

253

Arnesto had to think about this one for a moment. "No. Of course not."

"Finally. That's the first thing you've said all day that sounded like you." They sat there in silence until she got up. "I'm getting some aspirin, I have a headache," she said.

He suddenly grabbed her wrist. "Give me this."

"Give you *what*?!" she said, struggling to pull away.

"*This*. The surgery. I've never asked you for anything and never will again. I'll do whatever you want, forever, if you give me this one thing."

"Let *go*!" she said, breaking free and storming into the kitchen.

He heard her grab her keys and stood up and walked over to her. "I'll go. You can stay." They locked eyes. He looked at her, the woman he was in love with, going through one of the worst days of her life, and he had made it worse. She looked at him, the desperate asshole she barely recognized at the moment. He grabbed his keys and left.

He drove around aimlessly. Had he been a total idiot? He had hoped to overwhelm her; get her to agree while she was still in shock from the news and not able to think clearly. It hadn't worked, but for all he knew, it wouldn't have worked any better had he waited a day or two. She was a tough little broad. It was time for Plan B. Whatever *that* was.

Eventually, she texted him, explaining how scared and sad she was and how disappointed she was in him. He apologized and told her he would support her and respect her choices, whatever they were.

Of course, he didn't mean a word of it.

He gave her a little more time before he returned home with ice cream and her favorite anime on Blu-ray (Rochel's preferred version of

254

flowers and candy). The tension between them wasn't gone, but it was lessened.

The next day, he cautiously broached the subject again. "Have you given any more thought to—"

"I already made the appointment," she said to his surprise. "I'm meeting with the surgeon to discuss my lumpectomy." She stared at him as if she was already bracing for a fight.

It wouldn't be enough, not by a long shot. Still, Arnesto wasn't about to go down *that* dead end again. He bit his tongue and made his sincerest fake smile. "Okay."

This disarmed her a little. "You'll come with me?"

"Of course. Hey, let's go out tonight, someplace nice. Someplace pretentious and overpriced."

"Oh, so now you're going to make me get dressed up?" she asked, smiling.

"You can wear yoga pants for all I care. In fact, I *dare* you to wear yoga pants."

"I'm not wearing yoga pants."

"Okay."

* * *

That night they had a lovely dinner. Afterward, she agreed to go for a drive with him out into the country where they could park and watch the stars.

"Are you in a rush to get back?" he asked after a long lull in the conversation.

"No, why?"

"I'd like to tell you a quick story."

"Ooh, I like stories."

"You're not going to like this one."

She didn't respond right away, so he turned his head to look at her. "Go ahead," she said, sounding disappointed.

"Boy meets girl, girl meets boy, they fall in love. It helps they have so much in common. There are some differences, of course. She is, like, half his size"—she snorted at this—"but more than that, she is strong, so much stronger than he could ever be. And then... she gets cancer.

"Together with the doctors, they fight it with everything they have. Well, it's mostly her fighting with him cheering her on. But they fight, and they beat the cancer. Or so they think. But then it comes back stronger. No problem, she fights it again, and again she wins. But this time, she's barely even stepped out of the ring when it comes back again. They throw everything they have at it: chemo, radiation, surgery after surgery. They fight and they fight, and she keeps hanging on until she weighs little more than half what she started with and simply has nothing left with which to defend herself. My god she was strong, though. She never gave up even until the very end."

"This is a pretty shitty story," she said. "What happened to the boy?"

"He suffers. He doesn't know how to handle it all — remember, he isn't strong like her — and he never really gets over her."

"Does he stay with her the whole time?"

"Yeah, but that's not necessarily a good thing. He tries to take care of her, but he's not equipped to go through all that by himself. Sometimes they fight over the stupidest little things. Anyway, he spends the rest of his life regretting not having been more patient and taken better care of her."

"Good, he sounds like an asshole," she said.

He chuckled, but then realized she wasn't kidding. "Sometimes, he is."

"Is that it?"

"No," he said, "there's more. Afterward, her jerk family comes crawling out of the woodwork. They sue to have her buried near them in Jersey."

"What?!" Rochel said, disgusted. "They never cared about her when she was alive. Why do they suddenly care now? And she wants to be cremated."

"I don't know. The boy never figured that out."

"Well, does he fight?"

Arnesto sighed. "Yes, he tries. But the medical bills wiped them both out. Besides, for a while, he loses the ability to really care about anything. He puts up a meager fight but soon gives in. Her family is nigh impossible to deal with under the best of circumstances, but in his condition, forget about it."

"How's the funeral?" Aside from the mention of her family, she seemed to be enjoying the tale.

"Fine. Civil. Do you want to know what her tombstone says?"

"Yeah, tell me."

"It says, 'Here lies our beloved daughter, Rochel,' plus the dates of birth and death."

"That's it? That's... depressing. They even managed to make my death about them. Is there any more?"

Arnesto shrugged. "That's all I can... think of. How'd you like it?"

"I like the part where it was brief." She smiled, but it quickly faded.

"Actually, I could see my family pulling a stunt like that. But it's all moot because it's never going to happen."

"That's true. We can keep them out of the loop. It feels a little like sinking to their level, but we will ensure you get cremated this time."

"Or I could just, you know, not die."

"You're going to die."

"Wow, if this is how you're going to act throughout my treatment, then I don't want you there. I may not even want you in my *life*."

"What's left of it."

"Arnesto, stop it! What is wrong with you?! We're going to fight this thing and get through it. I'm not going to die."

"I'm so sorry, but unless we're more aggressive with the treatment, you are."

"You can't know that!"

"But I do!"

"How?! How can you possibly know?!"

"Because!" he screamed. "*I was there!*"

Picture It

Countryside
Silicon Valley, California
Friday, December 5, 2008
Night

NOW HE'D DONE IT. After so many years of not telling a soul, other than Pete, he'd blurted it out.

You know what? It was fine. Keeping her alive was worth the risk. Besides, she might not believe him and end up dumping him. In that case, she wouldn't be a loose end for long, *and* he wouldn't have to slowly watch cancer eat her alive.

Then again, he hadn't really confessed anything. She might've thought he'd gone insane. He had a crazy idea.

On the drive home, he stopped and put the car in park.

"Where are we?" she asked, looking in all directions outside the car. They were on the side of a road in the middle of nowhere, surrounded by fields. There wasn't a building, car, or person in sight. "Arnesto, just take me home."

He let out a long, deep sigh.

"Did you hear me? I said take me home, now."

259

"Wait, please. Let me tell you the rest of the story." He hurried his words, his mind going a mile a minute.

"You said it was over."

"There's more. The boy goes on living. And living. Finally, many, many years later he finds a way to send his memories back in time. To himself... me."

She looked around her seat. "Where is my — give me my phone."

"We need to talk about this. Think about it — how else would I know?"

She held out her hand. "Give me my goddamn phone!" When he didn't do anything but open his mouth to spew what she assumed was more nonsense, she opened the door and jumped out. She walked twenty feet down the road then stopped. "Where are we?!"

He calmly got out of the car and approached her. "I brought you here because I need you to hear me out. Please don't run off. It's miles back to the main road."

"You're fucking crazy, you know that?!"

"Please! I can prove it! Mr. Fuffles or Mr. Foofles or something, your imaginary friend as a kid!"

"Mr. Snuggles," she said, crossing her arms. She was only vaguely aware of the cold making her shiver. She was too scared for her life.

"Right, Mr. Snuggles. And *his* imaginary friend, Mrs., oh what was it, Mrs. Addictive..."

"Mrs. Attentive."

"Right! She was his friend because you didn't want him to be envious that you had an imaginary friend and he didn't."

"What is your point?!"

"You never told me about them! You've never told anyone about

260

them. Not even your parents because you knew, even as a young girl, they wouldn't approve."

They both stood there, unsure how to proceed. He tried desperately to come up with a better example but was too caught up in the moment.

"How do you know that if I never told you?" she finally asked.

"You will. One of our many, wonderful heart-to-hearts when you're… sick. It's kind of a deathbed confession sort of thing."

"Jesus Christ," she said, throwing her arms in the air in frustration. "You are so full of shit."

"Test me. Ask me anything."

"No."

"No?!" He was taken aback. "What do you mean, 'No'? You can ask me anything about the future and you don't want to?"

"You can't know anything about the future because it's impossible, so there's no point in asking you any questions. Can we please go now?"

He nodded and opened her door for her. "Whatever happens, you cannot repeat what I told you. For your own safety." She got in but shut her door herself in a small display of defiance. He ran around and sat in the driver's seat. "I can prove it to you. Give me until your appointment." He started the car but when he went to put the car in reverse, he hesitated.

"What now?" she asked.

"Your appointment," he said, as he started to drive. "I remember it. Tuesday, eleven o'clock with Dr. Hwang, right? We show up fifteen minutes early to fill out forms which takes five minutes. Then we sit there waiting for forty-five minutes or so. There's a smell in the air which displeases you. Let's see, what else…"

"Please stop."

"Okay. I'll shut up now. But you should know it's his daughter."

She couldn't care less what he was talking about, but on impulse asked, "What?"

"The picture in his office. You're going to ask if it's his granddaughter. Turns out Dr. Hwang looks older than he is. Anyway, it's no big deal. He's a nice guy. He laughs it off, but you feel embarrassed."

They drove the rest of the way home in silence.

When they arrived, exhausted, they went straight to bed. "I'm going to spend a few days at my friend's house," she said. "And I'm going to go to my appointment alone. I don't want you there." She rolled away from him.

"Okay," he said.

She felt relieved he didn't turn it into a discussion.

"Julie? Julie who snores?" Arnesto asked.

She rolled her eyes. "Yes, Julie." She was about to argue but realized she didn't know if Julie snored or not.

"I don't think she has her CPAP yet. I'm not going to tell you what to do, but I would humbly suggest you get as much rest as possible. Why don't you stay here, and I'll go?"

"I'll be fine. Goodnight," she said, carefully enunciating each word, her last shreds of patience evaporating.

"Goodnight," he whispered, letting her know the conversation had indeed concluded.

* * *

Julie proved to be a gracious host. She even had a spare bedroom for Rochel. After a fun evening spent drinking wine and bashing men, it was time to retire. Rochel got into her bed and played on her phone for a bit, then turned it off and closed her eyes. It seemed she would get plenty of rest after all.

Then she heard it.

It sounded like two jackhammers fighting inside a sawmill. Or two sawmills fighting *with* jackhammers. She turned on the light and confirmed her door was closed. It was no help. The sound, the most ungodly cacophony ever produced by a living mammal, was coming through their shared wall.

She got up, opened her door, walked to Julie's door, and quietly opened it. The sound got even louder. Julie wasn't much larger than she was. How in the hell could that little woman be making all that noise? How was Julie not deaf from her own labored breathing?

She quietly closed Julie's door and went back to her own room. Goddammit, Arnesto. He always was a lucky guesser.

After a couple rough nights, it was time to say goodbye. "Thanks so much for putting me up. And putting up with me," Rochel said, giving Julie a big hug.

"Anytime! I hope my snoring didn't bother you too much."

"No, must've slept right through it." She turned toward the door. "One question, though. This might sound weird, but did you say you were thinking about getting a CPAP?"

"No, I don't think so."

Rochel smiled. "Okay, thanks."

"I mean, we didn't talk about it, but I am thinking about getting one. Why do you ask?"

"Uh, somebody mentioned getting one, but I couldn't remember who. Thought it might be you. Must've had too much wine the other night."

She went home and saw Arnesto was still asleep, the well-rested bastard. She took a shower and got dressed. When she went out into the living room, she saw Arnesto had already gotten up and started playing video games.

They exchanged fake half-smiles, then she got ready to go to her appointment. That's when she saw the book she was reading on the couch. She wanted to bring it, but she had a problem. He would see her grab it and think she believed him about the long wait time ahead of her. *But what if it happened?* Long wait times happened in doctors' offices all the time. It would just be a coincidence. Why did she even care?

Because he was delusional, and she didn't want to enable him in any way.

Feeling flustered, she left the book and walked out.

As the minutes in the waiting room crawled by, she cursed herself for not bringing her book. It would have been the perfect distraction from everything going wrong in her life right then, which included, besides the cancer and her insane boyfriend, the smell. It wasn't awful, just... displeasing. It smelled like disinfectant with a hint of latex and a dash of anxiety.

This was not a lucky guess. Every doctor's office smelled like that.

Finally, she was called back. The clock said 11:35. She did the math in her head. Factoring in five minutes for filling out forms, and the extra five minutes she was early, the wait had been forty-five minutes... Okay, this time he got a little lucky.

The first thing she did upon entering Dr. Hwang's office was look for the picture Arnesto had mentioned. And there it was on the mantle behind his desk, an image of a young Asian woman. She looked around twenty maybe? Plenty old enough to be his daughter. Arnesto was wrong at last.

Dr. Hwang entered the room and introduced himself and apologized for being late. He seemed warm and personable. He gently examined her lump and was confident the lumpectomy was what she needed. He had performed thousands of such procedures and assured her it was trivial.

When their appointment was over, they stood and shook hands. She remembered the picture of his daughter and pointed to it. "Is this your... family?" she asked.

"Yes," he said, grabbing the frame and holding it out for her. "This is Hideko, my wife."

Rochel's jaw dropped partway. "She looks so young!"

"She's thirty-eight if you can believe it. People always tell me how lucky I am," he said, telling one of his canned jokes.

Rochel could see why. She thought he looked like he was in his fifties, though she didn't dare ask. He had very little hair left, but it was the bags under his eyes that defined his appearance. They looked like they had become a permanent fixture on his face a long time ago.

Dr. Hwang put the picture back, then grabbed another that had been on his desk facing away from Rochel. "And this is our daughter, Emily."

Rochel's heart skipped a beat. Emily looked like she was five!

"Would you believe," he asked as he put Emily's picture back on his desk, "people think she's my granddaughter? That's when I pretend I don't speak English." Another canned joke.

Rochel couldn't even feign a smile this time. Instead, she pulled out her phone. After a quick search, she held out a picture of her and Arnesto. "Do you know him? Has he been in here before?"

Dr. Hwang put on his glasses and looked at her phone. He shook his head. "Who is he?"

"Arnesto, my boyfriend."

"He doesn't look familiar to me."

"Dr. Hwang, what if — what if we were more aggressive? Could you — give me a double mastectomy?"

He had no idea where this was coming from. "Please, have a seat. Let's discuss it."

Chilling

LaGuardia Airport
Queens, New York
Thursday, January 15, 2009
3:10 p.m.

"REMEMBER, I WANTED to take the ferry," Arnesto said.

"If what you said is true, we'll be taking the ferry anyway," Rochel said, smiling.

"Alright, let's not talk about it anymore." He fidgeted with his phone, but Rochel could tell he wasn't into it. Either he was a nervous flyer, or he was good at acting the part.

"You know, commercial flying is perfectly safe."

He didn't respond, but she could tell he wasn't amused. He watched the woman behind the counter make an announcement, "US Airways Flight fifteen-forty-nine to Charlotte is now boarding all passengers."

"Here we go," Arnesto said as he stood up and put away his phone. He grabbed their backpack and slung it over his shoulder. There wasn't much in it, aside from one day's worth of clothes and some toiletries. He had bought all of it, including the cheap backpack, in California knowing he would probably never see any of it again. It was all for show so that later nobody would wonder why they hadn't brought a single bag on board with them. They had no checked luggage.

These were some of the details he wouldn't have had to worry about if Rochel had agreed to take the ferry. At least after this, there would be no way she could doubt him any longer.

"Wow, it's packed," he said as they boarded the plane and turned down the aisle. He shouldn't have been surprised — he couldn't even get them two seats together. This was a result of buying the tickets late so, as he had put it, "It would cause the least amount of disruption to these people's lives."

They went most of the way back when Rochel grabbed her seat in the middle on the left. He went a few more rows and took the aisle seat on the right. They didn't say anything when they separated. It was just one of his conditions that they "play it cool" so that nobody would offer to switch seats so they could sit together. Again, minimizing disruption. He didn't want to switch with another passenger only to have that person get injured in their new seat and wind up blaming him. In fact, he would prefer it if nobody remembered he was ever there.

He shoved his backpack under the seat in front of him, put on his seatbelt, and whipped out the safety instruction card.

"You won't need that," said the rotund man seated on Arnesto's right.

"That's good to hear," Arnesto said, scanning the card and putting it back. *Are you kidding me? All these New Yorkers and I have to sit next to the one who wants to be social? Or worse, he's probably from North Carolina.*

"Business or pleasure?" the man asked.

"Pleasure. Going to see the Carolinas Aviation Museum." Arnesto had done his research just in case somebody asked. Without realizing it, he had named exactly where the airplane was headed, eventually, as a display.

"Huh, taking a plane to see a bunch of planes," the man said. "If you like vehicles, you should come back next year when they complete the NASCAR Hall of Fame. People are real excited about that one."

"Oh, I bet," Arnesto said, doing his best to appear friendly.

"You know what you should see if you have time? The Billy Graham Library, it's wonderful."

"I'm Jewish, I'm not sure I'd be too welcome."

"Oh, no, they welcome everyone," the man said.

Right, that's why you guys lose the right to host the NBA All-Star Game in 2017. Come on, let's take off already.

After what seemed like an eternity, the flight attendants made their safety presentation. Arnesto paid close attention. Soon after, the plane began to pull away from the terminal.

Oh, god, here we go.

Arnesto looked over at the top right side of Rochel's head. Poor Rochel was finally about to enter his world once and for all.

As the plane taxied to the runway, Arnesto looked for empty seats but couldn't find any. Hopefully, there was nobody who couldn't take the flight because of him. More likely, he had saved someone from PTSD at the cost of some financial compensation. Either way, he didn't like changing someone's life like that. Saving lives was one thing. Denying them one of the most memorable experiences *of* their lives was another.

Maybe this was a mistake. He had always worked so hard to avoid these situations. What the hell was he doing putting himself in the middle of one? He was risking everything to, what, impress a girl?

Flight 1549 finished taxiing to the runway and was soon about to begin its final takeoff.

What if something's changed? What if I've done something in the past to change conditions for the worse? What if we've altered the distribution of weight enough to turn this would-be miracle into a disaster? I could scream. I could start screaming, get ejected from the flight, and nobody would ever know what would have happened.

Arnesto couldn't quite bring himself to scream. Seconds later, the plane was barreling down the runway then lifting into the air, leaving the nice, safe ground behind.

As the plane turned gently toward the left, he looked out the left side windows at the New York City skyline.

Wouldn't it be ironic if I prevented 9/11 but my mere presence caused 1/15?

He closed his eyes and tried to focus on his breathing to calm himself down.

He eyes snapped open when he heard the bang. There were some audible gasps from the passengers. As the plane's engines shut down, destroyed by the Canadian geese sucked inside, the plane became quiet.

With everyone else straining to look out the windows, Arnesto's view was even more obstructed, so he checked his seatbelt for the umpteenth time. He started to reach for the safety card again but realized it would be futile at this point.

Rochel looked back at him. He wasn't positive, but he thought he saw a fleck of terror in her eyes. He gave her a tiny nod in a weak attempt to reassure her, and she turned back around.

The plane had already begun descending, but it didn't look like they were over the water. Those buildings were starting to look awfully close...

In the excitement, he almost missed the captain's announcement to brace for impact, but there was no missing the flight attendants chanting, "Brace brace brace! Heads down, stay down!" After a few repetitions, Arnesto's mind translated their chant into, "Fuck fuck fuck! Fuck this, fuck you!" Clearly, they were much more skillful at their jobs than he would have been under such circumstances.

With people putting their heads down, Arnesto caught a quick peek and saw the plane had indeed moved over the water. He put his own head down and waited.

As the plane slammed into the Hudson River, Arnesto remembered the grainy video taken from a distance that showed the plane very quickly coming to a halt. At least, that's how he remembered it. In reality, it took much longer. He wasn't sure what was worse: the plane refusing to stop, the sound of the plane creaking under the pressure, or the smell of smoke now permeating the cabin.

Finally, the plane skidded to a stop with a little swerve at the end, another detail he didn't remember from the video. It didn't matter. They were alive.

Arnesto reached for his life preserver — one of the few passengers to do so — and noticed a sharp pain in his right shoulder. This bothered him, both because of the pain and also the fact that he didn't remember any injuries. He had only remembered that everyone lived. People made such a big deal about that detail, which was understandable, but they downplayed the fact there were a number of injuries onboard.

With so much forgotten information, Arnesto vowed to himself he would never get this close to an incident ever again.

The air that came in from the open doors was bitter cold — the water pouring over his feet, much more so. Arnesto had brought a hat and gloves but didn't put them on for fear of standing out from the crowd. He followed the other passengers out the emergency exit and joined Rochel on the right wing of the aircraft.

Four long minutes after the forced landing, the first ferry arrived. Fifteen minutes after that, Arnesto and Rochel boarded a ferry. Only five minutes later, everyone was rescued.

Rochel buried herself in Arnesto's chest. They both started to warm up again. They still hadn't spoken.

Arnesto finally broke the long silence. "Well, *that* was fun. Want to get back in line and do it again?"

Rochel said nothing. Normally, she had a wonderful sense of humor, but this time, she was not amused. Arnesto was fine with that. At least if she wasn't talking, she wasn't calling him out in front of others. He started to rub his hand up and down her back to help warm her up.

"Careful," she said, "I banged my elbow pretty hard."

It wasn't until they were checked out at the hospital that he saw the nasty bruise forming on her elbow. Thankfully, nothing was broken and both of them were released.

After they checked into a hotel room, he asked if she was ready to talk about it.

"The flight or... the other thing?" she asked, sitting on the edge of the bed.

He sat down in a chair. "All of it. Whatever you want."

"I believe you now," she admitted. "I guess I have for a while. I was just in denial. But the moment we hit those birds, I could no longer doubt you. I *had* to believe you, to know that you knew we weren't going to die. I keep thinking — you couldn't have warned them, could you. I mean, what would you even say?"

"That's right, I couldn't, not without exposing myself." He was proud of her. She seemed to get it.

"It's just that people were terrified. *I* was terrified, and I knew what was going to happen. And all those injuries, including mine…"

Arnesto sighed. "I'm sorry about that. I honestly didn't remember that part."

"So you can never warn people?"

"Sometimes I can. Remember on the ferry, when I pointed out the World Trade Center towers?" He told her briefly about the horrific events of 9/11.

She was incredulous. "So how did you stop them? Infiltrate their terrorist cell and take them out one-by-one?"

"No, I… sent an email."

"Oh," she said. "You still saved their lives. You're a hero."

"No, I'm not. Some years from now, a teenager from Pakistan named Aitzaz Hasan is going to sacrifice his life in order to stop a suicide bomber from blowing up his school. I only know because people repost his picture on *Imgur* all the time, whoring for upvotes. But the fact remains, this kid, who will only be fifteen years old, is far braver than I could ever be."

"Until you're in that exact situation, you can't know what you would be capable of." She got up from the bed. "The drugs haven't kicked in yet and my elbow is killing me. Will you help me get undressed?" As he stood up to help her, she asked, "Who else knows about this?"

"Nobody," he said. There were still some things he couldn't tell her. The last thing he needed was for Rochel and Pete to find out they shared the same huge secret. What if they couldn't resist talking about it with each other one day and a third party overheard? It was just safer this way.

"Thanks, I can do my bra," she said. She started to reach behind her with her good arm, then hesitated. She looked down at her breasts. "If your memory is fallible, maybe you remember wrong about my cancer?" He gently shook his head. "Okay, had to check," she said. "Guess I'll make that appointment with the surgeon." She removed her bra and he helped her put a t-shirt on. "Oh, I know. Does China take over the world?"

"This is your question? You can ask me anything and you want to know about China."

"There was an article in the in-flight magazine." She gritted her teeth. "I didn't get to finish it."

"I see. No, they never achieve world domination. Their economy implodes thanks in part to increased crackdowns on counterfeiting, their shoddy structures start crumbling en masse, and millions die in Hong Kong alone due to lung diseases attributed to what will become the worst smog in the history of the planet. I can't even warn them because they already know these things."

"That's awful! All those people and the environment... Dare I ask about global warming?" she asked.

"We're fucked," he said. She looked horrified, so he continued, "We don't go extinct or anything, unlike so many other species. We adapt. Though if you ever want to vacation in Florida, I would do it sooner than later. And as always, the people with money and power do alright," he said with an air of disgust. "And before you ask, yes, I have plenty of money."

"I have many more questions, but this was such a long day. Can we go to sleep now?"

"Of course," he said. He got undressed and they both crawled under the covers.

"Oh my god," she said, "We still have to fly home."

"We can drive if you prefer."

"No, it will be fine. Unless we can take your TARDIS...?"

Arnesto chuckled. "I left the key on the plane."

"That is the last time I trust an internet dating site."

* * *

"Can I tell you some stuff about the future?" he asked. They were finally home and had finished unpacking.

"Not today, I'm not ready."

"But soon, right? There's so much I want to share with you."

"Should you be telling me anything? Isn't that dangerous?"

"I will only tell you safe things. You should be excited, I know so much cool shit!" he said, holding out his hands like a fisherman exaggerating the size of his greatest catch.

"Arnesto, I... I can't be with you anymore."

"What?! Why not?"

"'Why not?' You kidnap me, tell me you're from the future, then you put me on a plane which lands in a river..."

"You made me do the third thing to prove the second thing which necessitated the first thing! And I did all of it to save your life."

She nodded. "Yes, you did. And I appreciate that, I really, truly do. But that's my point. If I never had cancer, would you have told me any of it?"

"I couldn't. Not knowing was for your own protection."

"Exactly. Because of my cancer, our relationship went from being completely based on lies to merely being founded on lies. That's still a heck of a lot of lying, Arnesto. I can't grow old with someone who always has me wondering if he's telling the truth. Or wondering if the next disaster is the one where he misremembers something and gets himself killed. Or wondering which day will be the one where government agents come pounding on the door."

"What if—" Arnesto stopped. He saw something he had never seen before. A tear rolled partway down her cheek before she quickly wiped it away.

She was crying.

In their handful of years together across two universes, he had never seen her cry. Not in dealing with her terrible family, not in facing cancer multiple times, not even in facing death.

But being in a relationship with him — *that* made her cry.

She sniffed hard and rubbed her eyes. "What are you thinking right now?" she asked in a gentle tone.

"How stupid I am. I honestly thought if I saved your life, we'd... Guess it doesn't matter."

"Do you regret it?" she asked. He didn't answer. "Arnesto?"

"No, of course not. I'm thrilled you're going to have that operation. And we did have a lot of great times together. Some of them twice. Listen, you can't tell—"

"I promise you I will never breathe a word of this to anyone." She grabbed her keys. "I'll stay with Julie tonight."

"Did she—"

"Yes, she got her CPAP." She gave Arnesto a hug. "You'll always be my hero. Please be careful." She opened the door and walked out of his life.

The Keys to Success

Katrina's House
Silicon Valley, California
Friday, August 26, 2011
Afternoon

"THANKS SO MUCH for doing this, Arnesto," Katrina said, gesturing for him to enter her (formerly their) house. "You're a lifesaver."

He looked at the photos on the wall. By now, it was an entirely different selection than he remembered. It had to be; they hadn't existed in his first timeline.

"No problem. It will be good to spend time with the boys," he said. If the cats weren't in the picture, there was no way he would house-sit for Katrina while she, Mike, and the kids went on their mini-vacation to Southern California. The main point of the trip was to see Mike perform with his band in some concert. Mike, the man who stole Katrina away from him. The man who knocked her up while they were still married. Would it have worked out between him and Katrina if Mike hadn't entered the picture? Probably not. But that was beside the point.

He became aware of piano music coming from down the hall. Guess they had a piano now?

"I know the cats will be thrilled to hang out with you," Katrina said, snapping Arnesto to attention. "I'm going to go check on the kids' last-minute packing." She turned toward the stairs but then looked back. "Oh, guess what! The kids all made honor roll."

Arnesto smiled; at least that was one positive that remained unchanged. "I'm not surprised. They have my brains."

She looked at him awkwardly. "Preston doesn't."

As if he needed that reminder. Wait, was she implying that Preston...

"He made honor roll, too. We put their report cards on the fridge, go take a look." She disappeared upstairs.

What the hell was she talking about — Preston aka Demon Child — made honor roll?! That would be a first. Arnesto walked into the kitchen, impressed by its tidiness, and looked at the report cards held by magnets on the refrigerator door. Nothing but A's and B's for Melissa, Carlos,... and Preston. Arnesto double and triple-checked the child's name, looked for evidence of tampering, and attempted to verify the paper for authenticity, but came up empty. Preston had in fact made honor roll. And it wasn't even the first time. Preston had made honor roll the term before, too, and had just missed it the term before that. Was Arnesto living in a parallel universe?! Oh, yeah, he was. But the differences never manifested like *this*.

Melissa had curlier hair and Carlos had a new birthmark, but they otherwise seemed identical to his children from his first life. Could Preston have received his own change that made him not a terror? And who was playing the piano?!

Arnesto walked to what used to be a guest room and peered in the doorway. He saw Mike sitting at the piano, but he wasn't the one playing. Seated next to Mike with his hands on the keys was Preston. He wasn't a prodigy, but for a child his age, he showed remarkable talent. Arnesto stood in awe with his mouth open, watching Preston finish the song.

"Good job, buddy!" Mike said when he finished. "This was one of my favorite songs when I was getting started. Oh, hey, Arnesto!"

Preston turned around. "Hey, Arnesto."

As the two musicians stood up, Mike admonished his son, "Remember, we talked about this. Unless he tells you otherwise, it's, 'Mr. Modesto.'"

"Hey, Mr. Modesto," Preston said.

"Arnesto's fine," Arnesto said, shaking off his shock. This was beyond trippy.

"Well, there you go," Mike laughed. "Why don't you see if your mom needs help?" he told Preston, who ran by Arnesto. At least, it sure looked and sounded like Preston. "Thanks for helping us out like this," Mike said.

Arnesto became aware that Mike was now standing in front of him with his hand out. "No problem," he said as he shook Mike's hand. *I am taller than you, smarter than you, wealthier, arguably better looking…*

"How's the games industry?" Mike asked. "Still doing independent contracting?"

"Yeah, it's good. Same old, same old. Are you excited about your concert?"

"I am. We're playing in front of fifteen thousand people."

Big deal, I've SAVED more lives than that. "Wow, doesn't that make you nervous?"

"Terrified. But once people start cheering and especially once you get past the first few notes, it all goes away and becomes this amazing rush."

Alright, that does sound kind of cool. Man, I hate this guy. "I wish you luck."

"Thanks. Oh, I think I hear the stampede. Excuse me." Mike walked to the front of the house. Arnesto followed but caught Katrina in the kitchen.

"Never go anywhere without snacks," Katrina said. "I believe you taught me that."

"That sounds like me," Arnesto said. "So, Preston's quite the musician."

"Isn't he though?"

"I have to ask — has he been a difficult child? At all?"

"I never know where your questions come from, Arnesto. But you know what, he was a little difficult in the beginning." She grabbed a couple of bottled waters out of the fridge.

"What happened?"

"He just... grew out of it." She turned to leave but paused. "Oh, the music helped. One time Preston started to throw a tantrum, but then Mike strolled in strumming his guitar, and Preston was mesmerized. Since then, he and Mike have had this incredible bond over music. I think we're ready now, come say goodbye to everyone."

Of course. It was the music. Katrina and Arnesto had tried everything with Demon Preston except music. Preston must have inherited Mike's skill and passion for melody. How could they have known? Arnesto hadn't even known Preston wasn't his child.

Arnesto followed Katrina to the entryway as everyone else came bounding down the stairs and out the front door.

"Hi, Dad! Bye, Dad!" Melissa said.

"Father," Carlos said with a handshake.

"Don't ask," Katrina said, rolling her eyes. She gave Arnesto a quick peck on the cheek.

"Bye, Arnesto," said Preston or his amazing doppelganger.

"See you next week," Mike said, shutting the front door behind him.

Arnesto watched through the window as their car disappeared down the street then he stood there appreciating the silence. Afterward, he sat down on the couch where Froggy appeared out of nowhere to jump into his lap. Schmedley also appeared, but wanting his space, he settled into a spot on the top of the far end of the couch. The cats must've been spooked by everyone running around and packing.

Arnesto thought about Preston. The boy's entire other life was so much the worse for wear. And why? Because he had been raised by the wrong man. In his own unique way, Arnesto had been the one responsible for Other Preston's troubles. There's no way he could have known, but it was still depressing.

"It was the music, Froggy," he said, petting the cat whose loud purr made him feel a tiny bit better. "Why didn't you tell me?"

Stretching over the armrest so as not to disturb Froggy, Arnesto reached into his bag and pulled out his laptop to check his email. There he read one of the worst messages he had ever received.

It was from his old friend Kabir at Smiling Axolotl Games. Kabir wrote, "Hey, I'm going to be in the area visiting my brother in a couple weeks. Want to fire up the SNES and play some Squid Wars?"

His heart sank. The problem wasn't playing video games with Kabir. Arnesto always enjoyed that.

282

No, the problem was that Kabir was going to show up in two weeks and tell Arnesto that Hiromi, their fellow tester, died in a fire a week earlier.

Or one week from now.

Fire It Up

Katrina's House
Silicon Valley, California
Friday, August 26, 2011
Evening

THUS BEGUN the moral dilemma of whether Arnesto should once again risk everything to save one life. Fuck it, Hiromi was a real nice guy. Of course he had to try. The issue was how.

What could he remember from the funeral? Not much. Lots of sobbing, people saying, "I can't believe he's gone," over and over. It was nice, about as pleasant as such a tragic funeral can be. Hiromi had looked good, very peaceful. Actually, that was something that had surprised Arnesto. After finding out Hiromi had died in a fire, it had been something of a relief to find out his death had been from smoke inhalation instead of having burned to a crisp. Made it easier for everyone to say goodbye.

Wait, there had been a brunch a week or so later. A bunch of the old crew had decided to get together in Hiromi's honor. Somebody had said something about the fire happening at night, possibly a dryer fire while they slept. Hiromi's wife, Yokiko, had made it out in time.

He obviously hadn't.

Tracking down Hiromi's address was as easy as looking up Hiromi's current employer on LinkedIn and then covertly following him home that Monday. It was only a slightly bigger hassle finding a fireman's mask, but he secured one by Wednesday, and returned to Hiromi's house in the wee hours that Saturday morning.

Hiromi and Yokiko lived in a cul-de-sac in a modest, one-story home. It was nice that there weren't any stairs to worry about. As an added bonus, Arnesto found a place to park farther down the main road where he could keep an eye on the house. It was also in the opposite direction from where Hiromi was likely to drive.

Arnesto settled in and drank his coffee, not that he needed it. The stress of the situation already held his mind hostage. Was there no other, safer way of handling this scenario? Warn them anonymously? Might be ignored while potentially adding a murder investigation. What about breaking in, planting a bunch of extra-loud smoke detectors? Right, might as well turn himself in right now. Same with starting a fire while they were out. There were too many variables, and above all else, he couldn't break his cardinal rule: Do not. Get. Caught.

The hours crept by. Finally, around 7:30 in the morning, he saw the garage door open and Yokiko leave for work. The night was a bust. Great, now he had an extra day to fill himself with self-doubt and preemptive guilt. After he went to bed, of course.

Easier said than done. Though he was plenty tired, the extra caffeine was wreaking havoc on his system. He only slept a couple hours that morning, plus a brief nap early that afternoon that only seemed to make him feel even groggier. Before long, he found himself back in the same parking spot in the wee hours of Sunday morning.

There was one difference — he forgot his coffee this time.

Was there anything else he should have brought? An ax? A battering ram? Nah, they would only add suspicion and complicate things. *Keep it simple, stupid.* Too late now, anyway. Man, he was definitely not as coherent tonight as he was the night before.

Around three o'clock, Arnesto tilted the seat back so he could give himself an unobstructed stretch. He closed his eyes for a second, but that was a second too long.

Ugh, who was smoking a cigarette outside at this hour? He raised his seat and looked around but couldn't see anyone. A quick glance at the clock revealed it was 4:47. Wait, that's not right. He must've fallen asleep!

He immediately looked at the house. It appeared illuminated, but it sure didn't look like there were any lights on. "Shit!"

He reached under the passenger seat and grabbed the mask and bolted toward the house, putting the mask on as reached the driveway. "*Fire!*" he screamed but felt muffled due to the breathing apparatus. He lifted the mask off his mouth, not wanting to reveal his entire face, and yelled, "Hey, fire!" He kept yelling as he banged on the front door.

He didn't seem to be having much of an effect. What a great plan he had! Yelling and screaming at a door, pure brilliance.

The door wouldn't give when he tried kicking it in, either. Maybe another door would be less sturdy? The fire seemed to be coming from the left, so he ran around to the right. As he did so, he saw the neighbor's lights turn on. At least someone besides him was awake. "Fire, call 911!" he yelled at the neighbor's house before completely donning the mask.

The back door had a screen on it, which he opened before starting

286

to kick the door itself. It definitely felt flimsier. On the fourth kick, the door gave way, crashing inward. There was no fire at this end, but dark, thick smoke came pouring out of the doorway. It wasn't like on television; he could barely see anything.

He felt along the wall and entered the first doorway he found. The room was small, and he realized when he grabbed the plastic curtain that he had found the bathroom. He stepped back into the hallway.

The mask must have clouded up, it couldn't possibly be this dark. He lifted his mask off his face for a second hoping it would give him a better view of the hallway. Instead, it felt like he had set his eyes and throat on fire.

Coughing and holding his mask firmly against his face with one hand, he continued to feel around with his other. He found the next doorway on the other side of the hallway and went inside. He bumped into the bed and quickly felt around, but it felt unused. It must have been a guest bedroom.

He took one step back into the hallway when he felt something grab his ankle. He reached down and felt the back of Yokiko's head and shoulders. She was on her hands and knees.

"Hiromi, help me!" she yelled while coughing.

"Keep going!" Arnesto yelled back.

"Hiromi!"

"Straight ahead, keep going straight!" He felt her let go of his ankle.

He pushed ahead, getting on his own hands and knees. The next door on the left led to what felt like a big room. It was the garage. He felt around for the garage door opener, but it didn't work. So much for going out that way.

At last, he reached the master bedroom. Once inside, he felt the top of the bed and all around it, but Hiromi wasn't there. Arnesto returned to the hallway.

It was getting warmer and the fire was getting louder. And closer. The hallway opened up into what must have been the living room and kitchen area — the far end of which was already on fire. He felt around the living room, but still no Hiromi. The flames beat him back into the hallway.

I'm too late, he must be trapped in the fire. I need to get out of here. NOW. I'm sorry, Hiromi. I'm so sorry.

Arnesto passed by the master bedroom and the garage but then remembered that one detail: Hiromi hadn't been burned. He had died from smoke inhalation, so where was he?!

Of course. Arnesto crawled as fast as he could into the master bedroom, went past the bed, and found the doorway leading to the master bathroom.

Now it was his turn to grab an ankle.

Hiromi lay face down unconscious on the floor. Arnesto yelled and shook Hiromi's leg, but there was no response. His friend badly needed oxygen, but if he gave him his mask, there might be two dead bodies instead of one.

Arnesto found Hiromi's other ankle, then taking one in each hand, started dragging Hiromi out. He quickly reached the hallway and heard the crackling all around him — the fire was on top of them. He could also make out the sounds of muffled yelling for a moment before the sound of an unleashing firehose at the other end of the house drowned them out.

Staying low, Arnesto dragged Hiromi down the hallway, bumping into the walls along the way.

At last, they made it out of the house into the yard. Arnesto flipped Hiromi over, grabbed him by the wrists, and pulled him another thirty feet. He then took the mask off and put it on Hiromi as he knelt down beside him.

"Is there anybody else in there?!" a firefighter yelled at Arnesto.

"No, but this guy needs help!"

"Alright, we've got him," the firefighter said, waving someone over. Arnesto got up and started walking toward the street. The firefighter saw this and asked, "Where are you going? You might be hurt, we need to take a look at you."

"I'm just going to my car," Arnesto said, which was technically true, although he had no intention of returning.

He felt like a zombie as he drove home. Any relief about the mission being over was offset by the fact that it was such a spectacular failure. He stepped into the bathroom and had a momentary shock at the blackened ghoul staring back at him in the mirror. There was a clear line on his face showing where the mask had been. He instinctively reached for the faucet but knocked over his deodorant. He picked it up and put it down a little too hastily and it fell over again. This time he grabbed it and threw it at the bathroom wall so hard it broke into pieces, leaving a nice glob of deodorant on the wall, right next to a fresh dent. "FUCK!" he screamed.

Arnesto took a few deep breaths, coughing as he did so, then began washing his face. Realizing he needed a shower anyway, he stripped and put his smoky clothes in a garbage bag which he placed on the washer. He then jumped in the shower and stood under the water cursing himself.

* * *

"Did you hear what happened to Hiromi?" Kabir asked from the right side of Arnesto's couch, his thumbs rapidly hitting the buttons on the controller as their virtual squid attacked one another. This was the moment Arnesto had been dreading all week. Arnesto briefly looked at Kabir, who continued, "His house burned down."

"Did they...?"

"They both made it out."

Holy shit, he's alive! Oh my god, I can't believe it. I did it, Hiromi's alive! Arnesto struggled to maintain his composure. "Well, that's a huge relief."

"They said he was deprived of oxygen too long, though. He's got some brain damage."

No no no! Now Arnesto struggled to hide having the wind knocked out of him. "How bad is it?"

"He's lost some motor control and his speech is slurred somewhat. They don't know if he'll ever recover. He's still himself, though, minus the Elvis impersonations. He was joking around when I went to see him."

"Well, that's something," Arnesto said as his squid died, giving Kabir another point. He hit "Retry" and they continued their battle.

"Yeah. Oh, and this is kind of funny, but he has rug burns on his face. I guess some idiot fireman dragged him out face down by his feet. I took a selfie with him; if you want to pause, I can show you."

"No, that's okay."

Pattern of Abuse

Arnesto's Apartment
Silicon Valley, California
Friday, September 21, 2012
Late Evening

PAIGE'S FAVORITE THING in the world was music. She kept droning on about it in the dating site's chat window.

Arnesto didn't mind. It made her happy and want to be with him. He knew if he could repeat history, he and Paige would go out a few times, have a fun little fling, then she would realize how little they had in common and end it. No harm, no foul.

Almost no foul.

Paige commented on another pop star, talking about how much she liked her latest album. Unlike most of the names she mentioned, he had actually heard of this one, though all he knew was that this rich, famous, talented singer had gone back to her dickwad boyfriend, the one who had beaten the crap out of her a few weeks earlier.

His all-too-quick programmer fingers typed back, "Now *there's* a woman you know you can hit and get away with it." It was a lame joke and he felt bad. He felt even worse when he realized he had made the same joke in his previous life. Then he remembered what was coming next.

He began typing an apology, but this time, his fingers weren't fast enough. Her reply was already in the chat window. She politely told him that having been a victim of abuse herself, she didn't appreciate his comment and would he please not joke about it again. He agreed and apologized.

While he cursed himself for repeating his mistake, they returned to happier topics.

Still, he couldn't help but think something was about to go horribly wrong. Someone was about to be abused to the point where it would change their life forever.

He focused on Paige's profile pictures. Nothing. He reread her entire profile, blabbering on and on about this or that band. Still nothing. He felt sure they would have a fling, she would end it, and he would never hear from or about her again.

Maybe it wasn't her.

He typed in a response to let her know he was still paying attention, then opened the website again in a new tab which he dragged to his second monitor. There he went through all the women he could find: his matches, women whose profiles he had previously viewed, women who had previously viewed *his* profile (a much smaller list), every conversation. He felt sure the victim was a woman he had met through a dating site.

But she wasn't on this one. Or maybe she was and had hidden or disabled her profile by now. He had certainly altered the timeline enough. It was quite possible she had only been online a short while and he had been so busy changing the universe that he missed his window.

He and the victim hadn't had a long-term relationship, or he would have remembered her. Yet somehow he felt he had dated her and seen her again after they realized it wasn't going to work out. But where? He must have... run into her? Downtown? No, outside downtown. On a walk...

Many walks! The remaining puzzle pieces fell into place in an instant. And the final picture was awful.

Her name was Angela. They had indeed met online and gone out a couple times. For whatever reason, the spark wasn't there, so they didn't pursue the relationship any further.

Several months after that, Arnesto had signed on to work for a company called Super Rad Gamez on a project called *OMG Totally Fashion!* It wasn't a game he could brag about having worked on, but, ridiculous names aside, it was a good company. It was the first game company he worked for that had both competitive salaries *and* didn't force its employees into frequent hundred-hour work weeks during crunch mode. He always had one or the other, but never both at the same time. However, soon after Arnesto started there, the company had shut its doors. Knowing this and still enjoying retirement, Arnesto had decided it wasn't worth working for them in this lifetime.

But in his former life, while he had been there, the company had a group of around a half-dozen people who liked to take brisk walks at lunch. He joined them sometimes on their strolls through the park downtown. It was often during these times on their way back that they encountered another group from a different company — the one where Angela worked.

She had always been warm and friendly when they had passed each other. Sometimes they had smiled and waved; sometimes they had exchanged brief pleasantries. Even though that was the extent of it, she had eventually friended him on Facebook.

It was there that he had learned of her murder.

For him, it had started in the morning — the morning after the conversation he was now having with Paige. He had checked his Facebook page and saw that someone had posted a cryptic message on her wall. "I'm so sorry, Angela!" it read. At the time, Arnesto had thought little of it.

But when he checked again that night, he realized something horrible had happened. He saw more posts on her wall, dozens of them, all saying basically the same thing, how sorry they were. He finally found a post that told of the man who killed her.

The man had spent time in the psychiatric hospital for the criminally insane, it was discovered after the fact. He had gone through the system and gotten better, but then when he was released, he stopped taking the meds that kept him stable.

He and Angela went out a few times, but she wasn't interested and called it off, at which point he became her stalker. He showed up at her place uninvited asking her to take him back. When she threatened to call the police, he went to his car, grabbed his gun, went back to her house, kicked in the door, and shot her. Then he drove himself to a rest area and shot himself.

Arnesto's mind back in the present, he knew he had precious little time to act.

He apologetically ended his chat with Paige and then tried to remember whatever he could about Angela, or more specifically, where she lived. Her house was... dark blue? There was a rickety wooden fence on one side... or on both sides? He googled her and found several links, but nothing with her address or phone number on it. Only a work email, which, it being a Friday night, she probably wouldn't check until it was too late anyway. He would save that as a last resort.

He also scoured a map of the city. She lived in a small, confusing neighborhood near both the river and the railroad tracks. He had had trouble finding it back when Angela had given him the address and directions. It would be a greater challenge now. He grabbed a couple caffeinated power bars and a water bottle and headed out.

The neighborhood was still confusing, but smaller than he remembered; it only took him a few minutes more to find her place than it had the last time.

Amazing, I'm actually early for once.

Arnesto slowly drove by the house. The lights were out, but he could make out a flicker through one of the windows. He found a place to park around the corner where he could make out her driveway through the trees. After going over in his mind one last time what he wanted to say to her, he took a deep breath and got out of the car. He felt like a creeper as he walked through the poorly lit neighborhood, but he still made it to her front door and knocked.

The door opened, but instead of Angela standing there, it was a twelve-year-old boy with long hair — Angela's son, William. He looked up at Arnesto expectantly but didn't say anything.

"Hi, is your mom home?" Arnesto asked.

William shook his head. "She's at karate," he said.

"Do you know what time she'll be back?"

"Soon. I have to go, my show's on," William said, shutting the door.

"Wait," Arnesto said, but it was too late.

Now what? Do I try again? Do I tell him to warn her? He might not even know anything about her relationship with that crazy guy. Arnesto decided it was best to leave the kid out of it, and he walked back to his car.

He sat in his car and wondered: What time were things supposed to go horribly wrong? What would her reaction be when he told her she was in danger? Did his interaction with William throw a new wrinkle into the situation? Wait a minute, if she was at karate, maybe he could try to find her dojo and meet her there as she was leaving. In fact, she might be more willing to listen to a stranger in a public place surrounded by her martial arts friends than outside her own front door.

He picked up his phone to search for local karate studios when he saw headlights ahead. It was Angela pulling into her driveway.

He got out of the car and hustled over, but by the time he reached the end of her driveway, she was already inside. Again he knocked on her door. This time, she was the one who opened it.

"Yes?" Angela asked. It's always an odd thing running into someone you used to know in a previous lifetime. He thought he detected a certain amount of fear in her eyes, but then, he was a strange man knocking on her door at night.

"Hi, Angela?" Arnesto asked in a soft voice, hoping William wouldn't be able to hear. "I just need ten seconds to talk to you about a certain ex who may have been bothering you lately. May we speak privately?" He stepped back and gestured toward her driveway. He thought she was going to agree but saw her look past him.

"Angela? Who's this?" asked the man walking up the driveway.

"Dale, what are you doing here? You can't just show up at my place—"

"I said, 'Who's this?!'" Dale said, sizing up Arnesto as he approached at a pace that only added to Arnesto's discomfort.

296

"Dale. This is my neighbor, Bob. I'm holding a package for him. Bob, come in," Angela said. Arnesto felt a tug on his shirt and realized he was "Bob." He stepped inside her home. "Give us a minute," she said to Dale as she followed Arnesto inside, closing and locking the door behind her.

"Who are you and why do you want to talk to me about Dale?" she asked, looking Arnesto up and down before running off into a back room out of view.

"He's crazy."

"Duh," came her voice from the back of the house.

"He's off his meds, and he's got a gun in the car. If he gets upset, he will not hesitate to grab it and come back and kill you."

She reappeared, the fear in her eyes unmistakable. She paused for a second, then walked over and held out an empty box.

"What's this?" he asked.

"Your 'package.' Don't let him see that it's empty or that your name isn't on it." Arnesto wished he could think so well on his feet. She always was brilliant. "Dale's a psycho, but he's never gotten violent," she clarified.

Arnesto tucked the box under his left arm with the top facing him so it would be concealed. "Not with you, yet. But he's tried to kill an ex before and thankfully was unsuccessful. My car's around the corner. Can we sneak out the back?"

"And go where?"

"Anywhere. The police station. We can call 911 on the way," Arnesto said.

"I'm sorry, this is too weird," she said, shaking her head. "It's not that I don't believe you, but I don't know you. You're not giving me any evidence, and you won't even tell me your name."

"I was trying not to get involved. I just want to keep you alive."

"Angela!" Dale yelled from outside.

Angela grabbed Arnesto's arm and turned him toward the door. "Thanks for the warning, but I can handle Dale. I promise I'll call the police at the first hint of trouble." She reached for the doorknob, but then Arnesto put his hand on the door.

"Wait, what does he drive?" She removed her hand and looked at him, wondering if she should tell him. "I want to get his license plate number. Just in case."

"He drives a gray Honda Civic. I don't know where he parked it. I didn't see it as I drove in."

Arnesto smiled. "Thank you. Good luck tonight. Do *not* underestimate him." He opened the door and stepped out. He gave Dale a quick nod as he walked by, keeping eye contact to an absolute minimum. He didn't hear anything as he walked down the driveway. Dale must have been waiting for him to leave.

He finally heard her door shut and turned around. Nobody was there. She must have invited him inside. *Goddammit.*

Arnesto walked back to his car and studied his map. He now had plenty of exit routes as well as a few possibilities for where Dale's car might be. Sure enough, he found the car a few streets over. He then consulted the map again to find a spot to park his own car around the corner from Dale's car. He grabbed a piece of string and a wire hanger he brought along for the occasion and walked back to the Civic. Then he walked around the car checking its locks and peering inside, but he didn't see the gun.

Trying not to appear conspicuous, he fashioned a loop about

halfway down the length of string then realized the car didn't have the type of lock that would open with that trick. He pocketed the string, then unbent the hanger and with great effort, managed to get it inside over the top of the front passenger side window.

However, try as he might, he could not get the hanger to unlock the door. How long had he been at it now? Five minutes? Ten? Screw it, he didn't have time for this.

He went back to his own car and opened the trunk, looking for something he could use. There didn't appear to be much. Some remnants of kitty litter he spilled that one time, a first-aid kit, a blanket, an ice scraper left over from his Massachusetts days… Finally, he lifted the carpet at the bottom to reveal the spare tire underneath. Apparently, his car came with a tire iron.

He hid the tire iron up his sleeve and crept back to Dale's car. There was still no sign of Dale or anybody else. He walked as nonchalantly as he could up to the passenger door, took the tire iron in his left hand and backhanded the window. It didn't break. He tried again, harder. It still wasn't enough. Tossing the tire iron to his right hand, he wound up and swung as hard as he could. Finally, the window shattered.

He didn't even bother opening the door, instead going straight for the glove box. He knew he shouldn't have been surprised to see it, but he flinched when he saw the gun sitting there on top of some papers. He carefully grabbed it by the handle, picked up the hanger which had fallen to the ground when he smashed the window, and hustled back to his car.

Not believing he was being followed, he put the items in his trunk and started driving away. He smiled, but he couldn't help feeling his job was not yet done. *I did it, I'm free and clear. Why can't I leave? Damn.*

He pulled over and looked at the map again. He found a spot where he could see Dale's car, but far enough down the street that Dale wasn't likely to spot him. He didn't know what would come first: Dale, an angry neighbor, or sirens (either because of Dale's actions or his own break-in). He did some breathing exercises while he waited.

At last, Dale appeared, walking quickly around the corner. It looked like he was cursing to himself as he stormed toward his car. When he realized his car had been broken into, he became visibly irate, waving his arms around as he paced back and forth. He even kicked the car a couple times.

Arnesto was really hoping Dale would give up and leave. Instead, Dale opened the trunk, got something out, and slammed the trunk shut. He started storming back to Angela's house when Arnesto realized what it was.

Dale had his own tire iron, of course.

Shit! Arnesto may not have prevented Angela's death after all. He had only changed the murder weapon while making the murderer even angrier. *Good job.*

Arnesto jumped out of the car and opened his trunk as fast as he could. *This is so fucked,* he thought as he grabbed the gun. He shut his trunk then sprinted as fast as he could after Dale.

When he was in sight of the house, Dale was already there, trying to kick the front door in. The door was starting to give. Arnesto knew Angela would be calling 911 if she hadn't already, but he also knew there was no time. He had to intervene.

"Dale!" Arnesto yelled as he slowed to a walk, the gun in his hand hanging at his side.

Dale turned to Arnesto. "That's my gun!" he said, walking the same

300

angry walk straight at Arnesto.

Arnesto stopped halfway across the street. He raised the gun and cupped it in his left hand, pointing it at Dale. "Dale, stop! Get down on the ground! I'm making a citizen's arrest!"

Without the slightest hesitation, Dale started running at Arnesto.

What the...?! Oh, right, he's crazy. "Fuck!" Arnesto yelled, as he turned and ran back down the street where their cars were parked.

Their running speeds were close, but Arnesto's legs were a little longer, he was in slightly better shape, and the pure fear he felt gave him the extra oomph he needed to start pulling away from Dale.

Arnesto realized he was one good tire iron throw away from being knocked out or worse. *Then Dale would have the gun again.* He briefly considered taking out Dale's tires but decided under the circumstances it would be best to unload the bullets into the brush on the side of the street. Arnesto fired. The noise was deafening as one shot after another went into the ground.

It wasn't until he was a short ways past Dale's car that Arnesto decided to look behind him. Dale was way back, still coming at him, but only at a fast walk. Dale stopped as they both saw the flashing police cruiser pass by their street as it approached Angela's house. Dale turned back to Arnesto and pointed behind him toward the house while he shouted something, but Arnesto's ears were ringing too loudly to hear what he said.

Arnesto said nothing but flipped him off.

Dale turned and started walking back toward the house. He realized that Dale's shouting must've been a threat to turn Arnesto into the cops. *Are you kidding me?! What, is he going to tell them? That I stole the gun he was going to use to murder Angela? Whatever. The police can handle it from here.*

Arnesto made it back to his own car, got in, and went home exhausted. It had been a long night full of violence and potential long-term hearing loss. He would anonymously deliver the gun to the police the next day.

When he woke up the next morning, first he checked his phone. No messages. Then he opened his front door. No police holding a warrant with his name on it.

Next, he checked Facebook. Nothing on his wall out of the ordinary. Just the usual nonsense posts from friends, including the myth about entering your PIN backward to thwart would-be muggers at the ATM.

After a quick search, he found Angela's page. Though a little disappointed her profile was still public to strangers like him, he was definitely relieved to see she was still alive and well. "Nothing like gunshots and the psycho ex bashing in your front door in the middle of the night to give you a heart attack," she posted. There were, of course, myriad comments from her friends concerned about her welfare. Angela answered many of the questions. Yes, she was definitely going to get a restraining order, for whatever good that would do. Yes, the police took the bad guy away. Yes, she and William were fine. No, she couldn't explain the gunshots she heard while she was busy frantically getting William out the back. Nor could she explain the mysterious stranger who had tried to warn her.

Arnesto was happy for the anonymous shout-out.

Finally, he remembered to check his online dating profile. There was a message from Paige, which read, "You disappeared kind of quickly last night. I think you're a really nice guy, but I don't think we'd make a good match. I wish you luck in your future dating endeavors."

And to think, his former self dated this chick! Whatever.

The Wrong Date

Kelley Park
San Jose, California
Saturday, November 17, 2012
8:56 p.m.

ARNESTO DIDN'T HAVE an extensive romantic background. He dated even less than his former self, since, of the small number of women willing to go out with him, he had already met some of them. No point in having another awkward first date with someone when you knew it wasn't going to lead anywhere.

That said, he did manage to date a new person every once in a while.

That's how he met Evelyn, a chipper go-getter several years younger. She was one of the rare women to contact *him* through the dating site first. She didn't have a picture posted, but she sounded like fun, so they agreed to meet for a walk through the park.

It was an excellent choice. It turned out Evelyn loved that sort of thing, maybe because it was a way to release some of her extra energy. She loved Mexican, too, so that's where they went on their second date. The conversation started off well, revealing they had a bunch in

304

common. Arnesto was beginning to feel a hint of chemistry.

But then she had to bring up the subject of work.

"So you're not working now, but you do a little contracting every now and then?" she asked.

"That's correct." He was almost finished with his enchiladas.

"What do you do with all your free time?"

"I play video games and watch movies and… stuff." He personally had no problem with his lifestyle, but it sounded a little embarrassing to say out loud.

"Do you travel?"

"I get around. When I need to." He did travel, though he didn't care for it. It was always stressful, and people constantly died almost everywhere he went.

"I'm having a hard time wrapping my head around this," she said. "I have two jobs, I'm interviewing for another job to replace one, I'm taking classes on the side, and I still feel like I'm not doing enough."

Uh oh.

She went on, "I don't mean to be rude, but I find your *complete* lack of ambition very unattractive." Did she have to emphasize the word, "complete?" Guess it was better than emphasizing "unattractive."

He paid the bill. She thanked him. They sat in awkward silence, and Arnesto realized it was time for a Hail Mary.

"So, what now, Netflix and Chill?"

"I only watch Netflix when I'm depressed," she said. First of all, that wasn't what he meant, but to be fair, the term hadn't been perverted yet. Second of all, who does that? He knew she would never be the one he could cuddle with on the couch watching a movie every night. "I need to go home," she said.

They walked out and she got in her car before he could even offer her a handshake. As he drove home, he wondered how someone with all he had to offer could have such bad luck dating. Then again, what did he have to offer? Lies? Secrecy? Low confidence and a *"complete* lack of ambition"? But he must have some good qualities. He hit it off with women like Katrina and... Rochel. He missed Rochel.

As he parked and walked to his door, he wondered where she was and what she was doing right then. Apparently, she was sitting outside his door waiting for him. Rochel saw him approach, gave him a slight smile, and stood up.

"Hi," she said.

It took him a second to get over the shock of seeing her. "Hi."

She looked him up and down and said, "You're ever so slightly dressed up. Were you on a date?" He nodded. "How'd it go?" He opened his mouth to speak but couldn't find the words. He was nervous seeing her again. Rochel laughed, "That well, huh?"

"I don't expect to hear from her again."

"Her loss. Arnesto, I need your help. Can I come in?"

They went inside and sat down. "Can I get you anything to drink?"

"Hot chocolate?" she asked.

"S-sure." *Who the hell asks for hot chocolate?* he thought. As he walked into the kitchen, he said, "Given your drink choice, this conversation is neither going to be brief nor serious, correct?"

He peeked out at her. She gave him a knowing grin in return but didn't respond.

He brought out a hot chocolate and gave it to her.

"Where's yours?" she asked.

"I don't want one."

"I wanted you to have one so it would make you more agreeable. Here, have some of mine." She held out her cup.

"No thanks."

"Arnesto, please, it's important."

"Fine." He took the cup and drank a couple sips. "Mmm, good. So, what—"

"My cancer's back. Don't drink all of it," she said, taking the cup back from him.

"What?! I'm sorry, I didn't know."

She took some sips of her own. "I know you didn't. It's okay. Ooh, that is good. See? Aren't you glad I didn't ask for water? What are you doing?" She noticed him closing his eyes.

"Let me think."

"No, Arnesto, it's okay—"

He shook his head. "We changed history when we saved you. Rochel, you, how do I say this, you never made it this far. I can't remember anything that might help at this point."

"I know. It's okay. Arnesto, there's nothing you can do. There's nothing *anyone* can do. I'm dying from cancer, but I've accepted it, and I hope you can, too."

"How long?"

"Maybe five months."

He winced and covered his mouth.

She put down the cup and grabbed his hands. "Arnesto, look at me. I'm okay. Well, emotionally. Not physically, *obviously*."

Was she joking?! "Could you hand me the hot chocolate?" he asked. He needed it now.

"Right?" she said, handing him the cup. "Hot chocolate is perfect for a conversation like this."

"So, if I can't help you, then how can I... help you?"

"Ugh, I feel sleazy for even having to ask, but you know my insurance won't cover nearly all my medical costs. So, yeah, I'm doing the gold digger thing."

"Money, of course. Yes, whatever you need."

"You're wonderful, Arnesto. I can't thank you enough. But there's more. Do you know why I broke up with you?"

"Because you're an idiot?" He was lashing out, but he wasn't angry at her, he was mad at the cancer. It was only her upbeat attitude that kept him from losing it altogether.

"Because I was afraid. Afraid of you, afraid of your memories, afraid of your lies."

"And?"

She sidled up next to him so that their legs were touching and rubbed her hand through his hair. "I'm not afraid anymore."

"You want to get back together."

She nodded. "If you'll have me. I should warn you, though, I'm not into long-term relationships."

"My god, you should leave the jokes to me."

"No, I'm dying, I can do what I want. Like this." She climbed on top of him and started kissing his neck, but then stopped. "One thing, though, no more lies, unless absolutely necessary. There's no more need, right? So if you have anything you want to tell me, sooner would be better than later."

"Agreed." They began kissing and caressing each other more heavily, and she introduced him to her replacement breasts. He whispered in her ear, "You know, despite the fact that our time together was so short, or perhaps because of it, you always were my favorite wife."

She tensed. "We were married?!"

He nodded, unsure of how she would react next. "We only did it so you could get on my health insurance, which isn't an issue this time."

She shook it off. "Whatever, tell me later. Take off your pants."

Breathless

United States
Late 2012 - Early 2013

ARNESTO TOOK ROCHEL on a whirlwind tour around the country, crossing items off her bucket list faster than she could add them. They ate exotic foods and stayed in luxurious hotel rooms. They golfed at Pebble Beach and mini-golfed at the Mall of America. They skated in Rockefeller Center and took a Segway tour around the nation's capital, catching the tail end of President Obama's second inaugural address. They saw *Spider-Man: Turn Off the Dark* on Broadway and Cirque du Soleil's *O* in Las Vegas. They watched from the stands as the Ravens edged out the 49ers in Super Bowl XLVII — once the power outage ended. They even made it to the Carolinas Aviation Museum in Charlotte to see what was left of the aircraft that had dumped them in the Hudson.

Until now, Arnesto had always shunned travel, seeing it as nothing more than a way of getting someplace he needed to be. Thanks to her, he remembered being much older and wishing he had seen more sights when he was able. He never imagined he could have this much fun.

When the list began running low, at his suggestion and after much

310

discussion, they decided to visit her extended family in Ireland.

She would never leave the country.

When they arrived, they received what to Arnesto felt like a hero's welcome — upward of a dozen relatives were waiting at Rochel's aunt's house, elated to see their little Rochie again and grateful to Arnesto for bringing her there.

Any misgivings Rochel had had about seeing her relatives vanished with their friendliness and hospitality. Had she been wrong about her immediate family back in the States? When that subject was broached, her aunts' and uncles' collective, profanity-laced tirade assuaged her fear. Arnesto heard phrases like, "bleedin' thick gobshite pox wagon," that he tried to file away in his brain for later use. Arnesto and Rochel had never laughed so hard together; she had tears streaming down her face.

At long last, Rochel had a real family again.

When the conversation turned more somber, the family insisted they stay "until the end" so that everyone could help take care of her. Though she didn't need it then, a few weeks later, Rochel started showing symptoms of decline. To her pleasant surprise, she learned she could have an eco-friendly funeral with a non-religious ceremony. She even picked out a beautiful willow casket in which to be buried in the family plot. However, to prevent any future turmoil with her relatives back in the States, she chose to protect her Ireland family by being cremated with her ashes spread around her aunt's garden. They did keep an urn with some decoy ashes in it to use as a peace offering should the need arise. As per Rochel's wishes, they agreed not to inform her immediate family until six months after she had passed, and they were also not to mention Arnesto. They knew Rochel's family would only come knocking if they thought they had money to inherit. *Such gobshites.*

Rochel's condition continued to deteriorate. Just over a month later, while surrounded by loved ones, she turned to Arnesto at her side, smiled, and said, "Thank you, Arnesto. I had a *grond* time." She then closed her eyes and slipped away.

The autopsy revealed that Rochel's cause of death was a tiny tumor on her pancreas that had spread atypically to her breasts, lymph nodes, and elsewhere. Nobody had made a mistake. It would be twenty years before medicine would be able to catch something as unlikely as that. Maybe if Arnesto had ordered the autopsy the first time she died… No, he couldn't even blame himself as he hadn't even considered time travel until many decades later. He felt too empty and numb for it to matter anymore.

* * *

When Arnesto returned to the states, his father was happy to pick him up at the airport. Since the events of 9/11 never happened, Karl was allowed through security and was waiting for him at the arrival gate outside customs. They gave each other a quick hug, then started the long walk toward the parking structure.

"What were you doing in Ireland anyway? Was this a game thing?" Karl asked.

"No, I was there for a girl."

Karl nudged him with his elbow. "What, couldn't find a date in America?" Arnesto couldn't help smiling at the dad joke. "So where is she? Do I get to meet her?"

Arnesto did his best to hide his pain. "We're not together anymore."

"I'm sorry to hear that."

"Nothing I haven't been through before."

"At least you got to see some of the world. I know you're not big on adventure. Actually, I'm glad you got into computers. It's nice not having to worry about you being in a profession that's unsafe. I was walking around the airport while I was waiting for you and saw a plaque down that way." He pointed toward the next concourse over. "What was his name, Roy something… Ray! Ray Carroll. The plaque didn't say much, just that he was a valued member of the security team who died in the line of duty. I mean look around." He waved his arm around the airport. "Seems like a safe place to work. But what do I know? You can't even go fishing without worrying about cars."

Arnesto furrowed his brow. "What?"

"Didn't you hear? This was a while back. Your aunt's boyfriend C.J. was in some fishing contest down south when the highway bridge above them collapsed. C.J. and his partner had just boated under the bridge seconds earlier."

"Whoa!" Arnesto was surprised. He hadn't known C.J. had been that close to the barge accident.

"At least that's how he tells it. You know how fishermen exaggerate. Anyway, only one car fell into the water. Seems there was a lull in traffic at just the right time."

When they reached the house forty minutes later, Arnesto felt relieved to be back home and able to spend some quality time with his dad. It was something he took for granted in his first life, and he knew there weren't going to be many more opportunities like this.

"I'm sure you're going to be awake a while yet, but it's past my bedtime," Karl said. "I have plans Monday and Tuesday during the day, but otherwise I'm free. You know where your bedroom is and where the remotes are, though I have no idea what's on these days. Oh, Monday's the Boston Marathon, so that's something to watch."

"Yes, I've actually been waiting for the marathon for some time."

On the Run

Boston, Massachusetts
Monday, April 15, 2013
10:15 a.m.

BEANTOWN. HOME to some of the country's most irate drivers and the country's oldest marathon. April 15, 2013. Patriot's Day, aka Marathon Monday. Arnesto pushed his way through the crowd near the finish line.

He tried to look excited in order to blend in, but being jostled around by a mob wasn't his idea of fun even when there *weren't* bombs present.

As was often the case when he couldn't remember a niggling little detail like the exact time of the explosions, he had arrived way early. Now he had nothing to do but wait. Wait and try not to look suspicious. He lingered toward the back of the crowd, able to keep an eye out for the suspects while appearing to watch the race. He also took note of the police nearby.

Once the initial anxiety began to wear off a little, he almost started to enjoy himself. It *was* exciting. He was right near the end of a 26.2-mile course that many had trained for months to attend. It was something he himself would never attempt, of course. He was starting to feel the effects of middle age and besides, he liked his joints too much.

Then he remembered why he was there. He vividly remembered the recording looking back from just beyond the finish line. It showed runners finishing then all of a sudden, BOOM, an explosion on the right side from behind the stockade which was itself behind a line of national flags.

Not this time. Not if he could help it.

He hung out in one spot for a while, then moved further down Boylston Street and back. He moved whenever he felt he had been in one place too long or when he found himself too close to someone smoking or shaking a cowbell. The hours crawled by. He spent more time watching the marathon than some of the runners spent running it. And with time came his old enemy, self-doubt.

Did he have the right marathon? It was definitely the right city. Like it did to so many other Bostonians, this attack felt personal. Was it the right year? Yeah, it had to be. Right event, right place, right date. The only unknown was when exactly it would happen. *Shouldn't it have happened by now?* Maybe something had changed. Maybe somehow he had prevented this. After all, it wasn't far from where he, the epicenter of alternate timelines, had grown up.

Right, wishful thinking. Either way, he couldn't leave. Just in case.

He began walking even further west down the street when he caught a glimpse of exactly what he was waiting for.

A white hat.

He couldn't see the wearer yet but could tell he was heading his way.

Arnesto quickly found a place to stop and observe. Mere seconds later, his view of White Hat became unobstructed. He fought off a chill as he immediately recognized the young man's face as he had remembered it from *Rolling Stone*. The magazine had put White Hat on the cover after he was caught, creating much controversy. As nonchalantly as he could, Arnesto dialed 911.

"Nine-one-one, this call is being recorded, what city?" the responder asked.

"Boston."

"One moment."

After a few seconds, another responder answered. "Hi, what's the emergency?"

"Hi, can you patch me through to Officer Maris?" Arnesto asked, recalling the name of an officer he had taken note of earlier. "He's working at the finish line of the Boston Marathon right now. This is an emergency."

"What's happening? Is there something I can help you with?"

"No, I can only talk to Maris, Officer Maris, can you put me through?" Arnesto realized he sounded strained. Maybe that was a good thing. The clock was ticking.

"I'm afraid I can't do that, but I can give you the number of his station."

"Uh, sure." Arnesto got the number and hung up. He then dialed the station. The person who answered asked how they could direct his call.

"I need to talk to Officer Maris, who is at the Boston Marathon finish line, right now. It's an emergency."

"One moment."

Finally, he was getting somewhere.

The phone rang a couple times before answering. "You have reached the voicemail of—"

"Fuck!" Arnesto mumbled to himself as he hung up. He paused for a moment then dialed 911 again. He didn't have a choice; there was nothing he could do on his own. They answered with the same response; Arnesto cringed on the word, "recorded."

White Hat passed his location, following a guy in a black hat with a similar backpack. Arnesto suddenly remembered. It wasn't a "he;" it was a "they." Of course, White Hat's older brother.

"What's the emergency?"

"There are two young men in black and white ball caps carrying bombs in backpacks walking east down Boylston toward the finish line of the marathon. They're crossing Fairfield now."

"Did you say, 'bombs?'"

"That is correct."

"And how do you know this, Sir?"

Seriously? "I overheard them talking a minute ago. One of them said, 'Drop the backpack in the crowd, walk away, then we'll set them off.' Oh, and something about, 'Allahu akbar?'" None of this was true, but it wasn't crying wolf if there actually *were* wolves — Islamic extremist wolves with bombs no less. "One's going to explode about fifty yards down, by Marathon Sports, the other, about a block west. Black ball cap with shades, white ball cap, backward, hair sticking out. Hurry, I'm getting the hell out of here."

"Sir, you need to stay on the li—"

Arnesto hung up. He went to break his phone under his sweatshirt but realized it might still be useful. It had taken the FBI several days and countless man-hours to catch the murderers, who had killed another

318

cop during that time. Maybe Arnesto could take pictures of the murderers and tip off the feds, speeding up their investigation and saving an officer's life. He decided to pursue.

When the brothers split up, Arnesto stayed with White Hat. Easier to follow, and there were a lot more police officers at the finish line where Black Hat was going.

White Hat stopped and joined the crowd, while Arnesto found a spot away from the street where he could keep an eye on him. He didn't like being so close to explosives, but he tried to take solace in the fact that this wasn't a suicide mission for the brothers.

White Hat began talking on his phone with someone. Who was he talking to? Was it his brother changing their plans? Arnesto had no idea if this was supposed to happen. The call ended and the suspect appeared to be dipping down. He was sliding off his backpack!

Instinctively, Arnesto walked straight toward him. *What am I doing?! No, I'm safe as long as I stay with him. I've got to help. I've got to try.*

Arnesto got a few feet away when the first bomb went off down the street. Like everyone else, he turned in shock and horror. Well, almost everyone else. When he turned back, he saw White Hat pushing his way through the crowd.

Arnesto grabbed the backpack. "Hey, you forgot your..." he shouted, putting on a show as he opened it up. One quick peek inside at the pressure cooker bomb was all he needed. When the FBI examined all the videos later, he would hopefully look like he was trying to do the right thing.

"Bomb!" he yelled, grabbing the top of the backpack with his right hand while pushing people away with his left. "Get away!" He threw the backpack as far and high up as he could over the barrier into the street. A few interspersed marathon runners would suffer far fewer casualties than a crowd. Hopefully.

He turned into the crowd, shouting, "Go! Go! Go!" as he brought his arms up to cover his own head. It was hard to move with so many people there. Still, there should be enough time. He realized he actually had no idea how far apart the blasts were. He had no idea they were only thirteen seconds apart. At least, they had been the last time. This time around, his interference by alerting the cops had, as it turned out, alerted Black Hat, speeding things up slightly.

He didn't feel the blast when it knocked him and everyone else around him to the ground.

At first, he couldn't hear anything, but soon heard a loud ringing and nothing else. There was white smoke all around.

As the ringing turned to screams and chaos, Arnesto realized he was unhurt, though he was shaken. He didn't know if there were casualties, but he didn't *want* to know. Not yet. Slowing getting to his feet and discovering he could walk, he knew there was still more he could do. Not tending the wounded, there were plenty of people to do that. No, it was more important to capture the suspects.

He took off in a run. It didn't take long to see White Hat intermittently walking and jogging ahead of him. Man, he wanted to tackle that guy and beat the shit out of him. But no, that wouldn't work for Arnesto for a multitude of reasons. Instead, he walked behind White Hat until they got to an intersection. Then, knowing which way he was going for at least the next block, he ran past him to the next intersection as fast as he could. He then turned around, phone at the ready, and started taking pictures in the general direction of the bombing, making sure the bomber was in the scene, while hoping not to arouse the bomber's suspicion. After White Hat passed, Arnesto looked through the photos, found a couple good ones that clearly showed the bomber's face, and sent them to the FBI.

He included the message, "White hat. It was him and his brother in the black hat. Get these assholes."

Finally, he destroyed the phone.

Building Violation

Dhaka District
Bangladesh
Saturday, April 20, 2013
Afternoon

BANGLADESH was a beautiful, verdant country. The heat and humidity were not unlike Massachusetts in the summer. After nearly being exploded in Boston, Arnesto felt he should probably get away for a little while, in case the feds were looking for the guy who threw the bomb. How could he have been so stupid?

He had another reason for coming to Bangladesh. It was because of something a coworker had said a couple days from now in his former life. He couldn't remember the exact words, but it was something like, "All those people died in that factory, but the media still won't shut up about the Boston Marathon."

Upon arriving, he paid the rickshaw driver and looked up at his target: Rana Plaza, an eight-story, dilapidated eyesore. Soon, it would be collapsing, with or without Arnesto's help.

He walked around it a few times, surveying the outside of the building. Points of entry, points of exit, and possible escape routes lead the list of which he made a mental note. Finally, he went inside.

He was surprised to see several shops — all he remembered of the place was that it was the site of one of the worst factory disasters in history. The factories were on the upper floors, including several floors built without a permit — in a building not intended for factory use — made from substandard materials — built on a pond. It's a wonder the building lasted as long as it did.

The shops were small and didn't appear to have many hiding places. Though the people were friendly to him, he was clearly a foreigner, and this made him feel even more conspicuous. His plan had been to hide somewhere until everyone went home for the night, but it was starting to look like he might have to break in after hours.

He almost didn't notice the camera crew until he was on top of them. After putting some distance between them and himself, he observed from behind a couple of other observers who had gathered. He couldn't figure out what they were recording, but the camera seemed aimed at the wall. Then he saw them.

Cracks. They were recording cracks in the wall. Cracks big enough to make one call a film crew. Had he missed them on his first pass or had they appeared since his arrival? One thing was certain — he was in the right place.

Someone ordered an evacuation soon after. Though it was unexpected, it gave him the opportunity he needed. Acting like he was supposed to be there, he alternated between directing evacuees and working his way upward. Eventually, he made it to the fifth floor, where he was able to sneak inside one of the now-deserted factories. He took note of his surroundings.

There were rows upon rows of sewing machines with some supplies scattered by the walls. At one end of the building were a couple of small offices while at the other end there was a generator. Behind the generator were a couple of small gas containers, while off to the side were a few large laundry carts that didn't look like they were being used.

With the building evacuated, this might be the perfect moment to bring it down. He walked over to the window and looked out, then immediately changed his mind as he ducked down. *Right, evacuated doesn't mean sent home, it means evacuated to right outside the building.* He cautiously raised his head to look out the window and saw roughly two thousand workers gathered a few stories below on the ground outside. *Can't exactly commit arson then run out the building in front of a few thousand eye witnesses. Besides, they're too close, they'll still get hurt.* He turned his gaze toward the entrance in time to see a few men in construction helmets enter the building.

He slunk down again, deciding to wait until the inspection team went back out. After a long wait, he heard what sounded like crowd movement, so he again peeked out the window. For once, history was on Arnesto's side. The workers were being sent home.

The building was his. There was no security, at least none that he saw, and there were no cameras watching the place. There also weren't any smoke detectors or sprinklers. Sure, this would help him in his pursuit of arson, but he needed to make it *big*. What good would one little fire do if people still showed up to work the next day, only to have the building collapse on top of them?

Looking over at the generator, he decided to step up his game. He lifted the first gas tank and shook it. Empty. He lifted the second gas tank but didn't shake it. There was half a gallon of gas inside. It would have to do.

324

First, Arnesto made sure he could, in fact, escape. The door leading out to the stairwell locked from the inside. From there it would be a cinch to run down the stairs and out a side door at the bottom. He couldn't access the other factories or shop levels, but if the fire was big enough, he wouldn't need to.

Second, he formed a makeshift fuse out of fabric and apparel. Unscrewing the gas cap on the generator, he stuck one end of the fuse inside while the rest continued down the side of the generator then along the floor between two rows of sewing machines. He then moistened the fuse with gasoline from the container.

Finally, he removed a lighter from his pocket and lit the far end. It took a moment, but the flame caught. He watched for a bit to make sure it progressed, then felt satisfied. He hurried out the door and down the stairs, then nonchalantly walked outside and away from the building. As he looked back, he could barely make out a tiny flicker in the fifth-floor window.

After a few blocks, he again turned to look at the factory. Shouldn't he have heard something by now? What if the flame went out? Should he go back? He still had some hours of nighttime left, though he hadn't propped the doors open, so he'd have to risk breaking a window —

BOOM!

The explosion was so loud that it scared him half to death even from three blocks away. The explosion had not only sent the burning wreckage of the generator into the floor below, it had also blasted a hole in the floor above, causing *that* generator to fall through as well. With so much heavy machinery tumbling through substandard building materials barely strong enough to hold the weight to begin with, the whole building collapsed in on itself into a massive pile of burning debris and sewing machines.

It didn't hurt that the gas canisters had been nearly empty because they had been used to fill the generator after repeated power outages.

Arnesto made it back to his hotel to gather his belongings, then took a cab to the airport to get the earliest flight home. A day-and-a-half later, he walked into his apartment, dropped his bag, and fell exhausted onto his couch. His phone buzzed, but he didn't feel like talking to anyone. He only decided to answer it when he saw it was Pete. Good, Arnesto wanted to ask him about any fallout from the Boston bombings.

"Pete," Arnesto said as he answered the phone.

"Hello, Mr. Modesto," said a pleasant but firm female voice. "I'm sorry we had to approach you like this."

The hairs on the back of Arnesto's neck stood on end. "Who is this? Where's Pete?" he asked.

"Mr. Modesto, we have Peter Morgan in custody, and we'd like you to come in as well."

Mementos

Arnesto's Apartment
Silicon Valley, California
Sunday, April 28, 2013
Afternoon

ARNESTO FROZE. This was it. He always knew this day would come, but that didn't make it any easier. He covered the mouthpiece and took a deep breath.

"Mr. Modesto? I know you can hear me."

"Who is this?" he asked. He looked out a side window and noticed a sturdy-looking man in a suit standing across the street. He looked out another window and saw another suit standing by a tree.

"We're not hiding from you, Mr. Modesto. We want to do this the easy way, and we know you do, too. In thirty seconds, you're going to hear a knock on your door, or you can come out on your own." The female voice was starting to sound more firm and less pleasant.

Arnesto looked around the apartment for answers, but his possessions seemed inconsequential all of a sudden. He went to the door and looked out the peephole. He saw another suit standing by one of the cars in the parking lot. After a quick sigh, he opened the door and locked it from the outside before walking down the stairs.

"Thank you, Mr. Modesto," said the woman on the phone. Please walk over to the street. We have a limo waiting for you."

Arnesto looked at his car and saw another suit standing next to it and still another walking toward him on the sidewalk.

"There's even more of them that you *don't* see," the woman said. "I suggest you not make them pursue you." He agreed; escape was not a viable option. "We appreciate your cooperation. I'll see you in the limo." She hung up.

As he approached the road and the suits closed around him, a limo pulled up alongside them. One of the three suits opened the passenger door for him, and Arnesto got in. There were four more suits inside, one in each corner, and Arnesto had no choice but to sit between two of them in the back seat.

Arnesto tried to figure out who they were. They weren't the police or FBI; they hadn't shown him any identification. CIA? They looked American, at least. He probably wasn't being kidnapped by the KGB, and they definitely weren't ISIS or members of the Yakuza. But they were all stocky men. How dangerous did they think he was, and where was the woman from the phone?

The man on his immediate left said, "Thank you for not kicking and screaming."

As Arnesto turned to face him, he felt a prick on the right side of his neck and fell unconscious.

When he awoke, he was in a cell. He felt disoriented and a little nauseous, more from whatever they had given him than the anxiety. He tried to take note of his surroundings. There was nothing in his cell except for himself, his cot, and a small, metal toilet. His clothes were different now: he was in a gray t-shirt, gray sweatpants, and white boxers, but nothing else. None of the clothes were his. This made him shudder. He had neither socks nor shoes nor any other possessions.

His cell looked out at a wall. Pushing his face into the bars, he could tell by looking left his cell was at the end of a hall, but looking right, he could only see more wall. There was also a camera in a protective bubble in the ceiling just outside his cell; they could see everything.

As he walked around his cell barefoot, he became acutely aware of his footsteps. He realized they were the only thing he heard. He coughed and snapped his fingers to make sure he wasn't losing his mind. He heard these fine, but otherwise, the hallway was perfectly quiet. Perhaps he was alone in this hall.

"Hello?" he asked. "Hello?! Is anyone there?"

There was no reply. Maybe an apocalypse had happened, leaving him the only survivor. Nah, he would've remembered that. Where was he anyway? Was he even in the United States?

He sat down on his cot and waited.

While he still wasn't feeling well physically, he was surprised he felt as well as he did psychologically. As he reflected on this, it occurred to him that a huge source of his stress was gone. No more would he spend his days wondering if he was being watched or when he would be captured. It had happened. He had sacrificed himself in order to save many lives, and now it was over.

It had taken a cell to make him feel free.

He lay down with his head toward the camera — so as to give them less to look at — and waited some more.

After what felt like an hour, he heard a door open and footsteps come his way, so he sat up. His cell door opened and two guards appeared.

"This way, please," the female guard said.

They were wearing suits, which didn't give Arnesto much information about where he was, only that it probably wasn't the kind of place that had visiting hours. The guards didn't even put handcuffs on him, which meant they didn't consider him a physical threat.

They led him to an interrogation room where he sat down behind a table in an uncomfortable chair. Soon after, a man came in and sat in the chair opposite.

He wore a suit that looked brand-new and custom-fit to his athletic build. His hair had a fresh ivy-league cut with a seamless part on one side, not a single hair out of place. Arnesto noted it was a shade lighter than black, as if the gray was just beginning to appear while still blending in perfectly with the existing color. The man looked to be of Hispanic descent.

"Mr. Modesto, hello. Do you know who I am?" the man asked, staring intently at Arnesto.

Say nothing except to ask for a lawyer. No, too soon. Your only chance is to act like any other suspect. Play the game, but only as much as necessary.

"I'm sorry," Arnesto said, shaking his head.

"You don't know who I am. Come on, take a guess."

This is odd. What is he doing? Arnesto squinted his eyes a little and tried to remember, but came up empty.

"I'm sorry, I don't think I know who you are," Arnesto said.

The man relaxed a little and looked away. Arnesto thought he seemed disappointed. "Let me paint you a picture. A cashier approaches a table full of agents, tells them there's a phone call. A young agent walks over, picks up the receiver and has a very interesting conversation. He hears a hesitant voice tell him to listen to a tape he left

330

behind at the Dr Pepper museum."

Oh shit.

"Can you believe that was twenty years ago when you called me? Of course now you know who I am. I'm Agent Whiteside. It is so good to finally meet you in person. Tell me, Arnesto. May I call you Arnesto?" He looked back at Arnesto who nodded. "How did you not predict your capture? Don't you know everything?"

There was a silence as if Whiteside expected an answer, but Arnesto chose to take it as a rhetorical question. He looked at the mirror and wondered how many people were watching him from the other side. He then returned his eyes to Whiteside.

"Okay, Arnesto, you're not omnipotent. Nobody is, right? The difference is, there's nobody else on the planet that I know of that can predict the biggest earthquakes of an entire decade. How did you do it?"

Lawyer time? No, not yet. There's still a chance. Play dumb and don't give him anything, not a single microexpression out of line.

"I can't predict earthquakes," Arnesto said.

"You can't... anymore? But you could before?"

"I've never been able to predict earthquakes." Arnesto was grateful to be able to say that truthfully.

"A computer program then? Some advanced tectonic plate simulator? I've never heard of a simulator that good, though. No? What about a weapon? You have some sort of sonic weapon that can perform extraterrestrial shockwave lithotripsy? I hope not, you might decide to hit us with one right now, heh!"

What is he doing, putting on a show for his superiors? This is a big deal, he must be one of their best. You don't get to be top dog by showing off, so that's

331

not it. Is he building to something?

"Did God come to you? Tell you when these earthquakes were going to happen?" Whiteside asked.

This question didn't seem to be rhetorical, so Arnesto said, "God has never spoken to me."

"Come on, Arnesto, work with me. We know you're the source. You're the guy who gave the list of earthquakes to Father Martin. You did the right thing. You've saved countless lives. We want to work with you on this, we really do. But you understand, that kind of power is too much for one person. Can you imagine what would have happened to you if some other country got to you first?"

So I am still in America.

"I know who Father Martin is from the news. But I've never met him. I've never spoken to him or had contact with him in any way," Arnesto said.

"Alright," Whiteside said. Without taking his eyes of Arnesto, he signaled somebody behind the mirror.

A moment later, an agent walked into the room carrying a briefcase, which he then opened and began removing its contents, placing them on the table in front of Arnesto. Whiteside studied Arnesto as this was happening. The other agent then closed the empty briefcase and set it down next to the table before walking out of the room.

Don't look at the items, maintain eye contact. No, wait, an innocent person would naturally look down out of curiosity. Look at them, but do not look surprised. Only look confused if anything, and be consistent.

Arnesto looked down at the items. The first was an old, faded piece of paper. It was one of his flyers warning about rioters should the officers who beat Rodney King be acquitted. The moment he recognized

332

it, it felt like all the air had been sucked out of the room. He had to focus on his breathing to keep from revealing himself. He was still in control, but just barely.

The second item was a cassette tape. Somebody, not him, had written on it, "David Koresh: Burn the Children."

The next item was a picture of a crater in front of a destroyed semi.

"I couldn't find a big enough piece of the Ryder truck. Oh, these go together," Whiteside said, sliding the next item next to the picture. It was a receipt of the car Arnesto had rented when he had tried to chase down McVeigh.

After that was a heating tile.

"That's actually from the Space Shuttle Columbia. I'm particularly proud of that item. That was the one piece I thought I would never get. They were reluctant to loan it to me, but under the circumstances… Of course, a threat to national security as big as yourself has to take precedence over leaving some piece of debris in storage."

Next was a copy of the police report involving a rental truck with a flat tire parked at one end of the Santa Monica Farmers Market.

The next item was a burned logo that said, "Jee." The letter 'p' had been broken off. Arnesto immediately recognized it from the 2005 Glendale train crash.

"Remind me not to ask *you* for a ride anywhere," Whiteside said.

Arnesto wanted to scream. Or pass out. Or something, anything. This was all too much. Instead, he looked up at Whiteside, whose eyes betrayed his excitement.

"I want a lawyer," he said.

"C'mon, Arnesto, I was really hoping we could talk about this. I have so many questions—"

"I know my rights. I'm not saying another word without a lawyer."

"We analyzed your DNA while you were unconscious. Took a full body scan, too. I know you're human, so you're not going to melt my face or explode or anything. You probably would have teleported out of here by now if you could have. Right now, in here, I don't think you're dangerous. But out there, on your own, you are a threat to national security. I just don't know how you do it. How do you do it, Arnesto?"

Arnesto crossed his arms. The two sat there in silence, glaring at each other. Whiteside let out a sigh then stood up. "Well try again soon," he said, starting toward the door.

Two agents came into the room to escort Arnesto out.

Arnesto jumped up out of fear. "What are you doing?! I'm an American citizen, I have the right to legal representation!"

Whiteside spun around and walked up to Arnesto. "In here, you have no rights! What, you think you were brought in for stealing Granny's purse?! I have you at the scene of every major event since the Kennedy Assassination. And believe me, we double-checked that one, too. Look, like I said, I know you've saved lives, though if you had worked with us from the start, we could have saved a lot more. But I can't let you go out there and risk getting picked up and tortured for information by one of our enemies. Look at these, Arnesto," he said, motioning toward the items. "I can't even imagine what we've missed, what we *don't* know. Good intentions or not, you've put this country at risk. If I got you a lawyer, I wouldn't be able to let him leave, either. We both know that's not something you'd want."

Arnesto sized up the man in his face. At five-feet-ten, Whiteside was a couple inches shorter than Arnesto, half a dozen years older, and twenty pounds heavier, all of it muscle. He was fearless, intimidating, and in control, like any good alpha male. Arnesto, the nonviolent omega male, suspected Whiteside was the last guy he would ever want to mess with.

Whiteside nodded to the other agents, who began to move toward Arnesto, but Arnesto walked out on his own. Whiteside then turned to the mirror and said, "He's going to put up a fight. He's smart but vulnerable. It will take some time, but I'll break him."

Alliances

Pete's Law Firm
Massachusetts
Monday, April 29, 2013
7:30 a.m.

"ARNESTO'S AN IDIOT," Pete said.

"What makes you say that?" asked Agent Huntley, Pete's interrogator, a strict-looking woman with all the charisma of a brick wall. She was in her early fifties but had no crow's feet due to never smiling. "His test scores were great, his GPA was high, he graduated college at nineteen."

"He couldn't have done any of those things without his... power," Pete said.

"And what exactly is his 'power?'"

Pete looked around the conference room. Besides Huntley and himself, there were two more agents with notepads seated on either side of Huntley, and two larger agents standing by the doorway, preventing anyone from coming in — or going out. At least those two weren't staring at him like the three across the table. Pete didn't know any of their names except Huntley's; their little group didn't seem too fond of introductions.

"You don't know?" Pete asked. "I was hoping you could tell me."

"Mr. Morgan, please. In all the years you've been friends, Arnesto never told you how he does it?"

"He once told me he was a god" — the lackeys immediately started writing on their notepads — "as well as an oracle, a time traveler, a visionary, a psychic, and what else, I know I'm forgetting some." As Pete was listing them out, the lackeys realized the value of this information and put their pens down.

"And what do *you* think? If you had to pick one?" Huntley asked.

"I always had this odd feeling that he might be an alien, but then I realized he's just sort of weird."

"Mr. Morgan, I must insist on your cooperation."

"I don't know how he does it," Pete said, throwing his hands into the air. "You want me to pick one, fine, he's psychic. Sometimes he knows things about the future. I don't know what else to tell you."

"Mr. Morgan, why aren't you rich?"

"Excuse me?"

"You have this friend who can see the future. We've been over both your finances. You're both well-off, but with his ability, you could both be extremely wealthy, yet neither of you is. Why is that?"

"Did he tell you about the time he convinced me to bet big on the Pistons and they lost?" Pete noticed their eyes widen at that remark, and continued, "Yeah, he's not always right."

"Perhaps he did that intentionally, to get back at you for something or to shake your faith in his ability?" Huntley asked.

"No, I don't think so. He's always done right by me."

"Has he?" Huntley rifled through her files. "Tell me about your mother. She died young, did she not? Did Arnesto try to warn you?"

Pete frowned. "There's an explanation for that. I told him beforehand not to interfere with my life."

"Did you specifically order him not to warn you about immediate family members dying?"

"No. What exactly is your point?" Pete asked.

"My point, Mr. Morgan, is that your friend Arnesto seems to enjoy playing God. If he's willing to sit by as his own friend's mother gets cancer—"

"That's hardly fair. He didn't make her smoke."

"But he could have stopped it. He could have saved her life."

"There's no way to know that for sure, Agent Huntley. But what about all the lives he *did* save?"

"Yes, let's talk about Oklahoma." The lackey on Huntley's left handed her a file. Huntley opened it to the first page. "Timothy McVeigh a.k.a. The Oklahoma Highway Bomber. They estimate Arnesto may have saved fifty lives, many of them children."

Pete put his hand up. "Hold on, fifty? Try almost four times that amount."

Huntley took out a pair of reading glasses and put them on. She then flipped past a couple pages in the report. "According to our analysis, the Murrah building's structure would have withstood the brunt of the blast. Two independent contractors agreed that no more than forty to fifty people would have died. Did Arnesto tell you the number was higher?"

"Much higher, yes," Pete said.

"Perhaps he was lying, embellishing his heroics knowing you would never know the truth?"

Pete's voice got quieter. "He wouldn't do that."

"He wouldn't what, lie?" Huntley asked. "Did you know less than an hour before the explosion, he lied to a police officer? He told the officer that he and McVeigh stayed at the same hotel the night before. Minutes later, that same officer was murdered by McVeigh. Did you know that? Here, read the report for yourself," she said, turning the report around and sliding it across the table to Pete.

Pete read the report, much of it being news to him. Still, he found nothing to contradict what little Arnesto had told him aside from Huntley's speculation which he didn't trust anyway.

"Seventeen people died in the blast," Huntley said, "most of them federal agents. If he had given them just a little more notice... But Arnesto has proven himself to be reckless. Here's one question I would love to have answered: What was he doing there?"

"I am happy to answer that. He told me he was worried that his warning was going to be ignored. *Again.* He went there as a last resort to try to stop McVeigh himself. Run him off the road if necessary."

"Mr. Morgan, does that sound like someone who has worked so hard to maintain his anonymity? Does that sound like Arnesto?"

Pete again looked at his interrogator and her lackeys. They all stared straight back, awaiting his response. Almost in a whisper, he said, "No, it doesn't."

"Was Arnesto working with McVeigh?"

"Oh, come on!" Pete said, jumping up and sending his chair wheeling backward a couple feet. "To what end?!"

"You said yourself, he felt the government was ignoring him. Maybe he wanted to send them a message then changed his mind at the last minute, or maybe it got out of hand, I don't know. Did he and McVeigh ever have any contact?"

Pete walked to the window and looked outside. As much as he wanted to, he couldn't avoid the question. "Yes. They spoke briefly in Waco two years earlier, during the siege. It was a chance encounter."

"Ah, yes, Waco," Huntley said as she opened up a different file. "Where Arnesto forged a disturbing recording in David Koresh's voice, which he sent to two different news stations before leaving a third for the FBI. Again, Arnesto chooses the most reckless path."

"It worked, didn't it?"

"Did it? Several people still died. In the meantime, he meets McVeigh, they have a nice little chat about how much they hate the government, perhaps establish a partnership—"

Pete sighed and sat back in his chair. "At his worst, Arnesto's actions were less reckless than your conjecture. I am cooperating with you, but I have to ask, how many more files do you have? Exactly how much more are we going to cover?"

"Mr. Morgan, I would suggest you cancel your appointments for the rest of the week and possibly the next." As she said, this, the lackey on her right started pulling out boxes full of files from underneath the table and setting them on top. "We've only just begun."

A Relaxing Conversation

Location: Unknown
Monday, April 29, 2013
Time: Unknown

THE NEXT DAY, Arnesto was brought back into the interrogation room where Whiteside was waiting for him.

"Good morning, Arnesto," Whiteside said, holding up the L.A. riots flyer from the day before. "I thought we'd start at the beginning. April 29, 1992: the Los Angeles riots. I'm sure it's not the beginning for *you*, but it's the earliest we have anything on you. So far.

He read from the flyer. "'If the officers who beat Rodney King are acquitted, the people may riot.' Why didn't you say, '...the people *will* riot?' It's more accurate, but I guess it also makes you sound more threatening. Were you afraid the people would take it as a call to arms? Or were you afraid that if you were caught, you would be charged with inciting the riot that nearly burned the city to the ground? Did you think that far ahead?"

After each question, he gave Arnesto time to respond, but Arnesto remained silent.

"Am I correct in assuming you're not going to answer any of my

341

questions? Alright, we'll give you something to help loosen you up a bit."

Two agents entered the room. One stood by as the other injected something into Arnesto's arm. Arnesto never said a word and put up no resistance.

"Amobarbital," Whiteside said. "Similar to Sodium Pentothal, though I couldn't tell you their exact chemical compositions. I bet *you* could, though.

"Anyway, let's get back to the riots. So, the night before, you stayed at that hotel, where you paid cash, but still gave them your license plate number, only with two of the digits transposed. You posted these flyers all over Koreatown, then got the hell out of town, went home, and watched the riots on television like everyone else as fifty-three people died. Did you feel that they brought it on themselves, that they deserved to die?"

Arnesto said nothing.

"That was the prevailing theory, by the way, until I told them, 'No, this guy loves saving lives. He was just a rookie, still learning.' I was right, wasn't I? Still not talking?"

Whiteside pointed at the guard to give Arnesto another dose, then waited for the chemicals to take effect. Arnesto had never felt so relaxed in his life, but he tried his best not to show it.

"Look, Arnesto. I don't blame you for L.A. One man working alone? Why should anyone listen to you? But here's the thing. You clearly knew it was going to happen." He stopped pacing to lean on the back of his chair. "Why didn't you stop the beating in the first place? You could have given King a ride the night he was pulled over. I'm sure there are a hundred ways you could have handled it. But you didn't, why?"

He resumed pacing as Arnesto was given a third dose. It was more than he could handle, and he passed out, falling forward onto the table. Two agents caught him before he slid onto the floor.

"Sir?" one of the agents asked.

"Fine," Whiteside said. "Give him the flumazenil, take him back to his cell, and keep a close eye on him."

Sometime later, Arnesto woke up in his cell without the foggiest clue how he got there. He wasn't even sure how much time had passed since they drugged him — a few minutes? Days? There was no way to tell.

Once again, they came to collect him. He stood up, felt the world around him begin to spin, and sat right back down. An agent offered him a small bottle of water from which Arnesto took a few sips before standing up again. This time, he didn't get dizzy and started to walk, but the agent stopped him, took back the water bottle, then motioned for him to keep moving.

"I thought we could skip ahead to the al-Qaeda Nineteen," Whiteside said as Arnesto sat down. "First of all, let me be the first to thank you for tipping us off. This was back in September of 2001. A little reminder in case you can't remember the past as well as you can see the future. There's no doubt in anyone's mind that you saved a great number of lives that day. Our analysts conclude that one or even two of those flights could have indeed been hijacked and flown into those buildings, killing dozens, possibly hundreds of people. Kudos. I mean that.

"Still, the way you informed the authorities could have been better. You emailed more than two dozen people. I get it, you wanted to get the word out. But you've heard of things being on a need-to-know basis, right? Well, a lot of those people didn't need to know. You created a small panic, causing several agencies to trip over each other before a plan of attack could be decided upon, and that wasted precious time. Speaking of, you gave them a little more than a day to stop what could have been the greatest terrorist attack on U.S. soil in history? Come on, Arnesto. Your email was not crafted last-minute. How far in advance did you know about the attack? And also, do you ever check your email?

"People had questions, Arnesto. I'm sure you felt you told them everything in the email, but maybe someone would have asked something that would have caused you to recollect one more little piece of information that could have helped. At the very least, you would have seen that they wanted to reward you. Jeez, you could have had the key to the city if you wanted. Or maybe guaranteed anonymity and a medal would have suited you better. You could have had some fun with it, but instead, you went and hid and made yourself look suspicious. Do you understand that, Arnesto?"

Whiteside leaned back in his chair, giving Arnesto plenty of time to respond, but Arnesto remained silent. "You *can* hear me, right?" Arnesto looked up in confirmation for a moment before returning his gaze to the floor.

"Right." Whiteside sat up straight and put his hands on the table. "I'm going to grab a coffee. Do you want one or can I get you something else? No? Be right back." He left and returned holding a coffee. He was also smiling.

Whiteside sat down, sipped his coffee, and resumed his questioning. "Staying on the subject of airplanes, let's talk about flight fifteen-forty-nine. I have to hand this one to you, I don't know how you did it. Miracle on the Hudson? You were the miracle, weren't you. Again, it was brought up, what if you were the cause? I shut that down in a hurry, Arnesto. It didn't fit, not at all. A guy like you with your power doesn't try to crash a plane while he's on it. No, you were clearly the hero. Which leads me to two questions.

"First, why did you bring your then girlfriend? You knew what was going to happen to the plane. You must have hated her."

Arnesto looked up, but quickly corrected himself. He couldn't let Whiteside know he had touched a nerve.

"You know what," Whiteside continued, I don't even care. Let me get to question number two: how did you do it, how did you save that plane?" He took a couple sips of coffee while he waited for an answer. "Come on, give me this one, I really want to know. You answer this one question, I'll get you out of that cell and into someplace real comfortable: all the amenities, all the video games you want. Are you going to let Sully hog all the credit?"

Not getting a response, Whiteside put down his coffee, stood up, and began pacing the room. "Damn, I was hoping you would give me that one. Here's the issue, Arnesto. There's not one shred of evidence you contributed to the events of that day. It was the geese, we know this. The problem is there's also not one shred of evidence you did anything to save those people. How many of them would be mighty unhappy to find out that they didn't need to have gone through that harrowing experience? How do you think US Airways would react if they found out you could have saved their expensive aircraft plus all those payouts after the crash? Where was the email this time?"

He sat down again. "What I don't like is that you're becoming reckless. Case in point, the Boston Marathon."

345

Right on cue, an agent entered the room carrying a laptop which she handed to Whiteside before stepping back out. It was ajar but Whiteside opened it all the way. He tapped the touchpad and Arnesto heard a crowd sound. Whiteside tapped the touchpad a second time then dragged his finger along it before tapping it a third and final time. Arnesto surmised that Whiteside had started, paused, then restarted a video. Whiteside put the laptop in front of Arnesto. "Play it."

Arnesto played the video. He saw and heard the crowd react to the first explosion, then saw himself pick up and throw the backpack containing the second bomb moments before it, too, exploded. There was nothing pleasurable about seeing how close he had come to death nor seeing how hard he and the rest of the crowd had been knocked to the ground. It was especially painful knowing this was how they had caught him.

"Your tip helped us apprehend the terrorists. That is, your second tip with the picture that you sent *after* the explosions. Your first tip, the phone call before the explosions, was ineffective."

Arnesto found himself replaying the video over and over and stopped.

"You really cut it close that time. Not just with the bomb, but with the investigation. Without your text, they were going to start taking a very close look at *you*. Instead, they arrested the brothers in record time and the FBI's investigation closed. *Our* investigation, however, had just caught a major break.

"Do you have any idea the resources we've spent trying to find you? It's a little embarrassing, to tell you the truth. But finally, we almost have you and then you go and flee the country. Did you — did you blow up a factory in Bangladesh? That's not like you. No, I get it, the building was going to collapse and kill everyone inside. Probably within the next day or two, right? How many, hundreds? More than a thousand? Right on, Arnesto. Sadly, the powers that be, and I can't argue with them, have a growing concern that left unchecked, you, with your newfound love of adrenaline rushes and possible addiction to explosions, may create an international incident, if you haven't already.

"Do you see now, Arnesto? Do you see why we can't let you run rampant?" Whiteside stood up and reached over and shut the laptop before picking it up and moving toward the door. "I want to help you, Arnesto. Let me help you save lives out there. I can get you anything you need, but I can't help you at all until you start talking to me."

Arnesto said nothing.

"Sleep on it," Whiteside said. "We'll meet again first thing tomorrow."

They met the next day and the next and at indiscriminate times after that. Arnesto soon lost track of what day it was as the agents and guards were careful to hide that information from him. Even his meals were served at random times.

Through it all, Arnesto never said a word.

* * *

After what felt like a couple weeks, Arnesto noticed he had gone several days in a row without hearing from Whiteside. Were they done? Had his adversary asked his last question? It seemed unlikely, but then, where was he? Time passed, and Arnesto grew more concerned that he had been abandoned.

It was with an ironic sense of relief that he was finally called back into the interrogation room.

"Hello, Arnesto, how have you been? Hanging in there okay?" Whiteside asked as Arnesto sat down. "Sorry to skip out on you like that, but your friend Pete gave us some new leads to check out. He cooperated quite a bit." He motioned toward some boxes that Arnesto hadn't noticed when he walked in. "Pete filled in a number of gaps in our intelligence and told us all sorts of things we didn't have a clue about: the Oklahoma bridge collapse, for instance." He paused to let that sink in. "You should know that we let him go in exchange for his cooperation. I hope you won't hold a grudge against him. What he did was for the good of the country."

Whiteside swiveled around in his chair, but then said, "Oh," and turned back to face Arnesto, clasping his hands and resting them on the desk. "We paid a visit to your family."

Arnesto did his best to remain stoic, but he had no idea if he was successful. He felt Whiteside probably noticed his increased heart rate. More than anything, he hated the way Whiteside paused after every couple of sentences. Was he merely gauging Arnesto's reaction, or was he rubbing it in?

"I'm telling you this as a courtesy. All we did was inform them that we were likely going to be working together and asked them a few simple 'background' questions about you. Your parents, your brother, your ex-wife, they were all surprised and proud to find out you would be assisting us with important, top-secret work. See? I didn't even have to lie to them. They didn't even seem disappointed to find out they shouldn't expect to hear from you for a while."

Whiteside stood up and walked over to the boxes, pulling out several large folders before returning to his seat.

"Now, back to business, shall we?"

Schooled

Location: Unknown
Date: Unknown
Time: Unknown

"REPORT," WHITESIDE SAID, not looking up from his monitor. He was drafting a reply to an email from his higher-ups who were demanding why weeks had passed without Whiteside being able to show progress. Just as Arnesto hadn't shared one word with Whiteside, Whiteside was having trouble coming up with the words to answer his superiors.

A male agent named Crowl spoke first. "Pretty much the usual. He sleeps, exercises, eats, and stares or meditates or whatever."

"Pretty much?" Whiteside asked. "I told you, if there's any deviation at all, no matter how trivial, I need to know about it."

"He's... uh..."

"He's playing with himself, sir. Masturbating," said the female agent named Stanfield.

Whiteside took his hands off the keyboard and looked at the other agents. He thought for a moment, then said, "Explain."

"He sits there playing with it," Stanfield said.

350

"And stares at the camera the whole time," Crowl added.

"How long?" Whiteside asked.

The other agents looked at each other. "A couple hours?" Crowl asked.

"Does he finish? Does he even have an erection?" Whiteside asked.

"Sir?"

Whiteside smiled and turned back to his computer. "He's not playing with himself, he's playing with *you*. Get him a magazine." When his agents hesitated, he continued. "Get him a girlie mag. It's okay. It's the incentive approach, which is in the manual you two are going to reread the moment your shift ends. Dismissed."

Arnesto did appreciate the magazine, more for the articles than the pictorials. While internet porn hadn't completely ruined airbrushed, softcore pictures for him, it was the words that gave him the most distraction from his predicament. He devoured the magazine, fearing that at any moment it would be taken away from him. When it wasn't, he reread it at a more relaxed pace.

He made up little games for himself, like trying to subconsciously count how many of a given letter was used while reading an article. Then he would go back and carefully count. He was always wrong, but never far off.

He stopped touching himself, not because he had succeeded in obtaining a magazine, but because he had failed at irritating Whiteside. Whiteside personally gave Arnesto a second magazine a few weeks after he had received the first.

"Thought I'd give you something a little more substantial," Whiteside said, sliding the magazine across the interrogation table. "Go ahead, look at it."

Arnesto never looked at anything Whiteside presented to him until he was ordered to do so. Aside from never speaking, Arnesto wanted to obey orders as best he could, but always did so without the slightest change in expression. He steeled himself and looked down.

It was a news magazine. The cover focused on some celebrity about whom Arnesto couldn't care less. Arnesto lifted his head.

"Look a little closer. Please," Whiteside said.

Arnesto looked back down at the magazine. In the corners under the large headline describing the celebrity's shenanigans were various cover lines in much smaller text. One of them mentioned a school shooting.

"There it is, under whatsherface's pregnancy, another school shooting, this one in Santa Monica," Whiteside said. "Feels like we've been having more of them lately. It bothers me, Arnesto, and I know it bothers you. Every time I see a headline like that, I think, 'Could he have prevented this? Could Arnesto have saved those lives?' Go ahead, turn to page sixty-eight, see if they got the details right."

Arnesto opened the magazine and flipped the pages until he reached the half-page article on the shooting. It was news to him. He recalled nothing of the event.

"I know, you can't stop them all. At least, I don't think you can. I'm not actually sure. But what I am sure of, is that, sooner or later, there's going to be an event where people die that you could have prevented. How long — how long is it going to be until that happens?"

Arnesto never made eye contact with Whiteside unless ordered to do so. He believed in giving away as little information as possible. Unnecessary eye contact might not only give something away visually, it could also reveal information by virtue of a simple change in behavior.

352

However, just this once, he couldn't resist.

He closed the magazine and looked straight into the eyes of his nemesis.

Whiteside stared back.

It was a silent battle, each man trying to find the other's weakness, and finding none. They tried to imagine what their opponent was thinking, what their motivation was, what their next move would be, and while they both knew they had similar goals, neither had any idea who was winning.

Arnesto was the one who finally blinked and resumed his usual downcast blank stare. To an outsider, it might have appeared as if this had given Whiteside the victory, but this was not the case. Arnesto had simply realized there was nothing more to be gained and ended the epic staredown. Likewise, Whiteside hadn't been staring in an effort to intimidate or establish dominance. He simply wanted to observe his unyielding captive.

"Get him out of here," Whiteside said.

Their short, mostly silent meeting had, unlike their other meetings, been ever so slightly productive, for each of them felt like they had barely riled up the other. It was better than nothing.

Sinus Trouble

Location: Unknown
Date: Unknown
Time: Unknown

"SIR, THERE'S SOMETHING you need to see," Stanfield said.

"Yeah, I know, I'm watching it now," Whiteside said. He restarted the video clip of Father Martin's latest announcement.

"Hello again, I'm Father Martin. I have received another message from my source, the person who speaks through me. My source is also the one to whom I am now speaking. In your message, you said there was another event approaching, and that if I didn't hear from you again by today, that I should make this announcement. Wherever you are, I hope you're safe and will be able to contact me again soon. Thank you and God bless."

"Sir, we know when Father Martin was contacted. Arnesto was here. Are we sure we have the right guy?"

"Positive. He set this up ahead of time. He saw us coming like he sees everything coming."

"What do we do now? People are anxious, sir. The stock market's crashing—"

"You don't think I know that?" Whiteside asked. "Take him to the board room."

"Sir, we both know he's as likely to give us false information—"

"*Any* information is more than we've got now. If he lies to us, great, at least we'll have something to rule out." He looked up at Stanfield, whose stoic expression betrayed a hint of disapproval. "Out with it."

"Permission to speak freely?" she asked.

"Yes, yes, say it already."

"He's not a terrorist, sir. He's not a spy. Whatever crimes he's committed, he only did so to try to save people. Is this how we treat one of our own?"

"Anything else, Agent Stanfield?"

She stared at him briefly before replying. "No, sir."

"Agent Crowl requested a transfer to another department; are you next?"

"No, sir."

"Good, then take him to the board room. And keep life support standing by. We can't afford to lose him."

Less than five minutes later, Stanfield helped secure Arnesto to a gurney, then lowered one end so his head was below his feet. He seemed a little bit tense to her, even though he wore the same lifeless expression to which the staff had all grown accustomed.

She leaned over him. "You know I don't want to do this," she said. "Give me something — anything — and this can stop."

She walked over to the shower overlooking the gurney and placed her hand on the nozzle. She looked at Arnesto, then nodded to another agent who placed a large rag over Arnesto's face. Then she turned the nozzle to full blast.

Time and again they waterboarded him. He coughed and gagged and sputtered as much as anyone would, but still never talked.

Sometimes Whiteside would be there himself to turn on the water or cover Arnesto's face or simply observe. Sometimes he was absent. It was his way of keeping Arnesto guessing.

One time, he walked in on the middle of a session. Upon entering the room, he immediately stopped and motioned Stanfield to come and talk to him in the hallway.

"Where's the clock that was on the wall?" he asked.

"I took it down. I noticed he was using it to time himself," she said.

"What, like some kind of high score?!" Whiteside put his hand on his head and took a few steps away before walking back. He looked inside at Arnesto. "That guy in there couldn't beat up my six-year-old niece, yet waterboarding can't get him to talk?"

"Maybe he feels he has nothing to confess. Sir, we've tried everything."

"Just about. Stanfield, where are we on the questioning?"

"We've covered all the major events, but—"

"'All the major events.' Great, he's given us next to nothing, while we've told him everything we know about him. He's playing us — again! You know what, cancel the waterboarding. Take him back to his cell. I have some phone calls to make."

For the next few days, Arnesto languished in his cell. Other than the on-site doctor monitoring the sinus infection he had acquired from the waterboarding, he had no contact with anyone. His physical energy was slipping, and his mental state wasn't far behind.

Maybe they were right and he was being selfish. They certainly would have saved more lives if he had worked with them. Maybe.

356

Would they have warned the other countries about the earthquakes, and if they had, what would they have expected in return? How much could he trust them? Right, like the government's ever been trustworthy... What was Whiteside doing now, collecting wood to burn him at the stake?

He didn't have to wait much longer to find out.

Arnesto was half-asleep when the sound of his cell door opening gave him a start. Great, if they were paying attention, and they always were, then they noticed his reaction and probably felt they were, at last, starting to get to him.

They led him to the interrogation room, where Whiteside was already seated. Arnesto sat down and tried to brace himself for whatever the agent was going to throw at him next. It was probably some brand-new torture designed solely for him and approved by some bought out congressperson.

Alright, Whiteside, hit me with it already. Whatever it is you think you've got, I'm ready.

Arnesto was not ready.

Without any emotion, good or bad, with the kind of stoicism only Whiteside could display, he said the two words Arnesto never thought he'd hear.

"You've won."

Concessions

Location: Unknown
Date: Unknown
Time: Unknown

"YOU DON'T LEAVE the country. Ever," Whiteside said. "Do you understand me?"

Arnesto was half ignoring him. It made it easier to avoid having any reaction to whatever the agent was saying. Even so, this conversation seemed different. Something had changed.

"Let's just say certain people have reconsidered your threat level. It seems you are actually more dangerous down here than you are out there. I think they were also impressed with how well you handled yourself under pressure, though they'd never admit it. I would hate to see what it would take to get you to confess anything.

"Here's the deal. You work for us now. You tell us what you know, and you let us handle it. I can't promise you any say in operations, but as you're the only one with any intel, I imagine you'll have quite a lot of pull.

"You get your life back, sort of. We'll be keeping an eye on you 24/7. That's the way it has to be, both for your protection and ours. So, you can leave this place, work with us, and go back to saving lives, or you can stay here. I know what *I* would pick, but frankly, I'm starting to think you're enjoying your time in this—"

Arnesto mumbled something, but his raspy voice was inaudible as he tried to speak for the first time since their initial meeting.

Whiteside opened his mouth, but it took him a second to register. "Could you repeat that please?" he asked.

Arnesto cleared his throat. "Do I report to you?"

Whiteside smiled. "I am your point of contact, yes. But technically, you're my boss. That means you're welcome to replace me if you choose. Under the circumstances, I would understand."

"How do I know you won't suddenly change your mind and put a bullet in my head?" Arnesto asked.

"I won't lie to you. If you fuck with us, if you do anything to hurt this country, if you force our hand, we won't hesitate to kill you. Or if we feel you've been compromised or you're not otherwise holding up your end of the bargain, we'll bring you back here. There's a lot riding on this, as you know. But as of right now, you are a free man, so to speak."

Agent Stanfield entered the room and deposited a bag containing Arnesto's personal effects on the table.

"Thanks, Lindsay," Arnesto said to the agent, who seemed taken aback. She stared wide-eyed at Arnesto, who turned and gave her an approving nod.

"Thank you, Agent Stanfield," Whiteside said, not altogether thrilled by her lingering. She nodded and left the room.

"One more thing," Whiteside said. "You've done a decent job of maintaining a low profile all this time. But it needs to be better going forward. We have some fake IDs you can use, but if you want, we can make one of them official — give you a whole new identity. You can even pick your own name. Anything you want, assuming the analytics department signs off on it. For someone who prefers leaving as little as possible to chance, it might make things easier for you. I would urge you to consider it, however, it's entirely up to you. Sir."

Arnesto stood up and took his bag off the table. He walked to the door and opened it with his free hand, but didn't walk out. He thought for a moment, then turned back to Whiteside.

"Call me Arnesto."

The End

Epilogue

School Gymnasium
Massachusetts
Saturday, August 17, 2013
2:15 p.m.

PETE WATCHED from the stands as his son Daniel, now ten, competed in the karate tournament. A well-built man sat down on his immediate left, distracting him from a much thinner man sitting down on his right.

"Boo," said the second man, giving Pete a start.

"Goddammit, Arnesto," Pete said as he gave his friend an awkward side hug. "You lost a few pounds in there. How are you? Am I allowed to ask?"

Arnesto leaned forward and gave the man on Pete's left a quick head tilt to tell him they needed space. They watched as the man walked to the next section and sat down again. "We're clear."

Pete looked at his friend. Arnesto appeared well-groomed and had a fresh haircut, but still looked like he'd aged ten years.

"I'm okay," Arnesto said. "At least, I was before I walked in here. Why does it smell like feet?" He looked around at all the barefoot competitors. "Oh, right. Can't believe I spent ten bucks on this."

"Is it true about the... waterboarding?"

Arnesto nodded. "It was horrifying. I still have to brace myself every time I take a shower."

"How did you get through it, I mean, without talking?"

"It wasn't easy. I almost cracked so many times. But I knew they wouldn't let me die. My knowledge is too enticing for them. I knew if I could just hold on... How about you?"

"It wasn't fun, but it wasn't torture, either. Arnesto, I told them everything." Pete hung his head in shame.

"You told them everything? Or *everything*?"

"I told them, wait, which is the good one? Whatever, I cooperated."

"I understand." Arnesto reflected on this. "You cooperated? Or you *cooperated*?"

"Arnesto, I revealed so much more than I thought possible. However, I don't have your memory, so I may have missed a few... *details*. Still, I blabbed. And I may have badmouthed you as well. I am so sorry."

"Please. I don't want your apology for *sticking to the plan*. You swore to me if I was ever caught and you were questioned, you wouldn't hold back. Other than how I do it, of course. This was always my mess, not yours."

Pete accepted this. "So what now?"

"I've come to say goodbye. I've disrupted your life enough." Arnesto scooted to the side to put a little more distance between them. Pete noticed Daniel running up to him and knew Arnesto didn't want Daniel to recognize him.

"Dad, did you see? I made it to the next round!"

"Great job, Daniel, go get 'em!" As Daniel ran off, Arnesto returned to his former position. Both men knew they had missed Daniel's match.

"Case in point," Arnesto said.

"I wish I could help, but I guess you've got a team for that now. If I may ask, what did Whiteside tell you exactly?" Arnesto filled him in. "It's not ideal, but now you can save lives without the danger or having to constantly look over your shoulder. One question, though. Why put you in charge?" He looked at Arnesto's chaperone pretending not to watch them from the next section. "I mean, no offense, but as such a valuable asset, wouldn't it have made more sense to keep Whiteside in charge and keep you as a top priority consultant?"

"Damn, it took me almost a week to catch that. And you're right, we must be using the same playbook. Just like you told them everything to placate them, they pretended to put me in charge to placate me. I'm pretty sure they only let me out to see what I can do for them. Once they realize how little that is…"

"They'll take you back. Jeez, that's awful. What are you going to do?"

"Don't worry about me. I've got a plan," Arnesto said, a knowing grin plastered on his face.

Pete chuckled and shook his head. "Nobody makes plans better than you. I almost feel sorry for *them*."

Arnesto shook Pete's hand. "Before I forget, you're not flying to Malaysia next year, are you? Well, don't." He stood. "Now if you'll excuse me, I've got to run."

Acknowledgements

Special thanks to:

Stina Campos, for her neverending support and feedback.

Ryan "Pete Morgan" Kelly, for keeping me sane in high school (the rootbeer popsicles helped!)

And of course...

You! Thanks very much for reading!

Edited by Dustin Schwindt, bookbutchers.com

Cover art by Adam deGrandis

About the Author

Two questions used to keep me up at night. First: what would I do if I suddenly found myself back in September 9, 2001 — two days before the horrible events of 9/11? Second: what would I do if I suddenly found myself back in homeroom in high school?

At some point several years ago, a light bulb went off and I realized I could merge the two and attempt to answer them both. And so, without really knowing what I was doing, I decided to write this book, and Arnesto Modesto was born.

Thank you for reading *Arnesto Modesto: The World's Most Ineffectual Time Traveler*! I hope you had as much fun reading it as I had writing it. Actually, considering all the hours I spent cursing to myself as I paced back and forth, I hope you had a lot *more* fun reading it than I had writing it. I complain but I would do it all over again. And you know what? Those two questions no longer keep me up at night.

This book is my first novel.

Other Works by the Author

This book is my first novel, so currently there *are* no other works by the author. That said, I have begun work on a number of short stories. Here are but a few (titles subject to change):

The Pacifier (aka Baby Hunter): a sudden mutation has spread around the globe causing newborn babies to be born with superhuman strength — and a taste for blood. He is Earth's only hope. He is: The Pacifier.

Tyrone Jackson and the Half-Court Dunk: the new star recruit learns that ball is a lot different when magic is involved. He has the skill to make balla history — if he can get past his ego and stop breaking the rules. A parody.

Quincunx: In the championship Scrabble game, one player makes a move no one saw coming.

Chasing CowQuest: His life was perfectly content until he receives a message from his rival that his world record score from decades ago has at last been beaten. How far will he go, how much will he risk to reclaim the title? A mockumentary.

The Part Where the Author Begs You for a Review

Reviews are everything to an independent author. If you have the time and inclination, please consider writing one. I would greatly appreciate it. Here are some reasons why you may want to:

1. You enjoyed the book and want to contribute to its success. Huzzah!
2. You hated the book and want to vent your frustrations.
3. You want to encourage others to read this amazing novel.
4. You want others to read it so they will suffer as you have.
5. You've never written a review before and figure this is as good a time as any.
6. You feel this book has too few reviews and deserves at least one more.
7. You feel this book has plenty of reviews and you want to jump on the bandwagon.
8. The previous reviewer wrote something you disagree with. How dare they!
9. You would like to read more of Arnesto's fantastic adventures and know leaving a review will encourage the author to write them.
10. You don't care about Arnesto at all and just want to fool the author into spending several more years writing a sequel (you have no intention of reading) for the lulz.

Contact

darrenjohnsonauthor@gmail.com

https://twitter.com/ArnestoModesto

Made in the USA
Columbia, SC
05 June 2024

36669612R00224